FIRE WEED

by

Terry Montague

Covenant Communications, Inc.
American Fork, Utah

Fireweed
ISBN 1–55503–407–1
Library of Congress Catalog Card Number 92–72487

First Printing: August 1992
93 94 95 96 97 98   10 9 8 7 6 5 4 3 2

Cover Illustraton: Wayne Andreason
Cover Design: Leslie X. Goodman
Author Photograph: Krisan R. Hardcastle

Covenant
COMMUNICATIONS, INC.

ACCLAIM FOR THE BOOK

Fireweed is an intensely emotional, complex, authentically detailed novel of the Saints' struggle to keep family and testimony intact in Hitler's Germany. Their brave battle will kindle your admiration while it wrings your heart.

Terry Montague, wise in human relationships, fills her story with richly drawn, real, and engrossing people who persist in the reader's mind long after the reading experience is over. She shows us ourselves—sometimes shocking our sensibilities, often casting light on our own lives, always challenging us to reexamine our values and the depth of our comittment to them.

Mary L. Smith, Author

Fireweed—a stirring story about an LDS German girl who watches the destruction of her world during Hitler's Germany. Her strength and love sustain her during loss of family and country. Her faith, nourished by God's love, helps her preserve others.

Montague's memorable characters bring to life the plight of the German people caught in Hitler's lies. Yet throughout the novel, each character's wonderful sense of humor and compassion reinforce the belief of hope and survival in the upheaval of a war ruined country. *Fireweed* should be read by everyone who sometimes feels overwhelmed by life's little problems.

Krisan R. Hardcastle, Artist and Illustrator

How This Book Came to Be

Except for the time I spent at school (I graduated from BYU), I've spent my life in Rupert, Idaho. I grew up in a small German community here. The community is descendant of the German colonies founded along Russia's Black Sea at the time of Catharine the Great. About the time of the Bolshevik Revolution, anti-German sentiment forced most of the Germans out of Russia. They came to America and settled in Nebraska, South and North Dakota, Rupert and American Falls, Idaho, the Palouse Valley in Washington and Lodi, California—anywhere there was homestead land. My grandparents, aunts and uncles, and the neighbors next door and across the street were all Russian-German. Everyone spoke German. The church we went to had services in German. We made our own sausage in the back yard and ate cheese dumplings on Sundays (that explains my figure). None of my relatives called themselves Russian in spite of the land they came from. My grandfather always said, "Just because the cat had kittens in the oven doesn't make them biscuits." Everyone was and still is fiercely German.

My dad was injured at the Battle of the Bulge and left to die. It was so cold his open head wound froze before he bled to death and he was able to stumble around the Ardennes for several days. He accidentally crossed behind German lines many times before he finally stumbled upon an American radio unit. He won't talk about that experience much. I often wonder if he felt confused at having an enemy he was so closely connected to.

While growing up I remember watching the show "Combat." I remember that in the show everyone who spoke German was a "dirty Kraut." I saw that same attitude in old Daffy Duck and Bugs Bunny cartoons. I refused to believe my tiny grandmother could be a "dirty Kraut." I was in the sixth grade when I started reading about Nazi Germany and the history of World War II Europe. Through my studies I tried to reconciliate my American heritage and my German ("dirty Kraut") heritage. I don't know that I did.

I've always wanted to be a writer and when my boredom started to drive Quinn (my husband) crazy he encouraged me to write. As I was trying to find a subject I met Norm Seibold, who is our County

Commissioner. His experiences as a missionary in Nazi Germany inspired me to write *Mine Angels Round About*. While I was researching that book, I talked to more than a half a hundred missionaries who also served in Nazi Germany. They'd say, "Let me run in the next room and get my album." Then their wives, several of whom were German, would start telling me their stories of the war. After *Mine Angels Round About* came out, I knew I needed to tell another part of the story—one from the German point of view.

This is where Lisel, Marta, Papa, Frau Heidemann and Kurt were created. It isn't easy writing a full length novel, but my characters helped me by showing up in my dreams and talking to me about themselves and what they were doing and what they should be doing and what I should be doing. They were real to me. So real that now, sometimes, I miss them and have to go back and read a part of my manuscript just to see them again.

I wanted to make their experiences real for the reader too. So I did something a lot of my friends had fits over. For the last several chapters of the book (about six weeks worth) I decreased my calorie intake to less than 800 a day to be able to realistically describe the hunger the characters felt and what that hunger did to them. I was very careful though. I drank adequate amounts of water and took some heavy duty vitamins. I didn't lose any weight, but I did lose my verbal skills. Often I couldn't finish the sentence I had started, a problem my husband will testify I didn't have before. This was particularly troublesome when I was invited to Logan to lecture on fiction writing. I'm still embarrassed about what happened there. Another phenomenon that happened is that I didn't have any emotional control and spent a lot of time crying. I don't know what I was crying about, but I was crying. I was also angry and very pessimistic—not like me at all. I also found out that when you're really hungry over a long period of time and you bend over you see bursts of light in front of your eyes and that standing too long makes you really dizzy. That was a miserable experience but I think it made a better story, and to a writer that is what matters most. What also matters to me personally is that through this writing experience I've bridged that gap between my American and German heritage and understand clearly now that human love and suffering is the same no matter what language you speak.

Terry Montague

Chapter 1

With her breath tight in her throat, Lisel Spann slid cautious fingers between the heavy draperies and parted them just enough to see the dark, cobblestone street below. Pools of summer rain glittered as a length of gray cloud shrouded, for an instant, the full moon. A gust of wind tore at the loose corners of a huge, wall-hung poster that proclaimed, "Ein Volk, Ein Reich, Ein Fuhrer." One People, One Country, One Leader.

No living thing moved on the street. But still Lisel watched—in silence, in darkness—waiting for a movement in the shadows of the tall brick house across the street.

"What are you doing in the dark?" her older sister asked as she came through the front door. "I can't even see to hang up my hat." Lisel heard her fumbling at the rack behind the door.

"Shhh," she whispered to Marta. "Some men are down on the street. They have been watching this building for the last half hour."

Marta moved with quick steps across the living room to the tiny alcove that served as a kitchen. "I did not see anyone down there," Marta remarked in a voice that suggested if Marta did not see anything, there was nothing to see.

"That is because you came through the back garden," Lisel replied.

Marta came up behind her and looked over her shoulder. "Your imagination has gotten the best of you again. There is no one down there."

Then a tiny, metallic glint betrayed the presence lurking in the darkness. "There!" Lisel said on a note of triumph. "I told you they were there."

Lisel sensed Marta's shrug. "So there is someone down on the street. They could be just ordinary German citizens, waiting for their ride."

Lisel glanced back at her elder sister. "And maybe cows chase rabbits," she replied.

Marta's mouth tightened in impatience but she said nothing. Even though Marta was only two years older than Lisel, Marta was always the grown-up, sensible, predictable one. She wore her soft brown hair in the same short, smooth style every day. She got up at the same time every morning and went through the same tedious daily routines of classes at the Red Cross nursing school, then shopping and housework. She never complained. She never went to movies, preferring to sit at home reading her textbooks or listening to music on the radio with her mending in her lap. When she became angry or upset, her warm, brown eyes flashed, but she rarely allowed herself to pronounce an angry word.

In contrast, Lisel, her red hair braided in long strands that hung on either side of her gamine face, her red-brown eyes that flashed her every emotion, frequently lost her patience, her temper, and her heart. She said everything she felt and often made a fool of herself. Her busy imagination took her out of the confusing, contradictory atmosphere of Germany to glittering, glamorous Hollywood where she danced, in a sleek pink gown trimmed with boa feathers, on the arm of Fred Astaire. She sang too loudly in church just because she liked the music, but her singing made the branch president cover his smile with his hand, the music director scowl, and the red come up in her papa's neck. She often shocked her father and provoked her sister. Everyone said she was that way because she was only sixteen, still a school girl. They said she would grow out of it. But Lisel hoped she would not. It would be like growing out of herself. Like growing out of life.

Marta plucked at Lisel's sleeve. "Come away from the window. What would Papa say if he found you in the dark, staring at strange men in the street?"

On cue, their father rounded the street corner and started down the block toward the apartment house. "I suppose we are about to find out," Lisel said.

Joseph Spann carried himself with the vigor and briskness instilled by years of military service—his back straight, shoulders squared, every movement precise. Lisel could almost hear the quick snap of his footsteps on the cobbles as he came nearer the dark, shadowed side of the street.

"He will walk right past them," Lisel said, and a sudden chill settled in her chest. On a night like this, a week ago, Kurt Heidemann, the boy upstairs, was ambushed and beaten in the dark. Lisel's dread quickened as her eyes followed her father's smart pace down the street.

Even in the humidity and heat of the August evening, Papa insisted on wearing his one remaining good suit, the gray jacket buttoned across the matching vest, the tiny clip with decorations from the World War on his lapel, the knotted tie, the creased trousers, now a little baggy at the knees, his worn but frequently blocked felt hat.

In another minute he would step into the blackness where the three men waited for something or someone in the dark.

Suppose those men waited for her father? Her father, who defended with valor the fatherland in the last war. Her father who, five years ago, gave up position and wealth to join the Mormon Church and whose greatest desire was to take his family to the temple of the Lord to be sealed together for eternity. For what cause would men lie in wait for a man like her father?

The answer sprang from the fear that gripped Lisel's heart like an icy hand. There was no just cause. Kurt's crime had been that he refused to join the local Hitler's Youth organization. These things happened and no one dared openly discuss or condemn them. But it would not happen to her father. Not if Lisel could help it. She tore back the draperies and jerked at the window latch. It jammed.

"What are you doing?" an astonished Marta demanded.

"We have to warn him!" Desperately, Lisel gripped the latch and pulled. Her fingernails tore as the tiny mechanism creaked free.

"You goose!" Marta cried in a rare outburst. She grasped Lisel's arms and dragged her away from the window. Her brown eyes shone as points of light in the dark. "How do you think Papa will react to having his youngest daughter shouting down the street to him? He will put you on bread and water until you have no teeth to chew with!"

Lisel tried to free herself. "But those men. Papa—"

"Papa can take care of Papa. Besides, if you call out, those men will hear you. They will wonder why you warn him. They will be suspicious of Papa and us too." Marta's argument made sense. But then, Marta always made sense.

Lisel stopped struggling.

"Come. Look." Marta pulled Lisel back to the window and the sisters leaned close to the pane so their breath mingled and clouded on the glass.

Unsuspecting, Papa approached the shadows. Lisel saw his head turn and his shoulders hunch slightly in surprise. The shadows wavered. Her father's footsteps slowed and faltered. Then he raised his arm in a stiff salute. Lisel held her breath; she could almost hear his reluctant, "Heil Hitler." His arm came down and he resumed his normal, brisk gait, crossing the street to the front of their apartment house. He disappeared from her view as he strode up the front steps. And still the men across the street remained in darkness.

Lisel let out a long breath.

"You see?" Marta said, "It was nothing."

Lisel's surge of relief was replaced by a prickle of resentment. Being shown not only wrong but foolish and impulsive by her older sister rankled. Lisel drew away from Marta. "You did not have to call me a goose," she protested. "And it could have been something. Those men could be SA or SS. Have you forgotten what happened to Kurt last week?"

The living room door clicked and swung open. Papa stood in the doorway. "Marta? Lisel?"

"Just a minute, Papa." Marta dashed to turn on the lamp.

Papa's heavy gray brows drew together in a frown. "What are you doing in the dark?"

Lisel rushed toward him. "Oh Papa, we were so worried about those men on the street!"

His frown deepened. "There are no men on the street," he replied and turned away from Lisel, carefully hanging his hat on the peg behind the door and smoothing his gray hair.

4

"But we saw them, down there in the shadows." Lisel declared, confused by her father's denial. "You walked right—"

Marta cut Lisel off in mid-sentence with a quick poke in her back.

Surprised, Lisel whirled on her sister. But Marta silenced her with a sharp look of warning.

Papa, ignoring the altercation, had settled in his favorite chair in the corner of the room, adjusted his wire-rimmed glasses, and was scowling at the front page of the *Volkishcher Beobachter*. The headlines screamed, "Chaos in Poland! Polish Soldiers Push to Edge of German Border! German Families Flee Polish Monsters!"

Lisel frowned.Why did the newspapers and the radio broadcasts continue to make such reports? They made everyone on the streets, in the shops, and even in the classrooms, ask, "Will we have war again?" Hitler said he would handle this new crisis just like he did the last one. Hitler said there would be no war. Everyone knew the Fuhrer did not want war at all. So why did the newspapers and radios continue to whip the German people into such a fever over war?

"Lisel?" Lisel blinked and looked up at Marta. Her older sister smiled knowingly. "Spinning dreams again?"

Lisel straightened her shoulders. "I was not. I was thinking about the state of the world," she replied.

"I wish you were thinking about helping me with dinner," Marta said and handed Lisel a stack of plates for the table.

Lisel pulled a face but took the plates.

Marta lifted the lid from a black iron pan. Steam billowed up from the contents, carrying with it the spicy aroma of smoked pork sausages. "The rain kept the lines at the butcher's short today," she said, "and Herr Schmidt found some nice fat sausages for us."

Lisel glanced at her father. He liked nothing better than a good sausage. But he seemed not to have heard Marta's remark. Papa had refolded the newspaper, unread, and laid it aside. He took his well-worn Bible from its place on the table next to his chair and opened it in his lap. With his index finger he absently riffled the top right corner of the pages.

"And the garden still has a good growth of green beans, thanks to Kurt. That boy can do miracles with a handful of seeds. With

Lisel as his assistant, of course," Marta added with a brief smile of acknowledgement to Lisel.

Lisel wrinkled her nose. She hated working in the garden, more than she hated setting the table. She laid out the place settings, watching her father as she worked. In a characteristic habit that showed his disquiet, Papa's mouth curved down beneath his wide gray mustache. He turned the thin pages of the scriptures inattentively, as though searching them but with some preoccupation that kept him from reading.

"The bread was no good today, though," Marta continued from the kitchen. "The baker said that though the Fuhrer ordered the wheat harvest to be in before the end of August, the bakery had only received half its regular quota and it was of very poor quality. I think he may have mixed sawdust into the flour again."

Perhaps the news from the Polish border upset Papa or perhaps the men on the street troubled him more than he would admit. His silence unnerved Lisel, and she struggled for a remark that would distract him from whatever clouded his thoughts. "We are having poppy seed cake for dinner tonight," she ventured.

Papa lifted his head and looked at Lisel, his brows rising.

"Marta had to use half our sugar rations for it," Lisel continued gamely, remembering the way Marta had poked her in the back.

Papa looked over at Marta, who spooned the green beans into a chipped china bowl. "Such a small treat will not bankrupt the household," she replied evenly.

"No," her father agreed, "and it has been a long time since we have had poppy seed cake."

"She did it because the missionaries are coming," Lisel blurted, irritated now because her father was not.

With a sobering glance at Lisel, Marta set the bowl onto the table. "The missionaries come every Thursday night to pick up their laundry."

Undaunted, Lisel went on. "I wonder if Elder Nolte knows how carefully you wash his collars and iron his sleeves?"

A faint pink rose in Marta's cheeks. "The Elders pay us well to wash and iron their clothes, and I give them both full value for their money."

"And sigh over Elder Nolte's cuffs," Lisel said with a mocking flutter of her lashes.

6

Marta's face flushed red. "Perhaps it is time you took over the laundry chores," she said, wiping her hands on her faded blue apron. "I would be glad of any help you could possibly make of yourself, though I doubt that would amount to very much."

"Marta! Lisel!" Papa's voice sounded sharp and harsh. "Is this how your mother and I raised our daughters to speak to each other?"

Lisel thrust out her chin in a defiant angle. "But she poked me," she protested, "and called me a goose!"

Papa's eyes, narrowed and questioning, went from Lisel to Marta. Then his shoulders sagged. "How I wish your mother were here," he said in a voice muffled with growing emotion. "Surely she could do better than any of my poor efforts." His chin dropped to his chest and his jaw clenched and unclenched as he fought back his grief.

Suddenly, Lisel felt ashamed. She missed her mother with her whole heart, but that was nothing to the aching loss she knew her father felt. And now to have prodded that ache, to have brought up the pain in her father's face, made Lisel horribly, dreadfully ashamed of herself. She rushed to him and threw her arms around his neck. "It's not your fault, Papa. Please don't say it's your fault." Hot, contrite tears welled in her eyes. "I was only being spiteful to Marta because I was angry with her." She turned to her sister. "I did not mean any of the things I said, did I, Marta?"

Marta crossed the room to her side and knelt next to her father's chair. "Of course, she did not mean anything, Papa. And I am sorry, too. I should not have lost my temper."

Papa's mouth tightened in a sad smile and he patted both daughters' hands. "This last year cannot have been easy for either of you. I am not the best father, being old enough, almost, to be your grandfather; and I am also a very poor substitute for a mother."

Lisel laid her face on her father's shoulder as she did when she was a child and in need of comfort. But now she needed to comfort him. The wool of his jacket was scratchy against her cheek and smelled of shaving soap. "You are a wonderful father. We have seen how lonely and unhappy you have been but always, your first thought has been for Marta and me. And we have been ungrateful and wretched."

"And you have been very tolerant with your young and inexperienced daughters' efforts at managing a household," Marta added with a coaxing smile. "Do you remember when I tried to make Mother's beef soup with a smoked ham? And you ate it without one word of complaint?"

A slight, wistful smile lifted the corners of Papa's mouth. "I remember how thirsty I was for two days afterward." Lisel and Marta smiled too. "Perhaps we do not smile enough in this house." Papa sighed. "Not like we did when your mother was alive."

Lisel took her father's large hand in hers. She knew what would comfort him, what would comfort them all. "Soon we will have saved enough money to go to Salt Lake City, to the Temple. Michael will be out of the Labor Corps by then and we will all four go."

Lisel went on, her enthusiasm growing. "All of us, even Mother will be with us in spirit. She could never bear to miss a celebration." She paused for an instant, remembering. "And we will be sealed together. A family forever. And no one and nothing will ever part us again."

Lisel saw her father's hopeful, pensive smile and the moisture gathering in his eyes. "Yes, that will be a glorious day. A day for great rejoicing."

"And," Lisel continued, gripping her father's hand even more tightly, "we will go during the time they will be having conference. And we will wait in the great tabernacle with the domed roof; and when the prophet, Heber J. Grant, strides in we will all leap to our feet and sing so the angels will hear us, 'We Thank Thee Oh God For A Prophet.' Lisel felt the goose bumps come up on her arms and the stinging under her eyelids. "And we will sit in the presence of the Prophet of God and hear his words."

Papa wiped away a tear that had coursed down his cheek. "It will be like Heaven itself," he said in a voice choked with emotion.

"Herr Spann! Herr Spann!" A thumping at the door accompanied the voice in the hallway.

"Is this Franz Muller?" Papa frowned as he rose from his chair.

"We must have a blackout," Herr Muller insisted when Papa

8

opened the door. "Your curtains are open," he said pointing with his pipe to the draperies Lisel had pulled open and forgotten to close when Papa came home.

Marta hurried to the window and drew the curtains together.

"The papers tonight said Poland is on the verge of attack!" Panting, Herr Muller pulled off his hat and mopped his bald head with a large white handkerchief. The climb to the second story had left the short, barrel-shaped man red-faced and out of breath. "And downtown the Wehrmacht is installing antiaircraft guns on the roof of the I.G. Farben building!" he said, waving his pipe wildly, his voice squeaking his excitement.

"You must come in and sit down, Herr Muller," Marta said with a worried frown.

"No, no, I see I have interrupted your dinner." Herr Muller tucked his handkerchief into his jacket pocket. "I have just come home and I want to get to my radio. Surely we will be at war any moment!"

"But the Fuhrer said we would not have war," Lisel insisted, though now a tiny doubt tainted her certainty. "The Fuhrer said—"

"The Fuhrer does not know horse manure," Herr Muller snapped. "These Poles are warmongers. Have always been warmongers from the start of time. But we will show them this playing with fire is going too far," he said, his face reddening even more. "The only smart thing Hitler ever did for Germany was to make an alliance with Stalin. The Communists will show him how to properly deal with those murdering Poles."

Lisel felt a stab of apprehension. If Herr Muller intended to say such things about the Fuhrer and the Communists in such an outspoken fashion, she wished he would go somewhere else to say them. She wished he would go downstairs to his flat and shut the door. She did not want to hear any more about war. She longed to tell Herr Muller so, but she knew what her father's reaction would be if she did. For once, she clamped her lips together and kept quiet.

Marta laid her hand on Herr Muller's arm. "Perhaps you would like to come later for a piece of poppy seed cake?"

"Cake?" Herr Muller turned to Marta. His broad face reflected a slight confusion while his thoughts shifted from war to pastry. He smiled. "Poppy seed cake?"

9

"The missionaries will be coming too. Perhaps we can make a little party of it."

His smile sobered. "Thank you very much Fraulein, but I do not believe this is a time for parties."

Smiling, Marta turned him toward the door. "Well then, if you will not come up to us, we shall have to bring a large slice down to you."

Herr Muller's head bobbed with pleasure. "That would be wonderful, wonderful. I do not plan to be out tonight." He glanced toward the window and lowered his voice. "There are some strange men on the street tonight," he said and clapped his hat on his head. "I think they are SA thugs. You should not go out either." He tugged at his hat's brim. "Good night, Herr Spann. Frauleins," he said with a nod to Marta and one to Lisel.

Lisel heard his heavy footsteps on the creaking, wooden stairs as he made his way, in the dark, down to his basement apartment. She swallowed back the lump of uncertainty that rose in her throat and, looking for reassurance, cast a glance first at her father, then at her sister. She thought, for an instant, she saw an exchange of wary, worried glances. And she knew they were trying to hide their anxiety for her sake . . . because they thought she was a child and would not understand . . . because they thought she would be frightened.

Her eyes went to the window with the blackout draperies pulled against the night. Questions circled in her mind. Who were the men on the street and what were they waiting for? And if the Fuhrer said there would be no war, why was the Wehrmacht putting an antiaircraft gun on the I.G. Farben building?

"Come, let us eat before the food is cold," Papa said. And together, the family knelt beside their chairs and prayed for peace.

Later, around that same table, the Spanns and the missionaries finished their poppy seed cake. Elder Grant Nolte, a tall, blonde and burly young man from Idaho, told humorous stories of growing up near the Tetons, speaking in slow, distinct English so the Spanns, who were learning the language, could understand. While Elder Robert Parker, his junior companion, dark, slight and bespectacled, laughed quietly, shyly. Papa, forgetting the black preoccupation that hung over him earlier, joined in the fun with his distinctive laugh that sounded more like a snort. Marta, her gentle face alight, followed Elder Nolte's every expression with sparkling brown eyes. And Lisel, watching it all, smiled and made the sounds of laughter, but at the shaded edges of her mind lurked the dark figures down on the street, the headlines in the newspaper, and the gun on the roof of the I.G. Farben building downtown.

"That poor, confused moose," Elder Nolte was saying through his laughter, "crashed through Aunt Edith's clothesline and charged through the middle of town with Uncle Cheney's red winter underwear flapping from his antlers!"

Marta brushed away tears of laughter and Papa, in a rare expression of lightheartedness, clapped one hand against another. Lisel managed to join the gaiety and, for a few moments, push away all her doubts. They laughed and laughed until their laughter faded and the only sound in the room was the ticking of the clock while the unspoken, ominous threat rose above them like a clenched fist.

From upstairs, the music from Kurt's phonograph drifted down to them. He was playing a banned recording of "Honeysuckle Rose." Lisel's eyes went to the ceiling. Did he not know, she thought with exasperation, they could hear it? Could the men out on the street hear it, too?

"That boy sure does like jazz," Elder Nolte said. His words were casual but his voice betrayed his concern.

"What a racket," Lisel exclaimed and, flipping back her braids, went into the kitchen where she took the broom from behind the door.

"Since they banned jazz, Frau Heidemann will not allow Kurt to play those records," Marta said. "She must be away from home tonight."

Lisel thumped the ceiling with the broom handle. "She probably smelled our sausages and is, at this moment, down harassing the butcher for sausages of her own." She thumped again, harder. The music stopped. Lisel felt the entire room sigh with relief. She replaced the broom in its dark corner and turned to see the four at the table, glum and silent.

At last Elder Parker spoke up. "The Mission President has warned us to be ready to leave at any moment."

The color dropped out of Marta's face. Papa's eyes widened with alarm. A sudden fear struck Lisel like a padded fist. If the prophet felt Germany was unsafe for the missionaries and called them out, that must mean war was coming. Germany was going to war.

"Are things as bad as that?" Papa asked.

Elder Nolte sighed. "On the way over here we ran into the postman. He was delivering draft notices. He said more than a million men had been mobilized. He said the roads outside the city are filled with trucks and tanks. All headed east."

"To Poland," Papa said with finality.

Lisel looked at her father and sensed he was thinking of his only son and she thought of him, too. "Does that mean Michael will be going to war?" she asked and felt the tightening in her throat and heard her voice rise. "Does that mean he will have to fight?"

Papa sighed heavily. "I pray not, Lisel. I pray not."

"Well maybe it's not really that bad," Elder Nolte said and tried to smile. "We were called out last year during the Czech crisis. Everyone said there would be a war then, too. But there was no war and we came back okay. Maybe that's what will happen this time."

Marta's dark eyes brightened; a hopeful smile lifted her lips. "Yes, maybe you will not go. Maybe there will be no war."

And maybe cows chase rabbits, Lisel thought bitterly. The newspapers said it, the radio said it, Herr Muller said it, and now the missionaries said it. Germany was going to war. The sharp, hot certainty rose and expanded in her chest until she thought if she did not get away from the table, away from the others' brittle, hopeless smiles and their eyes that avoided each other, she would explode. She had to get away. Lisel rose from the table and picked up her fork and empty plate. "I will wash the dishes," she announced and gathered the other plates and utensils.

From the kitchen, Lisel tried to block out the whispered talk of war from the table. She was sick of hearing about war. Sick of feeling so confused and frightened. Papa said in the last war,

Germans finally resorted to eating the fireweed shoots that grew out of the bomb craters in the streets.

Lisel pushed shut the cupboard door on a stack of newly washed plates. Old Frau Schatz, down the block, said she had lived through one war and that was enough. She said a doctor friend gave her a black pill, one that she kept in her stocking drawer, so she would never have to live through another one. Thinking about that black pill in Frau Schatz's stocking drawer, Lisel frowned down at the remainder of the poppy seed cake. Then she remembered the promise to take a large slice down to Herr Muller. Lisel slung her dish towel over her shoulder. Maybe Herr Muller should have come up for his piece, she thought. This was just the sort of party he would enjoy.

She cut a piece from the cake and laid it on one of her mother's best china plates. Later, Lisel decided, she would also take a piece up to Kurt.

"I am going downstairs," she told the four at the table but no one took note of her leaving. Because of the blackout, the hallway and stairs were dark and Lisel had to feel her way down, guided only by the sound of Herr Muller's radio. The happy waltz that rushed up to meet her seemed loud and raucous.

Lisel hated going down to the basement. The air was more humid there, dank. And the hallway smelled of damp earth and mildewing masonry. At the end of the hall, Herr Muller's door stood halfway open and a shaft of faint, bluish light streamed out. Lisel pushed open the door.

She reacted to the scene inside with surprise. Surprise that Herr Muller's radio spewed out such a merry tune while laying on its side on the floor. Surprise at the overturned chair and rumpled throw rug. Then she saw Herr Muller. He looked like a heap of bloodied rags in the corner of the room.

Lisel dropped the plate and ran to him. "Herr Muller! Herr Muller!" she called, bending over him. He did not respond. Blood poured from his nose, his mouth, and a vicious cut above his eyebrow. From his throat rose a groan and a rattle. He had been beaten and beaten badly.

Lisel leapt to her feet and ran. Across the ransacked living room, through the door, down the hallway. Her braids whipped around her face and her shoulders. Don't let him die. Don't let him die. Don't let him die. Her heart pounded out the prayer. Her legs pistoned up the dark stairwell. Lisel tripped once and caught herself on the wooden stair. She felt a splinter stab into her hand, up again and up the stairs. She knew who had done this to Herr Muller and her imagination supplied the horrible sight over and over again. But why? Her breath coming in hot, dry gasps, she burst into the apartment. "Papa! Herr Muller's been hurt. Those men from the street have hurt him!"

The scene before Lisel's eyes froze. Her father staring at her. Marta, Elders Nolte and Parker, wide-eyed, mouths agape.

Papa rushed toward her. "Get Kurt," he ordered. He brushed past her and down the stairs.

Lisel turned and ran, leaving Marta and the missionaries sitting stunned at the table.

On the top floor, Lisel burst through Heidemanns' door. Kurt was slouched in an old easy chair, a book in his hands. His blonde hair was rumpled and his shirt was off. For one ridiculous instant, Lisel thought how strong his bare arms looked. He looked up at her in surprise. "It's Herr Muller," she sobbed. "He has been beaten!"

Kurt leapt out of the chair and grasped Lisel by the arms. His face bore the mottled green and yellow of healing bruises. "Was it the men in the street?" he asked, tightening his grip on her arms.

Lisel nodded. "I think so."

Kurt swore under his breath and pushed past her and out into the hall.

Lisel followed, running behind Kurt to the basement. There, they found the missionaries standing, pale and grim-faced, in Herr Muller's living room, watching as Papa and Marta bent over the injured man.

Lisel's teeth wanted to chatter. She wrapped her arms around her waist to stop the sudden shivering that took her.

Herr Muller had roused enough to mumble barely coherent answers to Papa's questions. Marta knelt next to him, a slight frown between her brows as she tried to staunch the flow of blood from his head with the dish towel Lisel had lost when she fled his apartment.

14

Marta raised her eyes to Lisel. Marta's face, though pale, was as calm as if she had just looked up from a piece of needlework but her brown eyes betrayed her apprehension. "Run down the street and fetch Dr. Kettel," she said.

"No," Kurt exclaimed, kneeling next to the injured man. "I know a doctor, a safe doctor. We must get Herr Muller there." He looked down at the man. "You must get up, Herr Muller. You must try to get up."

"But he cannot be moved," Papa interjected.

Kurt looked up. His blue eyes burned in his bruised face. "We must get him out of this apartment, away from this neighborhood. It is not safe here for him anymore." He turned to Herr Muller. "You understand? You must get up."

Herr Muller nodded. Kurt wrapped his arms around the older man's chest and, straining, pulled him into a sitting position. Herr Muller groaned and slumped against Kurt.

He looked up at Elder Nolte. "It is five blocks," he said. "I will need some help."

Elder Parker put his hand on Elder Nolte's arm. "You can't get involved in this. President Reese said—"

"I'll tell President Reese myself. Tomorrow." Elder Nolte brushed aside his companion's hand. "You'd better stay here with the Spanns in case those men come back." Elder Nolte stepped forward and, together with Kurt, was able to get Herr Muller to his feet.

Kurt nodded at Lisel. "Get his coat and hat," he said.

Lisel did as she was told but handed Herr Muller's clothes to Marta. "Here," she said, "I must run upstairs." Lisel dashed down the hall and up the stairs to the top floor and into the Heidemanns' apartment. She found Kurt's shirt on the arm of the easy chair and his jacket in the closet. By the time she got back down to the basement, Kurt and Elder Nolte, with Herr Muller sagging nearly unconscious between them, were in the hallway. She stopped in front of Kurt and, feeling suddenly shy, held out his jacket and shirt. "You had best put these on."

The corner of Kurt's mouth lifted in a lopsided smile. "Thanks," he said, and while Elder Nolte supported Herr Muller, Kurt slipped into his clothes. Then he reached out and tugged at

Lisel's braid and winked a farewell. Lisel knew he meant the gesture as a comfort and she was grateful.

Lisel, Marta, and Elder Parker watched from behind the front door of the building while the trio—a German teenager, an injured old man, and an American missionary—clung to each other and staggered down one of Berlin's blacked-out streets and into the night. Marta glanced back into the dark apartment building. "Where is Papa?"

"He's still in Herr Muller's apartment," Elder Parker answered.

Marta nodded. "I suppose it could do with a little straightening," she said and turned and went down the stairs. Elder Parker followed, leaving Lisel at the door.

She stood there for a moment longer. "Please be all right," she prayed. "Please be all right." The sound of footsteps on the street drew her attention, and she caught sight of the postman, walking with slow, weary steps from door to door as he delivered the midnight summons.

Chapter 2

"Go at once to the C and A . . ."

LISEL STRAIGHTENED FROM THE PATCH OF VEGETABLES SHE WAS weeding and, flipping her braids over her shoulder, glared at the window on the top floor of their apartment house.

"Charming things are there today," the vocalists continued to the snappy fox-trot rhythm and then went on to name every item in the store.

Lisel had heard the song thirty-seven times that morning and counted each time with growing irritation. She pulled off her mother's tattered gardening hat and impatiently slapped it against her knee. Everyone who went to the C and A Department Store received one of those records and since it was the only record Walter Heidemann, Kurt's ten-year-old brother, had, it was the only one he played and played and played.

Lisel looked over at Kurt who, with his hoe, hacked at the tiny sprouting weeds with murderous intent. Perspiration glistened on his face and his bare arms and made his sleeveless undershirt stick to his back.

"You are very generous, Kurt, letting Walter use your phonograph like that," Lisel said with only a trace of sarcasm in her voice.

Kurt straightened and grinned his crooked grin at Lisel. He ran a hand through his blonde, wavy hair. "And you think I should be generous enough to lend him my records also."

"I think you should tell him to turn it off. Are you not tired of hearing about the good old C and A?"

"No," he replied with a jaunty shrug. "I like the C and A. Charming things are there today," he sang off key and executed a nimble little dance step among the tomatoes. Kurt did things like that only to annoy her. Lisel turned away from him with a snort of exasperation, clapped the hat back on her head, and went back to the hated weeding. She tried to block out the insistent music but Kurt continued humming along with the record, "Go at once to the C and A . . ." Lisel gritted her teeth and glanced over her shoulder at him.

Kurt was a handsome young man, despite the bruises that marked his face and body. Tall, a little thin maybe, but broad-shouldered. His eyes were a bright, clear blue under heavy brows, his lips firmly cut, and his jaw straight and decisive. But his high, thin nose had an odd crook in it, like it had been broken once and never set.

In the brilliant sunlight of the August morning, Kurt, humming among the cabbages, looked like a different person than the commanding and intense young man who spirited Herr Muller into the night only ten hours earlier.

A slamming door in the apartment building drew Lisel's attention. Two unfamiliar men had been moving boxes from Herr Muller's apartment to a horse-drawn wagon in the alley.

Kurt had said nothing about Herr Muller or the incident last night, and Lisel had felt his reluctance to talk about it. She had understood. She did not care to think about last night either; but now, watching the men as they hefted Franz Muller's easy chair through the garden, she felt that if she did not find out where Kurt had taken him, whether or not he was all right, whether or not he even survived, the huge cold lump in her chest would burst.

At last she asked. "What about Herr Muller?"

"What about him?" Kurt asked without looking up or breaking rhythm with his hoe.

"Well, is he all right? Where is he?"

"I heard he is going to live with his sister in Denmark. He had that arthritic knee and going up and down the stairs pained him. So he has gone to live with sister, in Denmark."

Incredulous, Lisel frowned at him. "I am not asking about his arthritic knee. I want to know—"

From between his teeth Kurt swore. He fastened blazing blue eyes on Lisel. Splotches of angry red stained his lean cheeks. "I heard he is going to live with his sister in Denmark." Despite the emotion on Kurt's face, his voice was normal, casual. "Going down the stairs to his apartment became too painful. So he has gone to live with his sister, in Denmark."

At last the meaning behind Kurt's words sank in. Herr Muller was still alive but in hiding somewhere, a fugitive. Usually a victim of her emotions, Lisel felt an odd emptiness. The combination of fear and relief cancelled each other out. "Well, then, I guess that is that." She moved to the weathered, wooden bench in the shade of an ancient peach tree and sat down. The morning sun shone through the leaves and made a lacy pattern of sunlight and shadow on the ground. The scent of the damp, warm earth trailed along with a lazy summer breeze. How many times had she seen Herr Muller and his fox terrier sitting just here, in the shade?

Lisel looked at Kurt who had gone back to hoeing but who was no longer humming. She longed to ask him why those terrible things had happened to Herr Muller, but she knew, if he knew, he would not tell her. He was protecting himself and, she realized with a surge of gratefulness, he was protecting her, too. But most of all, Kurt was protecting an old man who talked too much.

She looked down at the mound of earth at the base of the tree. "I never thought he would leave Maxi," she said in a quiet voice.

Kurt moved to stand next to where Lisel sat. She felt a gentle tug on one of her braids, a playful effort to cheer her. "Yes, Maxi was a good dog. A good friend to Franz," he said.

"I remember how upset your mother got when she found out Herr Muller was going to bury him here, in the back garden."

Kurt withdrew his hand. "Yes, she was upset," he murmured and turned back to his hoeing.

The men in Herr Muller's apartment had finished and were climbing into the wagon. "I wonder who is going to move in downstairs," Lisel said.

"We are," Kurt answered.

"No!" Lisel twisted around on the bench and faced Kurt. "You cannot move down there. It's horrible! It smells musty and there is no sunlight."

Kurt's lips became a tight line. "Mother says we need a bigger place."

And whatever Frau Heidemann wanted, Frau Heidemann got, Lisel thought.

"Hello!"

Lisel turned to see Elders Nolte and Parker parking their bicycles at the side of the house. They came through the garden toward her. Lisel knew why they had come and her heart, weighted with fear and foreboding, plummeted to the soles of her feet. She stood and pulled her cold lips into a smile as the pair approached. Elder Nolte led the way with his long strides, his blonde hair shining in the sunlight, and Elder Parker lagging behind, watched his footing among the plants. "You are leaving," she said when they got to where she stood.

"Yes," Elder Nolte replied. He seemed calm, unworried though Elder Parker fidgeted, jingling the coins in his pocket. "We're taking the boat-train to Copenhagen as soon as we finish saying good-bye," Elder Nolte continued. "We wondered if we could leave our bicycles here. Just until we get back."

"I think that would be all right," Lisel answered and looked over at Kurt, who stood aloof, leaning on his hoe, his blue eyes cool. "We could put them in the garden shed, could we not?"

"What if you do not come back?" Kurt asked.

Elder Nolte shrugged. "I suppose then, you could just keep them. You could use a bike, couldn't you, Kurt?"

"Not likely," Kurt replied with a brusque voice and turned away.

Surprised at first, Lisel glared at him then turned her attention back to the missionaries. "I am sure Walter would be glad for the offer. But maybe you will be back soon," she said to the Elders. "Have you told Papa and Marta yet?"

"No. We were just on our way up when we saw you out here," Elder Nolte said.

"I will put my things away and be there in a minute."

Elder Nolte nodded. He extended his hand to Kurt, who took it with reluctance. "The next time I see you, Brother Heidemann," Elder Nolte said with conviction, "we are going to have a long discussion, and then I will see to it you are baptized."

Lisel expected a rude rebuff from Kurt, but he only cocked his mouth sideways in a sardonic, lopsided grin and replied, "Not likely."

When the missionaries were out of earshot, Lisel turned on Kurt. "That was a fine piece of courtesy," she snapped. "After last night, I should think you would be a little more friendly toward them."

Kurt regarded her with narrowed eyes. "Are you going to marry one of them?"

Lisel rolled her eyes in disbelief. "And I have seen cows chase rabbits," she declared.

"Yes, and I have seen how those American missionaries come here with their fine clothes and their money and how the Mormon girls chase after them," Kurt replied bitterly. "They forget they are German girls and they only think of marrying rich Americans and going there to live."

Lisel drew herself up. "Kurt Heidemann, how can you pretend to know what other people think? I do not chase after any man and we do not plan to live in America."

"Then what about Marta?" Kurt returned warmly. "She is in love with Elder Nolte and I hear your family, all the time, talking about when you will go to America."

Lisel jerked off her garden gloves finger by finger. "I have explained all that to you before, Kurt. We are going to America so we can go to the temple in Salt Lake City. They have ceremonies there that will seal our family together forever. Even after we die we will still be a family and still live together as a family. Do you not see how important that is to us?"

"I see how foolish you are. Death is the only certain thing in this world. After that there is nothing. We are nothing. Your religion teaches you that after death there is a better life so you are indifferent to all that is wrong in this one. You ignore the hate, the violence, the atrocities committed now because you are contemplating a bright and glorious future on some pink and gold heavenly cloud." Kurt paused for a second, his face flushed. "You talk of your family and how important it is for you to go through this ceremony. You save your money so you can make this long trip. You make this great effort because you want your family to be together forever. What, then, about the German family? What great effort do you make for that family?"

Lisel's mouth dropped open and then snapped shut. "Kurt Heidemann, how dare you speak such rubbish! You do not know what you are saying." She slapped her gloves into the crown of her hat. "*I* do not know what *you* are saying. So it would be best if you did not say anything more to me ever again!" Lisel whirled and stormed up the garden path toward the house. He could put away the tools himself.

Lisel found her father and the missionaries sitting at the dining table with glasses of lemonade. They sat without speaking. Papa stared at the air, a worried line between his gray brows, his mouth drawn down. Elder Parker drew circles on the tablecloth with his fingernail and Elder Nolte watched Marta out of the corner of his eye.

Marta was in the kitchen, packing sandwiches and fruit into a basket. Her eyes were bright with unshed tears and her chin quivered a little as she worried her bottom lip with her teeth. Her sister's face alarmed Lisel. She had rarely seen her so upset.

It was true, the missionaries' departure worried and frightened Lisel, but she could see their leaving held another dimension for Marta . . . Marta, who might never see her Elder Nolte again. Lisel felt ashamed for the way she had teased her sister the night before. "Is there something I can do to help?" she asked.

Marta cast her a watery smile. "No, I have done almost all. We thought we would see them off at the train station." Her voice trembled. "And I wanted to give them a little something to eat along the way. It will be a long while before they get to eat again."

Lisel looked into the basket. Besides several wrapped, cold-cut beef sandwiches, in the bottom was a tin of cinnamon, the tea kettle lid, and a chunk of soap. She shot a sympathetic glance at her sister who was polishing a pair of red apples with such energy Lisel thought the skins would wear off. Then, without mentioning it, she took the cinnamon, the lid, and the soap out of the basket and put them back in the cupboard.

Marta placed the apples in the basket and frowned. "I thought I had put more than this in here."

"I think there is enough," Lisel told her. She tried to make her voice sound cheerful. "Copenhagen is not that far away, and there will be places to buy food along the way."

Marta glanced over her shoulder toward Elder Nolte. "But he is such a hearty eater. I would not want him to be hungry." She began rummaging through the cupboards again. "If only there were something more I could give him."

Lisel found a cloth napkin and tucked it over the food, hoping to keep Marta from sending the entire kitchen with the two Elders. "It looks wonderful just the way it is. Come on now or we might miss the bus."

Slowly, Marta closed the cupboard. "Yes," she said. "We might miss the bus."

At the stop, they did not have long to wait before the double-decker bus roared up to the curb. It had the advertisement, "Berlin Smokes Juno Cigarettes" and the slogan, "Right Is What The Fuhrer Does" painted on its side. A young woman sat in the driver's seat while the usual driver, now wearing a gray military uniform, stood behind her offering instructions. Lisel glanced at her father. His eyes narrowed on the uniform, but if he felt any emotion it did not show on his face. Yet Lisel sensed he was thinking of Michael and she wondered whether her brother, in the Labor Corps, like so many other young men in their early twenties, would also be drafted.

Lisel swallowed back her anxiety and she and her father made their way to the center of the bus and slid onto a bench, leaving Marta to sit next to Elder Nolte, while a frowning Elder Parker found a seat next to a bearded man who carried a huge paper-wrapped parcel on his lap. The bus, filled to capacity, was hot and stifling and smelled of human sweat even with the windows down. Despite the crowd, no one conversed, no one laughed. It was as though the passengers had been stunned into the brooding silence that had invaded the bus and even the very air held its breath.

At the next stop, a short young man boarded the bus. He smiled as he greeted some of the passengers and whistled a jaunty tune as he sat down. The woman next to him scowled. "This is no time for frivolity," she snapped and the young man quit whistling.

23

The railway station was in a state of wild confusion. Ticket lines snaked down the walkway and blocked the platforms. The Spanns and the missionaries threaded their way through the over-crowded station toward the gate of the noon boat-train platform. Arriving and departing trains filled the station with such an intense level of noise that Lisel wanted to put her hands over her ears.

Baggage handlers, spurred on by the frantic curses of the baggage masters, worked with furious disregard for the luggage they pitched onto the carts. Hundreds of soldiers, wearing their heavy winter uniforms, stood in clumps, nervously puffing cigarettes. Some paced, others sat in corners playing skat, and still others tried to comfort their weeping mothers, wives, or sweethearts. Vacationers, hearing the rumors of war, had cut short their holidays and jammed into the railway station in an effort to get home. At the edge of the platforms, groups of Jews huddled together, weary desperation etched on their faces.

Lisel sidestepped a pair of young soldiers who, with their arms around each other, sang the Horst Wessel song, "Oh, we'll go marching onwards, til nothing's left but shards, Today we're masters of Germany, Tomorrow of all the World . . ." They smelled of sour beer and Lisel wrinkled her nose in distaste. She felt Papa's firm hand on her elbow as he urged her to quicken her pace. "Disgraceful," she heard him murmur.

"Herr Spann! Marta! Lisel!" The three turned to see Albrecht Masur fighting his way toward them. He had been in school with Michael and went into the Labor Corps at the same time. Today he wore a gray army uniform that was too long in the arms and legs.

He rushed up to them, out of breath. Perspiration glistened on his forehead and lip. Lisel thought he seemed relieved to see them. "Are you here to see Michael off?" he asked.

Papa looked a little surprised. "No, our friends here are leaving the country," he replied and introduced the missionaries.

Albrecht acknowledged the Elders with a nod then turned back to the Spanns. "I thought Michael would be going with this call but maybe he is too valuable where he is."

Papa shook his head. "We have not heard from him for a week now. Last we heard he was still working on the West Wall."

Albrecht shrugged. "Maybe those fellows are not going. What fireworks they are going to miss. I'm glad I have the chance to show those murdering Poles what is what."

The muscles along Papa's jaw hardened into a ridge at Albrecht's enthusiasm. He changed the subject. "Where is your family? Surely they will be here to see you off."

"I don't know." Albrecht frowned, and, with a puzzled glance, looked around the platform. "I wrote them a letter when my conscription notice came through. I told them where I would be and when I would be leaving. Maybe with the draft notices going out, the mails are slow. Maybe they have not yet received my letter." Albrecht hitched up his shoulders with confidence. "Of course we will be back within a week. So there is really no need to worry."

Lisel looked at Albrecht's broad face, beaming with certainty and self-importance, eager for the glory of a proven warrior; and she felt a vague sense of unreality. Though he was older than she by four years, he looked like a boy playing soldier. He looked too young for such a deadly game. And he was no older than Michael. Would Michael be going to war, too? A cold stone fell through her heart. Had Michael written them a letter that was not delivered? Was he waiting in some noisy, overcrowded train station like Albrecht? Lisel's eyes darted among the crowd, searching for her tall, dark-haired brother.

"Well, I had better get back to my unit," Albrecht was saying while shaking hands with Papa. "If you see my parents would you send them to the lower platform?"

"Of course," Papa answered. He patted Albrecht's shoulder and sent him off with a smile that Lisel knew hid his troubled thoughts. She saw lines of worry form in Papa's face as he watched Albrecht make his way through the crowd. She felt her own throat tighten. Where was Michael?

"I think this is our train."

Lisel turned at Elder Nolte's voice. The train pulled into the station with a roar and a rush of air.

The two missionaries began gathering their hand luggage. From behind her, Lisel felt a shove and then a jostling push and she had to grab for her hat. The crowd on the platform surged forward, toward the already crowded train.

"I guess this is it," Elder Nolte said and offered his hand to Papa.

"God be with you," Papa said, as he shook each missionary's hand.

"And with you Brother Spann," each returned, solemnly. "Would it be all right," Elder Nolte asked Papa, "if we wrote to your family while we are away?"

"Of course, of course," Papa answered, "and we will be happy to write back to you."

"Good." Elder Nolte answered with an enthusiasm that sounded forced and hollow. He turned to Lisel with an affectionate smile and tugged one red braid. "We'll see you in a few weeks," he said. Lisel mustered a grin. "Yes, a few weeks," she replied and truly wanted to believe it. But a nightmarish certainty overrode her hopes and her smile froze into a stiff line. Elder Parker shook her hand. "Good-bye, Sister Spann," he said and Lisel saw the moisture gather in his bespectacled eyes. She felt the hot, mounting pressure in her own and knew, any moment, tears would spill over her lashes.

Lisel looked away as Elder Nolte said good-bye to Marta. She could not bear the despair that underscored her sister's gentle features. Not that Marta was not brave in saying good-bye to this man whom she secretly loved. She shook his hand cordially and, through unshed tears, a flicker of a smile rose at the corner of her lips then died. Elder Nolte was just as proper and correct as he had always been, but Lisel saw and even felt all the wrenching misery of that final parting. And suddenly, great, hot tears were coursing down her face and onto the front of her blouse.

The Elders had to fight their way into the already overloaded railway car. From where Lisel stood on the platform, she could see the passengers were crushed into every available square inch. Grim-faced men, both uniformed and civilian, frightened women, and weary children strained and sweated, holding their narrow places in the car while making room for the boarding passengers.

"Can you see them?" Marta asked as her eyes searched among the faces.

"No," Lisel answered, "but they must be there."

"We must wave just the same," Marta insisted. "Perhaps they can see us. They must see us wave."

As the engine began to roar and the heavy, iron wheels to turn, Lisel and Papa and Marta waved at the departing train, the departing missionaries—Germany's link to Salt Lake and the prophet. Lisel felt as if she and her family had been left adrift and alone. The scalding tears that brimmed over her eyelids magnified and distorted the scene to a hazy blur. But Marta, holding herself rigid, her face white, biting her bottom lip, did not shed one tear.

"We will go down to the lower platform now," Papa said when the train disappeared from view. "We cannot let Albrecht go without someone to see him off."

So Lisel, sniffling, dragging her handkerchief over her eyes and wet cheeks and feeling completely miserable, and Marta, walking in stiff silence, followed Papa back through the crowded station and down to the lower platform. They arrived just moments after Albrecht's train pulled out. Only a few people still remained— weeping women comforting other weeping women.

"We are too late," Papa said and he cast an anxious glance around the platform. "Do you see the Masurs?"

Lisel looked but Albrecht's parents were not there. They had missed their son's train. "No, Papa. They are not here."

"I do not see them either," he said with a sad sigh. "I guess there is nothing left for us to do but go home. Perhaps, there, we will find word of Michael."

They were halfway up the stairs when they met the Masurs hurrying down. Albrecht's father, grim-faced, clutched a letter in his hand. His mother still wore her apron over her faded, shapeless housedress. Her eyes were red from weeping. "Herr Spann," she cried out when she saw Papa. "Have you seen our boy? Have you seen our Albrecht?"

With a look of compassion, Papa reached out and took Frau Masur's hand and laid another on her husband's shoulder. "Yes, we saw Albrecht. His train has just left."

Frau Masur let out a small cry and then began to sob against her husband's shoulder. "I will never see my Albrecht again."

"Now Mama," her husband patted her shoulder, "Albrecht is a grown man. He will be all right." He turned agonized eyes to Papa. "We only just received his letter. It must have been delayed in the mail."

"Yes," Papa said, "Albrecht thought that might have happened. He wanted to see you but, of course, he was also very excited. He looked very proud and handsome in his fine uniform." Albrecht's mother stopped sobbing and looked up at Papa with something fragile yet hopeful in her swollen eyes. A trembling smile touched her lips. "Handsome?"

"And healthy and strong. Just the way you raised him," Papa added with a gentle smile. "You would have been proud of him."

"Yes," she said and wiped her eyes with the corner of her apron. "We are proud of our boy. He is a fine and loving son."

"Just as Michael is to you," Herr Masur said. His face had relaxed and he managed a smile. "I suppose you are here seeing him off too?"

Lisel looked up at her father and saw the anxiety harden his face.

"No," Papa replied. "We have not heard from Michael yet."

The couple exchanged glances, then Herr Masur extended his hand. "Well, I am sure you shall hear soon. Thank you, Joseph."

"Yes, thank you Herr Spann," Albrecht's mother said. "I know we will not have to worry about either of our sons."

The Spanns had turned and started back up the stairs when Lisel heard Frau Masur's anguished but resigned voice. "I shall never see my Albrecht again."

"Now, Mama, we will not think such things," her husband returned.

Lisel looked at Papa. His face was grave and thoughtful and again Lisel knew he was thinking of Michael. She turned her own eyes to the mass of people crowded in the station, but she saw no one who looked like her brother.

On the way through the station, they passed a platform where two young men were fighting, using bare fists, in a circle cleared by shouting men. One of the soldiers had blood on his face and his tunic was torn. Papa turned away from the sight with sorrow and despair in his eyes. "How can it have come to this?" Lisel heard him mutter.

From the street outside their apartment house, Lisel ran ahead. Her chest filled with a confusing rush of anticipation and dread as she pulled open their postbox. It was empty.

"The postman has not yet come," came a voice from above them. Lisel looked up and saw Frau Heidemann, Kurt's mother, leaning over the railing. She was an overbearing, demanding woman whose unstylish and soft appearance sometimes fooled people into believing they were dealing with someone of half her determination and slyness. "I expect all these draft notices have slowed things down."

Lisel did not like Frau Heidemann, but she tolerated her for Kurt's sake and was civil for Papa's. "Yes, I expect that is what happened." She made a move for her front door but Frau Heidemann stopped her.

"I noticed you were not home this afternoon," she said.

Lisel knew the older woman would pry and question until she found out just where and why the Spanns had gone. She longed to tell the woman to tend her own cabbage but she bit back the words. "We went to the railway station. The missionaries from our church are leaving."

"Leaving for good?" Frau Heidemann asked in a shrill voice. "Those Americans," she went on when Lisel had nodded, "are no better than sissies and cowards. A little rumor of war and they run home to hide their heads in their mothers' skirts. Pah!" she said with a derisive gesture. "Let them go then!"

With the sound of the front door opening behind her, Lisel turned to Papa and Marta. Each of their faces bore an anxious and worried look. "Is there anything?" Papa asked.

Lisel shook her head.

"Herr Spann! You must congratulate me," Frau Heidemann called. "I am moving today."

"Then, by all means, congratulations," Papa returned.

"We are taking the downstairs apartment now that Herr Muller has abandoned it." She turned and said something to someone behind her. "Ours is so cramped and stuffy. And such a filthy thing with the wind blowing in dust all the time. And so much of it with all the buildings going up in the city."

From behind Frau Heidemann, Kurt and Walter appeared, hefting their mother's favorite possession—a huge, gilt-framed mirror her husband had pilfered from a French Chateau in the last war. Lisel suspected Frau Heidemann had waited until she had an audience to move the mirror through the hall and down the stairs. Lisel cocked her mouth sideways in a grimace.

"Gently now," Frau Heidemann called to her sons. "That is a very valuable piece. It must be handled carefully." She slanted a look at the Spanns. "Ernst liberated that mirror in a terrible battle along the Loire. He received three wounds that would have been fatal to ordinary men, but Ernst was no ordinary man."

Lisel chewed her tongue on that one. Walter and Kurt were angling the mirror past the Spann's on the landing. Kurt's mouth was a taut line and his cheeks ran red. He did not look at Lisel and she remembered she was still angry at him so she stared right at him, daring him to look her way.

"The frame itself must be worth a thousand marks," Frau Heidemann continued, "but of course, since it was a gift from my Ernst," she paused and dabbed at her eyes with the corner of her apron, "it is much more valuable than that to me." Frau Heidemann preferred to think of her husband as "passed on" though everyone knew he had just run off one day—and probably for a good cause.

The front door of the building clicked open and a man and woman stepped into the hallway. He was a thin, flour-faced man with a pair of *pince nez* spectacles over a white walrus mustache. But behind his spectacles were alert, glittering eyes with a look hard enough to crack ice. She was a short, broad-bosomed woman with her iron-gray hair scraped back in a knot. He wore a party badge on his lapel and she a Women's League pin. Together they lifted their arms. "Heil Hitler."

The Spanns and Frau Heidemann returned the greeting. Lisel saw Kurt look up at the pair with narrowed eyes. And she saw that the man's glance went to Kurt with a flicker that hooded some thought that brewed in his hard, gray eyes. Lisel felt a shiver from deep within.

"We are Gustav and Elsa Wrobel," the man declared. "We have come to look at an upstairs flat." He snapped out the words in a dry, humorless voice.

"Ah, yes," answered Frau Heidemann. "I would be happy to show you the apartment." She beckoned the Wrobels up the stairs. "It is a lovely little place and my sons and I are so unhappy to give it up," she said as the Wrobels came up to the landing. "But they are growing so large now and they beg me so often for more room." Here Frau Heidemann shrugged. "So what could I do? I had to sacrifice my dear little home."

The three disappeared from view and the Spanns turned to their own apartment. "Did you hear that?" Lisel said when the door closed. "How could she say such things and not have her nose grow out to here?"

"We cannot judge another's actions," Papa said and, with a thoughtful frown between his gray brows, lowered himself into his easy chair.

Lisel bit her lip. Papa was right but she felt no remorse. Lies had short legs and would not carry Frau Heidemann far.

"I believe I will go to my room for a while," Marta said quietly. "I have some mending to finish."

Lisel knew that was only an excuse and felt a niggling worry at the back of her mind. She had never seen Marta seem so despairing before.

"She will get over it in time," Papa said, breaking into Lisel's thoughts. "I remember when your Mama and I. . . ." He broke off, retreating to some far off time and then his head dropped. His mouth tightened. "Perhaps one never gets over it after all."

A staccato rapping sounded at the door and Frau Heidemann's face appeared from around it. "Herr Spann, such glad news," she exclaimed and invited herself into the room. "The Wrobels have decided to take my apartment. I thought I would have such trouble getting rid of that hole and I would end up paying rent for two apartments. But they decided right away. Of course, they noticed how clean it was. I always must have things clean around me." She paused, looking at them, her head cocked. "But why are you so somber? I thought you would be happy for me."

A brief smile lifted Papa's mouth. "Of course we are happy for you. If we appear somber, it is probably that we worry a little over Michael. We have not heard from him in a week."

Frau Heidemann threw back her hands and began to laugh. "How foolish of me. I am becoming forgetful." She searched the pockets of her apron. "Michael was here this afternoon while you were gone. I thought he looked so handsome in his uniform. Ah

31

ha!" She produced a folded scrap of paper. "He asked me to give you this."

Papa took the note with trembling fingers. Lisel went to his side, her heart pounding in her throat, and, over his shoulder, read the hurriedly scribbled words.

Dear Papa, Marta, and Lisel,

I am sorry to have missed seeing you this afternoon. They say we will be back in a few weeks so I will come to you then. I am not frightened and you must not be frightened for me. I trust in the Lord to watch over me. His Will Be Done. Remember me in your prayers as I will always remember you. God be with you until we are together again.

Your loving son and brother,

Michael

Chapter 3

O<small>N</small> T<small>HURSDAY</small>, A<small>UGUST</small> 31, 1939, <small>THE NEWSPAPERS CARRIED</small> the broad banner, "Heavy Fighting in Gleiwitz!" According to the accounts, a German radio station in Gleiwitz, near the Polish border, was attacked and captured by the Polish army. The "gangsters" locked the station employees in the basement, made inflammatory speeches over the air in Polish, and then quickly retreated across the border.

The next morning—a gray dawn with low, forbidding clouds—home radios and loud speakers in shops and factories and on street corners blared a fanfare followed by the announcement, "The Fuhrer speaks!"

Hitler declared, "I have determined to speak with Poland in the same language Poland has been using toward us for months now. . . . My love of peace and my boundless patience must not be mistaken for weakness or cowardice. . . . Since early this morning at 5:45, fire is being returned, and from now on each bomb will be answered with a bomb!"

This announcement was quickly followed by declarations of war from England and France. Unlike similar announcements in 1914, these did not trigger a wild rejoicing in the streets. The German people were stunned and astonished.

An air of depression and anxiety invaded the Spann household and sent Papa searching his scriptures, once again, for solace. Marta became more withdrawn, and Lisel sat between two opposing emotions. First, an excitement, a swaggering, youthful confidence that the Fuhrer was always right, the Reich would gloriously prevail, and it would take no more than a couple of weeks to put the arrogant Poles into place. But then a more pervasive sense of fear and dread gnawed at the corners of her mind and went with her into sleep. After the declaration of war, more announcements followed. Listening to foreign radio broadcasts was declared illegal and Lisel wondered if Kurt would continue to monitor the BBC Channel Seven eleven o'clock news. She knew even the threat of imprisonment would probably not be enough to thwart his type of stubbornness.

Blackouts were to be total and mandatory. Homes must use the heavy blackout curtains and businesses must extinguish all lights after dark. Streetlights were eliminated. Bus headlights were replaced with a single, blue light that cast a ghoulish glow in the dark. Streetcar lights continued to have a faint light on their route numbers but the interior lights were hooded with black cloth. Policemen were allowed to use flashlights with a single red bulb, but civilians were threatened with a fifty-mark fine for the improper use of a flashlight during a blackout.

Hitler's Youth groups mobilized to paint curbs and street crossings with luminous white to warn those who must be out after dark. Gratings on the street were covered with sandbags that were also striped with the paint.

Five hundred thousand sick and infirm, elderly, and children under ten were evacuated from the industrialized areas of western Germany into the countryside.

That Sunday, the Spanns attended sacrament meeting as usual in the chapel on the second floor of a rented building. But the tone was somber as their branch president, wearing a uniform, said good-bye to his congregation. During the closing hymn, "God Be with You Till We Meet Again," several members of the congregation wept openly. Afterward there was no visiting. Branch members left the building and hurried home. Puzzled, Lisel followed Papa and Marta out onto the strangely empty street. Even the tram carried few passengers today. "Where has everyone gone? What has happened?" Lisel asked.

Papa and Marta exchanged glances. At last, Marta spoke up. "There is a rumor that seventy Polish bombers are headed for Berlin," she said.

The news came as a chill shock. Lisel divided the rest of that long day worrying about Michael and watching the brilliant blue skies over her home. She jumped at the sound of every vehicle that rumbled by on the street. Several times she checked the government issued gas masks her family received and traced her footsteps down to Heidemann's basement apartment, which had been designated as the building's bomb shelter much to Frau Heidemann's outrage. She counted each step and noted the time it took to go down the stairs. She filled a bucket with water and stood it next to their apartment door, in case of fire. And she wrote Michael two long letters. The first, full of her fears, she crumpled and threw away. Onto the second, a cheerful, chatty letter as if Michael were away on holiday, she fixed a stamp showing the Fuhrer in knightly armor. But since she had no address, she slipped the letter into the top drawer of her bureau. And she fretted.

If Marta was worried, she did not say it. However, she put a big kettle of laundry on the stove to boil and sat in the kitchen with her mending in her lap, something she never did on Sundays. Marta had frequently chided Lisel for sewing on Sundays, saying, "You'll have to pick out every stitch with your nose in the hereafter."

Papa retired to his scriptures, reading aloud from Exodus.

Two scriptures stuck in Lisel's mind that day: "Thou shalt neither vex a stranger nor oppress him: for ye were strangers in the land of Egypt"; and the second, "Thou shalt not oppress a stranger: for ye know the heart of a stranger, seeing ye were strangers in Egypt." Had the Polish vexed the German stranger?—or now, was it the Germans who vexed the Poles? She looked up at Papa and longed to ask but she held her tongue. He would only remind her that Exodus referred to the Jews. And though Papa never spoke of it, Lisel sensed her father's outrage at their government's treatment of the Children of Israel.

Supper that night was somber. Though another, stricter rationing had been announced, Marta had produced red snapper, stewed tomatoes, and cucumbers from the garden. Lisel did no more than pick at the food.

The daylight withdrew from the sky, leaving only the stars to light Berlin. Lisel began to relax. She had watched all day, but no

35

bombers had arrived. She sent a fervent "thank you" up with her prayers at bedtime.

Lisel had only been asleep a few hours when the shrill wail of air raid sirens startled her from sleep. At first, she could not make out the sound or its meaning. Then she was running, her heart in her mouth, expecting at any moment to hear the whistle of bombs overhead. "Papa, Marta," she called, snatching up the gas masks. Her father and sister appeared in their dressing gowns and slippers and the three stumbled down the stairs in the dark.

Frau Heidemann greeted them at the door with a flashlight that had a blue bulb. "The Wrobels are already here," she said in a hushed voice when she shut the door. Indeed the Wrobels had shown up, fully dressed and with their gas masks in place. They sat on Frau Heidemann's sofa as if they were some large specie of insect come for a visit.

Frau Heidemann motioned the Spanns to the dining table chairs and then pulled up a chair in front of her precious mirror, as if she were guarding it. Walter sat, upright with excitement at the kitchen table, his blonde hair ruffled by the mask, his eyes bright behind the goggles. He had pulled on his Hitler's Youth neckerchief over his striped pajamas.

Kurt leaned with one shoulder cocked against the bedroom doorjamb. He wore only his pajama bottoms, an undershirt, and an insolent, lopsided grin directed at Lisel.

She returned the stare until she realized Kurt was seeing her barefooted in her old cotton nightgown. Lisel jerked the gas mask down over her head and told herself she did not care that her hair, fluffy from her braids, bunched out under the hood. She dropped down on the kitchen chair, folded her arms over her chest and refused to look at Kurt. After a few moments, he ambled back to bed and left all of them sitting in the dark, straining for a sound from overhead, waiting to be bombed to death.

But death never came, except to old Frau Schatz, who kept a black pill in her stocking drawer. In her great haste to get to the basement that night, she slipped in the dark and fell.

On September fourth, the British bombed Cuxhaven and Wilhelmshaven. But in the lovely, balmy days that followed, there were no more rumors of attacking bombers. Air raid sirens remained silent, and life settled back into its old routine. Berliners spent weekends at the nearby lakes or in the woods of the Grunewald, where they swam, sailed, and picnicked. The war in Poland was so far away; it was as if it did not exist.

The Spanns received weekly letters from Michael, full of tales about army life and the people he met. If any of the family noticed that Michael avoided mention of the war or his part in it, they chalked up the omission to the importance of secrecy that went with troop movement and activity.

The Spanns even received a letter from Elder Nolte in Copenhagen to which Marta replied. The next envelope from Denmark was addressed to her and, for days afterward, Marta floated around the apartment with the high color returned to her cheeks and the laughter to her voice. She was convinced the crisis would be over in a few weeks and the missionaries would be returning to Germany.

About the second week of September, the first death notices with iron crosses began to appear in the papers.

> In a hero's death for Fuhrer, People and Country,
> died, on 2 September, in fighting in Poland, my
> beloved son, Theo Weber, aged 22.
> Dorothea Weber

> For his beloved Country, there fell in a battle
> in Poland, on 4 September, our only son, Albrecht
> Masur, aged 21.
> Heinrich and Magda Masur

The Masurs, like almost half of the families who ran such obituaries for their sons, husbands, and brothers, omitted the "died for the Fuhrer" in protest of Hitler and his government.

Toward the end of the month, Lisel and her friend, Grete Spengler, took the elevated railway, or S-bahn, through the center of Berlin to the Marmorhaus Theatre and sat through a double feature—*Carefree,* with Ginger Rogers and Fred Astaire, and a German production with star Kristina Soderbaum who, inevitably, committed suicide at the end of all her movies. The last shot of the film always showed her floating, like Ophelia, out to sea.

Lisel wrinkled her nose. "The Reich ministry ought to name her "the national floating corpse," she said as she and Grete walked the last few blocks home.

"I think that is a very disrespectful attitude," Grete insisted. "Kristina Soderbaum is a great artist and she uses her talents to show us the consequences of ignoring sound moral attitudes." She shuddered. "Imagine falling in love with a Czech."

"It was only a film," Lisel reminded her. "And not a very good one. I liked *Carefree* much better. So romantic. Such lovely music. Such lovely dancing." Lisel executed a little pirouette in the street. "Yam man," she sang off-key.

"Lisel," Grete scolded, "I cannot come out with you in public if you behave in such a frivolous manner. Besides," she grumbled, "Fred Astaire has a weak chin."

Lisel shot her friend a tease of a smile. "But surely you approve of Ginger Rogers. Blonde hair, blue eyes, and a high nose. She looks like the perfect Aryan to me."

"Frau Neuber says she bleaches her hair," Grete said with a frown that reminded Lisel that Grete did not like to be teased. "Frau Neuber even asked some of the girls if you colored *your* hair."

Lisel pulled up short and whirled on her. Her hand went protectively to her braid and she felt the anger rush into her face. "That old cow! How could she think such a ridiculous thing?"

Grete stepped back. The astonishment rose in her face. "Because she is new at the school and does not know you."

"Humph!" Lisel lifted her chin and marched forward. "Just let her make that accusation to my face. I will gladly tell that one what I think."

"Come, come. That was months ago and I am sorry I told you." Grete had to hurry to keep up with Lisel. "Besides, just last week she said you work hard, just like a good German girl, even if you do not look like one."

Lisel shot her friend a sideways glance. "So, does she think I was hatched from an egg? Does she think that too?"

Grete made an exasperated noise under her breath and rolled her eyes but kept silent nevertheless.

The pair walked on. In the middle of the next block a long line of sullen-faced people waited outside Schmidt's meat shop. The girls had to step into the street to get past and as they did, a young man, standing beside a huge basket, bent and pulled it out of Lisel's path. He smiled at her, nodded, and tugged the brim of his cap.

When they had passed, Grete sighed. "It is the same everywhere. When I am with you, no man looks at me."

Lisel looked at her friend, truly surprised. "And cows chase rabbits!" she declared. "And if you mean that poor fellow back there, he was only being polite."

"Well no one who was polite to me ever looked at me like that," she complained. "I will never find a husband."

The girls stopped at the gate of Lisel's back garden. "Grete, you are still in school. How can you think of getting married?"

"How can you *not* think of getting married?" she returned. "That is my responsibility. That is your responsibility. To marry and bear children." Grete hung her head, biting her lip. "But no man is interested in me and I do not understand. I am the correct nordic type, my blood is pure, I have the interests of the Reich at heart, and my hips are wide enough to bear many children."

Lisel reached out and took her friend's hand. "I think you forget marriages are supposed to grow from other things besides the color of your hair and the purity of your bloodline."

"Oh, I know," Grete returned wearily. "You still believe in that romantic fairy tale nonsense where a man and woman meet, fall in love, marry, and live happily ever after."

"That is how it happened with my parents," Lisel returned in defense.

Grete's brow furrowed. "That is true, but your parents were no different from the characters in a fairy tale." She held up her hand to stop Lisel's protest. "Your mother was a beautiful, pampered daughter of a wealthy family and your father was a handsome, dashing military officer, also of a wealthy family. And I can understand why your mother should fall in love with him. I would have myself, in that day. But that was the old times. These are modern times and we should behave in modern ways."

"And that means marrying without love?" Lisel snapped, feeling the heat of outrage rush into her face. "That means producing children in a family that is dictated by State specifications?"

"But that is the modern, correct way to create a sound, strong race." Grete smiled in a way that reminded Lisel of the way Frau Neuber smiled when she delivered the proscribed lectures on cultural and racial purity in school. "I know," Grete continued, "you want to marry a Mormon boy in one of your temples. You want to create a Mormon family. So why is your looking for a Mormon boy different from my looking for an Aryan boy?"

Lisel considered that for a moment. "The Mormon boy I am looking for is one who has the same beliefs I have and who has the worthiness to go to the temple. Those things have to come from his spirit. You are looking for things that come from the body only. That is the difference."

"But you cannot deny that men notice a woman's body first, that women notice a man's body first. I have a racially desirable body. It is a man's first instinct to take notice of my body. It is his duty to regard me as racially desirable." Lisel saw the sudden glisten in her friend's blue eyes and the rush of red to her cheeks. "At least they ought to regard me, but they look only at you."

Sympathetic, Lisel reached up and stroked Grete's shining, fair hair. "I know men look at me but they are thinking, 'What a scarecrow of a girl! She has a short nose like a pig's and hair the color of carrots! She must belong on a farm!'"

Both girls laughed and Grete dried her eyes with the back of her hand. "Maybe some men think you belong on a farm, but that is not what Kurt thinks when he looks at you."

"Kurt is not a Mormon boy," Lisel replied and then added sharply, "besides, I do not care what Kurt thinks of me. He is an insolent, crude fellow and I am not speaking to him."

"Good. Then maybe he will notice me."

Lisel thought about that as she had said good-bye and walked through the back garden. The idea of Kurt and Grete, Grete and Kurt, brought up an uncomfortable pressure in her chest.

"Lisel, you have come at last!"

Frowning, Lisel squinted around the garden. She saw Walter standing under the peach tree.

"Nobody is home and I have waited and waited for someone to come."

"Are you locked out?"

"No, I lost my glider in the tree and I can't get it down." Walter pointed a grubby finger.

Lisel came to where he stood and looked up into the tree. She could see the model airplane caught at the crotch of a limb. "Why don't you just climb up and get it out?"

"Mother said I was not to climb any trees. She said I would fall out and break my leg."

Lisel knew Frau Heidemann fussed over Walter but she had never realized it might be to this extent. "Have you tried shaking it out?"

Walter nodded. "And I got a rake from the shed but I still could not reach it."

Lisel picked up the rake and tried to knock down the glider but it remained stuck.

"Maybe we should get the ladder," Walter said, "and you could climb up and get it for me."

Lisel made a face. She propped one hand on her hip and, frowning, glanced around the yard. "I think we can find another way to get it down," she said. Then she spied Walter's leather-covered handball on the bench. She fingered the ball for a moment, bouncing it up and down in the palm of her hand.

"But Lisel, you might break my plane," Walter protested. "Can we not get the ladder?"

"Oh, I will not aim at it. I will just toss it close enough to shake it loose." Lisel sped the ball toward the trapped glider, but it flew wide. It sailed past the tree and came down in a direct line toward the Wrobels' bedroom window. Lisel held her breath. Walter put his hands over his eyes. But the ball only smacked sharply against the window frame and thudded to the ground.

Her lips clamped firmly together, Lisel walked over, picked up the ball and, again, took aim.

"Wait!" Walter called. He came dragging the old wooden ladder from the shed. "I brought the ladder for you."

Lisel looked down at the ball and then up at the Wrobels' window. "All right," she said, dropping the ball. "I will hold it and you climb up."

"No, no. I cannot do that. My mother said I would—"

"—fall and break your leg," Lisel finished with a sigh. She had half an inclination to leave Walter there to figure out how to get the plane for himself. But though he was sometimes a nuisance, she liked Walter. Lisel positioned the ladder under the tree and climbed up onto the lowest of the rough, brown limbs. There were two other limbs that looked sturdy enough to hold her weight and Lisel pulled herself to the next highest. From that point, the glider was only a few inches beyond her outstretched hand. She hitched herself over the coarse bark, with her bottom lip between her teeth. Her fingers curved around one balsa wing and she tugged the airplane free. "I have it," she shouted and sent it floating down to Walter. Then she knew she had made a mistake.

Lisel looked down at Walter's smiling, pink face. He was grinning with a devilish, lopsided grin. He looked just like Kurt. "You do not dare to move until I get down from here," she insisted.

But Walter was already dragging the ladder away. Lisel could hear him giggling. "You come back here!" she shouted and scrambled onto the lower limb. "Walter Heidemann, you come back here right now!"

It took a minute for Lisel to calm herself enough to consider the problem of getting down. She stared at the ground from between her dangling feet. Jumping was definitely out of the question. She would probably break her leg. Hanging from the limb where she sat and dropping the distance to the ground seemed more plausible. That way, she thought bleakly, she would only break her ankle.

Lisel's grim musings were interrupted by the sound of whistling—someone whistling "Honeysuckle Rose." And that someone was coming across the yard from the back gate and moving closer and closer to the peach tree where she sat. It could only be one person. For an instant, Lisel thought of escaping higher into the tree but there was no time now. Any second he would be directly beneath her. Lisel froze. She felt the heat coming up from her waist.

Kurt tilted back his golden head and grinned his crooked grin up at her. "Picking peaches? "

Lisel's teeth were clenched when she answered. "Not exactly."

"Must be model airplanes then," he said. "Though I would have thought the model airplane crop a little overripe this time of year."

Lisel drew herself up. "Would you please get the ladder from the tool shed?" she said, almost without moving her lips.

"When I was about ten, I had a model airplane," Kurt continued, smiling pleasantly. "We had a very pretty cousin named Frieda living with us then. And—"

"Kurt Heidemann, this is of your influence," she shouted with a sudden burst of anger. "Your brother got me into this. You get me out!"

"Perhaps if you shouted loudly enough," he continued, "one of the neighbors might hear you. Or maybe if you sang. You do have a very loud, very distinctive voice. Maybe someone will think the house is on fire and send a fire truck with a ladder."

Lisel glared down at him from narrowed eyes. "If you are not going to help me, do not bother offering suggestions. I can manage on my own."

Kurt's smile sobered. "And just how were you planning to do that?"

"I had the impression that was no particular concern of yours," she responded with a haughty lift of her chin and flipped her braid over her shoulder.

The line of Kurt's jaw hardened. "Wait a minute. I will get the ladder."

"Never mind. I would not want to take any of your precious time. You just go in the house and forget you ever saw me here."

Kurt's hands clenched into fists. "I am not leaving until you are down."

"Then step aside. I do not have the inclination to chat with you and I do not think you would care to break my fall." At that moment Lisel could think of nothing she would like better than to land with both feet in the middle of that hard, arrogant face.

His blue eyes widened. "You are not going to jump, are you?"

"Do I have a choice?"

Crimson stained Kurt's cheeks. He sputtered up at her. "You will break your—"

"I know," Lisel broke in angrily, "I will break my leg."

His eyes glittered up at her. "I am going to get the ladder and if you do anything idiotic while I am gone and *do not* break your foolish leg, be assured, when I get back, *I will!*"

"You fight with everybody else," she called after him, "you might as well fight with a girl!"

He responded by slamming open the shed door.

Lisel looked down at the ground and her hands went suddenly cold. She had never intended to jump. Why she said she was going to, Lisel did not understand, except that Kurt had goaded her into it. I probably would have broken my foolish leg just to spite him, she thought.

Kurt reappeared below her. "It is not there," he said. "Walter must have hidden it." His jaw jutted out at a determined angle that brought a nervous little flutter to Lisel's stomach. "You are going to have to let yourself down from that bottom limb," he said, "then I can get hold of your legs and lower you the rest of the way to the ground."

Lisel looked down at her green cotton skirt and bare knees. She did not like the idea of lowering herself down so Kurt could take hold of her legs. "I do not think—" she began.

Kurt snapped her off short. "Do you want to get down or do you want to stay up there?"

"I want to get down, of course, but—"

"Then do as I say!" he ordered.

"Only if you will close your eyes," she insisted.

"Close my eyes? Then understanding dawned on Kurt's face. "What rubbish," he declared. "Is this all right?"

Lisel looked down at his upturned face, not sure she could trust him. "Just make sure you keep them that way," she said as she repositioned herself so that she hung halfway across the limb on the stomach, her legs dangling in midair. Through her socks, Lisel felt Kurt's fingers grip her ankles.

"You will have to come down a little farther. You are too high yet."

Carefully, Lisel tried to lower herself but the scabby bark scratched through her cotton blouse and tore at the palms of her hands. In spite of her best efforts, Lisel began to lose her grip. "I am slipping," she wailed.

"No you are not!" Kurt insisted. "Hang on!"

As Lisel fell, she was aware that her foot struck out and caught something solid with her heel, followed by a muffled shout and a painful grunt. Lisel opened her eyes. Kurt was lying on his back and she was lying across his chest. His eyes were closed and there was a tiny trickle of blood at the corner of his lip. "Oh no," she breathed in horror. "Kurt! Kurt!" She gripped his shoulders and tried to rouse him with a frantic shake. "Kurt, are you all right? Please be all right!"

A low groan came from his throat and his eyes fluttered open for an instant before they winced shut again in a grimace.

"Kurt, please say you are all right!" Lisel pleaded. Frightened tears stung her eyes.

His eyes came open and focused on her. "I would be all right if you got off my chest," he growled.

Lisel rolled away from him and tried to help as he pushed himself into a more upright position. "Kurt, can you ever forgive me? I could not hold on longer, the bark was rough, and my hands hurt so." She blubbered on helplessly and tried to brush leaves and dirt from his hair and clothes.

Frowning, he touched his cut, swelling lip and scowled down at the blood on his fingers. He shot Lisel a side-ways look that made her heart shrink within her chest.

"Oh Kurt, I am sorry. I did not mean to hurt you."

His eyes blazing, he glared at her. "Did you know, when you cry, your eyebrows turn red?"

For an instant, Lisel was not sure of what she heard.

A sly grin pulled at Kurt's bruised lips. "But that is nothing compared to the color of your nose," he added and tweeked one braid.

Lisel gritted her teeth. She should have known Kurt would say something like that. Of its own accord, her fist doubled and shot out toward Kurt's face.

He ducked to the right and caught her wrist. "And it is the prettiest I have seen you look," he laughed. And then Kurt kissed her.

Lisel drew back in wonder and surprise. The taste of Kurt's blood was on her lips. "I do not think Papa would approve," she said primly.

Kurt's fair brows quirked up. "I *know* he would not approve."

"Mama would not like it either," a giggling voice piped in.

Lisel and Kurt turned to see Walter's impish face grinning at

45

them from behind a gooseberry bush. Both of them leapt to their feet. "That is the fellow I will thrash," Kurt cried and started toward his brother.

Walter jumped up and began to run for the house, but Kurt was too fast and both boys came down in the dirt, with Walter kicking and wailing with all the might of his lungs.

"Hold him! Hold him!" Lisel cried and threw herself at the pair. Dodging pummeling arms and thrashing legs, she dug her fingers into Walter's ribs and tickled the boy until he shrieked with laughter and they all collapsed, panting and laughing, on the ground.

"And what is this I come home to see?" said a stern voice from above them.

The three looked up to see Frau Heidemann scowling down at them. She wore her good hat and carried a shopping basket. "Kurt, how often have I told you not to torment your brother? And Lisel, I find you wrestling on the ground with boys? Is this what comes of having no mother?" She reached down and snatched Walter's ear. "I told you to stay clean today, and what do you do? You are like a pig."

Walter came to his feet, protesting, his face contorted with pain. "Ow, Mama. Let go!"

"I will let go when you are clean, like a human, again." She glared at Kurt and Lisel. "You two, go into the house. Lisel, I will speak with your Papa later." Then she marched off, tugging Walter along by the ear while he yipped and skipped along behind her.

Lisel felt the heat of embarrassment suffuse her cheeks. The idea of Frau Heidemann complaining about her to Papa made her want to run to her room and hide under the bed. She sneaked a look at Kurt. He returned the look and then they both began to laugh. "Papa will scold me for this," Lisel said, wiping away a tear.

"If he does, ask him about the upstairs maid his family had when he was ten."

Lisel's mouth sagged open. "And cows chase rabbits," she gasped.

Kurt shrugged. "Walter did not get that idea from me. I never told him about Frieda."

Lisel put her fingers over her lips to hold in the laughter. Somehow she could not imagine her Papa as a ten-year-old and even less could she imagine him deceiving the upstairs maid into a tree. But how she would love having him explain his part in it. The laughter spurted from between her fingers.

"I thought I told you two to get into the house!" burst Frau Heidemann who stood at the back door with her hand on her hip. "Must I drag you in by the ears?"

"Perhaps we had better save our ears," Kurt said out of the side of his mouth. And they both ran into the house.

That night after supper, when Marta had settled to study the care of infants from her textbook, Papa had opened his newspaper and Lisel was in the middle of *Gone With the Wind*, Papa looked over the top of his paper at Lisel. "Frau Heidemann said Kurt had a cut on his lip this afternoon. She thought you might have had something to do with it."

Lisel did not look up from her page. "No more than any upstairs maid would have had."

Papa cleared his throat and when he did not say anything, Lisel looked up. Papa had raised the paper as if he were reading but Lisel saw that the sheets were shaking.

By October, the war in Poland was over. Michael sent word that he had received leave and would be coming home. The news launched Marta into a flurry of trading and bargaining with neighbors and shopkeepers over ration points.

Lisel was glad to see her sister busy and distracted from her sorrows. Only days before, she had received a letter from Elder Nolte. He told her the missionaries were being taken from Denmark. They would all be sent home, he said, to the United States. Once again, Marta had retreated to her room. Only the prospect of seeing Michael and the challenge of fixing him good, home-cooked meals again brought her out.

Lisel did not escape the excitement and anticipation. She thrilled to the idea of having her family together again.

Michael came home looking tall and bronze and fit. But there were new lines around his mouth and between his dark eyes and the skin of his face seemed taut and strained, as if it had been stretched too tightly over his bones.

On his second night home, Marta invited the Wrobels and the Heidemanns for dinner. She produced knockwurst soup and rolls, a roast beef with spicy gravy, fresh potatoes boiled with one of Kurt's sweet onions, and a cold cucumber salad made with real cream. For dessert, there was Michael's favorite: an apple tart made with cinnamon and dusted with powdered sugar.

"Did you kill any Poles?" Walter asked eagerly, his mouth full of tart.

"Of course, he did," Frau Heidemann answered for him. "Do not talk with your mouth full." Walter swallowed. "How many did you kill?"

Lisel held her breath. She did not want to hear Michael's answer and was glad, during the past two days, when Papa and Marta and even Michael had avoided the discussion of war and Poland. She sneaked a glance at her father. He was studying his plate while Marta watched her brother, her brown eyes tense.

Michael sent the boy a faintly amused smile. "I am afraid you would be disappointed in me, Walter."

A silence fell over the table. "Do you mean you did not kill any Poles?" Walter asked, shocked.

A teasing gleam lit Michael's dark eyes. He lowered his voice. "Not a one."

Lisel blew out a relieved breath and her heart began beating again.

"I served on the Polish front in the Great War," Herr Wrobel said through his wide brush of a mustache. "Perhaps I know the place where you were stationed."

Michael looked down at his plate. "Hochlinden," he said and when he looked up again Lisel saw something strange in her brother's eyes. Something horrible. "I was at Hochlinden."

A frown made a crease between Herr Wrobel's white brows. "But Hochlinden is the place where the Poles crossed when they attacked Gleiwitz. The papers said there was terrible fighting there."

Michael shrugged. "I did not get there until after the fighting was over."

"Then what did you do there?" Lisel asked before she could stop herself.

Michael's smile was faintly apologetic. "I was on burial detail."

"What is burial detail?" Walter asked his mother.

"Hush, Walter, and eat your dessert," she answered hastily.

Michael looked directly at Walter. "Burial detail is when you bury things. Dead things. Like horses. Like men."

Horrified, Lisel put down her fork and pushed away her plate.

"Did you get to bury dead horses?" Walter asked, delighted. His mother cuffed his ear.

"Every service performed for the Fuhrer and his inspired cause is a glorious one," Herr Wrobel declared. "And no service is too small or menial." He turned to Walter who was rubbing his ear. "When that great man told us that in five years we will not recognize Germany, he did not mean that he could do these wondrous things by himself. He meant for us all to help him, to serve him, to give everything—even our lives if we have to. And because we all love him, we serve him, without question.

"Did I tell you once, how I met the Fuhrer?" Frau Heidemann put in. "It was before he was Chancellor. He flew over our town in an airplane and I was doing my shopping when he came into the town in a marvelous black Horch. I had just bought a bouquet of daffodils because my Ernst so loved daffodils, and the Fuhrer's car stopped just where I stood. I was not even thinking but I reached up and put the flowers into his arms. He looked down at me and it was as if he could see right into my soul and then he took my hand." Dramatically, Frau Heidemann lifted her hand and all the eyes at the table followed it. "And he said, 'Thank you, madam.' Just like that. And it was as if electricity went from his fingertips into my hand and up my arm and my whole body tingled." She looked around the table solemnly. "From that day I knew he was the true savior of Germany."

"Wonderful. Wonderful," Frau Wrobel said, sighing. She shook her head. "To have touched his very hand."

Suspicious, Lisel snatched a slanted look at Kurt. His face flushed a bright red to the roots of his blonde hair.

Herr Wrobel made a move to rise from the table. "It is time we went home now. Göering will be speaking tonight and I know it will be something very important. Perhaps you will turn on your radio in a quarter of an hour?" It sounded more like an order than a suggestion to Lisel. They shook hands all around.

"Delicious, delicious," Frau Wrobel offered Marta and she blushed with pleasure.

"Lisel, see the Wrobels to the door," Papa said to her.

At the door, Herr Wrobel leaned toward Lisel and said, in an undertone, "I am sure Michael's superiors are treating him poorly. When our Friedrich came home he brought canned sausages, some lard, and even a goose!"

Back at the table, Walter turned to his mother. "But Mama, you never told us about meeting Hitler," he said.

Frau Heidemann shrugged. "When you talk to the baker, you talk bread. When you talk to the butcher, you talk wurst. When you talk to Nazis, you talk nonsense."

Lisel chewed down on her lip and, for her own sake, resisted the urge to laugh.

"Come now, it is time you were in bed." Frau Heidemann took Walter's arm and pulled him to his feet then glanced at Kurt. "You, too."

"I want to talk to Michael for a while," Kurt said without looking at his mother.

"All right," she replied as she pulled Walter through the front door, "but do not stay long."

"But Mama, I want to stay too. I want to hear about the dead horses," Walter whined as his mother pulled shut the door. The Spanns heard the pair arguing all the way down the stairs.

Papa smiled a resigned smile at Michael. "So you see, nothing has changed."

Michael stared at his father, then suddenly, his face crumbled and he buried his face in his hands, his shoulders heaved and tears squeezed out from between his clenched fingers.

For a moment, they all sat there, stunned, listening to Michael's sobs. Then, Lisel flew around the table and knelt at his side. "Michael, do not cry. Please," she pleaded, snatching one of Mama's linen napkins from the table and wiping at the tears that rolled down the front of his hands. "Please Michael, tell me why you are crying."

Michael lifted his head. His tormented eyes were reddened from weeping. His mouth twisted. "Can you tell me where Herr Muller is?"

Lisel straightened away from him. Herr Muller? She fought with herself for an instant and decided to tell Kurt's version. "Yes, Michael, I can. You remember Herr Muller had that arthritis in his knee? Climbing up and down the stairs to his flat pained him and so he moved to his sister's in Denmark."

Michael's face filled with anger. His eyes went to Kurt. "Where is Franz Muller?" he demanded.

Kurt's face was very still. "We put him into the hands of someone I trust."

Michael looked down at his hands and he started to laugh. A wild, bitter laugh. "Hands you could trust all right." Then he looked up at Kurt. "You put him in my hands. I buried him in a field outside Hochlinden."

Kurt's face went stone white. Lisel felt her breath catch in her throat.

"But Michael," Papa grasped his son's clenched hands. "How can this be? Herr Muller was not at Hochlinden."

"Papa, do you not see? That raid on Gleiwitz was a hoax. The blackshirts came dressed in Polish uniforms, fired a lot of shots, and pretended to take over the radio station. Then, when they left, they left bodies . . ." Michael's voice cracked. "They left bodies in Polish uniforms so it would look like there had been fighting. But the bodies were of people who were dead before." Michael shielded his eyes with shaking fingers. "The bullet holes did not even have blood around them. And the uniform on Herr Muller did not fit him."

Lisel gasped. She remembered the last time she saw Herr Muller, with Kurt's arm about him, as they struggled down the dark street. And she remembered how frightened she had been. She squeezed her eyes shut on the image. She heard Papa's stern voice.

"You are not to repeat this story. Do you understand me, Michael? You are to tell no one."

Then came Michael, bitterly. "And who will Kurt tell? What has he told already?"

Lisel heard the scrape of Kurt's chair on the floor and his rapid footsteps to the door. She lifted her head but Kurt was gone.

Chapter 4

Lisel's thoughts were too clouded, too unsure to allow her to sleep that night. She got up from her bed, careful not to wake Marta, wrapped her quilt around her and wandered to the bedroom window. It overlooked the back garden washed with the moon-blue light that stole the color from the autumn vegetation.

A moaning night wind drove tattered clouds across the moon's lop-sided face and made the eaves of the old house creak. Lisel could hear the rustle of the dry, yellowing leaves on the peach tree.

She wiggled her toes against the bare, cold floor and thought of the old rhyme, "On St. Gall's day, in the barn the cow must stay." She decided there were probably lots of cows in barns on this October sixteenth.

Last week, she and Kurt had dug out the dead and withered plants in the vegetable garden. They left only a few tomato plants that still bore reddening fruit. Tonight the tomatoes were shrouded in old newspapers that shook and rattled in the wind.

Of all the shadows that belonged to the night, one did not. Lisel caught the movement and leaned closer to the window. She felt a stab of alarm as she saw a figure hurry across the garden. Although the figure wore a dark jacket with the collar up around his jaw and a cap over his hair, Lisel recognized him just the same.

With caution in his movements, Kurt pulled open the toolshed door and went in. Seconds later, he emerged with Elder Nolte's bicycle. He eased the bike through the back gate and disappeared into the darkness.

Lisel stood there, her heart pounding in her ears. Where could Kurt be going this time of night? Surely not an errand for his mother? Another thought flashed through her mind. Maybe a girl. Maybe Grete. An instinct told her that was not right either. He was not going on an errand for his mother or to see Grete or any other girl. Whatever secret thing Kurt was doing, it had something to do with what Michael had told them at dinner.

Her mind's eye burned with the image of Kurt's face across the table. Was it grief she saw in his shocked expression or something else? Michael would not lie. But the whisper in her heart told her Kurt was neither a conspirator nor a murderer. So why did he allow Michael's accusation to hang there, unanswered. Why did he run away? And now this stealing away in the dark? Was this also a reflection of shock and grief? Or was it guilt?

Lisel wanted to go to Papa now and tell him what she had seen, but she knew what Papa would say. He would insist she dreamt the whole matter and send her back to bed.

Lisel chewed her bottom lip. She would solve this riddle. She would sit here at the window and wait for Kurt to come home. Lisel thrust out her chin. She would confront Kurt and demand an explanation.

A shuffling sound from the ceiling made Lisel glance up. Someone was moving around just over her room. Someone was moving around in the Wrobels' bedroom.

Lisel's eyes went to the back gate where she last saw Kurt. Had the Wrobels been watching the back garden and also seen Kurt leave? Lisel shivered a little and pulled the quilt more tightly around her. Herr Wrobel did not seem to like Kurt much, but Lisel doubted he would stay up at night just to see if Kurt sneaked out the back garden.

Lisel tucked the quilt snugly around her, settled with her elbow propped on the window sill, her chin in her hand, and watched the back gate, waiting for Kurt.

Lisel awoke to Marta's hand on her shoulder. "What are you doing here? You will catch pneumonia," she declared.

Lisel squinted against the bright sun streaming in through the window. "Oh no," she gasped. How could she have allowed herself to fall asleep? She pushed herself to her feet. Arrows of pain shot through her stiff back and neck. One leg was asleep. She had probably missed Kurt all together. Lisel limped to the cupboard and pulled out her clothes. She felt as cold as death and her numb fingers fumbled over the buttons on her blouse. Looking in the pitted mirror over the bureau, she quickly braided her bright hair.

"Where are you going?" Marta asked as Lisel went through the door. "I need you to help with breakfast. Today is Michael's last day, you know."

"I will be back in a minute," Lisel called over her shoulder and hurried out the flat, down the stairs, and into the back garden. Elder Nolte's bicycle was in the shed, just where it had always been, as if it had never been touched.

Lisel walked slowly back to the house. If she went downstairs and confronted Kurt now, she would have to do it in front of Frau Heidemann. Lisel dismissed the idea with distaste. She would wait until she could speak to Kurt alone.

The morning sun was warm on the top of Lisel's head, and a yellow peach leaf drifted down from its lofty branch to settle on her shoulder. She paused to detach the leaf and, as she glanced up into the tree, caught sight of a pale figure in the Wrobels' bedroom window. Herr Wrobel was staring down at her in a way that made an icy chill run up Lisel's spine. She lowered her eyes and ran into the house.

She found Marta fussing over a pan of simmering gruel. Her face was pale and shadows circled her eyes as if she had not slept well either. "I wish I had better," she complained, wiping her hands on the corner of the faded blue apron. Her lips were a tight, disappointed line. "I remember when Cook fixed eggs and sugar-cured ham and huge cups of hot chocolate." Marta paused, a wistful look in her brown eyes. "Do you remember the thick slices of bread she made with white flour? The butter we used! Now it seems sinful." She frowned at the cereal she had prepared for Michael's last breakfast at home. "Our servants ate better than this," she said. "I wish I had more to give him. I would not want him to be hungry on his way."

Something in Marta's tone made Lisel think of that day nearly two months ago when the Elders left. She sensed that Marta thought of them too. The missionaries had not come back.

Perhaps Michael would not return either. Lisel sent that thought packing.

She slipped an arm around Marta's waist. "But a good, hot cereal is just the thing for a fall morning." She gulped back her own distaste at the gruel. "We still have some of that whole milk Frau Heidemann let us have from her ration card; and with a bit of peach preserve, we will have a feast. Besides, if our servants had eaten this, they would have been much healthier. Do you remember old Johann? He always had a cold and what asthma!"

Marta sent her a grateful smile. "Nobody will be able to eat this if our menfolk do not come out of the bedroom."

On cue, the bedroom door swung open. Papa, in his suit and tie, and Michael, in his gray uniform, appeared. Both their faces had a pale, strained look. Michael managed a wide, unconvincing smile. "What a delicious aroma!"

"Lisel was just saying how she loves a nice, hot bowl of gruel for breakfast," Marta returned with a bit of a twinkle in her brown eyes.

They all laughed, understanding Lisel's preferences and sympathizing with them. "But," Michael added, lifting Marta's hands and kissing them, "it was prepared with the hands I love best in the whole world."

"What about *my* hands?" Lisel protested, with mock indignity.

Michael bowed over Lisel's fingers. "We both know I prefer your beauteous knuckles to those of your older sister's; but we both also know if I say such a thing, she would poison my gruel."

"She certainly would," Marta interjected and began to spoon the thick, grayish cereal into a breakfast bowl.

"Marta, a moment," Papa said. His face was grave. "This is Michael's last morning with us for some time. And so, accordingly, he has asked that I pronounce upon him a father's blessing. I thought it would be best if that was done before breakfast."

"Of course, Papa," Marta said and scraped the gruel back into the pan. Several times a year, since Papa had received the Melchizedek priesthood, he had frequently blessed each of his three children. At the beginning of a new school term and again when Michael went into the Labor Corps. These were sacred times for Lisel, who loved to hear her father's resonant voice, full of the Spirit, pronounce blessings of counsel and comfort. She thought of the blessings she had received under his hands and her heart warmed. So many times when she was unhappy or confused, she sought out those memories and held to them. She always found an ease and a relief there. Lisel knew Michael and Marta felt the same way.

Papa pulled a dining chair away from the table and motioned for Michael to sit down. Lisel found a spot on the sofa next to Marta. Her head bowed, her eyes closed, Lisel waited for Papa to begin.

"Michael Joseph Spann, by the authority of the Holy Melchizedek Priesthood which has been conferred upon me, I place my hands upon your head and pray for the Holy Spirit to attend this gathering of my family whom I love so dearly. I humbly submit myself to that Spirit that I may give you this blessing and I pray that he will direct me in this endeavor. I pray that I may give you the blessing that you will need as you return to your military unit."

Papa paused. Lisel knew he was gathering his thoughts, waiting for the promptings of the Spirit.

"I exhort you, as you return to your unit, that you will be mindful of the counsel and comfort found in the holy scriptures. I exhort you to keep them near you and refer to them often. Remember the Lord heareth the prayer of the righteous and blessed are they who put their trust in the Lord. Pray without ceasing, Michael, and trust in the Lord, thanking him in all things.

"Remember Michael, always obey your superiors and pray that you will never be called to do anything that is contrary to the teachings of the gospel which you know to be true. Keep ye from false matters. Be mindful of those around you who will also benefit from the gospel. Teach them by your example.

"And now I bless you, Michael, as you leave our family circle—"

Papa paused. He seemed to be grappling for words. Lisel could hear the seconds ticking on the clock on the wall. At last, Papa began again but his voice had changed. It had a faraway tone, as if he called from some other place. Yet it struck Lisel with such power, she felt the impact somewhere below her heart.

"And now Michael, as you leave the circle of our family, I pronounce upon you a special blessing that you will survive the terrible conflict and destructions that will come to us all."

Lisel's eyes flew open and her head jerked up. Papa's face had paled. His hands trembled on her brother's dark, bowed head.

"You will bear your trials with humility and faith and endure the suffering you must, remembering always God's great love for you. Remember his Son's sacrifice for you, and in your darkest hour you will be encircled in the arms of his sustaining love."

Lisel looked at Marta. Though Marta's eyes were closed, Lisel saw the shock in the tight, horrified line of her mouth.

"Through deprivations and afflictions he will guide and protect you. Your family, both living and dead, will watch over you and administer to your body and soul."

Lisel forced her head down and squeezed her eyes shut. She could hear Marta weeping next to her and she felt the tightening in her throat. Why was Papa saying such terrible things? How could he say them? She wanted to jump up and make him stop. But she could not move.

"Remember these things, Michael. Remember how your mother and I love you. Remember how your sisters love you."

Lisel heard Papa's voice tremble and break. For that moment she heard his muffled sob. Hot tears started from behind her eyelids.

"Remember, our prayers will be with you unceasingly and when we are reunited, it will be at a better time and a better place, and we will embrace one another and never be parted again."

Lisel had a vague sense of her family, restored and whole, arms around each other, smiling into each other's eyes. She was filled with an overwhelming sense of oneness, of wholeness, of completeness. Of total peace.

"I bless you with peace of heart that you will not worry about your family. I bless you with confidence of spirit that you may do those things which you must do. I bless you with comfort.

"Now go forth with gratitude and rejoicing in your heart for the great blessings of the gospel. The Lord loves you and is joyful because of your desire to serve him. Remember these precious things and cherish them in your heart.

"I humbly pronounce these blessings on you as your loving father and beseech the Lord in fulfilling them in the name of Jesus Christ. Amen."

Lisel, tears burning her eyes, lifted her head. She saw Papa's ashen face. He put a shaking hand to his brow and with his other hand, grasped the back of Michael's chair. Lisel saw his shoulders slump and knew he would fall. She ran to his side and wrapped an arm around him. "Papa, come and sit down," she begged.

With Marta's help, they lowered Papa into his easy chair. Wearily, he let his head drop back against the chair and he closed his eyes. Lisel reached up and touched his face. Though he was pale, his skin burned.

Michael joined his sisters around their father. Papa opened his eyes and the two men looked at each other, and they reached for each other, their hands joining.

Michael's eyes misted, his voice tightened. "Thank you, Papa."

Papa nodded. "My son," he said with a thick voice.

"Let me get you something, Papa," Marta said, anxiously. "What can I get for you?"

Papa shook his head. "I am fine. Just a little dizzy. Just a little weak." A faint smile showed just below his gray mustache. "The Spirit is much stronger than I. But perhaps Michael would like his breakfast now."

Marta jumped up and ran to the kitchen.

Lisel took her father's hands in hers. "Papa, what did those things mean?"

Papa shook his head. "I do not know, little one. But we must trust the Lord and not question."

Lisel knew in her heart she should be satisfied. But she was not. Her heart accepted those things her father had spoken and she recognized the calming spirit that accompanied them, but she was frightened just the same.

"I cannot serve this cereal," came Marta's anguished lament. "It is overcooked and like rubber. I will have to make more."

"No, do not bother." Michael smiled at Marta and then wrinkled his nose. "I think I am not so hungry for gruel this morning anyway."

Marta's face crumpled. "But I wanted to give you such a nice breakfast and all I had was this cereal. Now even that is ruined."

Michael went to Marta's side and looked down into the pan on the stove. "I would not say it is ruined. Wrap it in newspaper and I will take it back with me. It should be handy for patching tires."

"You ungrateful fellow!" Marta cried, trying in vain to suppress a smile. She smacked Michael's shoulder with the spoon.

"Ouch! I am being attacked! Help, Papa!" Michael cried out in mock terror.

Papa eyed the pair with loving forbearance. "It seems Marta does not need so much help," he said wryly.

They all laughed. Michael scooped Marta into his arms and held her. Lisel ran to them and threw her arms around the pair. "I will help you, Marta," she cried and poked her fingers into Michael's ribs. Shouting with laughter, Michael freed himself from his sisters.

"Now children," their father broke in. "You must stop. Frau Heidemann will come up here, thinking we are herding cattle."

"Only if she has need of manure!" Lisel giggled.

Michael and Marta clamped their hands over their mouths.

"Even so," Papa said sternly, "you must not be so noisy."

"Yes, Papa," the three said in contrite unison and then, together, burst into laughter.

Breakfast was leftover bread, peach preserves, and a hot drink made of roasted ground barley and a little molasses. They all worked at keeping the conversation lighthearted and happy. Lisel talked and laughed most of all, if only to keep from worrying. Her efforts were of little use, however. All the while she worried about Michael. She worried about Kurt. But most of all, she worried about the things Papa had said in his blessing. Things of destruction and affliction.

Michael did not want to say good-bye at the railway station and, as they embraced at the apartment door, he teased Lisel about her red nose when she cried. Lisel knew he meant her not to cry for his sake.

Then, Michael left his family standing on the stairway, all of them trying desperately to smile. Lisel ran back into the flat and to the window, where she watched her tall, dark brother in his gray uniform stride off down the street. Marta and Papa joined her in time to see Michael turn and lift his arm before he went around the corner.

They stood there for a moment, no longer able to see their brother and son. Out on the street a few men in work clothes walked or rode bicycles; women with their shopping baskets over their arms hurried to the lines that would quickly form outside the shops. The morning sun had not yet warmed the city and most people blew spouts of clouded breath in the chill, fall air. Today might be any ordinary day in Berlin. Except for this one thing— Michael was leaving. Remembering her promise, Lisel choked back the tightness in her throat and gritted her teeth.

"He will be back at the front by nightfall," Papa said absently.

Marta tried, in vain, to stifle a sob. She put her hand over her mouth and ran from the room.

Lisel felt her chin begin to quiver and the tears burn her eyelids. "Poor Marta," she said in a voice that squeaked, "having to say good-bye so much."

Papa laid a gentle hand on Lisel's shoulder. "Fortunate Marta," he corrected. "She has a sister who thinks of other's feelings before her own."

Lisel's own emotions were too raw for her to consider. She pushed them aside with a wry smile. "Right now, I am thinking half of the city is queuing up outside the shops and if one of us does not get down there, we will have no supper."

Lisel saw Papa's look of concern as he glanced at the closed bedroom door. They could hear Marta's muffled sobs. "I think it is time I tried my hand at the shops," Lisel said. "I am sure Marta lets the grocer bully her into taking inferior merchandise."

Papa's smile was loving. "I am certain you would not let the grocer bully *you*."

Checking once more, Lisel pulled the ration cards from her pocket. Blue for meat; yellow for fat and dairy products; white for sugar, jam and marmalade; green for eggs; orange for bread; pink for flour, rice, cream of wheat, oatmeal, and tea and coffee substitutes; and purple for sweets, fruits, and nuts. She looped her arm through the shopping basket and buttoned the last button on her jacket. She supposed she should go to the grocer first, then the butcher.

Lisel pulled open the door to find Frau Heidemann standing on the landing outside the Spanns' apartment. Her eyebrows flicked up in surprise and, for an instant, it flashed through Lisel's mind the older woman had been waiting there.

"Ah, Lisel," Frau Heidemann said with a wide smile, "I was just about to call for Marta. We market together almost every day."

And cows chase rabbits, Lisel thought. "Marta has extra studies today, so I am doing the shopping for her."

Frau Heidemann's smile widened and, in Lisel's eyes, Kurt's mother seemed pleased. "Then you and I shall go together. I am sure you could use some guidance." She leaned toward Lisel and lowered her voice. "I suspect Herr Schultz cheats Marta. But he would not dare when I am there. No, no. You have no need to thank me. I am delighted to help."

Lisel doubted Frau Heidemann's generous offer was so simple. She was up to something, Lisel was sure. But what? Maybe it had something to do with Kurt. Well, Lisel was up to something too and it was definitely about Kurt. "I would be grateful for your help," Lisel answered and hoped she sounded eager.

"I saw your brother leave this morning," Frau Heidemann said as they walked along the street.

Lisel wondered how Frau Heidemann managed that. The basement apartment windows did not face the street. "Yes, about an hour ago."

"Kurt seemed quite eager to talk with him last night," Frau Heidemann went on. "He stayed very late, I think. Anyway, I did not hear him come in."

Lisel glanced sideways at Frau Heidemann. Was she trying to find out what time Kurt left their apartment? The contrary corner in her personality urged her to turn the implied question. "You must be a very sound sleeper," she said.

Lisel saw a slight confusion draw Frau Heidemann's brows together. But then, because she had an opening to bring the conversation back to herself, Frau Heidemann sighed. "Oh, how I *wish* I could sleep through the night. Even the slightest noise awakens me. I am such a delicate sleeper." Lisel listened to Frau Heidemann's recitations with one ear. So, even Kurt's mother did not know where he went last night, though she knew he had gone. Lisel also knew, eventually, Frau Heidemann would get back to

Kurt and find a more pointed way of asking Lisel what she knew about his midnight errand. Out of dislike for the woman, Lisel decided to take the obtuse course and pretend to know nothing at all.

The line at the grocer's had already stretched down the block and reached the corner. Lisel looked up the long line of women. She might be here for hours, she thought with dismay. Stuck in a line with Frau Heidemann. Hoping to avoid any further conversation, Lisel pretended to be engrossed in a poster on the wall next to her. It showed a grinning, skeletal figure perched atop an attacking British airplane. The figure was aiming a live bomb at a building with a solitary light burning in its window. "The Enemy Sees Your Light! Black Out!" the poster said with bold lettering.

Impatiently, Lisel looked up the line again. It did not seem to be moving. She counted three more posters between herself and the grocer's door.

Frau Heidemann had begun a conversation with a woman ahead of her. The woman was short with a pudding-bag body and black frizzled hair. Lisel felt a small rush of relief. At least Frau Heidemann would not be questioning her about Kurt in front of these other people.

Another woman moved into line behind Lisel. Frau Heidemann greeted her with, "How is your son today, Frau Schiller."

"Better today, thank you," Frau Schiller replied in a flat voice, as she pulled the shawl more closely around her face and turned away.

Lisel saw the woman's eyes were red and swollen, as if she had been weeping.

"Had his leg blown off in Poland," Frau Heidemann whispered out of the side of her mouth.

Lisel stared at the woman in horror. It had not occurred to her that some men came home from Poland maimed. She thought of Michael, thought of him being wounded on the battlefield, coming home without a leg or an arm. Dread sank through Lisel.

From the next block, a band played a jaunty tune while Women's Party League members collected donations from passers-by. Their sign said, "Consider the poor. Give to Winter Relief."

"They say this winter will be a bad one," Frau Heidemann explained when she saw where Lisel's gaze took her.

"The worst in years," the black-haired woman added.

"I suppose we can be thankful our soldiers are being well taken care of," Frau Heidemann said with a sigh. "My neighbor said her son came home from Poland with a goose!"

The other woman threw up her hands in astonishment. "We have not had goose this whole year. And it does not look like we will have goose next year either. Not with this new rationing."

Lisel reached into her jacket pocket and felt the edges of her cards. The new cards allowed each person, each week, one pound of meat, five pounds of bread, three-quarters pound of cooking fat, three-quarters pound of sugar, and one pound of the ground roasted barley that most Germans used as a sort of coffee. Only children were allowed milk. Men had a coupon for a small bar of shaving soap, intended to last four months. And women, though the Fuhrer discouraged smoking for females, were allowed a few cigarettes.

Lisel stared at the cigarette coupon and wondered what Marta had been doing with it. Surely they could trade it for other points.

The black-haired woman clutched at Frau Heidemann's sleeve and lowered her voice. "Have you heard about that new recipe?" When Frau Heidemann shook her head, the other woman continued. "First you take your coal ration card and light a nice, hot fire. Then you dip your meat card in a combination of your egg and flour cards and fry until crisp in your fat cards. Serve it with your steamed vegetable card and your boiled potato card. Pour your milk card into your coffee card and sweeten it with your sugar card. Remember, before you sit down, however, to wash your hands on your soap card and dry them on the rest of your ration cards."

Frau Heidemann opened her mouth, wide, and laughed. Lisel turned away, embarrassed rather than amused.

The line moved forward. Lisel ignored the conversation between Frau Heidemann and the black-haired woman and studied the heavy block lettering on the next poster. "The Needs of the People Before the Needs of the Individual," it read.

"Look at this," came a shrill, angry voice.

Lisel glanced around to see several women clustered around another who had just come out of the grocer's. She held a tin of herring that had been opened. "The grocer said he has to open all tins so no one can hoard them!" she declared. "How am I supposed to carry an opened tin of herring? It will surely spill before I get home."

With indignation, everyone agreed but moved forward in the line. Lisel stepped ahead like everyone else but decided not to buy anything in a tin.

The next poster showed a family around the dinner table. Lisel read the caption, "Bread For All The People."

"And splinters for all the gums," Frau Heidemann said in a wry tone.

The black-haired woman nodded. "The last loaf I bought tasted more like my bedpost than bread."

Amusement glinted in Frau Heidemann's eyes. "Do you know the difference between Germany and India?"

With a grin of anticipation, the black-haired woman shook her head.

Frau Heidemann repeated the question to Lisel who tried to look away. Whatever the joke, she was sure it was one that would get them all into trouble.

"The difference between Germany and India," announced Frau Heidemann, nearly bursting with laughter, "is that in India one man starves for millions and in Germany millions starve for one man!"

The black-haired woman cackled. Lisel wanted to laugh. If only it had not been Frau Heidemann who told the joke and if only she had not told it in public.

"Hush. Be careful!" came Frau Schiller's stern voice. Her grief-etched face was grim. "If you talk like that you will end up in a concentration camp."

"Pah!" Frau Heidemann said with a snap of her fingers. "I am a good German woman and my poor husband gave his life for the fatherland in the last war. No one would accuse me."

From around the corner at the end of the block, rumbled a dark green, armored truck. The women in the line fled back from the street, flattening themselves against the wall as the truck passed. The SS driver glanced neither to the right nor left.

Lisel cast a sideways glance at Frau Heidemann. The older

woman's face was blank. She and the black-haired woman did not speak again and the line moved forward in silence.

Last night, Michael had implied that Kurt was involved in not only Herr Muller's death but some horrible conspiracy that included the SS. But Kurt and the SS? That was too ridiculous to comprehend. Besides, Kurt had been a loner. He had even refused to join Hitler's Youth, though it was the law that all boys over nine participate. Perhaps Michael was wrong. Yet the question still haunted her. Whether Kurt was involved or not, Lisel did not doubt that somehow the SS was behind Herr Muller's death.

At the grocer's door, a poster on the left announced, "All This We Owe the Fuhrer," and on the right, in the window, "German-owned Business."

Frau Heidemann waited for Lisel to make her purchases, much to Lisel's discomfort. Despite that, Lisel bought a dozen small, mealy-looking apples, a quarter pound of butter, a loaf of bread, and, miraculously, three brown eggs. The only vegetables available were in tins, so reluctantly, Lisel settled for one of peas and one of pickled beets, which the grocer opened on the counter.

She and Frau Heidemann were just leaving when they heard Frau Schiller's pleading voice. "But certainly you can spare my boy some whole milk."

The grocer, a small, thin man with a long nose, shook his head. "How can I sell you milk if you have no coupons for it?"

"But my boy . . ." Tears made Frau Schiller's voice tremble. She began again. "My boy was badly injured. Now nothing stays in his stomach. If only he had some whole milk, I am sure he would feel better."

Lisel's eyes reached out to the little grocer, pleading with him for Frau Schiller's son. The grocer hesitated, conflict on his face. "But Frau, if I sold milk to someone who has no coupons, I would make trouble for myself and my business. Then where would my customers go? You must see this."

Lisel saw the despair in Frau Schiller's bowed head and slumped shoulders and her own heart contracted. The woman nodded. "Yes, I see. My son gave his leg for his country, and now his country cannot spare a cup of milk for him." She turned to go.

"Just a moment, Frau Schiller." Frau Heidemann put her hand on the other woman's arm. "My Walter does not like his milk. I must argue with him to drink it. Perhaps if you took mine . . . ," Frau Heidemann took a bottle of milk from her basket and held it out to Frau Schiller, "you would save me an argument."

Open-mouthed, Lisel turned to Frau Heidemann. Never had she known this self-centered, stingy woman to offer anything to anyone unless she expected something in return.

Frau Schiller took the bottle with trembling fingers. Tears spilled over her eyelashes and ran down her cheeks. "Thank you," she whispered and clutched the milk to her chest. "I have not always thought well of you. Now I can see I was wrong."

"What eyewash," Frau Heidemann returned, ungraciously. "And you need not mention it to anyone." Her tone seemed almost angry and she turned with a fierce, threatening look to the grocer. Lisel stepped through the door ahead of Frau Heidemann, wondering what her neighbor thought to gain by giving her milk to Frau Schiller. Frau Heidemann was not known as a compassionate woman nor was she patriotic enough to offer the milk to a soldier defending his country. What common thing prompted one woman to come to the aid of the other?

Lisel stopped dead on the street. Frau Heidemann had given the milk to Frau Schiller because they both had sons. Both worried about their sons. And, Lisel realized with a jolt, both loved their sons—Frau Heidemann just as much as Frau Schiller. Lisel knew then she had been wrong to think she could deny Frau Heidemann any knowledge of her son. Lisel would tell her what she knew.

"What are you doing?" Frau Heidemann demanded in a vinegarish voice. "If we are to buy meat today, we must hurry."

"You gave her that milk because of Kurt," Lisel said. "Because you are just as worried about Kurt as she is about her son."

Frau Heidemann's undersized chin thrust forward. "Who said I must worry about Kurt?"

"You worry because you do not know where Kurt goes when he leaves and you do not know what he does."

The defiant challenge dropped from the woman's face and Lisel saw the concern and anxiety there. Her voice held the same pleading as Frau Schiller's. "Kurt has such affection for you, Lisel.

Does he tell you? Do you know where he goes at night?"

Lisel wished she could say something to comfort but she only shook her head. "No. But I am worried for him too."

Frau Heidemann considered that, then with a sigh full of weariness, "Well, I suppose there is nothing I can do for my boy, except hope he will be wise."

"Yes," Lisel agreed. "There is always hope."

The pair finished their marketing and parted without speaking. Lisel was aware something elemental had changed in her feelings about Frau Heidemann but she was not sure what that change meant.

Lisel found Marta and her father sitting at the dining table. Papa had his bankbook open and their household money stacked neatly in front of him.

Marta looked up at her with a wide, welcoming smile. "Lisel, how sweet of you to do the shopping for me. You must be tired." She took the basket from Lisel's hands.

"Be careful," Lisel said. "The grocer opened the tins of peas and pickled beets so we will not be tempted to hoard them."

Marta made a face. "Who would be tempted to hoard pickled beets?"

Frau Heidemann's name nearly jumped out of Lisel's mouth, but she bit it back. "What are you doing, Papa?"

Papa looked up at Lisel, pulled off his glasses, and rubbed his eyes. "I have made a decision today, Lisel. I have decided to take the money we have been saving and use it to collect our genealogy."

Lisel stiffened. Her voice rose with surprise. "But does that mean we will not be going to Salt Lake?"

"No, it only means we will have to postpone the trip for a while yet. Michael cannot go while he is in the army and we cannot go without him. We will wait until we can all go, and then we will take our genealogy also."

"But how long will that be?" Lisel felt as if they had been waiting forever, struggling to save the money.

Papa made a helpless gesture with his hands. "I do not know. They say the war will soon be over so Michael may be discharged at any time. Then we will go just as soon as we have the money."

Lisel looked at the bankbook lying open on the table. The amount was not large but it was almost enough. "Why can we not go as soon as Michael comes home and then collect the genealogy afterward?"

Papa's dark eyes, so much like Michael's, met Lisel's with a level, steady gaze. "Lisel, do you remember Michael's blessing this morning?"

Lisel nodded.

"Then you must remember in that blessing was the promise Michael will be watched over and administered to by his family, both living and dead. Then, how can we partake of the blessings of the temple without making sure they are able to partake of them too?"

Lisel wanted to argue, if only to soothe her disappointment, but she knew her father was right. To get to the temple now, they would have to wait until the end of the war and they would have to have more money. Lisel could do nothing about the war. It would be over soon anyway. But, she thought with growing resolution, perhaps she could do something about the money.

Chapter 5

LISEL STOOD AT THE STREETCAR STOP AND SHIVERED IN THE biting November wind. She turned up her collar and tried, with little success, to pull her arms into the too-short sleeves of last year's winter coat. New rationing allowed each individual only one hundred points for clothing per year. A new coat used sixty points. Lisel supposed her old woolen one was better than anything she could buy new anyway. Wool and cotton, no longer available, were substituted by a poor quality fabric made of cellulose and dubbed by some as Black Forest wool because it swelled like a bud in the spring when the weather warmed and changed colors in the fall when the weather cooled.

"Where is that streetcar?" grumbled an old woman. She wore a tightly buttoned, ankle-length gray coat and a rusty black felt hat with four faded and tired-looking red feathers in the band.

An unshaved worker in a tattered coat answered her. "We still have five minutes to wait, Grandmother. The tram is not yet late."

"Is it too much to be early for a change?" the old woman argued. Her mouth pursed with irritation.

Everyone, it seemed, was a little irritable these days as a result of long lines, short supplies, and long working days. At least *some* people had working days. After three weeks of looking for a job after school, Lisel had spent almost all her carefully hoarded pfennigs on trams and buses. From the cafes on Friedichsstrasse to the markets of Invaledenstrasse and even from the good old C and A, she heard the same thing. Without the government-issued employment booklet, no one got a job. And since she was a student, she was not eligible.

One sympathetic shopkeeper had suggested she ask family and friends to help her. Sometimes, he said, good connections were of more value than an employment booklet. But Lisel was not eager to ask family and friends. She knew her father would not approve of what she was doing; but she was sure that after she found a job, he would not make her give it up. They needed the money too desperately.

Lisel stamped her feet, trying to force some warm blood into them. This year there was no rubber for overshoes and no leather to repair her old shoes that had a hole in the sole. Her toes felt like ice cubes. To keep her mind from her freezing fingers and toes, Lisel studied the advertisements and posters on the corner kiosk. One poster encouraged a one-dish meal the first Sunday of the month. The money saved from not eating during the rest of the day was to be contributed to the government for armaments. The poster's caption read, "The Meal of Sacrifice for the Reich." The illustration showed a smiling husband and rosy-cheeked children being served steaming bowls by their proud wife and mother. It made Lisel feel even colder.

"Here it is. Here is the tram at last," the old woman said as the high, narrow cars clanged up to the stop. Several waiting passengers boarded the last car designated, "For Jews Only."

Lisel stepped aside and allowed the old woman, who smelled strongly of moth balls, to board ahead of her. Inside the car, Lisel slid into an empty space on a seat beside her.

"Your nose is violently red," the old woman observed.

Lisel put a hand to her nose. She could feel neither her fingers nor her nose. "I suppose it is because I am cold," she answered, trying not to smile at the woman's rudeness.

"Filthy cold," the woman muttered. "It's too cold too early, I say." She squinted at Lisel. "Why are you not out galloping around some football field with the rest of Hitler's Maidens?"

Lisel shrugged. "Because I am too busy trying to find a job."

The old woman raised both her hands in astonishment. "A job, you say? Humph! You will never find a job in this Germany. There are no jobs. Only slave labor."

"What is this you say?" demanded a man on the next seat as he turned to face her with a hard stare. He had a long, narrow face and cold gray eyes. Lisel saw the party badge on his lapel and tried to shrink into her seat.

"More Germans are working now than at any other time in history. In 1933, six million were unemployed but now the Fuhrer has eliminated unemployment. He has created four million new jobs and at the same time built the Autobahn and the West Wall."

"Pah!" the old woman replied. "My grandson is one of those four million with a new job. He works outdoors, even in the winter. He shovels dirt for 50 pfennigs an hour and they charge him 15 pfennigs a day for a filthy straw-tick mattress in an unheated shack and 35 pfennigs for a bowl full of putrid soup. That is not work; that is slave labor. We might as well go back to 1933 and turn our backs on Hitler and his filthy Nazis!"

The man's face had gone red and his eyes bulged. "My good woman," he sputtered, "every loyal German wants to work and our Fuhrer has made it possible. All of us must sacrifice in order to progress. In sacrifice will come our glory!"

"Then glory stinks." The worker from the tram stop spoke up, "In 1933 I was still earning a wage in my own trade, as a printer. The money was not much, but I was at home enough that I could help with the garden. My family ate. Not pork roast every night, but we ate. Now, I work fourteen hours a day in the Siemens Electrical plant and my wage keeps going down. I make sixteen marks a week. I ask you, how can my family eat on sixteen marks a week?"

The other man drew himself up, "As I said, sir, we must sacrifice our individual pleasures for the good of the whole German race."

The old woman raised her fist in the man's face. "The German race would have been much better off," she shouted, "if that fool assassin had put Hitler in the ground two weeks ago."

The man's eyes bulged, his lips clamped shut, and he snapped around to face the front. Lisel saw the scarlet on the back of his neck and the stiff, angry set of his shoulders. She shifted uncomfortably in her seat. Would he call the police when he got off the tram?

Lisel put her hand on the old woman's arm. "Please, Grand-mother, speak more softly. Others can hear you."

"So let them hear me!" She wagged a finger at Lisel. "Hitler cooks with water just like the rest of us; and when he has run out of steam, his turnips will burn."

The woman continued to mutter, her fists clenched in her lap. After a few moments, however, she relaxed and turned to Lisel, patting her hand. "I am afraid I have a terrible temper and I say too much. Now I have embarrassed you." Her smile was sweet, angelic.

In view of the other watching passengers, Lisel decided not to return the woman's smile. They might think Lisel approved of what the older woman said. Instead she whispered, "I have a terri-ble temper too, but I only have to imagine my father's face to keep me from saying too much."

The old woman wheezed with laughter. "I am afraid my father, rest his soul, had the same effect. That makes you and me alike. I have decided to help you find a job."

"Oh no, you really do not have to do that." Lisel only wanted to get off the tram at the next stop and never see the old woman again. "I am sure I will find a job soon."

The woman put a gnarled finger to the side of her nose and closed her eyes. "I have it," she said at last. "My nephew's brother-in-law owns an appliance shop; perhaps he will have need of someone to clean up."

Lisel was about to refuse the offer but she hesitated. It was the first prospect she had had. And had not the kindly shopkeeper told her that family and friends were better than an employment booklet? "Do you think there might be a chance?"

The old woman nodded and winked a wrinkled eyelid. "But of course there is always a chance. And if that is not right, we will try my cousin's bakery. Then we will go to my neighbor's son who owns a music shop."

Clanging its bell, the streetcar rolled to a halt. And the old woman grasped Lisel's arm. "This is our stop," she said.

They were in Neukolln, in south central Berlin, a grim, work-ing-class neighborhood known to be mostly Communist. To Lisel's eyes, everything seemed gray, the street, the cheerless, stone-faced tenements that rose from the cobblestone pavement, the unsmiling workers hurrying to their shifts, and the poorly dressed women and their thin children. All gray.

"I must go to the tobacco shop first," the old woman said and started down one of the narrow streets. The shop had a huge Star of David painted on its front window. It also had two SA officers at the door.

The sight of the dun brown uniforms, the clubs slung from their belts, filled Lisel with a conscious foreboding. To be in a Communist neighborhood, one that was known to be violently anti-Nazi, was one thing. But to encounter the SA, there was another. It smelled of trouble. Lisel hung back, slowing her steps.

"Come along, girl," the old woman beckoned impatiently with her bony hand.

"But there are SA there," Lisel said in an undertone. Now, she regretted getting off the tram with the old woman.

"Pah, who cares about them? They are only thugs with acorns for brains."

A tiny voice of caution warned Lisel to find an excuse to leave the old woman and go back to the tram stop. To go home and help Marta with dinner. Then another, more determined voice reminded her how much she wanted a job . . . how much she wanted the money. She heeded the second voice and followed the old woman up to the tobacco shop door.

"Do you enter Jewish shops, Grandmother?" one SA man asked when she tried to brush past him.

"It is not your business what I enter," she replied loftily.

The other officer put his hand on her shoulder. "It is every good German's business to buy his goods in a German-owned business. You are a good German, are you not, Grandmother?"

The color rose in the old woman's face and she shook off his hand. "You are no one to question me, Nazi," she said, aware that a few people had stopped to watch. "Stand aside!"

Lisel saw the man's eyes narrow, saw his jaw tighten. She clutched the old woman's arm and was prepared to drag her away. "Come. We will find your tobacco somewhere else," she coaxed.

But the old woman dug in her heels and would not budge. "I shop *here*," the old woman declared belligerently. She cast her eye at the growing group of people who surrounded them, "and no one tells me I do not." She faced up to the officer, so much taller than she, and lifted her chin. "Get out of my way, you filthy Nazi!" Her clenched hand came back.

"No!" Lisel shouted. She made an instinctive grab for the old woman's arm. She missed.

The man's head bobbled with the blow. He staggered backward, a stunned look on his face. A murmur of astonishment rose from the crowd. Blood started from the man's mouth. His eyes filled with determined vengeance. He raised a threatening fist.

"No!" Lisel darted between the man and the old woman. From the corner of her eye, Lisel saw the other SA man slide his black jack from his belt.

"She is only an old woman," Lisel pleaded. A brief hesitation rose in the officer's eyes. The blood from his cut lip ran down his chin. "I will take her away and you will forget her folly."

With a sharp elbow, the old woman jabbed Lisel out of the way. "So you would strike an old woman," she said loudly enough to be heard down the street. "See here! See here!" she shouted. "This Nazi would strike an old woman!"

Suddenly, the crowd seemed much larger. Their eyes shone with resentment.

The officer's lips thinned. His jaw made a hard, angry ridge. "This does not concern you," he shouted at the crowd. "Return to your homes!"

Someone, a tall, broad-chested man with black, curly hair, answered with an obscenity. The other SA man turned and ran down the street to a call box on the corner.

"One would beat old women while the other runs away!" the old woman jeered. The crowd laughed.

Spurred by the laughter, the tall man with black hair reached out and knocked the cap off the SA man's head.

The officer's face purpled. "Go back to your homes," he snapped out in an authoritarian voice. "Go back to your homes. If you do not, you will be under arrest!"

Lisel's blood went cold. An internal voice told her to run. She tried to turn and push her way through the wall of angry people but she was hedged in.

"You heard me! Return to your homes!" the SA man shouted.

The black-haired man shot a fist toward the officer. Clumsily, he tried to dodge it, but the blow caught him in the chest. His breath went out in a painful bark. He reeled backward and went down on the cobblestone. Lisel heard the "thwack" as his head hit the curb.

With an indrawn gasp of surprise, the crowd recoiled and stood staring at the downed man in shocked silence. Then two men rushed at him with their fists. Lisel jumped back in horror. In reflex, she turned to fight her way to the open street. Beyond the crowd, she saw the other officer running toward them, pulling his club from his belt.

Instinctively, Lisel knew his target would be the eye of the storm, the old woman. Lisel's mouth went dry. The crowd had engulfed and carried the woman away, but Lisel caught a brief sight of the black felt hat and its red feathers. There was no way to reach her before the other SA man reached the shouting mob.

Lisel grasped the coat of the tall, curly-haired man. "You must stop this! You must stop this!"

The man's lips drew back, revealing rotted teeth. His mouth formed a vile curse. His wide, flat-fingered hand shot out. Lisel felt the blow on her shoulder. She reeled, clawing at the air for balance. Then, the hard cobblestones rushed up to meet her. Her breath left her body in a painful rush. Stars burst in front of her eyes. A booted foot came down close to her face. Lisel flinched away and threw her arms over her head. From down the street came the sound of a siren, wailing high on the cold air. Everyone froze in a listening silence. Some cried out in fear. Some in anger. All ran. Feet and legs churned past Lisel. Dizzy with fear, she struggled to rise. A knee caught her on the side of the chin and she slammed against the street. Lisel felt like a dry leaf in a whirlwind. Searching for some stability, she fought her way to the curb, crawling on hands and knees, and threw her arms around a lamppost.

"Stand up!" a harsh voice ordered in a cold, hollow echo.

In an attempt to clear away the ringing in her ears and the blinding pops of light from her eyes, Lisel shook her head.

"You will obey!" the voice barked.

Lisel felt a rough hand seize her head. Fingers dug into her hair. She was hauled to her feet by her scalp. Pain shot across her head and down her neck. She cried out.

The SS officer gave her hair another jerk and thrust his face into hers. His Aryan-blue eyes glinted. His words came from between gritted teeth. "You will do as you are told! You will do it quietly! Without struggle!"

Lisel winced at the pain and nodded.

"Get in the truck." He prodded her with his club.

Lisel turned to see the back double doors on the Black Maria gapped open. Another officer was forcing the old woman into the truck. She thrashed out at the man with her fists and shrieked, "Filthy Nazis! Filthy Nazis!" over and over again. Her black felt hat lay on the street. The red feathers were scattered and broken on the ground. Lisel saw the other SA man, the victim of the mob attack, sitting on the curb with his head in his hands. Blood ran from between his fingers. He spat out a broken tooth.

The policeman gave Lisel a shove toward the truck. "Let's go."

Then, like an image in a fading dream, Lisel saw her father standing at the apartment window, Marta at the stove in their tiny kitchen. "I cannot go with you. My family is expecting me home for dinner." A bruising stab to Lisel's ribs cut off her breath as the officer prodded her with his club.

"You will be fortunate, indeed, if you ever see your family again," he snarled. "Get in!"

Stunned by a whirling panic, Lisel climbed up the steps and into the Black Maria. The heavy, metal doors clanged shut behind her and closed off the light. Inside, the truck smelled of sweat and vomit and fear.

The truck rumbled then leapt forward. Lisel fell back onto a metal bench. In the darkness she could hear the old woman's curses. Horror crawled over her skin and she began to shake.

At the Gestapo Headquarters on Prinz-Albrectstrasse, SS officials took Lisel's identification papers and her clothing and locked her in a narrow, windowless cell.

In a shocked stupor, Lisel sat, unmoving, on the comfortless pallet with her legs drawn up, her head on her knees and waited for the nightmare to end.

Sometime in the chill of the night, however, reality forced Lisel to lift her head and look around. She was not awakening from some bad dream in her own bed, in her own home but in a Gestapo prison, alone and cold. Grave cold. And, with a nightmarish certainty, she knew she would never see her family again. Anguish clutched at her. Lisel wrapped her arms around her knees and rocked back and forth on her pallet.

Papa did not know where she was. He would have begun to fret when she did not come home that afternoon. She had said she might go to the cinema with Grete that day. In her mind, Lisel saw him go to Grete's house. She saw the puzzled concern that drew his gray brows together when he discovered she was not there. She saw the anguish grow in his troubled eyes as the day grew dark. She saw him standing at the apartment window, watching, worrying, sick to his very soul. And Marta. Elder Nolte lost to her, Michael gone to war, and now this new pain. Because of her!

"Oh no!" Regret tore at Lisel's heart. "Please forgive me. Please!" Only later, when Lisel's eyes were raw from weeping, her body exhausted and her soul drained, did she consider her future. Only last month, two boys from Hannover, who had been caught stealing a woman's purse during a blackout, had been executed. Was that her fate? An icy finger touched her heart. She was afraid of pain. Would she be shot, like those two boys? Or maybe the scaffold. People accused of treason were taken before Germany's highest court, the blood court, found guilty, and beheaded. Executions were filmed and played on newsreels at the cinema. Leaflets, daily distributed on the streets, announced beheadings and hangings.

Tormented and sick inside, Lisel threw herself onto the pallet with her arms over her head, trying to shut out the terrifying visions. Despair racked her. Her lips moved in desperate vocal prayer, begging for relief, for escape, for forgiveness.

Lisel was so intent on her pain, so desperate in her seeking, it did not occur to her there would be an answer to her prayer. At least not the answer she received.

Lisel was almost surprised with the sudden, healing warmth that reached into her heart. Then, like a balm, Lisel felt her mother's comforting presence. She felt it so surely that at first she sat up and looked around, thinking she might see her. But with her mother's gentle touch on her braids, Lisel lay back down, at last quiet and at rest.

Only one ache remained. That was for her family. Especially Papa. This time he would be grieving for *her*. And this time, she would not be there to comfort him. She would not be there to tell him she loved him. Lisel realized it had been weeks since she had told him. A renewed pain of regret clenched in her chest. If only she could tell him now!

Then the plan came clear. Using her fingernails, Lisel ripped up a thick splinter of wood from the pallet and scratched three words into the plaster wall next to the pallet. "I love you."

Then, healed, Lisel slept.

Because of the darkness in her cell, Lisel was not aware of the passing of night into day. No one came to her cell. A combination of cold, hunger, and exhaustion numbed her into a kind of weightless separation. She was resigned to the sentence that would eventually come.

Sometime during the afternoon, her cell door opened and a woman guard brought in her clothes. "You are to dress quickly and come with me."

Lisel's cold fingers fumbled as she buttoned her blouse. Her heart beat with a sluggish rhythm in her chest.

The female guard led Lisel to a small office, unadorned except for the large portrait of Adolf Hitler that stared sternly down at her. The blonde, fortyish woman behind the desk wore a military uniform. She lifted her arm. "Heil Hitler!"

Completely empty of emotion, Lisel returned the salute.

"You are Lisel Spann?" the woman asked.

Lisel nodded.

"What were you were doing in Neukolln yesterday afternoon?"

Lisel told her.

"And do you know this woman who enlisted you in rioting?"

Lisel had no energy to refute the allegation. She shook her head.

The woman's eyes narrowed as she studied Lisel. "Her name is Gertrude Hoffmeyer. She said you tried to prevent her from striking the SA officer. When we questioned him, he revealed that you tried to stop the aggression against him. That is to your advantage."

Lisel felt the woman's eyes on her. Did she expect her to react in some way? Lisel did not know. She felt boneless and weak, standing there, waiting for her sentence. And she felt something else. Impatience to get it over with.

"Why were you looking for a job?"

"My family and I are trying to save enough money to collect our genealogy." The words came to her lips with no expression. "I thought if I had a job I could help with the money."

The woman nodded. "I believe that to be a worthy objective." She flipped open a folder on the top of the desk. "This report says you have not completed your year's term of farm labor. It also says you have not attended the compulsory meetings of the League of German Maidens." She pinned Lisel with a look. "You know it is the Fuhrer's wish and a law that every young woman join the League."

"I have been busy with school."

"Yet your teacher's reports say you are but an average student." She paused as she glanced over the pages. Then she looked up at Lisel again. "The Fuhrer believes that in the education of women, emphasis must first be placed upon development of the body and character. Only later is consideration given to mental development." The woman studied Lisel. "Physically, you appear to be sound. Perhaps we need to apply our efforts to the development of your character. And perhaps we can also offer you the opportunity you desire."

Lisel waited, unsure of what the woman meant.

"Therefore, I believe the proper course in this case would be to remove you from school and enter you directly into Compulsory Service."

Remove her from school? "My father places great importance on learning. He would not approve of me leaving school."

"Would your father approve of your involvement in a riot in Neukolln?" She flipped the folder shut. "I believe your behavior has been dealt with in a most lenient manner. You should be grateful for your Fuhrer's generosity in offering you this job. You

will return to your home and await word of your assignment."
She stood. "Heil Hitler."

Home? A faint shaft of hope, almost too narrow to be recognized, showed itself. She was not to be executed. She was going home. Lisel's despair fell away. Tears of stunned relief burned her throat. "Thank you." The words came out as a hoarse whisper.

At the door, she turned again to her interrogator. "What will become of Frau Hoffmeyer?"

"Frau Hoffmeyer's case has been turned over to a higher court," the woman answered dispassionately.

Lisel knew that meant the feared blood court. Another measure of sadness weighted her heart.

The female guard led Lisel down a hallway and into a wide corridor, lined with wooden benches. On one of the benches a haggard old man slumped between a young man with his hat in his hands and a tired-looking woman. She looked up at Lisel and Lisel saw she had been crying. "Marta?"

"Oh Lisel!" Her sister threw herself into Lisel's arms. With Kurt's help, Papa stiffly pushed himself to his feet and, with great rivers of tears coursing down his face, limped toward her. Lisel left her sister's arms for her father's. She wept against his shoulder.

"Papa, I am so sorry."

Chapter 6

THE NEXT MORNING, LISEL AWOKE FROM A HEAVY, DREAMLESS sleep, still weighted by the effects of the valerian drops Marta had given her. She squeezed her eyes shut. She wanted to flee back into unconsciousness and the muffled comfort of not knowing and not feeling.

"Are you awake, then?" Marta asked from a chair in the corner of the room.

Lisel saw the smile on her sister's gentle face. A sudden, buoyant sense of relief and gratitude swelled within Lisel. The nightmare was over. She was at home, in her own bed, with her own family. The family she thought she would never see again. Then she remembered what she had to tell Papa.

Lisel sat up and pushed the hair from her face, expecting to see him there beside Marta. "Where is Papa?"

"He will be home soon." Marta closed the book she had been reading. "He will be pleased to see you are awake. You have been sleeping for seventeen hours."

"Seventeen! But I will be late for sch—" Then Lisel remembered. She was not going back to school. She was to wait for her Compulsory Service assignment. Dread came rushing at her. She might be assigned somewhere far from Papa and Marta, away from everything she knew and loved.

Marta must have read Lisel's sudden anxiety. Marta sent her a teasing smile. "After seventeen hours you are also very late for dinner."

Lisel returned the smile. "Perhaps I can make up for it by having dinner and breakfast at the same time. I am empty to the bottom of my feet."

"Good," Marta pronounced. "Put on your dressing gown and I will warm some of the chicken soup Frau Heidemann brought last night. That is, if you feel you can eat chicken soup so early in the day."

Lisel grinned. "Right now I could eat chicken *feathers*."

She finished the bowlful of steaming broth, filled with thick noodles and chunks of very tough but delicious meat and stared with regret at the bottom of the bowl. It had been months since she had had chicken. Poultry had disappeared from the market with the beginning of the war in Poland. She had heard that only people who bought goods on the black market even *saw* a chicken nowadays. Lisel knew of one person with the audacity to come up with a chicken. "Did you say Frau Heidemann made this?"

"She was very kind yesterday," Marta answered as she dried a pan.

The memory brought humiliation like a hot, sharp pain in the chest. "I cannot say how sorry I am, Marta. You must have been badly frightened."

Marta put the pan in the cupboard and shut the door. "Judging from the way you looked yesterday, I would say you also had a good scare."

"When I first saw you and Papa and Kurt in the corridor, I did not recognize you," Lisel admitted. "For the first time, Papa looked like an old man to me."

"Papa was badly shaken, that is true. But I think things might have been much worse without Kurt. After we searched and searched, he was the one who found you."

Lisel looked up. "How did he do that?"

Marta paused in her washing up. "I did not ask him. He came late at night, after midnight, and said you had been. . . ." Marta paused and chewed her lip, reluctant to say the word. "He told us, one of his friends had seen the incident in Neukolln and saw the Black Maria take you away."

Kurt's involvement added an even more disquieting element to Lisel's predicament. It triggered questions in her mind. Questions about Kurt and about his friends. But they were not questions Lisel could ask aloud. At least not of Marta.

"Grete was here last night," Marta said, shaking out a damp

dish towel and hanging it on the rack next to the sink. "She said to give you her best." There was something restrained about Marta's comment, as if she were struggling with some unpleasant thought. Lisel guessed what it might be.

She put her spoon in her bowl and took it to the kitchen. "I suppose Grete was shocked when she heard," Lisel said, allowing Marta an opening.

Marta's ordinarily calm face looked, for an instant, regretful. "No, I think Grete was more concerned than she was shocked." Marta frowned down at her hands, reddened by the washing up. "She said her mother would not allow her to come here again."

"Oh." Lisel should have expected something like that from Frau Spengler. But she did not expect, nor realize, until that moment, her foolhardiness was not only her disgrace but her family's also. The revelation sent shame pulsing through Lisel.

Marta put a hand on Lisel's shoulder. "Allow some time, Lisel. Frau Spengler will forget soon enough and things will be more normal again."

Lisel nodded. "Yes, you are right," she answered, but did not believe it. What would ever be normal if she was sent away from her family?

Lisel turned as she heard the familiar footsteps on the landing. Today they were slower and heavier.

"That must be Papa," Marta said and Lisel heard a strange and tense edge in her voice. She turned to her sister with the question on her lips but, just then, Papa pushed open the door.

His eyes brightened when he saw Lisel there. "You are awake at last."

Lisel went to him and put her face against his shoulder. She felt the rough wool of his coat and smelled the sharp scent of his shaving soap. "I love you, Papa."

Papa patted her shoulder indulgently. "Yes, little one, you told me yesterday."

"And I will tell you every day," Lisel said fervently and looked into his face. It seemed grayer today, and thinner and so care-worn. She knew she had been the cause of this suffering and her heart contracted with remorse. "Can you forgive me, Papa?" she asked, tears tightening her throat.

"What is there for me to forgive? Your desire to help collect our genealogy? Your desire to prevent violence? That is nothing to forgive." He held her away from him. "Now, let me hang up my hat and coat."

Papa turned from Lisel but not before she caught a look that passed between him and Marta. It communicated a weary defeat.

Puzzled, Lisel glanced at Marta. She had busied herself in the kitchen, but Lisel saw the way her lips had thinned and tightened. Marta was worried about something.

Lisel drew in a deep, steadying breath. "Where have you been, Papa?"

With an abstracted air, Papa smoothed his jacket and lowered himself into his easy chair. "Just an errand," he said and opened his scriptures. He riffled the top right corners of the pages with his index finger.

Lisel knew he was shutting her out, unwilling to talk. In alarm, she turned to Marta. "What is wrong?"

Marta's eyes flitted to Papa. With a sigh, he closed his scriptures, pulled off his glasses, and rubbed his eyes. "I have been to see your Uncle Leopold today."

Confusion made Lisel think she had not heard right. "Uncle Leopold? But Uncle Leopold was the one who sent us away when we joined the Church. He said, as far as the family was concerned, we are dead. Why would you go to see him?"

Papa made a helpless gesture with his hands. "I was worried that your Compulsory Service assignment would be somewhere far away from us. I thought, since he had such strong connections with the Party, he could arrange for you to be close by, so that you would not have to leave home."

Lisel was almost afraid to ask. "What did Uncle Leopold say?"

Papa's jaw clenched and his mouth, beneath his wide mustache, turned down. "He would not even see me."

The rejection came like a slap in the face. Lisel had always believed they had not kept in contact with the rest of the family because they chose not to. It did not occur to her, until now, that the family chose not to see *them*. Then Lisel realized how much more of a blow Papa had suffered. He and Leopold had been brothers and friends and business partners until the day Papa announced his intentions to join the Church. That was the day Leopold had renounced him.

Lisel knelt beside Papa's chair and put her arms around his neck. "You need not have done that for me. I am not afraid of where I will go," she lied. "Perhaps they will send me someplace wonderful. You know how I would love to see new places. Perhaps somewhere in the mountains where I can swim and hike in the summer and ski in the winter. I would love that so much!"

Papa smiled down at her and Lisel felt warmed all over. "Yes I am sure you would love that," he said. "But consider your sister and your old father. Life would be too quiet here without you. We would be forced to buy a parrot."

Papa's little joke surprised Lisel and she giggled. "Then you must name it Frau Heidemann so you could say, "Frau Heidemann, shut up!"

Marta could not quite suppress a chuckle.

Sternly, Papa looked at Lisel, though he struggled with the shape of his mouth. "We must not make jokes at Frau Heidemann's expense, Lisel. She has been very kind to us in these last two days."

"Of course she has been. And I did not mean to sound ungrateful. But I wonder, with chicken so scarce, if she has not given you your parrot a little early."

Their laughter stilled with a tap at the door. Marta ran to answer it and found Herr Wrobel, his face hard-edged and cold. His eyes went to Lisel and a sudden chill ran up her spine. She looked away from his stare and pretended an interest in the upholstery on the arm of Papa's chair. Undoubtedly, he had heard of her troubles and was intent on showing his disapproval. Lisel felt her cheeks warm.

"I was downstairs when the postman came," he said and he handed an envelope to Marta, "so I thought to bring yours to you."

Papa rose from his chair. "Thank you, Herr Wrobel. Will you come in?"

Lisel prayed he would say, "No," and was grateful when he made his excuse and left.

When she looked up she saw Marta staring down at the letter. Her face had gone pale. Lisel knew it had come.

"That one is for me," she said with assurance. Lisel rose and moved to where Marta stood. The letter, in a long, white envelope was addressed to her and was stamped, "From the Office of Regional Party Headquarters." Lisel took the letter. Her anxiety made it tremble a little in her fingers. She wished she did not have to open it. Lisel looked up. Her eyes went from Papa to Marta and back. Worry showed in both faces. Lisel resigned herself. She ripped open the end of the envelope.

The letter addressed her by name and began by stressing the great war effort and her personal commitment to the Reich's welfare. She hurried through it, looking for her assignment.

"You will therefore report to the Wittenau Munitions Works at 3 P.M. on November twenty-second for a twelve-month term of service."

Lisel's breath went out in a long sigh of relief. She looked up at her father. "I am to be at the Wittenau Munitions Works," she said. "I am to remain in Berlin."

The rest of the day was like a holiday. No school and the prospect of the new job near her home made Lisel lighthearted. The gray sun shone through the leafless branches of the peach tree as she hurried across the back garden to the gate. The squeak of the toolshed door slowed her, and she pulled up short beneath the peach tree as Kurt came out. He was wearing his dark blue cap and a gray scarf over his black coat. They stared at each other. Lisel thought Kurt looked tired. Dark shadows showed beneath his blue eyes; they seemed dull and lifeless.

Kurt stepped toward her. "So you are not to be sent from us then," he said with a stiff, restrained politeness.

His uneasiness frightened Lisel a little. She remembered how he had stood apart from her in the corridor last night. How her father had embraced her and Marta had embraced her, but Kurt had not even spoken to her. Just stood there, his pale eyebrows drawn together, his mouth a grim line, and his jaw hardened.

"I was assigned to the Wittenau Munitions Works," she replied, and thought she saw a flicker of relief behind his eyes but she was not sure.

Ever since Michael made that terrible accusation, Kurt had behaved oddly, avoiding her when he could and treating her as if she were a stranger when he could not. It was as if he knew she would ask him questions he did not want to answer. And in these last weeks, though suspicions plagued her, Lisel missed the Kurt she knew. Not this one who stood looking at her with such cold, forbidding eyes. Not this one who had some mysterious connection to Prinz-Albrectstrasse. But the one who comforted her by tugging her braids. The one who teased her. The one who had kissed her in the garden. She wished he would come back. She wished she could find him again. But where to look?

Lisel stepped closer to him, her eyes searching for some warmth of friendship in his face. "I have not thanked you for what you did for us," she said and was surprised that the words brought a stinging moisture to her eyes. She blinked them back so he would not see. "You were very kind."

Kurt closed his eyes as if he, too, had to block out the memory. Then he looked down at Lisel, and she saw the anguish in his eyes and knew his coldness was only an attempt to hide his concern for her. Her heart warmed.

The color rose in his cheeks. "That was a monumentally stupid thing for you to do," he snapped.

Lisel smiled, glad to see the old arrogant Kurt surfacing. But he scowled. "I suppose you think this is funny," he accused. "It was not so funny what that adventure did to your father and to Marta."

Lisel looked down at her hands. She knew she was being scolded and it made her glad. She looked up at him. "Was it not so funny for you too, Kurt?"

For an instant, she thought he was going to swear. But instead, all his pretense of harshness fell away and the expression in his eyes spoke his feelings. "Oh, Lisel," was all he said as he moved toward her and clutched her against him.

Lisel closed her eyes and pressed her face into his throat. She felt his arms tighten around her, his heart beat rapidly against hers, his face hard on the top of her head. And she knew, instinctively, what she felt from him was his own torment and his need to be comforted in it.

She and Papa and Marta had been able to comfort each other but no one had comforted Kurt. Lisel wrapped her arms around his waist. "It is all right now, Kurt," she murmured against his shoulder. "Everything is all right."

"I thought I would never see you again. I thought you had gone from my life having lost your trust in me." His words came like a rumble from his chest. "In my heart, I saw you dead."

Lisel remembered the night in that icy, dark cell and remembered she had seen herself dead too. But his other fear was not true. She knew that now. "How could I not trust you?" she asked him, looking up.

As if he did not hear her, Kurt looked down at her with pain-narrowed eyes. "Then to have seen you there, in that place and you were so . . ." He looked away from Lisel, struggling with the words. He swallowed hard. "I wanted to hold you then and touch you just to know that you were still with me, still here. But you would not see me." His voice cracked. "I realized then, you believed every kind of criminal thing about me, and I felt as if I had seen you dead all over again."

Lisel reached up and put her fingertips over his lips. She did not want to hear these things. They cut right to her heart. "Oh Kurt, I saw you but you seemed so far away. You had been avoiding me so much. And some of the things I knew you were doing seemed so suspicious. I did not know what to think, except you had turned away from me."

He was looking down at her now, as if he was listening, a dawning comprehension on his face.

"I do not know how to say how sorry I am," Lisel went on in a rush. "I am so sorry that you should have had to go through this because of me. I—"

This time Kurt put his fingers over her lips. "Lisel Spann, did anyone ever tell you, you talk too much?"

Lisel gaped at him. This was the Kurt she used to know. The one who pulled her braids and teased her and kissed her in the garden. Happiness filled her chest and she threw her arms around Kurt's neck and kissed him, full and hard, on the lips.

He seemed to enjoy it for a moment then gently pulled her arms from around his neck. "I doubt your Papa would approve." He smiled as he chided her.

"I know your mother would not," she giggled in return. "But I would kiss you again right in front of all of them."

"And someday, I will let you kiss me in front of them. But not now, Lisel. Not for awhile." Kurt grinned. "At least not until I have no fear of my mother pulling my ear."

Frau Heidemann's face flashed across Lisel's mind, and she knew there was something she had to tell Kurt. "Can we sit down for a minute?"

He frowned. "Are you ill?"

She smiled and shook her head. "I only want to tell you something I learned while I was in . . . while I was in jail."

Kurt's face sobered. "What is it?"

"I discovered that the most important thing between two people is, no matter what other cares or involvements they have, that they love each other. And it is love that sustains them, and comforts them and helps them endure any trial."

Kurt looked puzzled. "You want me to tell you I love you?"

"No," Lisel came back, surprised. Then she smiled, touched and warmed, and lifted her fingers to his cheek in a caress. "I am trying to tell you, your mother loves you."

"My mother?" Kurt's brows drew together. His face hardened in stubbornness. "My mother loves only herself."

"That is not true," Lisel protested. "She loves you and worries about you. She knows you go somewhere at night and she is frightened for your safety."

Kurt became very still. "Did she tell you this?"

Lisel nodded.

He stood abruptly and moved away from her. She felt a sudden chill. "I think there are too many women meddling in my life," he said. The words struck out at Lisel in anger. He turned and strode through the garden and into the house.

Lisel sat there on the bench beneath the peach tree, stunned and confused. She had thought she had found her Kurt again. But now she realized those things she did not know about him outweighed everything she did know. And for this moment, the thing she knew best was that he had hurt her.

Lisel had to run the last block to the Wittenau Munitions Works. She had decided, in order to save a few pfennigs a day, to walk from the flat to the train and from the train to the factory. But on that first day she had miscalculated the time and was late.

A graying, middle-aged secretary named Frau Segler led Lisel to the Works manager's office. He was a lean-faced man with wire-rimmed spectacles, a narrow jaw and a chin that disappeared into his neck. Herr Bauer did not look up from his paperwork when Frau Segler laid Lisel's notice of assignment on his desk. He glanced at the sheet. "You are late," he said, scribbling a note.

Lisel opened her mouth to explain, but he cut her off.

"The State believes young women must be educated as Spartans in the Labor Service. You will learn the endurance that befits a member of our race. You will not be petted or coddled. You will renounce cosmetics, wear your hair in a modest, simple style, tied in a scarf if necessary, and dress in a manner that makes coquettishness impossible." He sounded as if he had made the speech thousands of times. Lisel felt insignificant standing there, while he scratched notations on a notepad and gave her her orders.

"Your shift begins promptly at 4 P.M. I trust you will make the necessary effort to be punctual. At no time and under no circumstance are you to discuss your work here with anyone. Your wage starts at 35 marks a week from which we will automatically deduct 90 pfennigs a week as your contribution to Winter Relief. Meals are served in the cafeteria at 8 P.M., the charge is 4.90 per week. Your normal work day is from 4 P.M. until midnight, but since these are unusual times, you will stay on the job until 2 A.M. You will have Sundays off.

"You will need a physician's signature to excuse you from work if you are ill. Herr Oswald Hahn is your supervisor. You will report to him in the grenade division for your specific assignment. Do you have any questions?" For the first time Herr Bauer looked up. Lisel saw that his eyes were large, gray, and completely impersonal.

She shook her head.

"Good. Heil Hitler," he said, flipped back his arm in an absent salute and went back to his paperwork.

Frau Segler led Lisel to a neatly ordered cloakroom and told her to leave her belongings there. Then she led Lisel to a long, low-ceilinged room. Rows of silent women bent over large trays of hand grenades, scrubbing away at them with wire brushes.

Frau Segler beckoned to a man at a huge desk on the far end. He rose and marched toward the pair with his shoulders rigidly back and broad chest out. As he came closer, Lisel saw that his angular face held a stern, disciplined look. His hair, which might have been red, like hers, was shaved almost to the scalp. He was also very short.

Lisel realized Herr Hahn must have had his shoes reinforced with boot tacks and metal-coated heel rims, for when he clicked his heels, it sounded like a pistol shot. His right arm came out in a stiff, precise salute. "Heil Hitler!" he barked.

Lisel raised her arm and answered.

Frau Segler made the introductions. "Herr Hahn will show you where to work," she explained.

"You will follow me," he commanded in a sharp voice and turned and marched down one of the long rows.

Lisel followed, trying to keep up with his smart pace without running.

Herr Hahn stopped short at a gap between two women and turned sharply to face Lisel. "This will be your station, Fraulein. You are to clean the threads of the grenade like so." He took a wire brush from the tray on the table and snatched up one of the grenades, a metal cylinder about eight inches long. With a quick twist of his wrist, he whisked the brush over the threads. "Then it must be oiled like so." Herr Hahn showed her. Then he held out the brush to her. "You try."

Lisel took the brush and chose a grenade from the tray. Carefully, aware of his scrutiny, she scrubbed at the threads.

"No! No, Fraulein! We are making weapons, not scouring the front stoop!"

Lisel heard the woman next to her laugh under her breath and Lisel felt the heat rise in her cheeks.

"Watch carefully," Herr Hahn commanded. He snatched the brush and grenade from her hand. "Like so," he barked and showed her again. "It must be quick. It must be efficient." He shoved the brush back at her. "You try again."

Lisel took the tool and picked up a grenade. She made another attempt to copy Herr Hahn's movements. But the grenade was too smooth to grasp firmly and her nervousness made her clumsy.

Herr Hahn shook his head and swore. "When will they stop sending me such simpletons?" he declared and swore again.

Again, Lisel heard the woman laugh. She gritted her teeth

against the insult, an act which also served to hold back the angry words that leapt to her tongue. Lisel grabbed another grenade and tried again. This time she was more efficient. She slid a sideways glance at Herr Hahn, knowing better than to expect any praise or encouragement.

He merely glared at her. "This will never do. You are much too slow!"

Lisel grabbed another grenade, whisked the brush across the threads, oiled it, set it in another tray and had hold of another grenade when she realized Herr Hahn had marched off to his desk at the other end of the room.

For three hours, Lisel kept up the furious pace, only needing to renew her anger by looking at the little man behind the big desk.

When the break bell rang, the women in the grenade room hurried to the bathroom. Lisel, not familiar with the routine, was late getting there and late coming back. When she returned, she found Herr Hahn waiting for her with a stopwatch.

"You are late!" he snarled. "Since this is your first day, I will be generous with you; but hereafter you will be back at your station at the appointed time or you will make up the time with an extra hour's work."

Lisel swallowed back her anger. Tears of frustration wanted to rise in its place, but she dashed them away with the back of her hand. Her legs had begun to ache from standing for so long on the concrete tiling, and her hands were raw and bleeding from her clumsy attempts with the wire brush.

Lisel felt a gentle nudge from one side. The young woman next to her offered her a sympathetic smile. "It is always hardest at first," she whispered, making sure her head was down so Herr Hahn would not see their conversation. "Do not despair so. It will become easier."

The quiet words of encouragement brought a swelling of gratitude within Lisel. She sniffed back her tears and nodded. "Thank you."

At the dinner break, Lisel lined up with the other women in the commissary, first to pay 15 pfennigs for her meal and next to receive her bowl of knockwurst soup (which was more soup than knackwurst), a small, hard roll, and a steaming cup of barley coffee.

Lisel sat down in the first empty chair she found. The back of her legs ached and now, as they relaxed, cramped. Lisel grimaced. The women around her talked and laughed as if five hours on their feet was nothing at all.

"Are you feeling better?" The young woman who had stood next to Lisel at the grenade trays sat down beside her. She wore her brown hair short with curls that framed her wide, friendly face. When she smiled, Lisel saw one tooth was chipped.

"I believe my legs are now an inch shorter than when I came," Lisel said ruefully.

"I was over nine feet tall when I started," the young woman returned and then laughed."You will be used to it soon enough. But when you stop noticing how much you ache and how tired you are, you will only be bored." She finished with the salt and passed it to Lisel. "I am Susanne Brecker," she said and offered her hand.

Lisel introduced herself. "Have you been here long?"

"Only eight months. Four to go," she said and made a face at the barley coffee. "This stuff gets worse every day. Not that there is much that improves here over time. After you have been here for a while and become more accomplished, your wages go up. And then you might also be reassigned to the bullet division. At least there you get to sit down."

Lisel stirred her soup around her bowl with the back of her spoon. There was something she needed to ask if she was to get along here and she hoped Susanne was the one to approach. Lisel began slowly. "I do not think Herr Hahn likes me," she said cautiously.

"Herr Hahn likes no one," Susanne answered. She leaned toward Lisel and lowered her voice. "We call him the 'little rooster' behind his back."

Lisel smiled at the comparison, but it did not calm her concern. "But if he likes no one, how do you get along with him?"

Susanne's eyes narrowed. "A good girl does not want to get along with that one."

"Oh." Susanne's meaning was clear enough and Lisel thought it over with mounting distaste while she finished her soup.

"See here." Susanne took her arm as they returned to their work stations. "Do not worry so about Herr Hahn. Just do your job and mind your own business. You will adjust well enough."

Lisel nodded. "I will try." But the prospect of twelve months standing at the grenade trays with Herr Hahn looking over her shoulder stretched out bleakly before her.

At 2 A.M., her legs, back, and head throbbing with exhaustion, Lisel stumbled onto Wittenau's blacked out streets. She followed the other women, now silent, for a mile to the train station. Ahead of her, Susanne glanced back then stopped long enough for Lisel to catch up.

"How did you like your first day at the Wittenau Munitions Works?"

Lisel sighed. "Does it really get easier?"

"No, I suppose it does not," Susanne replied and then shrugged. "You only learn to not take so much notice."

At the train station, Lisel leaned her head against the bench back and closed her eyes. Of her first day's work, she earned thirty-five pfennigs an hour. She spent fifteen for the bowl of thin soup and five for her train ticket. She made a rapid calculation. America seemed farther away than ever.

Chapter 7

LISEL STEPPED ONTO WITTENAU'S NIGHT-DARKENED STREET. The chill January air stung all the way to the bottom of her lungs. Overhead, the sky hung low, starless.

She heard Susanne groan when the cold hit her. "I cannot ever remember being this cold before," she grumbled.

"No one has ever been this cold before," Lisel answered and pulled her old coat more tightly around her. Not that it did much good. "If we walk fast, we will be warm."

"If we live until next May, we will be warm," Susanne came back. "No one shall hunger or freeze," she said, sarcastically repeating the newest propaganda slogan.

Lisel sighed. "I wonder how they made that illegal."

"I do not know," Susanne returned. "But it means we must all be arrested."

Everyone in Germany, it seemed, was cold and hungry. Although during the Christmas week, everyone got an extra quarter pound of butter, a hundred grams of meat, and four eggs instead of one, it did not seem enough. Then, with the worst cold in fifteen years, cellars full of potatoes froze. The rivers iced over so thickly, fishermen could not go out in their boats. Even the coal barges were unable to get down the river. No one had coal. No one had heat.

On top of that, a gas shortage was declared. Gas could be used for cooking, but hot water for bathing was limited to Saturdays only. And there was no gas at all for heating homes. Lisel lived, worked, and slept in her coat and knitted hood. Her fingers were forever shriveled, stiff, and numb.

"You know what they say," Susanne said, her voice muffled by her scarf. "January with snow and chill presages grain on every hill."

"If that is so, we should be able to build Hitler's Germany out of loaves of bread."

The two girls clung to each other and made their way down the middle of the icy street. Sidewalks during a blackout could be dangerous places. There were lampposts to walk into and fire hydrants and wall-hung mailboxes and drifts of snow.

Susanne clutched at Lisel's arm and whispered. "There is someone over there, hiding in the doorway."

Lisel stared into the darkness and could barely make out a tall, shadowy figure. It stepped out. "Lisel!" The voice came as a whisper but she recognized it just the same.

Kurt had avoided Lisel for months and, at last, she gave up trying to speak to him. Now, she was not only puzzled by his appearance but annoyed too. "Susanne, can you go on ahead?"

Susanne glanced doubtfully at the figure. "Will you be all right?"

Lisel nodded. "Do not wait for me. I will take the later train."

When Susanne left, Kurt beckoned to Lisel from the doorway. Lisel came to him slowly. She would not run just because he crooked his finger.

"Why who is this?" She feigned politeness. "I believe it must be Kurt Heidemann who used to be my neighbor. What could you possibly be doing in Wittenau in the middle of the night?

Lisel saw Kurt's shoulders stiffen. His eyes were two flashing pinpoints of light. "You are the most knuckle-headed woman I know," Kurt growled. "I am here because I wanted to talk to you."

Lisel folded her arms across her chest. "You have no time when I want to talk to you, it seems. But when you want to talk to me, you just stroll up any time and any place. Perhaps I do not want to talk to you now. Perhaps I think there are too many men meddling in my life."

Lisel heard his snort of impatience. "If you do not want to talk to me then all you need do is listen. I have not the heart to argue with you. I do not wish our last words together to be words of anger."

Lisel's resolve fell with a clatter. She saw the torment in his eyes and the sadness that pulled at his lips. "Why Kurt, what is the matter? What are you saying?"

"I am saying good-bye, Lisel. I cannot tell you where I am going and you must tell no one you saw me here."

"I do not understand this," Lisel began and had a sudden insight. "Does your mother know you are leaving?"

The muscle along his jaw came out in a stubborn ridge. "No," he said. "And you will not tell her you saw me tonight."

"But how can I do that?" Lisel raised her voice. "She will be worried about you."

"You need not concern yourself so much with my relationship with my mother," he replied sharply.

Lisel felt a spark of anger. She grasped Kurt's arms and would have shaken him except for his size. "You are being unfair. Your mother loves you more than you know. If you do this to her then she loves you more than you deserve."

Kurt shook off her hold on him. "What do you know about my mother?" he demanded. "Do you know she poisoned Franz Muller's little dog, Maxi? Do you know she went to the Central Bureau for the People's Welfare and denounced Herr Muller to them? Not once, but several times." Kurt's voice broke. His mouth twisted. "And do you know why? Because she wanted him out! Because she wanted his flat!"

Lisel felt the warmth rise in her face. "Do you imagine that cows chase rabbits too? Who told you such rubbish? Those mysterious friends of yours? The ones who see everything? The ones who see right into Gestapo headquarters and know what happens there?" The long-suppressed suspicion popped out of Lisel's mouth and she saw Kurt's face harden, his eyes become cold.

"Yes, some of my friends *do* see into the Gestapo but only because the SS must be watched. We must know what they do so we can protect ourselves and every good German."

Deep inside, Lisel never believed Kurt was a spy for the party. She never believed he had anything to do with Franz Muller's death. But neither could she believe Frau Heidemann had anything to do with it either. "This is not true, about your mother, Kurt. This cannot be so. You cannot think this is so."

97

Kurt stared down at her, his lips a thin, angry line. "What I cannot think is that you will understand. You, who believe all the world is love. That all one must do is love. You are a fool, Lisel. Your beliefs have made you a fool."

The accusation affronted Lisel's dignity. She lifted her chin. "*Your* beliefs have made you blind—the worst kind of blindness there is because you do not want to see. If you could see, you would know your mother, despite anything she has done, loves you with a love that is above any of the ideologies you risk your life for. And that is the love you spurn so easily. How can you feel no shame?"

"I am only ashamed of my mother," Kurt said and his tone told Lisel there was no changing his mind.

Lisel sighed her resignation, though she could not give up her discontent. "Then I suppose you must go."

He ignored her bitter tone. "Yes."

Lisel saw his pale brows draw together. He lowered his voice. "You must be very careful now," he said. "They are still watching you. They sent the Wrobels, at first, to watch me. Now they are watching you, too. And your Papa and Marta."

Lisel felt a stab of alarm. "But why would they watch Papa and Marta?"

His brief smile was bitter. "They watch everyone on the merest suspicion." He took Lisel's hands. His breath was warm on her face and suddenly she longed to feel his arms around her again.

"Promise me you will be careful."

Lisel nodded. She knew he could see the gathering tears in her eyes.

"Do not cry," he whispered and gathered Lisel to him. She slipped her arms around his waist and lifted her face. His lips touched hers in a brief, sweet kiss. Then he held her against him. She felt the warmth of his throat against her cheek and the steady rhythm of his heart.

"I am sorry," Kurt whispered into her hair.

"You do not have to go," she argued. She heard the tears trembling in her own voice.

With his fingers beneath her chin, he lifted Lisel's face to his and kissed her again, gently. "Good-bye Lisel." Kurt's arms dropped away from her and she felt the cold, night air close around her.

She stood there, alone, for a moment, watching him disappear into the darkness. Then she wiped her tears from her face with the back of her wrist and stepped out onto the dark street.

Lisel expected Kurt to reappear again in a couple of days. But days passed, then weeks, then months. Frau Heidemann told everyone Kurt had joined a special unit of Hitler's Youth that was being trained for the most elite level of the SS. She said the special training unit's assignment and its location was so secret, even she did not know.

Lisel did not know who believed such a story. But no one, not even Walter, mentioned Kurt's name again. Lisel, however, thought of him often and remembered him with a sad, aching loss.

Papa began organizing their genealogy early in the year. He started with the records he had kept in the family Bible. He wrote letters. Results came in with satisfying regularity at first. With excitement, Lisel and Marta watched as Papa filled in the lines on the sheets.

Then, as Papa researched more distant ancestors, the search became difficult. Sometimes, the letters came back with an apology. "We do not have the staff to help you, but you are welcome to look for the documents you requested yourself."

Marta finished her training at the Red Cross school and was assigned to the Kurmack maternity home. Everyone knew Kurmack was a Lebensborn or "fount of life" maternity home—a home where girls of pure blood delivered babies fathered by specially chosen men of pure blood, usually members of the SS. The girls were not married to the fathers of their babies and usually left the infants in the home to be raised by the State. The girls were hailed as patriots in giving children to the Fuhrer.

Most Germans did not approve of the program, however, and quietly denounced it as immoral.

Marta did not speak of her work while she was with her family, but Lisel knew by her sister's preoccupied and solemn manner that she was not happy at the Kurmack home. Only when she spoke of Elder Nolte did her eyes light and color brighten her face.

With Marta's new job, shopping for the family became a problem. Marta left at seven in the morning and returned home at nine at night, when all the shops were closed. Lisel got home after three in the morning, slept until noon, and then tried to do the marketing. But by afternoon most of the shops were out of merchandise. And she had only until two o'clock, when she had to leave for work, to find shops with anything left. Then she had to take what no one else wanted.

At last, Lisel began getting up after only five hours of sleep in order to get to the markets early enough to buy food. Most of the time, the process took her right up to two o'clock and even then she did not get what the family needed. Exhaustion made her slow and clumsy at work and Herr Hahn made her work an extra hour if she did not meet her quota. That meant another hour less sleep.

Finally, Papa decided they must choose another course. Though it meant he must lose his income and pension, he resigned his part-time job at the bank to take over the household duties.

At first, Lisel thought they might manage on her wage and Marta's. But she had not counted on prices going up. Though the government said it had frozen prices, manufacturers and retailers found more and more ways to add extra charges. In August 1939, the price of margarine was sixty-three pfennigs a pound. But by January 1940, it had leapt to ninety-eight pfennigs a pound. And the items in the marketplace, though their prices increased, were of poorer and poorer quality. Soap, of which each person was allowed only two ounces per month, was extended with sand. The sand soap was harsh and gritty and left the skin raw and feeling scummy.

More and more often, Papa came home from the shops with grim lines around his mouth and between his eyes. And, it seemed, there was never enough food. The extra egg per person during Easter week in 1940 meant next to nothing.

In March 1940, Susanne was due to be released from her Compulsory Service assignment. By January, she had already found a job with a bakery and was counting the days to her release. But at the end of February, Herr Bauer called her into his office. He explained there were not enough workers to fill the positions left vacant by those being released from Compulsory Service. He offered her a seven-mark-a-week raise and a transfer to the bullet division if she agreed to stay. Susanne refused.

On her last day, Susanne went to Herr Bauer for her employment booklet. Herr Bauer refused to surrender it. Susanne had no choice but to stay. Even with the transfer and the raise in wages, Susanne was bitter.

Lisel also felt her friend's disappointment along with a pang of alarm. She worried whether she would be released in November or forced to stay, like Susanne.

At the end of March, the newspapers were full of the news of an important discovery. Documents had been found in Poland that revealed President Roosevelt and ambassadors Kennedy, Bullitt, and Biddle were conspiring to force Germany into war with America.

Lisel worried as she cleaned and oiled her grenades. Would they have a war with America? Would the Lord protect them, she and Papa and Marta and Michael? She remembered the scripture in Nephi. It said the wrath of God was upon all those who gathered to make war on America. Did that also apply if America was the one making war?

In April 1940, Germany invaded Denmark and Norway and headlines in the *Volkischer Beobachter* declared, "Germany Rescues Scandinavia!"

Usually, by this time, Lisel and Kurt would be laying out the garden. Lisel thought she would be glad she did not have to do that hated chore this year. But she was not. She missed Kurt. And she missed the carefree girl she had been. Where was the girl Kurt had kissed in the garden on a summer day long ago? Now a pale, tired-looking Lisel stared back from the mirror.

In May, Holland, Belgium, and Luxembourg fell. Joseph Goebbels, Hitler's propaganda minister, explained that the occupation of those countries was merely a defensive measure. England and France, he said, had planned to use them to get at Germany.

Michael came home at the end of May. There were new, harder edges to his body and face and lines of strain around his eyes and between his brows. Of his military service, he only said he had

101

been in Denmark. Most of the time, he slept. But sometimes, when Lisel came into the flat during the early morning, she heard his voice and Papa's talking low in the bedroom. Marta told her Michael often cried out in his sleep and awoke shaking and sweat-covered. When he left to rejoin his unit, he could not say when he would be discharged from the military.

In the middle of June, loudspeakers in factories, shops, restaurants, and street corners blared out national and party anthems followed by the announcement that Paris had been captured. Then the current hit was played, "We March on England." There was no cheering. No celebration. Glumly, the Germans went back to their activities without comment.

Lisel heard the news with mixed feelings. How tired she was of war! Tired of hand grenades! Tired of worrying about Michael, now somewhere in France. Tired of worrying about Kurt! Tired of ration coupons and long lines! Tired of being tired! But surely, the war was almost over. The newspapers said by Christmas. Then Michael would be home. By Christmas, she would be finished with her Compulsory Service. A bold doubt reminded Lisel of Herr Bauer's refusal to surrender Susanne's employment booklet. Her hopes pushed it away.

By Christmas, they would have their genealogy. By the new year, if they were careful with their money, they would be in America. By the new year, they would have gone to the temple.

Grete began dropping in again that summer, usually on Sunday afternoons when Lisel was home. She talked of school and the people they both knew and of movies she had seen and of a handsome officer she had met. Lisel wondered if Grete was more impressed by the black Horsch the officer drove than by the officer himself. But then Grete would go on and talk of marriage and babies and the house she wanted to live in.

Lisel listened with indulgence. She did not share Grete's romantic aspirations with any enthusiasm. Lisel's daydreams had more to do with sleeping and eating than with boys. And when she did think of men, she thought of Kurt and was saddened. Of course, most of the men had been drafted. Now, their LDS branch was made up of women, children, and older men. They had even lost two branch presidents to the military in the first six months of the year.

In the middle of July, Hitler offered Great Britain a no-strings-attached peace. He said there was no reason Germany and Great Britain should war against each another. If there was war, it was only because Great Britain forced it.

Within four days, the British bombed Bremen, Hamburg, Paderborn, Hagen, and Bochum.

Hermann Göering, Hitler's defense minister, had promised that no enemy aircraft would ever penetrate the Reich. Now, resentment soared and morale plummeted. The Germans had been promised peace, but they had gotten only bombs.

To Berliners, Gôering made further assurances that though enemy aircraft might fly over Germany, they would never reach the capital. He even told them not to worry if an air raid siren went off. They should become alarmed and hurry into the shelters only if they heard the antiaircraft guns.

So, when the women in the Wittenau Munitions Works heard the wail of air raid sirens one night in late summer, they paused only long enough to look up from their trays of grenades. But then, within moments came an unfamiliar sound. Like a loud, harsh barking. For a heartbeat, Lisel stood listening, puzzled. Her blood chilled. "It is the gun," she said under her breath, not quite believing it. "It is the antiaircraft gun!"

Lisel caught a glimpse of Herr Hahn as he leapt upon his desk. "Get to the cellars!" he screamed. "Get to the cellars!"

Then everyone was running. Pushing for the doorway. Fighting for the stairs. Behind Lisel, she heard the rolling balla-balla-balla sounds of flak. The women scrambled, stumbled down the dark stairs. They crowded into the cellar beneath the Munitions Works. It smelled damp and musty.

Herr Hahn slammed down the cross piece that barred the heavy door and fought his way to the center of the room, where he stood under a single bulb that hung from the ceiling. "Calm yourselves! Calm yourselves!" he shouted at the women. "You will each find a seat on the benches or sit on the floor. If you have your gas mask, put it on. But above all, be calm."

Lisel fought her way to an inside wall where Susanne stood, as if in shock, her normally cheerful face drawn and pale and her brown eyes glazed. "We must sit down, Susanne," Lisel said, taking her friend's icy hands and pulling her to the floor, where they sat with their backs against the wall.

Around her, she heard the other women weeping and swearing and praying. Lisel's teeth wanted to chatter but she gritted them. She squeezed Susanne's hands. "It will be all right soon," she said. Dumbly, Susanne nodded. Tears streaked her face.

Lisel shut her eyes on her own burning tears and sent up a fervent appeal. "Father, protect me. Protect Papa and Marta and Michael and Kurt."

From overhead she heard the hum of an aircraft as it flew low over the Works. Then, again, the bark of the antiaircraft gun. Heavy flak fell with a wuuu-ummm sound then a slow rolling echo.

"Why are they doing this to us?" Susanne cried out. "Why are they doing this?"

Lisel put her arm around Susanne's shoulder. "Hush now. It will be all right soon." Lisel heard the returning hum of the airplane. She tilted back her head as if she could see skyward. But there was only the white plaster of the ceiling above her. From the movement of the sound, Lisel knew the aircraft had banked and was circling back. As it drew closer, the sound became angrier, the hum a fierce buzz. Lisel pulled in a deep breath and squeezed it in her throat.

Then she heard it. The shrill whistle of the plummeting bomb. Next to her, Susanne screamed. Lisel pulled Susanne down. They both crouched low to the floor, their arms over their heads.

The explosion rocked the walls. The light went out. Lisel heard the bursting, shattering glass from the windows upstairs. She heard the panicked screaming of the other women. Plaster dust from the ceiling swirled around her and she choked. It seemed any moment the walls would give way. But they stood.

For three hours, the women of the Wittenau Munitions Works huddled in the dark cellar and listened to the battle above them. Lisel and Susanne held each other. Under her breath, Lisel prayed. "Please protect me, Father. Please protect Papa and Marta and Michael and Kurt. Please make it stop."

Some of the time, repeating the prayer blocked the sounds of aircraft motors and bombs and explosions. Some of the time, horrifying visions of Papa and Marta under tons of brick flashed with searing clarity through her mind. Some of the time, she thought of Michael and wondered if this was what it was like for him. Except she knew it must be worse. Michael would be outdoors, unprotected from bombs and bullets and shrapnel. And some of the time, she wondered where Kurt was and prayed for him too.

She prayed for the antiaircraft gunners. And some of the time, in her desperation to have it end, she prayed the gunners' mark would be true. Some of the time, Lisel envisioned her own death and knew she could not survive the night. The basement of the Wittenau Munitions Works would be her grave.

The "all clear" came at nearly three-thirty. Lisel and Susanne pulled each other up. "It is over then?" Susanne asked.

"Yes," Lisel answered. The bombing was over but the fear was not. She must get home to Papa and Marta.

Lisel followed the other women out of the cellar. Her legs ached and her knees shook under her weight. She hesitated at the doorway, certain to the bottom of her heart that her world had been destroyed. Papa and Marta were crushed beneath their burning apartment house.

"What a mess," she heard one of the women declare. Lisel stepped into the workroom. Glass was everywhere. Tables were turned over. Grenades scattered across the floor. An odor of phosphorus hung in the air. She ran to the glassless window. Next door in an empty lot, a huge black crater smoked. Lisel searched the city in the direction of her home. The red glow of firelight showed where bombs had fallen. But, to Lisel's surprise, the glowing spots were few. A tiny hope let itself shine. Perhaps Papa and Marta were safe after all. With anxiety at her heels, Lisel ran toward the door.

"Workers!" Herr Hahn shouted.

Reluctantly, she stopped. There would be serious trouble for her now if she left. Stilling her feet, she turned.

"Our glorious defense system has defeated the enemy and driven him out," Herr Hahn said. "Now, we must also defeat the enemy. We will prove our superiority by finishing tonight's quota along with our quota tomorrow night."

Lisel waited only a second more before she bolted for the door. A hundred women came right behind her.

The scheduled train was late that morning. Someone thought the tracks might have been damaged in the bombing. A huge knot of worry tightened in Lisel's stomach until she thought she would throw up. She fought back her nausea by pacing the wood floor of the dark, crowded railway station.

Mutely, Susanne sat on a bench, her fingers bunching and un-bunching. Some women, like Susanne, sat in silence, muffling sobs. Other women, in frustration, decided to walk to their homes. Lisel dismissed the idea. For her, the walk would take hours and if Papa had survived, he might try to come to Wittenau for her and they would miss each other. She would wait here for a train.

At last, with the sun shining dully through low, gray clouds, Lisel boarded her homeward train. Then, she ran all the way to her street. Nowhere did she see any damage at all. Her heart nursed a renewed hope.

At her corner, Lisel leaned against the lamppost, breathless and weak with relief. Her apartment house still stood, tall and stone-faced, looking as it had always looked. "Thank you, Father," she breathed.

At the other corner, Frau Heidemann and Walter were collect-ing rubbish from the street. Lisel's heart warmed toward the pair, up so early, working so hard and with such haste. Walter turned toward her and raised his arm. Lisel waved back. Her heart felt light enough to float all the way to the apartment house. Nothing had changed at all.

Lisel was halfway down the block when she saw Papa come out the front door of the apartment house. He looked the same as he always did with his good gray suit that was just a little baggy at the knees . . . his carefully knotted tie . . . his frequently blocked hat. Tears made of gladness welled in Lisel's eyes.

"Papa!" she called to him. He had always scolded Lisel for shouting in public, but today she did not care if he scolded her. She felt like shouting and singing and dancing in the street. "Papa!" she cried again and hurried toward him.

He opened his arms to her. "Lisel! We were so worried. I was on my way to Wittenau to find you."

"Oh Papa, I love you," Lisel said and kissed his cheek. Papa chuckled. "Yes, little one, you told me that yesterday."

"But yesterday was so long ago and I was so frightened." Her voice squeaked a little on the words. "I was so frightened that something would happen."

Papa patted her shoulder. "Nothing did happen and we should be grateful, Lisel. The Lord has blessed us with great bounty."

Lisel put her hand through the crook of Papa's elbow and they turned to go into the building. Papa paused, frowning. "What are the Heidemanns' doing out here in the street?"

"The British dropped leaflets last night," Lisel explained. "The Heidemanns' were out here picking them up when I came."

Papa bent and scooped up one of the sheets of paper. He read, "The war which Hitler has started will only go on as long as Hitler does."

Papa's frown deepened. "It seems the British have an odd idea about who has begun this war," he said. He looked at the Heidemanns. "Perhaps we should help."

Lisel glanced up and down the littered street. She felt wearied to the very bone; but, at that moment, if her Papa had asked her to fly to the moon, she would have found a way. "We can use my bag," she said.

"Herr Spann! Herr Spann!" Frau Heidemann rushed up to them. An anxious smile twitched at her lips. "What are you doing?"

Papa straightened with a handful of leaflets. Surprise lifted his gray brows. "We are helping you clean the street," he replied.

Frau Heidemann stared at the paper in Papa's hand and eyed Lisel's bulging bag. "We need no help," she insisted. "No help at all. You must be exhausted. You should go lie down for a while. Walter and I will take care of the paper."

Something in Frau Heidemann's manner puzzled Lisel. "You are being very helpful," she said. "But this is too much for you. Let me call the Wrobels to come and help us. The Schmidt family down the street has lots of children. If we ask them to help, this will be cleaned up in no time."

Frau Heidemann's pale eyes bulged. "No! No! You cannot do that!" An inner conflict showed itself in her face. At last she grimaced with resignation. "If you call them there will not be enough."

107

"Enough?" Papa questioned. "Enough what?"

"Enough paper," Frau Heidemann hissed through her teeth and shook a fistful of leaflets in his face. "Have you seen the price of toilet paper lately? Why should I buy it at such inflated prices when I can get this for free?"

Papa scowled with distaste at the leaflets in his hand. His lips twitched beneath his mustache. The color of indignation stole up his neck and face.

Lisel had to suck in her lips and bite down to keep from laughing. After seventeen years with Papa, she had learned there were times to laugh and times to be silent. This was a time for silence.

Papa made a growling sound deep down in his throat and for an instant Lisel was sure he would throw down the paper in disgust. Instead, Papa stuffed it into his pockets. Then he reached down for another handful. "Well, will you stand there with your mouth agape or will you help?"

"Papa, you do not actually mean you would . . ."

Forcefully, Papa jammed another handful of the leaflets into his jacket pocket. "Frau Heidemann is right. The price of toilet paper is too high!"

Chapter 8

WHENEVER RAF BOMBERS DID NOT FLY OVER BERLIN, THE radio announced that the aircraft had been turned back by the Reich's glorious defense system. On other nights, when the British attacked Berlin, the radio stations went silent so they would not serve as beacons.

In August 1940, the RAF began dropping a new weapon—an incendiary device that looked like a small plastic envelope and had, pasted inside, a tablet of phosphorus. The package was dropped wet; but when it dried, it burst into flame. Fortunately for the Berliners, August had been a wet month, so few of the envelopes did any damage.

The real damage was to the Germans' morale. Most people, having worked long hours during the day, were kept awake by air raid sirens and bomber attacks at night.

The Chief of Air Raid Protection suggested that Berliners try to get a couple of hours of sleep before the bombers arrived. The humor-loving Berliners soon created a joke out of that suggestion. If people arrived in the air raid shelters and said, "Good morning," everyone knew they had been asleep. If they arrived and said, "Good evening," everyone knew they had not been asleep. If they arrived and said, "Heil Hitler," everyone knew they had always been asleep.

In the cellar below the Spanns' flat, no one mentioned that particular wittism; though each evening when the sirens went off, Frau Heidemann sweetly asked the Wrobels how long they had been asleep.

Papa and Marta made light of the situation, pretending to Lisel the nightly loss of sleep was no inconvenience. Yet Lisel saw the shadows of strain and exhaustion behind their eyes. Lisel did not suffer the same dehabilitating loss of sleep since she slept during the day and spent the hours of the bombing attacks in the cellar beneath the Wittenau Munitions Works. But she did suffer from exhaustion.

In order to make up for the loss of work during the raids, Herr Hahn pushed the women harder, increasing their hourly quotas until the pace was murderous. And he increased their shifts by another hour.

The bombings went on. The railroad yards, stations, and freight houses were hit. The three main stretches of railway lines were knocked out, creating chaos among commuters. The gas works, a rubber factory, and Siemens Electrical Plant received significant damage. At a branch of Duren Metals, two workers were injured when they tried to put out a fire on the roof.

Some nights, the women of the Munitions Works emerged from their cellar to find the night skies above them lit by huge fires on the ground. They could see from the destruction around the Works that it had been the intended target. "They missed us again!" they exclaimed. "What poor shots."

Of course, they did not comment on the lack of success of the antiaircraft gunners. Though huge searchlights pierced the skies and searched frantically during a raid, they rarely spotted a RAF plane. It was even more rare that a bomber was brought down. The Germans decided the British had painted their aircraft with invisible paint.

The newspapers ran broad headlines. "Revolting Crime: Murder of Children at Bethel!" "The British Island of Murderers Will Have to Take the Consequences of Its Malicious Bombings!"

The interruptions caused by the air raids created many new shortages, mainly of metal. All over the city, iron fences came down and loads of pots and pans found their way to the foundries. When party workers went door to door asking for any nonessential metal items, Marta told Lisel that Frau Heidemann's ornate mirror frame became suddenly carved wood and sported a new coat of white paint. After that, the frame exhibited some unusual characteristics. While the Spanns and Wrobels waited out an air raid in Frau Heidemann's dark basement flat, the frame glowed with an eerie greenish light—like the curbs that had been painted phosphorescent white. The Wrobels scowled with such fierce intent at the mirror and Frau Heidemann that from then on, she covered the mirror with an old sheet.

As the end of Lisel's Compulsory Service term approached, she began looking for a new job. Since most of the younger men were in active military duty, there were more positions available, though many were no better than what she had at the Munitions Works. However, anything was better than working with Herr Hahn, so Lisel continued to search.

In October, Herr Hahn interrupted Lisel's work with a tap on her shoulder. "You will follow me," he ordered.

Lisel's heart sank lower and lower as Herr Hahn led her to the Munitions Works managing office.

This time, standing at Herr Bauer's desk, he smiled at Lisel and gestured for her to sit down. His thin face was paler and a little more lined now. His long, thin lips had taken on a worried droop. "Our records show your term of service is nearly over," he said pleasantly, though his tone questioned.

Lisel nodded. She knew what was coming and fought back the anger and despair and frustration that made her want to strike out at the man. She clenched her hands.

"Our records also show you have served here well. We have been pleased with your work."

Lisel thought of Herr Hahn and how he shouted at her if she fell behind her quota. She remembered the names he used. She thought of how he stood outside the lavatory with a stopwatch and called out the time, in seconds, she had been in there.

Herr Bauer watched her, expecting some reply.

Resentment tightened her mouth. "I wish to let you know I have found another job in a grocery shop." It was not strictly the truth. The shop manager had not promised her the job, but he had suggested she come back and talk to him in another month.

Herr Bauer's mouth made a tight circle in his long face and he tapped his finger on the desk. "We had hoped you realized the great importance of your work here and would be willing to stay with us. We are even prepared to offer you, if you decide to remain with us, an additional seven marks a week."

"Seventy marks a week would not induce me to stay here!" Lisel blurted.

Herr Bauer's eyes, cool and flashing, narrowed with something that looked like annoyance. "I regret you feel that way, Fraulein. I also regret—"

"That you will not allow me to apply for my employment booklet," Lisel finished, with a dangerous heat growing in her face. "You will force me to remain here, whether I want to or not!"

"You have a temper to match your hair," he observed. "Perhaps that is not a profitable match."

"Perhaps not." Lisel stood. "But it seems, if you will not allow me my booklet, you will be compelled to tolerate it." She turned to leave.

"You have not been dismissed, Fraulein," Herr Bauer reminded her. Lisel heard the threat in his voice. She knew she should have been more discreet, and she knew her defiance would only bring more trouble. But at that moment she only thought of standing at the endless grenade trays for another year. Another year with Herr Hahn and his stopwatch. Another year of huddling in the cellar, waiting to be bombed to death. Hot tears of anger and frustration burned her eyes. Lisel snatched at the doorknob and yanked open the door.

On the other side, Herr Hahn jumped back. Lisel regarded him for an instant with all the contempt she felt, then strode past him and out into the hall.

She heard him coming up behind her. She heard the sharp crack of his boot tacks on the tiling. Anger quickened Lisel's pace but not enough.

Herr Hahn grabbed her arm and jerked her around. His strength surprised Lisel. She struggled against his grip, but he pinned her against the wall with his weight. His breath was on her face and he smelled of boiled cabbage.

Lisel opened her mouth to shout. "Scream," he sneered. "I will enjoy silencing you."

Lisel shut her mouth. She knew he wanted her to be frightened. He wanted her to struggle. In defiance, Lisel willed a pretense of calmness. She stopped struggling.

Herr Hahn grinned at her. One pale eyebrow arched. "Your interview with Herr Bauer did not go well?"

Lisel gritted her teeth. "Was the door so thick you could not hear?"

Herr Hahn's laughter made an ugly sound. He reached up and fingered one of her braids. "Perhaps your work would become easier if you made an effort to make more friends." His hand slipped onto her shoulder and slid down her arm.

Lisel stiffened. She saw his spreading smile as he read her alarm. Her heart sent out a desperate prayer.

"Perhaps you would feel closer to me if you realized how much I know about you." He leaned closer to Lisel so all she could see were his pale eyes. "For instance, if you knew I have seen your files. I know about the riot you provoked in Neukolln. I know you have seen the inside of a cell on Prinz-Albrectstrasse."

"Then you should also know there is no one so willing to report to Prinz-Albrectstrasse than one who has been a guest there." The words came out of Lisel's mouth before she knew she spoke them. She heard them with a tremor of surprise. And they had a shocking effect.

The color dropped from Herr Hahn's face and his eyes bulged. He jumped away from Lisel as if he had been burned. "You dare to threaten me!" he shouted. His lips trembled with his words. "You know nothing to threaten me!"

In astonishment, Lisel watched as the little man darted down the long hallway. His sharp, hurried footsteps sounded like gunshots. He paused at the door of the grenade room and raised his fist. His mottled face seemed to swell. "You know nothing to threaten me!"

Lisel stumbled back to her place in the grenade room. Her hands shook as she picked up the wire brush and grenade. What had she said to anger him so? Lisel glanced up at Herr Hahn. He sat at the end of the long room behind his large desk and scowled at her with such evil, Lisel had to look away. A strong, decisive warning from deep within her told her not to ever be alone, not in the Works or on the walk to and from the railway station.

Lisel remembered and remained cautious. The added threat increased the strain and by Christmas 1940, Lisel was ill from exhaustion. Doctor Kettel wanted to write her a note, excusing her from work for a few days, but she held off. The People's Welfare was coming to the Works that week to pass out a package of cocoa, some lard, and a bag of nuts. Lisel felt she could not miss the chance for the much-needed food.

The food situation was even worse than before. There was no fresh fruit at all. Last year's severe winter had seen to that. The occupation of Holland helped with vegetable and dairy products, but there was little meat to be had anywhere.

After receiving the food, Lisel did take the "forced" vacation. She spent the first few days sleeping. But one day she felt well enough to go to the cinema with Grete. The movie was romantic, just the kind Grete enjoyed so much. And Lisel surprised herself by enjoying it too. The story was about a couple who met at the 1936 Olympics, fell in love and then lost touch. During the popular Sunday radio program, Request Concert, the couple was reunited and lived happily ever after.

Afterward, Lisel and Grete returned to the flat to enjoy a rare cup of hot cocoa, thanks to milk from Holland and cocoa from the People's Welfare.

The girls and Papa and Marta sat around the table sipping the delicious cocoa, telling stories, and laughing. The day seemed so normal that Lisel almost forgot all that had happened in the last year and she was, once again, a schoolgirl.

Lisel and Grete were finishing the washing when Walter came to the door. He was eleven now and growing fast. With his blonde hair, blue eyes, and lopsided smile, he resembled Kurt so much it made Lisel's heart ache to look at him. More and more often, he was drawn to the Spanns' apartment out of simple loneliness. Seeing him, Lisel felt a pang of remorse that they had not saved some hot cocoa.

"We are telling jokes, Walter," she told him when he settled at the table to watch the two girls. "Do you know any?"

Walter cocked his mouth sideways and he screwed up his eyes. At last, his face cleared and he smiled. "I know one about a fisherman."

"Oh no," Lisel protested. "That is the same one you tell all the time. Tell another one."

Walter stuck out his chin in an obstinate gesture. "I will tell my joke or you will not get your mail." He reached inside his sweater and produced three, long, white envelopes. "Two of them are from America."

Marta sat up straight. "Let him tell his joke," she urged, "so we can have our mail."

Lisel sighed. How many times had she heard that silly story? "All right Walter, tell your joke."

Walter beamed. "Do you know why the fisherman took a clock and a hammer to the river?"

Lisel, Grete, and Marta all answered in unison. "No, Walter. Why did the fisherman take a clock and a hammer to the river?"

Walter was laughing through his tightly clamped lips and made a buzzing sound. "So when the fish came up to see what time it was, the fisherman could hit it over the head with the hammer."

Lisel, Grete, and Marta all groaned. "Now give us the mail, Walter or we will use a hammer on you," Lisel threatened and tugged at his ear.

Walter stuck his tongue out at Lisel and defiantly tossed the envelopes to Marta. Lisel responded by tickling Walter until he screamed and wiggled away from her.

"This one is for Papa," Marta said, reading the address. "It is from the Hannover Bureau of Registry."

Papa reached out and took the envelope. "This must be the history I sent for."

Marta checked the other two letters. Lisel saw her face flush with the first one, but she frowned at the second. "This one is also for you, Papa. From Elder Nolte."

Lisel saw Papa's eyebrows rise as he looked at the familiar handwriting. She knew the missionary had not written to Papa since that first letter after the evacuation.

"Well, what does he say?" Lisel asked impatiently.

Marta and Papa looked up at each other. Marta's face glowed, her cheeks pink, her eyes sparkling. Papa's held a questioning look.

"What shall I answer him?" he asked.

Marta flew across the room to her father and threw her arms around his neck. "Tell him yes! Oh, tell him yes!" She wept and laughed at the same time.

"Am I to be left out?" Lisel cried as she watched the scene with bewilderment.

Marta turned to Lisel. She saw the happy tears shining on her sister's cheeks. "Grant has been released from his mission. He has asked me to marry him. He is going to come for me and we are to be married!"

Lisel ran to Papa and Marta and threw her arms around them both. Then Grete and even Walter got caught in the moment and joined the embrace. They all laughed and they all cried. Except Walter, who escaped the flat when a sobbing Grete started kissing everyone.

"When is it to be?" Lisel asked. "When is he to come?"

Marta scanned her now-crushed letter. "He says it will be as soon as he has a job and can earn enough money."

"That will not take long," Lisel declared. "In America, everyone earns lots of money!"

Grete clapped her hands together. "You will be a beautiful bride and I will help you. We will design your wedding gown ourselves. From my magazines, I have cut photographs of the most beautiful gowns." She grabbed her coat and hat. "I will go home this instant and get them." Grete rushed out the door and slammed it behind her.

Lisel, Marta, and Papa all laughed. "She is more excited than you are, I think," Papa said to Marta.

"She could not be more excited than I." Marta clutched her letter to her chest and spun around the room. "I believe I must be dreaming."

Despite Marta's joy, a worrisome thought gnawed at Lisel. "When Elder Nolte comes for you, does that mean he will be staying in Germany for good?"

Marta's brows drew together and she caught the corner of her lip between her teeth. "No," she said slowly. "He is coming to escort me to America so we can be married in the temple. He wants us to live with his family in Idaho."

The room fell silent as the meaning took form. "You will be moving away from us then," Lisel said.

"But of course she will be moving away," Papa said. Lisel heard the underscoring disappointment in his voice. "The scriptures say, when we marry, we must leave our fathers and our mothers and cleave only unto our spouses. Marta must go where Grant takes her."

"It need not be that way, Papa," Marta interjected. "I know we decided that after we had gone to the temple we would return here, to Germany. But that was before I knew Elder Nolte. That was before we had family in America. Now we will have all of Grant's family as our family. It will be like a home for us there. We could live happily there, Papa. I know we could."

Lisel had only imagined life in America, where everyone was a member of the Church. Where wards had their own buildings. Where the chapels were filled for sacrament meeting. But until this moment, it was only a wistful piece of imagination. Now, the thought struck Lisel like a thunderbolt and left her breathless. "Marta is right!" she exclaimed. "It would be wonderful for all of us to be together in America."

Papa moved away from the girls and sat down in his chair. "Leave the fatherland?" he said with a troubled frown. "Leave your mother?"

Lisel had not thought of that. She did not want to leave Mama in a lonely grave with no one to tend to it. She thought of the small plot with only a narrow slab for a headstone. President Dieter had said that Mama was now in a joyous place, and Lisel had felt comforted by it. Now she knew what she must say.

She went to Papa's side and, kneeling there, took his hand. "Papa, you know Mama is not there."

Papa turned his eyes to Lisel. His mouth turned down and he nodded. "Yes, little one, I do know that. Only the body she once inhabited rests there now, but I cannot help but feel that is part of her, too. A small part of her. It is difficult to think of leaving even that one small part." Lisel heard his voice tremble and saw the moisture build in his eyes. "I loved her so much."

Lisel put her arms around Papa's neck and pressed her face against his shoulder. "And she loved you, too, Papa. She loved all of us." Her own tears slid down her cheeks. "Do you remember how she longed to go to Utah, to the temple?"

Papa ran a tender hand over Lisel's braids. "You are trying to tell me she would not want us to stay here because of her. You are right, Lisel. I would want the same for you. But I am such an old man. I do not know if I can stand so great a change."

Marta knelt next to Lisel and said, "But we were going to America anyway. There would not be so much change. Lots of our friends have already gone. With Grant's help you and Lisel can be settled near some of the people we know. And you would be near your grandchildren." A small flush rose in Marta's face. "Besides, Papa, in America, there is no food rationing. There is no clothing rationing. No coal rationing. And no war."

"We would be close to the Prophet," Lisel added. "And, Papa, you could go to the temple whenever you wanted. We would be able to go to conference all the time. I would find a Mormon boy to marry, just like Marta has. And Michael would find a Mormon girl."

"Please say it will be so." Tears welled in Marta's eyes. "I cannot bear to be separated from my family and I cannot bear to be separated from my Grant."

Papa put his hand over Marta's. "But that would mean we would have to wait for Michael to come out of the army. And we would have to wait until Lisel is released from the Munitions Works. That may be a long time."

"Everyone says the war will be over in a few months," Marta argued.

"And I can leave the Munitions Works anytime I want," Lisel said. "I will only forfeit my employment booklet, and I am sure I will not need that in America."

"Besides, while we are waiting for Michael to come home, we will be able to save more money," Marta came back. Her face brightened with the possibilities. "And we will have more time to collect our genealogy."

Papa nodded thoughtfully. "Perhaps you are right then. But we have another problem. In order to finish our genealogy, someone will have to travel to the cities and search the records. Which of us can go?"

Lisel and Marta looked at each other. Neither one had vacation time yet and neither could afford to give up even a few days work—the money was needed too badly. And Papa was needed at home. Lisel looked back at her father. She knew the words before they came to her lips. "You and the Lord will solve that one," she said.

Papa's mouth lifted in a wide smile. "With such faith, we cannot fail. We will inquire of the Lord."

1940 slipped into 1941. Michael came home from France for two weeks during the last of January. He wore his uniform now as if he had never worn anything else, though it was in need of mending and patching. Happily, Marta obliged with the repairs.

Like last time, Michael did not speak of his military service; but unlike last time, he seemed moody and was frequently away from the flat.

One night, Lisel came home and found him smoking in the back garden. Even in the dark, she detected embarrassment in his face. "There is not much else to do," he offered as an explanation.

Lisel put her arms around him and kissed his cheek. "You are my brother and I love you no matter what you do. When this war is over, we are going to the temple. We cannot go without you."

Michael nodded. "I will be there," he answered. "But do not expect the war to be over soon."

"I expect only miracles," she replied.

In February 1941, Rommel landed in Africa. Yugoslavia and Greece fell in April, and Crete was taken in May. Hitler announced the Reich would be victorious in 1941. Lisel breathed a sigh of relief.

The war would be over by the end of the year. By Christmas, Michael would be home. By Christmas, they would have found a way to complete their genealogy. By the New Year, Grant would come. By the New Year, they would be in America. And soon after that they would all be sealed in the temple.

One night, in the middle of May, Lisel came home to find Marta curled up and dozing in Papa's chair. "What are you doing up?" Lisel whispered.

"I wanted to tell you something," Marta replied.

From the tightness in her sister's voice, Lisel knew the "something" was not good news. Alarm sent her heart into her throat. "Michael's hurt!" she blurted.

Marta snatched Lisel's hand. The warm grip calmed her. "No, this has nothing to do with Michael."

"Then it's Kurt!"

Marta shook her head. "No, no. This has to do with Grete."

Grete was hurt? "What has happened?" Lisel demanded.

"Grete has entered the Lebensborn program."

For an instant, Lisel could not make the two connect. Grete used as a breeding machine for the Reich? Grete producing an illegitimate child? Then things clicked into place. It was a ridiculous notion.

"I blame myself," Marta continued. Her voice was muffled, the darkness shielded her face. "I was so caught up in my dreams of marrying Grant and the home we would live in and the children we would have." She broke off. "Did you know, after the first of the year, Grete came over several times a week while you were at work?"

Lisel knew Grete had been visiting, but she had not thought much about it. If she had, she would have realized Grete had been drawn by Marta's romantic dreams because Grete had the same dreams herself.

"If I had only realized where our talks were leading her," Marta said, covering her face with her hands. "I would have been more discreet. I would have been more careful."

Lisel pulled her hands from her sister's face. "This is not your doing. Grete has been thinking of this for some time. For at least a year or more."

"But I could have—"

"Only if cows could chase rabbits," Lisel interrupted. "I suppose, because of Grete's Nordic type, she has had a lot of pressure put on her. And being an only child, living with a widowed mother, I understand how Grete has come to long for a family the way she does. She has had the most terrible crush on Papa ever since I can remember just because she longed for a Papa of her own. Now maybe she thinks having a baby will give her the feeling of family that she so desperately wants. I will go over in the morning and talk to her."

"But you cannot. She is gone." Marta sketched a helpless gesture with her hands. Today, I went to her house. Her mother told me." Marta wiped at her eyes with her fingers. "Oh Lisel, you should have seen Frau Spengler. She was so grieved, so unhappy.

Anyway, she said, Grete is in a maternity home in Hannover. She is due to be delivered at the end of the year."

Chapter 9

BORED, LISEL STOOD IN THE LONG LINE OUTSIDE THE GROCER'S and studied the back of the man ahead of her. He was only a stump of a man really, not much higher than her shoulder. His white hair bristled out from under his shapeless, felt hat. His neck was crisscrossed by deep lines, and beads of perspiration glittered in the creases. Once, his collar must have been white. His suit jacket was too big, making her wonder whether it had belonged to someone bigger or whether the man had lost a lot of weight.

He did not look much different from many people on the street nowadays, Lisel reflected. A little worn. A little thin.

The shopkeeper had his radio on and the loudspeaker outside the store blared out a popular tune.

> *You're not virile, but charming,*
> *You're not clever, but gallant,*
> *You're the type of hero I like best, Bel Ami."*

The little man did not look like anyone's hero. He did not look like anyone's Bel Ami. But with so many men away, even *this* little man would be welcome at many women's tables.

Lisel sighed and looked away. Thanks to a moderately well-aimed bomb two nights before, she had several days off—a forced but welcome vacation away from Herr Hahn and the grenade trays while repairs were made. Wanting to give Papa a small respite from the household chores, Lisel offered to do the marketing. The woman behind Lisel snapped her newspaper, straightening the page. Lisel glanced back and scanned the front page. The headlines were the usual inflammatory statements about Churchill and Roosevelt and bomber damage reports and the demand for reprisals. There was also an article by Goebbels saying the Russian farmland—the best in the world—was in the hands of those who were least able to farm. He claimed the superior German farmer could manage the land better than any other farmer in the world. That he could grow two stalks of wheat where Russians could only grow one.

If that was so, Lisel thought sourly, why were Germans lined up outside of shops all over the country. Why did the State tell people how much they could eat? Lisel had heard the explanation over and over again. The State needed the food to feed the troops. But most importantly, the State reassured its people, the food was being stored against hard times. A famine like the one that followed the last war would never afflict Germany again.

Lisel supposed that explanation should be enough but it was not. She was tired of the complicated rationing system and tired of not having enough to eat.

"All this we owe to the Fuhrer . . ." were the square letters on the wall poster where Lisel stood. She read the familiar phrase with cold gratitude.

When they got to America, Lisel knew things would be different. She would go to bed at midnight and not get up until noon. She would burn so much coal, she would not have to sleep with any blankets on the bed. And when she woke up, she would drink a quart of whole milk and eat sausages and eggs and white bread with mounds of butter until she was sick. She would have seven pairs of leather shoes, one for each day of the week, and she would throw away the wooden clogs she had been forced to buy when her leather shoes had worn out. She would be invited to parties every night and, at one of them, Fred Astaire would see her and ask her to dance. The fantasy grew each time it filled Lisel's mind. And, as with most fantasies, it eased her bitterness.

The line inched toward the doorway. Ahead of her, the small man hitched forward with an awkward limp. Lisel noted his difficulty and when she looked closer, she saw that his gnarled, spotted hands shook. His age, his shabbiness, his infirmities touched her. She put her hand on his arm. He turned and Lisel saw that through his thick glasses his eyes were a rheuemy blue, yet they appeared sharp and full of intention. And despite his shabby attire he was clean-shaven. "What is it?" he asked in a surprisingly cultured voice. He reminded Lisel of a schoolmaster.

"I only wondered if you needed some help, sir. I can take your market basket if it is too heavy for you to carry."

His eyes narrowed and Lisel read the suspicion there. "No thank you," he snapped and turned away.

Lisel's surprise turned to indignation. She felt her face warm. Did he think her a thief? Was she to be rewarded for her kindness with harshness? Lisel glared at the back of the man. Then her annoyance collapsed into shame. The man had no market basket. He was too poor even for a basket. Poor and old and crippled. Pride had made him harsh. Lisel's compassion for him doubled but he wanted none of it.

Lisel lapsed again into her favorite daydream—going to America, going to Salt Lake, going to the temple of the Lord where her family would be united for all eternity. It brought a rash of goose bumps up on her arms. She could hardly wait. Yet, wait she must. Wait for the war to be over so Michael would be free to go with them. Wait until they had saved enough money to make the trip. Wait until they had collected their genealogy. The word "wait" made Lisel want to scream.

Yet everyone said any day the war would be over. The Spanns' savings had almost reached the amount Papa had said they would need. But in the collection of their genealogy, the Spanns had seen disappointment.

They knew they must find a way to go to the cities where the records were kept and do the research themselves; but, so far, they had not determined how that could be accomplished.

The family talked about engaging a professional genealogist, but the fees were much too high to afford, even with their savings.

They thought about hiring someone to do their marketing so Papa could go. But who, among their friends, was willing to use the extra time and effort, even for the extra money? And the Spanns worried that in these times the temptation to take advantage of someone else's coupons might prove greater than friendship.

Despite those disadvantages, Lisel knew their answer lay in one of those solutions. Papa said the Lord would clear the path. He would show them which to choose. And so the Spanns turned to the Lord and waited for his guidance. Papa said they must be like the followers of Alma who were enslaved by Amulon. They must wait in patience and cheerfulness, having faith. Lisel had faith and she could be cheerful, but she waited with restrained impatience. Every week, bombing raids destroyed more and more of Germany's buildings—some of them buildings where records were kept. And so, while Lisel prayed for guidance, she also prayed their records would be spared.

The line outside the grocer's moved forward enough that the small man with the limp was inside. Lisel waited her turn near the door and studied, with little interest, the new poster. The illustration showed an automobile, newly designed by the State. It was a tiny, egg-shaped vehicle. The caption read, "For every member of the people, a people's car."

"But I will take anything you have!"

Lisel recognized the little man's voice, sharp now and raised in desperation. Alarm rose in Lisel's chest. Was the grocer out of food? Several other women crowded around Lisel at the door, listening, clutching their bags and baskets with worry.

The grocer had come from around his counter and put his hand on the man's shoulder. Lisel saw the discomfort and sympathy in the grocer's face. "See here, my friend, this is but a small shop. It only requires myself and my wife and my daughter to do business."

"He is looking for a job, poor man," the woman behind Lisel said and clucked her tongue in sympathy. Everyone went back to their places in line.

But Lisel stood watching. Her heart contracted as the man pled. "But I can sweep floors. I can clean your counter. Look here." The man rubbed his own handkerchief over the counter. "You see, I can make it shine for you. And I will work for half of any other hireling. A quarter even."

"It is not that I would not give you a job if I could," the grocer replied. "But I cannot pay you anything for your work. There is barely enough for my family. Surely, you can find work in one of the factories."

The man's shoulders slumped, his now dusty handkerchief hung limp in his hand. "I have tried in those places." He shook his head slowly. His voice was toneless. "They say I am too old and too crippled."

"You must have some training," the grocer protested. "Something that has supported you for these years."

The man's smile was bitter. "I was a university professor. But where are my students? They are not in the classrooms nor the libraries. They are carrying guns for the Reich. They are lying beneath the ground for a madman's delusion. I have no one to teach."

"I am sorry, my friend," the grocer said.

"So am I," the small man replied and turned away.

Lisel saw the despair that sagged his face, the dull hopelessness in his eyes, the resignation in his heavy step as he came toward her. She searched her heart for something to offer the man. She had no useful material things to give. She could think of no position at the Munitions Works to suggest to him. Lisel's sympathy, compounded by her inability to help, frustrated her.

Lisel knew, as the man limped toward her, that he would know she had heard the exchange and see the pity in her eyes. He would be angered even more. The least she could give him was his dignity. She thought to lower her eyes, to turn her head away so he would not see. Yet, though she tried, she could not take her eyes from the man nor could she move her head. It was as if her neck and head were paralyzed. Panic flamed inside her chest. She tried to lift her hand, but it remained at her side as if unbidden. Her legs had turned to stone.

Lisel stood blocking the doorway. The man could not get past her and she could not move, neither to go forward into the shop nor to step aside to let him pass.

He looked up at her and scowled. "What is this? Let me pass," he ordered.

With a mighty effort, Lisel struggled against her weighted, unyielding body. She tried to speak, but her tongue found no words. Lisel turned to her only other resource. "Father," her heart cried out, "what would thou have me do?"

The answer came in a bright, white flash of understanding. Her heart swelled and her limbs were loosened. Lisel reached out and gripped the man's twisted hand. It felt strong and firm in hers, and for an instant he appeared tall and youthful and engulfed in light. Just like a classical hero in shining armor. Her Bel Ami. "What did you teach at the University?" she cried.

His face hardened, his nostrils flared. "Young woman, what do you mean by this insane display?"

"I mean to hire you if you will answer my question," she said, nearly laughing with joy and relief.

The man pushed Lisel's hands away. "I am a research genealogist," he replied in icy dignity. "I taught records research."

Lisel cried out in pure gratitude and she threw her arms around the surprised man who struggled against her embrace. "Young woman! Young woman!" he protested.

"But I have a job for you," Lisel said and laughed again. "You must come with me to meet my Papa."

The man eyed Lisel with skepticism. "What kind of job?"

"Papa will tell you when we get home," she said, carefully pulling him down the sidewalk by the arm.

The woman who had stood behind Lisel called to her. "But if you leave now, you will lose your place in line."

"It is of no matter," Lisel called back. "I have no need of food today."

And so Papa and Gunter Pinsel, Lisel's certified genealogist, struck a bargain. Professor Pinsel's fee was fully half of the Spanns' savings, but it was also only one-third of the price other genealogists had asked of them.

That night, as Lisel approached the Lord on her knees, it was with great humility of heart and gratitude that the British bomber had, at last, hit its mark and allowed Lisel to find Professor Pinsel. And for once, the night sky was filled with silence and peace.

The next day, the repairs at the Wittenau Munitions Works were completed and Lisel went back to work. At the beginning of the shift, Herr Hahn stood up on his desk and made an announcement.

"Workers!" he crowed. "Though the enemy inflicted great damage upon our building, he did nothing to damage the strength of our hearts. In only three days, we have repaired the roof of the Wittenau Munitions Works, proving, once again, the German superiority. Now we, as workers, must prove our superiority in production. We must increase our nightly quota by one quarter."

The groan that went up from the women at the grenade trays filled the large room. Herr Hahn scowled his disapproval but continued.

"I have discovered that much of the damage occurred because the windows of this room were left closed during the air raid. Beginning tonight, a worker will be assigned every night as window warden. It will be her duty, when the sirens sound, to open the windows."

Lisel glanced around the room at the large, multipaned windows. A chill came up her spine. Even moving quickly, it could take a woman several minutes to open all of them. In those several minutes a bomb could strike the Works. And a woman left unprotected near so much glass might be seriously injured or killed.

Lisel's mind filled with the ghastly image. What would it be like to be caught in a bomber attack with no shelter? She glanced around at the other women at the grenade trays. The same thought had occurred to them too. Many were studying the windows, their faces pale.

"The assignment of window warden is an important one," Herr Hahn went on. "Her efforts may well save our building and thus preserve the important work we do for our country's defense. The window warden for tonight will be . . ."

The room fell silent. Lisel held her breath.

". . . Fraulein Ursula Bonse."

Lisel looked to the tall, thin, unbeautiful Ursula Bonse. Her eyes bulged in her ashen face. Her hands gripped the edge of her tray, her fingers white.

"We must congratulate Fraulein Bonse," Herr Hahn said, "for being chosen as first window warden."

Ursula looked as if she was trying to smile but only succeeded in pulling her lips back from her teeth in a deathly grimace.

Lisel said a quick prayer of thanksgiving that she was not chosen and then added a request of speed for Ursula. The girl's life might depend on how fast she could move tonight.

When the first sirens sounded, the women paused for a heart-beat; their eyes went to Ursula Bonse. The tall girl seemed frozen, staring up at the ceiling, her brush still gripped in her hand. Lisel saw her frightened hesitation and felt the seconds of time speed past her. The words rose straight from her chest. "Run, Ursula!" she shouted.

Ursula jumped as if shocked and sprinted toward the windows. The other women reacted too. They fled toward the cellar door. Lisel followed, glancing back at the unfortunate Ursula. The latches and frames on the new windows yielded reluctantly, and as Ursula struggled with them, she wept aloud.

Lisel slowed and allowed others past her. Ursula was only halfway round the room and the women just ahead of Lisel had already disappeared through the doorway that led down the stairs. Perhaps, she could go back. There may be time if she went back to help.

A sharp blow between her shoulder blades sent Lisel sprawling through the doorway. Her breath left her in a rush. "Move along, Fraulein!" Herr Hahn bellowed from behind her.

Lisel stumbled down the stairs. "But Ursula is still out there!" she cried when she saw him push shut the heavy door. He slammed down the cross piece. "You cannot lock her out!" Lisel protested in a burst of outrage. "She may be killed!"

"Go to your place, Fraulein!" Herr Hahn ordered. "Go to your place now or I will put you on report."

An angry reply leapt to Lisel's lips but never got beyond them. "Lisel!" Susanne had hold of her arm and was dragging her down the stairs. "You must get to your place."

Lisel tried to pull away from her. "But we cannot let him do this. If he can do this to Ursula, he can do this to you or to me or anyone here."

Susanne spoke to her from between gritted teeth. "It will be worse if you fight against him!" Susanne jerked her down hard onto their customary spot on the floor.

Lisel realized she could not free herself from Susanne's grip and gave up. She glared up at Herr Hahn, who stood at the top of the stairs near the door. He sneered back at her, showing his small, yellow teeth, daring her to challenge him.

129

"Oh, he is evil, that one," Susanne said. "He chose Ursula to punish her."

Lisel turned to Susanne. "What harm could Ursula Bonse do to justify this?" she demanded.

Susanne's eyebrows quirked up. "She complained to Herr Bauer, that is what. She told him Hahn had been trying to fondle her. Herr Bauer called Hahn into his office." Susanne shrugged. "No one knows what was said, but Hahn has been making Ursula's life a hell. She gets less time in the bathroom and her quota is higher."

Lisel remembered the day last November when Herr Hahn had pinned her against the wall. She remembered his touch on her hair and her shoulder. She remembered his face so close to hers, the smell of his breath, the implied threat in his words. And Lisel shuddered with revulsion.

From outside, the antiaircraft guns began to bark, the sounds of flak rolled through the skies and, at last, came the whistling of the falling bombs. Underscoring it all was a dull pounding at the stairway door. "Let me in! Please, let me in!" Ursula wailed and the raw desperation in her voice made Lisel's hair go up on her arms.

The women in the cellar looked at one another with horror-widened eyes, asking the question of one another. At last, Lisel leapt to her feet. "Open the door!" she shrieked at Herr Hahn. "Open the door, you swine!"

Rage purpled Herr Hahn's face. "The regulations say I must not open the door until the all-clear," he snapped.

"And what do regulations say about the value of a worker?" Lisel came back. The cold rage inside her made her tremble. "What would the party say if you allowed a worker to be injured or killed?"

Herr Hahn's face swelled and colored. His eyes glittered, cold and black like a snake's. His mouth exploded with incoherent obscenities, and Lisel flinched but did not give ground.

"Open the door!" she demanded.

Herr Hahn glanced around the cellar room. All eyes were on him. He came back to Lisel and something of hesitancy showed in his eyes. His lips twitched. Then, abruptly, he turned and pulled up the crosspiece.

One of the women ran up the stairs as he opened the door. Ursula lay sobbing and babbling behind it. "I have wet myself. I could not help it," she wept. With soothing words, the woman got Ursula to her feet and helped her down the stairs.

Lisel looked up at Herr Hahn with a loathing so strong it brought up a bitter taste in her mouth.

Herr Hahn pushed shut the door and replaced the crosspiece. Then he faced the cellar of women. He thumped his chest with one fist. "Hahn values each worker!" he shouted. His jaw was an angry ridge. His mouth shaped the words with ugliness. His eyes returned to Lisel with a vicious glare. "No one can renounce Hahn to the party! Not even a Gestapo spy!"

So he still believed she had that power. Well, that was fine with Lisel. Let him believe it. She dropped down next to Susanne. Her arms and legs felt numb and her hands shook.

"You are a fool, Lisel Spann," Susanne said. Her voice was harsh. Stunned, Lisel turned to look at her. "Do you think he will ignore your insolence tonight? It will be *your* turn next. And then mine because I have been your friend." Susanne's lips thinned over her chipped tooth and turned down. "Well, I have no desire to be punished for your indiscretion. I can no longer be your friend." Susanne stood up and moved to the other side of the cellar.

Lisel felt a stone fall through her heart. "Wait, Susanne," she called. "I only did what every woman here knew had to be done."

Susanne did not look back or answer her. Lisel turned to the woman beside her. "Ursula could have been killed," she said.

The woman mumbled something Lisel did not hear and turned away from her.

For the rest of the air raid, Lisel sat alone, ignored and shunned by her cellar-mates. Puzzled despair closed around her heart.

When the all-clear sounded, the women moved up the stairs to the grenade room, each being careful not to brush against Lisel.

She returned to her grenade tray. She felt dried up and hollow inside. She had defeated Herr Hahn's evil plan, but she had lost more than he. She looked up at the little man. He was watching her. There was malice in his eyes and in the upward curve of his mouth. He knew what her defiance had cost her. The hair on the back of Lisel's neck rose. If she had no friends among the women, where would she turn for protection? Only while Herr Hahn believed her a threat was she safe.

Six days a week, Lisel had to face the loneliness of the Wittenau Munitions Works and the hatred of Herr Hahn. She was never called as window warden, and she began to suspect the women viewed her with even more uneasiness. She suspected some hated her because they believed she was a Gestapo spy. Others simply thought her dangerous and avoided her. Once, she caught Susanne looking at her and saw a brief flicker of regret in her former friend's eyes. But never again was a woman shut out of the air raid shelter—that was Lisel's one solace. No one thanked her for it. Not even Ursula Bonse.

At home, Lisel did not discuss her work or confide to her family about Herr Hahn. There was such a glow of happiness within the flat, she could not bear to darken it with her problems.

Marta was caught up in plans for her wedding. She floated when she walked and hummed all the time. Nearly everything she said was punctuated with "When Grant comes . . . When Grant comes . . ." She lived for his letters.

Papa, too, watched for the postman every day. And almost every day, he was rewarded by some news from Professor Pinsel. Another name found here. A date there. With great satisfaction, Papa entered each name and date on the genealogy sheets. While he copied, he hummed his favorite hymn, "Lead, Kindly Light," in double time. Lisel and Marta watched with grateful expectation. Each line took them closer to America.

Sundays were Lisel's favorite days. With Papa and Marta, she attended Sunday School and sacrament meeting in their small, rented chapel. She had a chance to meet with people who smiled and spoke to her, to hear the gospel, to sing the hymns. And sing she did. With all her heart. Until Marta elbowed her.

After the meetings, they had dinner together like they had before the days when Lisel had to go to the Munitions Works. Marta cooked and Lisel set and cleared the table. It felt like they were a whole family again. It felt good and right. One Sunday toward the end of June 1941, headlines in the *Volkische Beobachter* declared, "Two-faced Jewish-Bolshevik Rulers in

132

Kremlin Lengthen the War for the Benefit of England! Germany
Must Bring a Reckoning to the Moscow Traitors!"

"But we had a treaty with Russia," Lisel said, kneeling at
Papa's chair. "What does this mean?"

His face was grave, but he smiled and patted her hand. "I do not
think it means anything," he answered. "We will wait and see."

They only had to wait until the next Sunday.

> The State Defense High Command announces that in order to
> counter the danger threatening from the east, on 22 June 1941 at
> 3:00 A.M., the German State Defense thrust forward against the
> mighty advance of hostile Russian forces. Air Force squadrons
> swooped down in the early morning darkness upon the Soviet
> Russian foe. In spite of the enemy's numerical superiority, the
> Air Force secured mastery of the skies in the east and demol-
> ished the Soviet Russian Air Force.

The radio went on to warn of Russian attempts at infiltration
and admonished Germans to watch the skies for Russian para-
troopers intent on sabotage.

Lisel went cold and numb. More war. Michael would be going
into Russia now. Two years ago when he was first drafted, they
said the war would be over in a few weeks. There had been two
years of fighting and death and women in black on the streets.
Would there be two more years? How much longer would they
have to wait before they could go to America? "How much
longer?" she asked Papa.

He shook his head. "I do not know. Perhaps not too long. But
we must not think of what is keeping us from going to America.
After all, we are not yet ready to go. Professor Pinsel says he has
more research to complete; and since we hired him, we must save
more money. We must concentrate on the things we must do and
have faith that we will be able to do them."

Lisel only nodded. That evening, she sat at the living room window and brushed out her braids. The window was open and she
could smell the scent of blossoming geraniums. Twilight had
made long shadows on the street; and after a warm day, several of
their neighbors stood on the walk below the flat and discussed the
news. Lisel could hear Herr Wrobel's voice. He was excited about

this war with the Russians. He had never trusted them, he said. It was time, he said, the Germans showed them who was superior after all. Then, having conquered the rich steppes, Germany would produce quantities of food that would astound the world and again prove Aryan superiority. He made perfect sense. He sounded just like every State speech, radio broadcast, and newspaper article. It would be only a matter of weeks, he said, before the Russians were under control.

Lisel put away her brush. A certain voice from deep inside her said this war with Russia would not be over in a few weeks. Michael would not be home before Christmas and they would not be in America by the New Year.

She drifted into a troubled sleep, haunted by dreams of Michael in his uniform, her grenades tucked in his belt, a cigarette between his frowning lips, Grete with an eagle-faced child in her arms, and Kurt, lost somewhere and calling in the darkness for his mother.

Chapter 10

MICHAEL WAS NOT CALLED INTO RUSSIA UNTIL THE END OF September in 1941.

That same year, one evening in early October, Lisel believed her prayers had finally been answered. The radio broadcasted a special speech by Adolf Hitler.

"The Russian giant has been beaten to the ground, and he will never rise again!" he screamed. Then he declared England, at last, was close to defeat, and the war was quickly approaching its end.

Lisel heard the speech over the Works loudspeaker while she stood at her grenade tray. She wanted to believe it. She sent up a desperate prayer that it would be so. But when she looked around at her fellow-workers, she saw they heard the news with no reaction except grim silence. Then they all went back to work.

For days afterward Lisel watched the papers, searching for some assurance that the war was coming to a close. At first, the headlines announced new breakthroughs and victories. "The Final Victory, Heralded by Decisive Battles in the East, Is at Hand!" they cried.

Herr Wrobel nearly burst with his enthusiasm. "It is incredible what a superior military force can do. To have captured such vast ground in such a short time and with only a few casualties! And to have done it in all that snow and the cold. I have been told that despite the early Russian winter, we will be in Moscow and Leningrad and Stalingrad in a week and then, when they are captured, all of Russia will fall. Why, by next year, German settlements will be established all over Russia and then what we will show the world! What we will show the world!" Frau Wrobel clasped her hands together, her face shining. "There is no one like our Fuhrer. Such a wonderful man!"

Lisel allowed herself to be encouraged by such talk. But by the second week of October 1941, the headlines were less positive

"Movements in the East Are on Schedule." "The War in the East Is Proceeding According to Plan." Then there was nothing.

At the end of November, each household received a flyer from the Department of State Defense asking for used winter clothing, wools and rags. Lisel thought little of it until that night in the cafeteria, she overheard Renate Anders's worried voice. "But it is so cold there, and my Heinrich has only his summer uniform."

Lisel sat there, listening. The last time she saw Michael he had worn his summer uniform, and his pack held no winter gear. Had the State Defense not anticipated such an early snow on the Steppes? That would mean Michael and two hundred and forty thousand of Germany's men were stranded in the middle of a Russian winter with nothing but their summer uniforms?

The Spanns went through their winter clothing. They gave Papa's only other sweater, Mama's coat with a fox collar. Marta and Lisel both gave their pairs of gloves.

Newsreels showed Germans cheerfully handing over their coats and hats, gloves and sweaters, and ski equipment to the State Defense. But the happy unity the drive portrayed was only a pretense to hide the people's disheartenment. A gloom settled over Berlin. The Germans who still believed in prayer, prayed.

The news from the front, when there was news, was sketchy and though it seemed positive, was not encouraging. More and more women in black appeared in the streets as well as more and more wounded soldiers. Returned soldiers spoke of cold that froze oil in the trucks and tanks. Of severed supply lines. Of comrades frozen to death in their sleep.

Pressure at the Munitions Works increased. Workers' hours were increased by another two hours. Lisel's work day increased to twelve hours, with no increase in wages. More workers were brought in, most of them older men and women who would not have been considered for factory work a year ago. And because of the pace, many collapsed. Some nights, Lisel hoped for an air raid just so she could sit down. And some nights, sitting in the cellar waiting for the all-clear, she fell asleep with her head on her drawn-up knees.

After one such night, Lisel made her way home by a back street. It had been a moonlit night, one that, two years ago, might have inspired poets and lovers. But now the moon illuminated Berlin like no spotlight could. The bombers took advantage of the clear skies and managed to hit a couple of buildings and a rail line. It was the rail line Lisel took to get home, so she was forced to take another train and walk a mile and a half home through the cold.

Lisel tucked her chin into her collar and hurried down the narrow street to the back gate. It shrieked on its rusted hinge. Grimacing at the sound, Lisel carefully pulled it shut, so as not to awaken anyone in the house. Then, worried that Herr Wrobel's scowling face would be at the window, she glanced upward.

For an awful moment, Lisel stood there, trying to comprehend what her eyes saw. It was the confirmation of all her worst fears. Against the dawning sky, the roof over the Wrobels' apartment was no more than a gaping hole, edged by spars of blackened lumber. The windows were gone and part of the outside wall torn away so that Lisel could see into the bedroom. The walls and what was left of the furniture and the ceiling were black and blistered. The lingering, bitter odor of burnt wood stung her nostrils.

"Those filthy British!" The cry tore from Lisel's throat and she ran for the backdoor. "Please let Papa and Marta be all right," she prayed. She stumbled over burnt rubble and heard the crunch of broken glass under her flying feet. She jerked open the backdoor and let it slam behind her. The stairs were still intact. She flew up them. Lisel had expected the hallway to be burnt and was confused to find it undamaged, except for the stained walls and soaked carpet.

She paused at the apartment door, with her hand on the knob. Suppose she found the flat destroyed and Papa and Marta dead? A cold dread rose in her throat until she thought she would choke. She drew in a deep, steadying breath and pushed open the door.

Lisel had to wait a moment for her eyes to adjust in the dim light. The familiar shapes of furniture presented themselves in the gloom. She stepped forward with her hand outstretched. Her fingers found the dining room table. The top was smooth and cool to her touch. Then Lisel realized, though the Wrobels' flat had been destroyed, hers had been untouched. But what about Papa and Marta?

Lisel heard a rustle. "Lisel?" It was her papa's voice, slightly slurred with sleep.

She turned to the sofa and saw her father struggling to sit. "Papa," she said, going to him. "Are you all right?"

"Yes, little one. But we had quite an adventure tonight. One of those incendiaries came down on the roof. I am afraid the Wrobels have lost their home."

So that was why Papa was sleeping on the sofa. Lisel's heart warmed toward her father. "I love you, Papa."

Lisel could almost see Papa's indulgent smile. "I told the Wrobels they could stay with us until their flat was repaired."

From the damage on the roof, Lisel knew those repairs could take weeks. A sharp uncertainty closed over Lisel's heart. She dropped down next to Papa. "But you know who the Wrobels are. You know what Kurt said about them."

Papa patted her hand. "I only know they are without a home. How can I not share what I have, seeing their need. Besides, Kurt was inclined to see a spy around every corner. I am sure he was wrong about the Wrobels."

"But the Heidemanns have more room than we do," she objected. "They should be the ones to take them in."

"I do not believe the Wrobels would enjoy sharing a flat with an eleven-year-old boy. Besides, this is a good opportunity to let the Wrobels see that we pose no threat; and we may even be able to show them something of the gospel." Though Papa's voice was gentle, his tone told Lisel he would hear no argument. "You are late coming home," he said, changing the subject.

"The tracks were hit," she replied. "I had to walk from the Richterstrasse station."

"Then you must be very tired," he said. "Go on to bed now and do not worry more about the Wrobels."

Lisel nodded. She would go to bed, but she could not put away her uneasiness at having the Wrobels in their apartment.

She found Marta already dressed and brushing her short, brown hair in the mirror over the bureau. "I thought I had better start breakfast a little early," she told Lisel, "since we are to have two extra places at the table."

Lisel frowned at her sister in the mirror. "Do you think this is a good idea?"

Marta shrugged. "It is what Papa wants."

"But Kurt said they are dangerous."

Marta faced her. "Dangerous to whom? We do not carry on subversive activities in our home. We have no need to fear them. Especially now that Papa has been so kind. Come on, help me get breakfast. Then we can all eat together."

Lisel followed Marta into the kitchen. Papa was up, looking a little less than dignified in his nightshirt. "I will dress in your bedroom," he said to the two girls. He gathered his clothes and shut their bedroom door behind him.

Marta bent and lit the stove while Lisel collected plates and utensils. "Lisel," Marta said. Her voice was hesitant.

Lisel turned and looked at her.

"I wanted to tell you about Grete."

Lisel knew what was coming. Ever since Grete had transferred from the Lebensborn home in Hannover to Kurmack, Marta had seen to Grete every day. And nearly every day, Marta mentioned Grete. But this morning, Marta's tone was different.

"She has had her baby?"

Marta nodded. "A boy. It was a hard delivery. The physician said he was not sure Grete would survive, but she was better last night when I went off shift. The physician said she should not try to have any more children."

Lisel stared down at the fork in her hand. Poor Grete. How she had longed for a husband and family. Now, with no husband and no hope of more family, Lisel's heart ached for her friend. Perhaps this one child would be enough for her. "Is the baby healthy?"

"He seemed to be. A big baby though. Over eight pounds." Marta looked up as Frau Wrobel came into the kitchen.

She patted her pulled-back, iron-gray hair and smiled apologetically. "I am afraid, without my own combs and brush, my poor hair must be a sorry sight."

Marta shook her head with a smile. "You look fine. Maybe after breakfast we will check to see if it is safe enough to go up to your flat. Not everything could have burned."

Lisel remembered the state of the roof and doubted there was anything of value left, but she remained silent. She continued to lay out plates and glasses and utensils.

"I heard you talking about a baby," Frau Wrobel said. "Did you say eight pounds?"

"Yes," Marta answered."The mother had a difficult delivery. You remember Grete Spengler?"

Frau Wrobel pulled out a chair and sat down. "Oh yes. She is Lisel's friend." Frau Wrobel turned questioning eyes to Lisel.

"Grete and I were in school together," Lisel answered, unwilling to offer any more information than that.

"I do not suppose you approve of her participating in the Lebensborn program?"

Lisel knew Frau Wrobel intended the question to sound innocent but Frau Wrobel was not good at artifice. Lisel ignored Marta's look of warning and straightened her shoulders. "No, I do not approve. I was raised with the old-fashioned values my father and mother taught me. Values like purity before marriage and the sacred nature of the husband and wife relationship."

"But not every woman will have the opportunity to marry," Frau Wrobel returned. "Should she be deprived of motherhood because there are not enough men?"

"Should she be deprived of her virtue because the State wants more soldiers?" Lisel did not mean that to slip out. And she could see by Frau Wrobel's raised eyebrows and pursed lips, she had been indiscreet as well as rude. Lisel felt the heat of chagrin in her face. She glanced at her sister. A slight tinge of color had crept into Marta's face and she gripped the back of the chair so that her knuckles paled. Lisel swallowed hard. "I am sorry, Frau Wrobel. Papa would be ashamed of my speaking out that way. I suppose I am a little tired."

Frau Wrobel did not appear to be greatly appeased by Lisel's apology. While the three women prepared their breakfast of oatmeal with dried peaches and barley coffee, Frau Wrobel occasionally glanced in Lisel's direction with a cool, disapproving appraisal.

Had Kurt not warned her? Had she not promised to be careful? And the first thing Lisel did was criticize a government program in front of a government spy. For Lisel's part, she wished someone had cut out her tongue at birth. She used it far too much. But now, with the Wrobels in the same flat, Lisel realized she must use it less.

When Herr Wrobel and then Papa joined them, he explained that the family had prayer both morning and night. He invited the couple to join them. Herr Wrobel replied with a decisive "No thank you."

Papa's prayer was a little longer than usual today. He was thankful their lives had been spared and asked that the Wrobels would have their belongings restored to them soon. Lisel peeked out from between her eyelids. Herr Wrobel's hard eyes narrowed on Papa with stony disapproval. A sudden chill of apprehension chased down Lisel's spine. But Papa, lost in his prayer, did not feel the threat. He went on to ask for protection for Michael in Russia and continued safety for themselves. Remembering the look on Herr Wrobel's face, Lisel added a silent prayer that the Wrobels' apartment might be quickly repaired.

Halfway through breakfast, Walter made an appearance. His boyish face had a long, doleful expression and his lower lip was thrust out. He dropped down on the sofa.

Papa put down his spoon. "What is it, my boy?" he asked.

"Mama said I must go to an evacuation camp," Walter replied.

Lisel felt a stab of loss. First Kurt. Now Walter.

Papa got up from the table and sat down next to the boy. He put his hand on Walter's knee. "There will be many boys just your age," he said. "And special activities and games."

Walter did not look impressed. "I do not want to go."

"But it sounds just the thing for a boy like you," Papa said. "Why would you not want to go?"

Walter shrugged. He refused to look up at Papa, and Lisel saw the boy's chin had begun to tremble. Intuitively, Lisel knew the answer. Walter still needed his mother and he still needed familiar things around him. But how could a boy, almost, but not quite grown, admit that and not humiliate himself?

"A good German boy does as he is told," Herr Wrobel said

141

sternly. "He does not cling to his mother and weep that he does not want to go."

Walter looked as if he had been struck. Tears of humiliation rose in his eyes.

Lisel had to grit her teeth to keep from saying the words that leapt to her lips. She could not even allow herself to look at Herr Wrobel. Instead, she turned to Walter. "I hear the boys sleep in bunk beds."

Walter blinked back his threatening tears. "Like the ones in the army and the labor corps?"

Lisel nodded. "And the ones cowboys sleep in, in America."

Walter's brow creased. Some of the anguish faded from his eyes. "I have never slept in a bunk bed before."

"In the Great War, I slept in one that was three men deep," Papa added. "And what an experience that was." Walter's face turned to his, brightening with curiosity.

Papa patted his knee. "I was just going out to gather the burnt lumber in the back garden. Some of it should still be good for kindling. Would you like to come along and help?"

Walter nodded vigorously. Then his young face flushed. "But I am not sure how much is left. Mama has already gone out this morning."

Lisel bit back a grin.

Papa smiled and ruffled Walter's blonde hair. "We shall see, shall we?"

Marta insisted Lisel go to bed after breakfast and Lisel gratefully complied. She shut the bedroom door so she did not have to hear Marta's polite conversation and Frau Wrobel's equally polite but probing questions.

Lisel brushed out her braids in front of the mirror. The thought of having the Wrobels as guests for a prolonged time troubled her. Herr Wrobel with his watchful stare and Frau Wrobel with her transparent questioning, sent dread shivering through her.

Not that she would argue with Papa's charitable impulse, but that it should be extended to someone as dangerous as the Wrobels frightened Lisel. She would almost have preferred to bring vipers into the house.

Lisel heard Walter's calling voice in the back garden and she wandered to the window. The sun was well up now and she could see the heaps of burnt rubble in the back garden. Papa and Walter were poking through them.

With sinking regret, Lisel also saw that the patch of gooseberry bushes had been crushed under a pile of the rubble and, worse yet, one side of the peach tree had burnt almost to the trunk. And it seemed, for that moment, much of what had been pleasant in her life, had come down to ash and smoke.

Her eyes went again to Papa and Walter. They were laughing together and Lisel was glad to see Walter smile. He had seemed so inconsolable earlier and Herr Wrobel so cruel. Lisel thought of the cold man and wondered what sort of father he had been to his son, Friedrich. He must have been a very different little boy than Walter or a very unhappy one.

Walter had found a short piece of lath and Papa was trying to show him how to throw it so it spun on the air. She wondered if Papa was again telling Walter stories of his own childhood, like how to get girls up into trees.

How long ago that seemed. Now Kurt was gone and Walter leaving. A new idea took form in Lisel's mind. Why had she not thought of it before? If Walter was going to an evacuation camp, there would be even more room in Frau Heidemann's apartment, and Papa could not argue that the Wrobels would not enjoy living with an eleven-year-old boy.

If only there was a way to bring it up to Papa and convince him. Perhaps the Wrobels would think of it themselves when they realized how cramped they all would be in the Spanns' small flat.

Lisel turned away from the window and crawled under her quilt. She stared up at the ceiling. A huge water stain blotched the plaster and made it crack and pucker in several places. Lisel squeezed her eyes shut. Tomorrow she would try to find Papa alone and convince him of the rightness of her idea.

But she could not convince him. Papa disregarded the idea as inhospitable, but a thoughtful look in his eyes told Lisel he might welcome the idea if it came from the Wrobels or Frau Heidemann.

So the Spanns and Wrobels lived together for a week of strained courtesy. Then, in the second week of December 1941, Herr Wrobel announced there would be a special radio broadcast.

The Spanns were usually conscientious about listening to the broadcasts but, with the Wrobels, who had been appointed radio wardens for the building, they were even more careful about attending to the message. So, the group of them gathered in stiff expectation around the small wireless set. Lisel thought the announcement might be something about the Red Army in Russia. She hoped it was the final declaration—one that said the war with Russia and Britain was over. She did not even care who won it, just as long as it was over.

The program began with the usual fanfare and the announcement that the speech would be delivered from the German Parliament. Then: "The Fuhrer speaks!"

Hitler began by ranting against President Roosevelt and his "millionaire Jewish backers." He insisted *they* were mainly to blame for the war.

> It fills the German people, and I believe, all decent people throughout the world, with profound satisfaction that the Japanese government, after years of negotiating with this swindler, has finally had enough of being subjected to scorn and indignities. The President of the United States may not understand why we are so gratified; in which case he merely shows his mental limitations. But we know that the aim of his entire struggle is to destroy one country after another. As far as the German people are concerned, it does not need alms from Mr. Roosevelt; it merely wants what is right. And it will safeguard this right to life, even if a thousand Roosevelts should conspire against it. I have therefore ordered today that the American diplomatic personnel have their passports returned to them—

At that point, a roaring tumult of applause and cheering rose from members of the parliament and drowned out Hitler's words.

Lisel turned to her Papa. "What does this mean?"

Papa's face had gone deathly white. "I am not sure," he stammered, but Lisel saw he struggled with some terrible realization.

"It means war," Herr Wrobel interjected. "Our Fuhrer is declaring war on the United States of America."

His words hung in the air for a second. The sounds of cheering continued to pour from the wireless. At last, understanding struck Lisel like a clenched fist. Her blood ran like ice. She turned to Marta.

Her sister's face looked ghastly. Her widened eyes had dilated until they seemed black. Slowly, she pushed herself from her chair.

"I believe we would all agree that this declaration is long overdue," Herr Wrobel was saying in his calm, cold voice.

Marta had gotten to her feet and staggered toward her bedroom as if in some terrible trance.

Lisel stood and made a move to go to her.

"Fraulein Spann!" Herr Wrobel's voice cut in. "You must not leave the room until the Fuhrer's speech is over."

Marta continued her unsteady path to the bedroom door as if she had not heard.

"Fraulein Spann!" he snapped again. "It is a law that no one leaves the room while the Fuhrer speaks!"

"Herr Wrobel!" Papa's voice filled the room and overrode the staticky sound of applause from the radio. "This is not your home to give orders!"

The bedroom door closed behind Marta with a soft "click."

Chapter 11

CHRISTMAS 1941 HAD BEEN UNENDURABLY DISMAL AND NEW Year's Eve day was a gray, cold, and forbidding twenty-four hours. Lisel and Papa listened to the midnight broadcast of the bells of the Cologne Cathedral, which was followed by a particularly rousing rendition of the "Horst Wessel Lied." Lisel heard the opening strains of the Nazi anthem with anger and bitterness. She wanted to kick over the wireless set and crush it beneath her wooden clogs. Instead, she gritted her teeth while tears of frustration burned her eyes. Papa had tried to console her, patting her on the shoulder while he fought back his own emotions. And thus, Papa and Lisel spent the first hours of 1942.

Papa blamed himself. He said he should have known better than to bring the Wrobels into the apartment. He had been outraged to discover their betrayal when, the day after Hitler's declaration of war on America, the Wrobels went to the Central Bureau for the People's Welfare and denounced Marta for leaving the room during the Fuhrer's speech.

The outcome of Marta's interrogation by the Bureau might have been more serious but, in the end, they decided since Marta had never before been reported for any kind of misconduct and because her nursing skills were valuable to the Reich, she would be spared severe punishment. But because she knowingly disobeyed the law and because of her emotional involvement with an enemy, she was to be removed from her family, a discipline the Wrobels had suggested. So Marta was sent away to a military hospital in Frankfurt.

Marta showed no reaction to the sentence and seemed to be confused by Lisel's and Papa's distress—as if her staying or going was a thing of complete indifference. And when they saw her off at the railway station, her good-bye was only a vague gesture, her eyes passionless. Lisel knew Marta's lack of emotion was no indication of her true feelings—it was because Marta was so bruised within her heart that she had nothing left for anyone or anything else.

Lisel's own feelings of violation and betrayal turned her grief into bitter anger. She was even glad the Wrobels had only moved downstairs with Frau Heidemann instead of somewhere else in the city. With them so close, she would not forget how much she despised them. Her hatred had become a sweet pain. It was something to cling to—now that so many other things had been denied her.

There would be no more dreams of living in America, no more dreams of going to the temple, no more solace in knowing her entire family—Papa, Mama, Michael, Marta and herself—would be joined as one for all the eternities. Somehow, that seemed to be the Wrobels' fault, too. Now all that was left was for the promise in Second Nephi to be fulfilled.

In the last month since Hitler's declaration, Lisel had searched the passage over and over again for some measure of allowance. Some way of escaping what must come. But over and over again, her search was fruitless.

> I will fortify this land against all other nations.
> And he that fighteth against Zion shall perish, saith God.
> For he that raiseth up a king against me shall perish,
> for I, the Lord, the king of heaven, will be their king,
> and I will be a light unto them forever, that hear my words.
> Wherefore, for this cause, that my covenants may be fulfilled
> which I have made unto the children of men,
> that I will do unto them while they are in the flesh,
> I must needs destroy the secret works of darkness,
> and of murders, and of abominations.
> Wherefore, he that fighteth against Zion, both Jew and
> Gentile, both bond and free, both male and female, shall perish;
> for they are they who are the whore of all the earth;
> for they who are not for me are against me, saith our God.

147

With a weary sigh, Lisel pulled off her work gloves and laid them on her tray next to the unfinished grenades. She had heard a smaller grenade was being developed, a weapon more efficient. A weapon that would be less cumbersome than the long metal canisters she scrubbed and oiled now. A weapon even more deadly.

She paused at her tray and stared down at it. A new idea of horrifying shape formed in her mind. She was helping make weapons to kill Americans, perhaps even American Mormons. Maybe even someone who was a missionary in Germany. Maybe even Robert Parker or Grant Nolte.

Lisel reached out and clutched the edge of her tray. The passage in 2 Nephi said "male and female." "He that fighteth against Zion, both *male and female* shall perish. For they who are not for me are against me, saith God." Did that mean that by her standing here at this grenade tray, scrubbing and oiling weapons to be used against people of Zion, she was against God?

The possibility chilled Lisel to the core of her soul. She jerked her hands away from the tray as if it burned her skin. Then she spun away from it and ran from the room. Down the long hallway, to Herr Bauer's office. She reached out and snatched at the doorknob. It refused to turn. Lisel rattled the door. It was locked. The lights behind the door's opaque glass were dark.

Lisel looked up and down the hall, willing Herr Bauer to come along. At last she realized he would not come to the Munitions Works this early. She dropped down on the wooden bench opposite the office door and waited. The minutes ground into eternities as she waited and watched. Perhaps she could go to the Works entrance and watch for him there. But what if he came in by another door? Maybe she could meet him at the railway station. But the trains would be crowded this time of morning, she might miss him. Could she find his address and go there? Would he still be at home?

Lisel's tormented thoughts turned and twisted, searching for some way to get to Herr Bauer, to end her anxious waiting. Please let him come, she prayed. Please let him be here soon.

At last, footsteps sounded in the hallway and Lisel swung around to see Herr Hahn striding toward her, his heels cracking on the floor. His yellow eyes narrowed when he saw her there and he frowned and slowed his pace.

"Heil Hitler," he said and saluted.

Halfheartedly Lisel returned the salute. Herr Hahn was the only person she knew who still insisted on saluting everyone he met.

"So, you are not yet gone home," he said. The observation came smoothly from his lips, but Lisel knew he was asking what she was doing there. She decided to ignore the question. And though she knew it was unwise to be here, alone with Herr Hahn, she decided to ignore him too.

He hesitated for a moment, then sat down next to her. "You are waiting for Herr Bauer?"

Lisel wished he would take his boiled cabbage smell and go away. Perhaps if she did not answer him, he would leave.

"He does not come in for another hour," Herr Hahn continued. "You will have a long wait."

Another hour! Papa would be worried. But she could not leave now, not with Herr Hahn watching her. He might even get to Herr Bauer first, thinking she had come to denounce Herr Hahn for whatever illegal scheme he was involved with, and fabricate something with which to accuse her. No, she could not leave. Lisel continued to watch the door but she did not speak.

"You must have something of great importance to discuss with him if you are willing to wait so long."

Lisel continued to sit in silence.

"I, also, am waiting for Herr Bauer." He propped one of his jack-booted feet on his knee and leaned back, sliding his arm along the back of the bench until his fingers touched her shoulder. "Perhaps we will wait together."

Lisel felt the heat of repugnance rise in her face and she wanted desperately to flinch away but forced herself not to move from the pale, fleshy fingers at her shoulder. She knew he was not waiting for Herr Bauer. He was waiting for her. He was waiting to find out what she had to say to Herr Bauer. Well, let him wait. He could listen all he wanted to; after today, it would not matter what he did.

The sounds of more footsteps brought Lisel around to see Herr Bauer's secretary, Frau Segler, bundled against the winter morning, burdened with paper-wrapped parcels and a shopping bag, coming down the hall toward her.

Herr Hahn jumped to his feet with the salute. "Heil Hitler."

Frau Segler attempted the salute and gave up with a mere, "Heil."

Herr Hahn came forward. "Let me help you." His words were courtly and his manner so solicitous, the middle-aged secretary flushed like a girl.

"Oh, thank you, Herr Hahn," she gushed as she transferred her packages to his arms and fished in her pocketbook for the office keys. She did not even notice Lisel until she had settled herself at her desk. Frau Segler looked up at Lisel with a slight frown of recognition and inquiry. "Yes?"

"I must speak to Herr Bauer," Lisel said.

Frau Segler's lips tightened in impatience. "I believe you do not have an appointment."

"I will wait until Herr Bauer has a moment to see me."

Her lips tightened even more. "Then you had better sit down. Herr Bauer has not yet arrived and Herr Hahn came in before you."

"No, no," Herr Hahn protested. "Ladies always before gentlemen. I will wait until Fraulein Spann has finished."

Frau Segler smiled broadly. "How considerate you are, Herr Hahn. If only more young men were like you."

Lisel sat down on one of the worn leather-upholstered chairs and tried to block out the conversation between Herr Hahn and Frau Segler, which consisted mostly of cloying flattery from Herr Hahn and undignified giggling from Frau Segler.

Another hour passed before Herr Bauer made an appearance. He must have come through a back entrance because the first Lisel knew of his presence was when he opened his office door to speak to Frau Segler. He frowned when he saw Lisel there.

She stood. "May I see you for a moment?"

Though Herr Bauer looked as though he would have preferred to send her away, he nodded and held open the door.

"What is it?" he asked, sitting down behind his own desk. He did not offer Lisel a seat nor did he bother to lift his eyes to look at her. He was busy copying columns of figures from one ledger to another. "Well," he said, impatiently.

"I have come to request my employment booklet. I wish to leave the Munitions Works."

Herr Bauer leaned back in his chair, steepled his fingers, and studied Lisel over the top of them. "It is not very flattering that you should wish to leave our work force here in Wittenau. Perhaps you could explain why you want to leave."

His pale gray eyes made her uneasy, cautious. Lisel chose her answer carefully. "My sister, who lived with my father and me, has been transferred to a military hospital in Frankfurt. My father does not work and with the loss of my sister's income, I need to make more money to support us." It was not totally a lie. Though Marta sent what little she did not need to live, the Spanns' budget was stretched to the limit; and they had even discussed the possibility of discontinuing Professor Pinsel's services.

"Surely with fewer people in the household, your expenses are less?"

"Our rent is not determined by the number of people in the flat," Lisel replied.

"Just so," he acknowledged. "But with housing such a scarcity right now, perhaps you could take in someone left homeless by the bombing."

Lisel thought of the Wrobels, then realized Herr Bauer had deftly turned her away from her intention. "I have been here now for three years. That is two years longer than my original assignment. I would like to find other work."

"Surely this job is as good as any other," he argued. "And, with such a shortage of workers, you are doubly serving our Fuhrer by remaining with us. Our Fuhrer expects sacrifices from his workers. Can we achieve his glorious objective without some sacrifice? Without each of us putting aside our own comforts for the good of the whole people?"

"I am sure there are other ways I can serve the Fuhrer," Lisel said, unmoved.

Herr Bauer scowled. "If all our workers shared your attitude, what would become of our valiant warriors in the battlefield? Do you wish them defeated and destroyed?"

"Of course not!" Lisel exclaimed. "I have a brother in Russia." On impulse, she decided to be candid. Perhaps Herr Bauer would understand honesty. "I have friends in America. I do not have the heart to make weapons to destroy my friends."

Herr Bauer's eyebrows rose. "Your loyalty is commendable, Fraulein Spann, but misplaced. These same Americans you defend have been plotting for years to annihilate you, your family and your country."

"That is not true!" she protested. "They are our friends. We are members of their Church. My sister is even engaged to a young American man."

"It is widely understood that with the declaration of war, Germans who were married to Americans have had their marriages nullified. The State takes even less notice of an engagement. As for an American religion or any other religion, we need no God but our Fuhrer. We recognize only our Fuhrer as the savior of Germany." He met her eyes with an arch look. "Any alliance with any enemy is against the law, and anyone who has sympathy for the enemy is gravely suspect. I am sure you would not want to fall into that category. It would be uncomfortable not only for you but for your father and sister."

Lisel saw plainly through the veil of threat. She stared at him in quiet frustration. "I do not understand why you will not let me go."

The hardened edge dropped from Herr Bauer's face. He made a weary, helpless gesture with his hands. "The quotas are up and because of the shortage of workers and bombing raids, production is down. Most of our workers are underfed and many are over age. Yet the State Defense continues to demand more. I cannot afford to lose anyone." His lips formed a small thoughtful circle in his thin face. "But I can understand how you feel, Fraulein, and I am not totally unsympathetic. Perhaps it is time you took a small vacation. Say to some place quiet, in the country perhaps?" He took up his pen. "I can arrange that for you." He looked up at her.

Lisel knew he expected some show of gratitude, but she had none to give. She turned and walked to the door, pulling it shut behind her.

"You may go in now, Herr Hahn," Frau Segler said.

Lisel moved into the hallway on legs with no feeling. The other battles of her life had not seemed as hopeless as this one. Yet she knew, somehow, there had to be a solution. The passage in 2 Nephi also said, *"I will be a light unto them forever, that hear my words."*

"I have heard thy words," her heart cried out in rebellion. "Where is the light?"

"Your interview with Herr Bauer was unusually short."

Lisel started. How had she not heard Herr Hahn coming up behind her? "Yours must have been even shorter," she replied sharply.

"Herr Bauer was too busy to see me," he said.

Lisel knew he lied. He had followed her into his office, and now he was following her out. She knew she ought to be wary, but for this moment she did not care about Herr Hahn or his threat to her.

"You must consider yourself a very clever girl," Herr Hahn was saying through a yellow-toothed smile. "You made me suspect you were a spy planted by the Gestapo."

She stopped at the Munitions Works exit and faced him, hoping she looked less intimidated than she felt. "How do you know I am not?"

"I listened through the door," he admitted with no shame. "Someone who has such close friends in America would hardly be trusted at Prinz-Albrectstrasse."

Lisel saw his logic. Herr Hahn was no longer frightened of her or what he thought she knew. She felt a sharp stab of uncertainty, of vulnerability, like being in an oarless, rudderless boat. She grasped at the only device that floated toward her. "No one is trusted at Prinz-Albrectstrasse but the Gestapo will listen to anyone."

Herr Hahn's amusement made an ugly sound. "That will no longer work, Fraulein," he said and, turning, whistled as he strode out onto the street.

Lisel could hear the fading sound of his boot tacks on the cobblestone. A chill came up her spine. She would have to be very, very careful now.

Lisel did not confide in Papa about Herr Hahn, but she went to him with her worry about working in the ammunition factory. "We will inquire of the Lord," he said simply. And they did, searching the scriptures and fasting. But when no immediate solution was revealed, Lisel worried that the heavenly silence was punishment for being "against God."

Papa had patted her shoulder. "Do not lose faith, little one. God has heard us and we must trust him to do what is best."

So, Lisel returned to the Munitions Works each afternoon and scrubbed and oiled the grenades and over each one prayed that it would not be the cause of harm to any person. One evening, as she returned from her dinner, she saw Ursula Bonse hurrying away from the grenade tray where Lisel stood. She approached it slowly. Ursula's tray was at the other end of the workroom and the tall girl rarely had cause to come near Lisel's place. She looked down at the tray, and between two grenade canisters, she saw the corner of a slip of paper.

Lisel looked up, glancing around the room. The other workers were, like Lisel, returning from their dinners. Ursula was already working over her tray, her face expressionless. Herr Hahn was nowhere to be seen.

Lisel caught the corner of the slip with the end of her wire brush and pulled it forward alongside one of the canisters. The hastily penciled words stared up at her. "He is planning something. Be careful!"

"Workers!" Lisel looked up to see Herr Hahn standing on his desk. "The German people have suffered much at the hands of the British night pirates. With their bombs they have destroyed homes, schools, hospitals, and orphanages. They have murdered our little children, our sick and wounded, and our aged parents. Now, we have a greater threat. The Americans are joining our British enemies, and we can expect even more terror attacks, more destruction, and more murders at their hands."

Lisel crushed the note into her damp palm. Some warning instinct came from deep inside her and made her heart pound faster. Herr Hahn was leading up to something. Something that had to do with her.

"The Americans believe themselves to be strong and clever. We must prove them otherwise. We will work with much fervor to reach our quotas, and we will use all our means to thwart their plans.

"In the past, the British have attempted to destroy this munitions factory. But because of their mental and physical limitations, they have failed. The Americans will now try. We will see that they, also, will fail.

"Among our workers is one who knows these Americans well. She has had them in her home. She attends, even now, their Church, still operating in Berlin. She has had them teach her their language. In short, she knows how they think."

The workers had begun to glance, with furtive measure, around the room, and one by one, their eyes had all reached Lisel. She had made no secret of her Church affiliation. She had even told Susanne about her family's plans to immigrate.

"Therefore we will leave to her the security of this building. From today forward, the responsibility of window warden will be permanently assigned to Lisel Spann." Herr Hahn's eyes came to Lisel. There was malicious amusement there. "Congratulations, Fraulein Spann."

For an instant, Lisel was not sure of what he had said. Was not sure it was her name on his thick lips. But the workers were staring at her, some sympathetic, waiting for her reaction. For one dreadful moment, Lisel felt a cold, dropping sensation inside her chest, a fear desperate enough to make her sick. But she knew Herr Hahn would enjoy any display of panic. Instead, Lisel drew in a steadying breath. "I am grateful for the honor," she said, "and I will serve you faithfully."

The sneer dropped from Herr Hahn's lips. Pure hatred flashed in his eyes. From the other workers, however, Lisel saw looks of surprise and approval and even respect.

Later, however, when the sirens sounded, none of the workers even glanced back at her as they fled down to the basement. Lisel ran to the first window. She remembered how Ursula had struggled with it. "Father, help me," she whispered. The first window slid open easily and the second and the third and all the rest. Behind her, Lisel heard the shutting of the heavy basement door. Then the shifting thud as Herr Hahn secured the crosspiece. And Lisel knew there was no one behind the door to insist Herr Hahn open it for her. If the Works was hit, she would have no protection.

That knowledge should have terrified Lisel but, standing at the Wittenau Munitions Works window, looking across at the dark buildings of Berlin, seeing the brilliant explosions in the night sky, hearing the barking sounds of the antiaircraft, she felt an extraordinary peace. All was well.

She was safe and secure. And, as if there was a silken thread of love stretched over the miles, Lisel also knew Marta in Frankfurt was safe tonight and Michael in cold, faraway Russia and Kurt, wherever he was. Papa would be at Frau Heidemann's dining room table with his scriptures in front of him; Frau Heidemann sitting sentinel in front of her precious mirror; and on the sofa, the Wrobels waiting out the attack in their gas masks.

The Wrobels . . . the very thought of the Wrobels woke the bitterness within Lisel, and she found herself gritting her teeth. It seemed so unfair. She and Papa and Marta wanted only to live together under the commandments of Christ . . . wanted only to be worthy to go to the temple. And the Wrobels had taken advantage of her family's kindness and succeeded in tearing Marta away from them. Now the Wrobels were sitting safe and untouched, arrogantly certain that what they had done was correct.

Outside, the dark sky thundered with the sound of guns and flashed with explosion and fire. Out there, somewhere, people were being maimed and killed, their families shattered forever, their homes reduced to smoldering rubble. And in her bitterness and resentment, Lisel wished that for the Wrobels. Wished violent ruination on them. Wished all the covenants of 2 Nephi on them.

Lisel saw a sudden blaze light in the dark dome of sky over the Munitions Works. A rolling cannonball of sound burst above the building next door. Bricks and tile and lumber spewed in all directions. Air and dirt blasted through the open window where Lisel stood and knocked her to the floor.

Instinctively, she rolled over on her stomach and scrambled into the tiny space beneath Herr Hahn's massive desk. Lisel's panic helped her wedge herself into a tight ball so that even her skirt hem was tucked safely into the space.

Another explosion rocked the sky like a clap of doom. Lisel forced her head down onto her knees. She felt fear suffocating and blocking her breath. "This is not fair," she thought and was surprised to hear her own voice in protest. "It is the Wrobels who deserve this death—not me!"

Chapter 12

THE SCREAM TORE FROM LISEL'S THROAT. SHE JERKED UPRIGHT, wide-eyed. Her heart hammered inside her chest with such force she had to fight for each breath, dragging it in and out of her lungs. Then her eyes focused. She was no longer crammed under Herr Hahn's desk. She was at home, in her own bed. Her glance went to the alarm clock on the night stand. Lisel had only slept four hours.

She squeezed her eyes shut and fell back onto her pillow, but she knew she would not be able to go to sleep again. Ever since the dream terrors had begun two weeks ago, when she had been assigned Window Warden, she had been existing on less than five hours of sleep a day. Now, her hands shook almost all of the time and frequently she found herself crying for no reason. Loud noises brought out a cold, sticky sweat on her skin. Then there were the nightmares, confused, terror-filled episodes of bursting lights, explosions, and shattering glass that catapulted her into a shaking consciousness.

Lisel shivered under her quilt and pulled it closer. Despite its warmth she could not stop trembling. Not for a while anyway. She told herself she was beginning to get used to it. She would cry a little, then she would stop shaking enough to get out of bed, wash her face, dress, braid her hair and pull her mouth into enough of a smile so she could convince Papa she was not sick, body, heart, and soul. "I guess I am just a little tired," she would say when he frowned his concern at her.

She stepped out into the living room. Quiet but for the ticking of the clock, the flat was dim in the winter light. Lisel frowned, trying to think where Papa might be. Then she remembered. Today was Friedrich Wrobel's funeral.

She did not understand why Papa wanted to attend. Not after what the Wrobels had done. When she asked, he had looked at her with great sadness. "Because they are mourning, little one. They need us to mourn with them. They need us with them now." Lisel did not say it but she had thought how she needed her sister with her now. The Wrobels had taken Marta away. She was not sorry Friedrich Wrobel had been shot down by the British. She was not sorry they would not even have his body for the funeral. Was that not what she wished for them? Her only regret was she was too tired to enjoy the vengeance.

She went to the tiny window above the kitchen sink and took, from the outside sill, a bottle of rhubarb juice. It was cold and bitter stuff but it suited Lisel's mood. Her fingers were numb as she tipped the bottle forward. She tried to hold it tighter. Her hand began to tremble. The stream of juice snaked in the air and splashed across the cabinet top. Lisel gripped the bottle tighter. The smooth glass slipped from her fingers and crashed to the floor.

Lisel stared down at the broken glass and the widening pool of juice. It was nasty drinking, that juice, but it was all they had since apple juice had disappeared from the market. Even rhubarb juice cost money and ration points. She felt the familiar sting of heat behind her eyelids and fought back her tears as she picked up the glass and mopped the juice from the floor—a messy effort since she could not make her stiff, shaking fingers hold the cloth.

At last, with a cry of defeat, she threw down the cloth, snatched her right hand with her left and, weeping her frustration, smashed it again and again against the edge of the cabinet. The throbbing pain raced up her arm and reached some point in her brain capable of reason. Lisel looked down at her hand. Through the blurred haze of her tears, she could see the spreading, swelling bruise and feel its ache with every pulse.

She slumped down to the floor, her knees up, her head down and sobbed—sobbed for herself and her lost dreams; sobbed for Marta; sobbed for Papa. Of what use was she now to him? Now, when she should be sustaining him, she was only another troubled shadow in his life. And she had no resources left for herself. She realized that for the last several weeks, since the declaration of war between Germany and America, she had allowed the habit of prayer to slip away. So what was left?

Lisel sat there on the floor for a long time, hollow and without will. At last, she was roused by the sound of footsteps on the landing outside the flat door. Then a tap.

Lisel struggled to her feet and went to the door. It was Grete. The pair stared at each other for a moment before Grete smiled a smile that was more a gesture than an emotion. "Lisel, how glad I am to see you," she said.

Instinctively, Lisel reached out but flinched when Grete squeezed her bruised hand. Grete stared at it with dismay. "Why, what have you done?"

"I was pouring some juice," Lisel said with a vague gesture toward the kitchen. "I am afraid I made quite a mess."

Grete pushed past her. "Let me help you," she said. She picked up the cloth and began mopping the pool of sticky juice. "You ought to go see Dr. Kettel. Maybe you broke a bone."

"No, I think it will be all right. It is just bruised."

Grete straightened and frowned at Lisel. "You look thin like a stick and pale like you fell in the flour bin."

Lisel had not realized how much she missed Grete's vinegarish observations. Lisel allowed herself a smile. "If only we had a flour bin with flour in it."

This time Grete's smile reached her eyes and Lisel saw there had also been a change in Grete. Her face was thinner and her blue eyes, dark-shadowed. But her figure was fuller and rounder. The body of a woman who had not long since delivered a child.

"Marta said you had been ill. You are better now?"

Grete shrugged and rinsed the cloth in the sink. "I was not that bad. They made more of a fuss than was necessary." She faced Lisel. "The doctor said I was fit enough to have another next year."

Lisel heard the lie. Marta said Grete would never have another child.

"And of course," Grete continued, "I probably shall. It was all such a glorious experience." Her wide smile was brittle, on the edge of breaking. "And it was such a great honor."

159

Lisel knew Grete was hiding her real feelings, though not very well. "When will you bring your baby to meet us?" she asked.

The color rose over Grete's cheekbones and she looked down at her hands. When she looked up, her smile was even wider and even more strained than ever. "Why, what makes you think I have kept him? He is much better off being raised by the State. They have such marvelous facilities for raising children and they can do it with so much scientific understanding, much more than any of our mothers or fathers had. Why a child raised in that environment cannot help but be, not only biologically perfect, but perfect in all other ways also."

Lisel struggled to keep the shock out of her face. All Grete had ever wanted in the world was a family. To have given up her only hope of even a small one stunned Lisel. And she felt a sorrow for the little boy being raised with no mother and no father. But she saw Grete was waiting for some response, some gesture of approval. "I suppose he will be raised with lots of other children," was all Lisel could think to say.

Grete nodded energetically. "Oh yes, the nursery is so light and cheerful and the grounds so big, much bigger than a garden in the city, with lots of trees and grass to play on." Her eyes shone, over-bright. "And so many nannies to love him."

"That sounds wonderful," Lisel tried to agree.

Grete's smile faded. The pair sat in silence for a moment until Lisel recognized Papa's footsteps on the stairs. "I am sure Papa will be pleased to see you," Lisel said.

Papa's gray eyebrows rose when she saw Grete. "Well, well, Grete," he said, "how are you?" His voice betrayed his discomfort and his face flushed when Grete hugged him.

"I am marvelous," she responded. "But I have missed being here with the Spanns so much that I could not stay away a day longer."

Papa patted her shoulder, then discreetly put her away from him. "I am sure we have all missed you too."

Grete's eyes glistened and she blinked rapidly. "I wanted, especially, to see you, Herr Spann. I have something wonderful to tell you."

Papa hung his hat on the peg behind the door then turned to

face Grete, smoothing down his coat. "And what is that?" he asked, kindly.

"Well, you know, I never knew my own father; and when it came time to name the baby, I wanted to give him a name that meant something to me." She clasped her hands in front of her. "So I named him Joseph. After you, Herr Spann." Grete waited, her face shining and expectant.

Lisel saw the shock and distress flash across Papa's face then he smiled and took Grete's hand. "Thank you, Grete. I am greatly honored."

Grete blinked back the tears that welled in her eyes. "I hoped you would be."

Papa's blue eyes went to Lisel. She knew he was frowning inside, worrying over the weariness in her face. Then he smiled. "Good morning, little one," he said and touched her braids.

"Good morning, Papa. How was the funeral?"

Papa shook his head and Lisel saw the sorrow in the lines around his mouth. "So many State funerals nowadays. So many young men taken from us."

Lisel suddenly thought of Michael, so far away, and she knew Papa thought about him, too, and worried often.

"If you will pardon me," Papa said, "I believe I will just go to my room for a little rest."

"He is not ill?" Grete said after Papa had left the room.

"No, just worried, I think," Lisel replied. "He worries about Michael and about Marta and about me. It makes him tired."

Both girls turned as the apartment door clicked open.

"Hello, Frauleins." Frau Heidemann slipped through the front door and dropped onto the sofa. "I thought I would allow the Wrobels some time alone." Her sharp eyes went to Lisel. "What is the matter with you? You look ill."

"Just a little tired," she responded automatically. Lisel had not seen Frau Heidemann in a while. The older woman had changed also. Her unstylish hair was fading from light brown to a yellow gray and there was a soft line of sagging skin along her jaw.

"Who is *not* tired with bombing every other night," Frau Heidemann complained. She looked at Grete. "So you have had your baby."

Bright color rose to the roots of Grete's blonde hair. "Yes," she said, smiling with forced enthusiasm. "A boy, over eight pounds."

Frau Heidemann's lips pursed. "Eight pounds is big but not as big as my boys were. Kurt was nine pounds and Walter eight-and-a-half. Terrible labor delivering those two. I nearly died both times and lost all my blood. I did not have a single drop left in my body at the end. The doctor said he did not know how I survived such a terrible ordeal. He said the pain alone would have killed any other woman."

Lisel saw Grete's eyes widen. "But these things are not necessary any more. At the Kurmack home they taught me ancient Teutonic secrets to make it all easier. And it was so wonderful. Not at all like other women say it is."

Frau Heidemann snorted. "How could it be different? Women all have their babies the same way. And it all spells pain and agony."

"But it need not be that way," Grete protested. "In the labor room, there was a huge picture of our Fuhrer just above the bed and if you had a pain you could look at the picture and the pain went away. It was marvelously effective. And if you had a really strong pain, you just called out his name and the pain disappeared. A real miracle. Just saying his name gave you mystic powers."

Frau Heidemann threw back her head and laughed out loud. "I remember pains like that. I also remember calling out my husband's name and the only thing that would have made me feel better would have been to get my hands around his throat. That was because I was angry at him for getting me into such a predicament. But of course you probably did not know the name of the man who put you there, did you?"

Grete gasped and her face went white. Lisel felt the heat rise in her own face. She scrambled to find a way to distract Frau Heidemann away from the subject of babies and their fathers. "What was the funeral like?" she blurted.

Frau Heidemann's face went blank for a moment as she shifted from birth to death. Lisel was surprised to see a measure of pain in the older woman's pale eyes. But then Lisel remembered Frau Heidemann also had sons to worry over.

"I suppose it comforted the Wrobels a little," Frau Heidemann answered. "It is a terrible thing to lose a son."

Lisel knew Frau Heidemann was speaking from experience. Was not Kurt all but lost?

Frau Heidemann's brows drew together. "What amazed me was how differently people grieve." She met Lisel's eyes and Lisel saw a new, thoughtful depth there. "I would have expected Gustav to be the strong one. But he is not. He has been walking around for the last week, bent double with his grief, not even able to talk. Elsa has been the steady one. Not that she does not grieve. But Elsa made the decisions and the arrangements. And it was Elsa that comforted Gustav. I never would have guessed she was the strong one."

Frau Heidemann shook her head. "There is too much sadness in the world today. I remember how Berliners used to love to laugh. Now," she shrugged, "even the most ridiculous of things does not even make us look twice. Like that huge green net they have draped over the Exhibition Hall on Kaiserdamm to make it look like a meadow. Hah! Even the stupid RAF pilots could see it does not look like a meadow. It looks like a giant joke but nobody laughs about it."

"This is not a time to laugh," Grete said gravely.

Frau Heidemann flapped her hand at Grete. "This is just the time to laugh—when we feel the saddest." She looked at Lisel. "You must hear lots of jokes at that place where you work. Tell us one."

Many of the other workers did not often speak to Lisel, let alone tell her jokes. But, on occasion, she overheard things. She shrugged. "Do you know what Hitler said when he discovered Great Britain had tried to confuse the Luftwaffe by building false airfields and equipping them with wooden airplanes?" She looked from Frau Heidemann to Grete and back. "He said, 'That is no matter. We are dropping on them wooden bombs.'"

Grete managed a polite smile while Frau Heidemann laughed loudly. "You see. A little joke, a little laughter makes us all feel better."

Uncomfortably, Grete shifted in her chair. "I believe it is time I must leave."

163

Lisel tried to smile a message of sympathetic understanding to her friend, but secretly Lisel felt relieved Grete was leaving. Lisel stood and saw Grete to the door.

"I am so happy to have seen you again," Grete said. "I am so happy to share my joy with you."

Grete spoke of happiness and joy but her eyes said something else. Lisel reached up and touched her friend's pale cheek. "I have missed you. We will see each other again soon?"

Grete nodded but she did not speak. Her chin quivered and a sudden shimmer rose in her eyes.

"Perhaps we will go to the cinema sometime?"

Again Grete nodded. "Good-bye then," she said in a watery voice. Then a little louder: "Good-bye Frau Heidemann. It was good to see you again." And she was gone.

Lisel returned to the sofa.

"Well, she is as friendly as a peeled potato," Frau Heidemann said sourly. "And she did not convince me of her great happiness."

"This is a difficult time to be happy," Lisel responded.

Frau Heidemann's eyes narrowed on Lisel. "You do not look like a bouquet of violets yourself," she said. "What have you done to your hand?"

Lisel looked down at the bruise. It had swollen so she could not move her little finger.

"You had better see Dr. Kettel. It looks like you have broken a bone."

In the end, Lisel had gone to see Dr. Kettel. The bluish swelling on the side of her hand made it difficult to hold her wire brush and her production dropped radically. Then, during the air raids, she could only use one hand. It slowed her so much two windows were broken before she could get them open. Herr Hahn had said nothing in front of the other workers but raged at her in the hall outside the grenade room. Through her exhaustion, Lisel only stood and watched his lips form and reform around his enraged words. Her lack of response seemed to make him even angrier.

"No, it is not broken," Dr. Kettel said, frowning at her hand through his bifocal lenses. "But it is very badly bruised. It would be better if you did not use it for a while."

He looked up at her. His thick black hair, peppered with white, stood out as if he had forgotten to comb it and his tie was slightly askew over a shirt that was missing a button.

"I am not so worried about your hand as I am about the way you look, Lisel. Your color is not good and you are too thin."

Lisel shrugged. "I guess I am just a little tired."

Dr. Kettel frowned. "It is more than 'just a little tired' when a young woman of eighteen cannot keep her hands from shaking. I would say you are under a great strain."

He leaned forward and examined Lisel's eyes. "I would also say you are suffering from sleep deprivation and malnutrition."

Lisel managed a smile. "Just like everyone in Berlin."

Dr. Kettel shook his head. "Most of us can make up for lost sleep with a nap before the raids begin; and there is enough food, though it is dull and unpalatable, to keep us from starving." He leaned back in his chair and held Lisel with a piercing look. "Why is it, Lisel, you are not eating or sleeping?"

Lisel could not help it. The entire story poured out and by the time she finished, to her great embarrassment, she was weeping into Dr. Kettel's wrinkled handkerchief.

Dr. Kettel's brow furrowed. "In this case I can be of little help. I can recommend to your employer you take a rest cure and I can give you drops to help you sleep. Beyond that, I can do nothing. That may be, however, enough to save your health."

Lisel went away with a bottle of valerian drops in her pocket and a note to Herr Bauer. She was not surprised when, three days later, she was called into his office.

Herr Bauer scrutinized her with a scowl. Lisel knew what he was seeing. She was too thin. Her skin had gone a sickly, grayish color and her hair was a dull, red brown. There were bruises of exhaustion beneath her eyes.

"Your physician says you are unfit to continue to work here," he said. "I think you are pretending. You have badgered me about issuing your employment booklet before and found your efforts to no avail. Now, by the careful use of a little makeup, you convince some quack that you are ill."

Lisel replied with a sigh. He was going to lecture her and send her away again.

"However, I see that you are determined to leave here and, with this letter from Dr. Kettel, I cannot keep you. But I will not pass on a favorable recommendation to your next employer."

Lisel blinked and stared at him. "You are releasing me?"

"Have I an alternative?" he queried sharply. Lisel saw the flash of displeasure in his eyes.

"When? When do I leave?"

Herr Bauer's lips tightened. "It may take some time to process the paperwork. We will notify you when it is ready." When Lisel told Papa the next morning, a smile lifted his face. "Oh Lisel, how blessed we are! What a marvelous thing the Lord has done in hearing our prayers."

Lisel tried to share Papa's fervent gratitude. But all she could think was it was Dr. Kettel who did the marvelous thing. And that Herr Bauer would find a way to delay her paperwork. She was just too tired to consider anything beyond that.

The following Sunday night after Papa had gone to bed, Lisel stayed up a while longer. She was used to being awake during the night and sometimes did some mending or a little laundry but most often she read. Lately, however, she was unable to concentrate and sometimes could not remember what she had read from one page to the next.

So, after having at last left her book, she turned to the wireless set. Absently she turned the dial. A symphony concert. A replay of an official speech. News. A lecture on root crops. Lisel smiled at that one. It made her think of Kurt. He was the only person she knew who would have enjoyed a lecture on root crops. But then Kurt would at this moment be tuning in to the Channel Seven BBC German Language News Broadcast.

Lisel stared at the dial. She knew how to tune in to the broadcast. Everyone did, she supposed. That was why such severe punishments were given to those who were caught. Black listeners, they were called. She had never tried it and remembered being mildly curious why Kurt would risk so much for just a news program. But she had never asked him. Perhaps it was time she knew for herself.

Lisel twisted the volume control knob to its lowest setting, then carefully turned the frequency dial. The speaker buzzed and whined until, at last, a voice came clearly through the static. Lisel had to lean forward with her ear against the speaker to catch the words. "This is the BBC German Language News Report." Followed by the first four notes of Beethoven's Fifth, the famous V-For-Victory code that had become the BBC's trademark.

There was news of fighting in Africa and the resistance in Greece and France, of a Communist uprising in Germany. Lisel frowned. She had heard nothing of an uprising. Perhaps the British communications lied just as much as Nazi propaganda did. The announcer read a list of German pilots who had been shot down.

"Franz Barsch, killed; Heinrich Hauptman, captured alive; Max Wieck, wounded, captured alive; Egon Schiller, killed; Alfred Schroeder, wounded, captured alive; Friedrich Wrobel, captured alive . . ."

The announcer's voice went on but Lisel did not hear any more. Friedrich Wrobel captured alive? Could it be he was truly still alive though the German government had told his parents he was dead?

Were the British lying? Saying he was alive when he had been killed? Lisel reached up, snapped off the set and sat, without moving. Why would they announce some "killed," some "wounded and captured," and some "captured alive"? It did not make sense unless the British list was truthful. Lisel had to believe it. Friedrich Wrobel was still alive, held as a prisoner somewhere in England—and his parents thought him dead.

Lisel looked inside herself. Should she tell the Wrobels their only child was still alive? Or should she let them go on mourning and suffering? Something cold hardened Lisel's heart. Why allow them any consolation? What did they allow Marta? What did they allow Papa and herself? Besides, Lisel thought bitterly, the Wrobels would probably have no second thoughts about denouncing her as a Black Listener. She would tell them on the day cows chased rabbits. She would let them weep and mourn the loss of their son. And she would be glad for their sorrow.

Chapter 13

Lisel's release came three days later. Frau Segler called Lisel into the office and, without a word, handed Lisel her employment booklet. She could only stare at it in her hand.

Lisel had waited two years for that moment. Now she was not sure how to react. Was she not supposed to feel happiness and relief and gratitude? Yet when she searched inside herself, she found none of those. Only sorrow. Not because she would miss the Munitions Works. Lisel grieved for the two years of her life she had been forced to sacrifice for this evil cause, for the two years of grueling labor, for the two years of facing Herr Hahn every day, for the year of cowering in a dank cellar wondering if her family was safe. And she grieved that she did not feel happiness and relief and gratitude.

In silence, Lisel turned and left Frau Segler. From the grenade room doorway, she viewed rows of workers with their heads bent as they scrubbed and oiled, scrubbed and oiled, scrubbed and oiled. Though she knew each one by sight and name and disposition, they seemed as alive and individual as machines.

At the end of her shift, Lisel straightened her tray and cleaned her wire brush, as she had every day. She felt no more tired than she usually did but she moved with a strange apathetic slowness—detached and lethargic, like a sleepwalker.

Lisel was the last one out of the grenade room and glanced back as she went through the door. She could smell the odor of oil and metal mingled together. The other shift would not arrive for another half hour so the room was empty. Lisel recognized the same emptiness within her. She had come to this room as a six-teen-year-old girl with the desire to make the money her family needed to complete their genealogy. She had great dreams of going to America—to the temple in Salt Lake City. Now, only two years later, she left this place grieving the loss of her desires and dreams. She left this place a woman aged beyond eighteen by frustration and disappointment. The early morning sky, shrouded in low winter clouds, was devoid of stars or moon. Lisel's footsteps made a curious, hollow sound on slick cobblestones. Ahead of her, she heard the muffled voices of her former coworkers as they hurried to the train station, heard Susanne's laughter float back to her. Lisel could make out shapes. Tall, ungainly Ursula Bonse's lopelike walk. And even farther ahead, Herr Hahn's choppy movements as he marched on his short legs.

The notion that she would not walk down these streets again flitted vaguely across her mind. She could not imagine it. Nor could she imagine not standing at the grenade tray again. Perhaps if she knew what job she would be doing after this, she would not feel as troubled. But the fact was, Lisel had long since given up looking for work because she had not believed she would ever be allowed to leave the Munitions Works.

Now, the fact gradually declared itself. Tomorrow she would not be coming here to Wittenau. Then another fact made itself clear. She would also not be earning her seven marks. That realization came with a jolt of alarm. She and Papa depended on that money to live. She would have to find work now, in a hurry.

Overhead, the clouds parted and sent a shaft of bluish moonlight across Wittenau. A few stars shone like glittering eyes. Lisel heard the engine roar of the early morning train and blinked with surprise to see it standing at the station. She was later than she thought.

Lisel quickened her footsteps into a fast walk and then a half-run. Breathless, she dashed into the station just as the train was moving away. She pulled up short and stared at the last car as it disappeared in the morning darkness. The car had the customary "V" painted on it with the slogan, "Wheels turn for victory." She breathed a tired, resigned sigh.

There would not be another train for at least a half hour and if she sat down, her ankles and feet would begin to swell. So Lisel paced the train station, dark and lonely at this hour.

Only a few minutes had passed when the wail of air raid sirens ripped across the sky. Lisel's eyes went up to the station ceiling in astonishment. The sirens had sounded their warning during the night but no bombers had come over Berlin, probably not so much because the Luftwaffe had turned them back as the clouds had kept them away.

But a raid now? It would be daylight in an hour. Surely, even the RAF was not so foolish. Nevertheless, Lisel headed for a building down the street where the basement had been converted to an air raid shelter. The basement was darker than the one at the Munitions Works and more dank and musty-smelling than Frau Heidemann's apartment.

Lisel sat in the blackness with a half dozen other workers, either leaving their workplace late or going early. All of them expressed surprise the bombers would come over at such an hour. Several said someone set off the sirens by mistake, that they would not have to wait long for the all clear. Someone else, an older, faded looking woman who had come in after Lisel, sighed heavily. "How much longer can this war go on? I am so tired of the whole thing."

A tall, paunchy man from the corner answered her. "It will not be long now. Those British have about had it. In a few weeks, they will be begging us for peace. A few more weeks and it will all be over. You will see."

From overhead came the thundering sounds of the antiaircraft guns. Then cannon from the chasers. Lisel clapped her hands over her ears.

A nearby explosion shook the earth around and beneath the shelter. Lisel was thrown from her seat. She heard the crack of wood and masonry as the walls twisted with the force. Someone screamed. Someone called out in prayer. Dust swirled in clouds that choked. Underscoring the commotion came the hiss of severed pipes. Lisel smelled the sharp, piercing odor of gas. A rumble near the stairway spewed more dust. Lisel gagged on the contaminated air. It was truly the end. The building above her was collapsing. She would die, crushed to death, in the dark, buried beneath this building with people she did not know. For the first time in weeks she cried out in prayer. Not for rescue, not for mercy, but in bitter questioning. "Why?"

"Gas! It is gas!" Lisel recognized the tall man's voice. A new dread shot through her. Lisel scrambled to her feet and reeled toward the stairway, her hands over her mouth and nose. She collided with someone in the dark. Someone else pushed her. Lisel pushed back and fought her way over the heap of crumbling rubble that blocked the way to the stairs. From behind, someone shoved her forward and she stumbled. The smell of gas came stronger.

Lisel gained the stairs, lost her grasp on the twisted, splintered railing and groped for the wall. The man ahead of her broke through the door into the early morning and Lisel followed. The cold air hit her lungs like ice water. The atmosphere smelled of smoke and sulphur and stung her nose and burned her eyes. She ran into the street. The dawn was a dirty yellow.

Lisel felt something fall into her hair and something else pelted her shoulder. Her first thought was that it was hailing. Then she realized it was not hail but ash and flaming cinder and shards of metal shrapnel falling from a burning sky. With freshened fear, Lisel ducked her head, threw her arms over her hair and sprinted down the street toward the railway station. The distance seemed miles and miles. Sparks eddied around her like tiny, flitting, orange birds. A smoldering cinder fell against the skirt of Lisel's coat and she slapped at it with her bare hand, sobbing between gritted teeth with fear and anger. Fear for her life and anger because the cinder had left a black hole in the aged-thin wool of her only coat. Lisel ran on, over the slick, uneven cobblestones.

A shout brought up Lisel's head and she saw, in a recessed doorway, three people, their faces turned toward her in expectation. One beckoned. Lisel swerved and pitched toward them. They reached for her. Lisel felt their hands on her arms, pulling her into the doorway. One banged her back with the flat of his hand, putting out sparks that scorched her coat.

An explosion shook the sky. The four cowered farther into the doorway and covered their faces. Lisel's breath burst in and out of her lungs. Whether from the exertion of running or the fear, she did not know. Both were the same.

"She is a German," one of them said. Lisel heard the loathing in the man's voice. Then she heard him spit and felt the splatter near her foot. She turned and looked into the grim faces of her three rescuers. The shaved heads, stubbly beards, and pallid skin of the two men made them look almost identical. Their pale eyes blazed at her with the same identical hatred. They wore the badge of the Polish slave laborers, a purple "P" over a yellow diamond.

"So she is German." The woman shrugged. "She looks as bad as we do."

The woman also wore the letter on the front of her coat. She might have been older than Lisel. It was hard to tell. Her face was gaunt, her complexion jaundiced and flaky.

"I say we turn her out," the first man snarled. The anger in his voice was as hot as the swirling sparks. "Do the Germans allow us shelter during the raids? Why should we share ours with one of them? I say we turn her out."

Lisel glanced out to the street, to the hail of shrapnel and flaming cinder. A nearby fire stained the morning sky with red. And in the distance, black smoke rose in rounded masses until it looked like some blossoming, poisonous flower. Lisel gritted her teeth and clenched her fingers into her palms. They would have to fight her to put her out in that.

"Turn her out? Is that all?" The other man closed in on Lisel so he blocked her from the street. "What satisfaction is there in merely turning her out? I say we give to these Nazis what they have given to us." He grinned, showing a row of blackened, decayed teeth. "When they find her body, they will think she was killed in the air raid." The threat brought Lisel to herself. She had just run through a street raining with death and clawed her way out of a collapsing building. She had spent several weeks, unsheltered, in a room of shattering glass and the last year huddling in an air raid shelter. She had been in a street brawl between the Nazis and Communists, arrested by the Gestapo and imprisoned at Prinz-Albrectstrasse. Death no longer held the threat it once did. From this moment, she was no longer frightened. Only contemptuous.

Lisel drew herself up and faced the Pole with a stare of scorn. "It would take more than a couple of ragged scarecrows like you to kill me," she sneered.

172

The Pole blinked his surprise. Then his face twisted with fury. He took a menacing step toward her, his claw-like hands reaching for her face.

"Stop it!" the Polish woman commanded. She clutched at the man's arm. "If you act like a Nazi, you become a Nazi."

The hatred in the man's eyes burned with vengeance and his long, loose lips drew back in a snarl. "Nazis deserve no compassion."

"But because of the Nazis, the Poles understand compassion. Therefore, we can be more generous with it," the woman came back softly.

Like a vague echo, Lisel heard Papa's voice. "Thou shalt neither vex a stranger nor oppress him: for ye were strangers in the land of Egypt."

Lisel felt the heat of shame pulse in her face. Shame that these strangers lived principles she only knew. Shame that her own people should oppress another people in such a degrading way. Shame at being a German. But even when the Pole dropped his hands, Lisel's shame was not stronger than her angry pride. Though she should have remembered these people took her into their shelter, Lisel turned from them. And when the all clear sounded, she ran down the street to the railway station without looking back, mocking those who had humiliated her. At the ticket window, Lisel learned there would be no more trains for the rest of the day. A bomb had destroyed a section of tracks and the rails would have to be repaired.

Lisel walked a mile to a bus stop and waited a half hour. The bus was so overcrowded, she had to stand. On the route, the bus had to skirt a crater created by a bomb that had also burst the sewer lines beneath the street. The stench of the raw sewage made Lisel want to gag.

She changed buses twice and walked another three-quarters of a mile home. Papa was watching for her from the window of their flat. When he saw her coming, he came down the stairs to meet her at the door. Wearily, he put his arms around Lisel and she laid her cheek against his shoulder. She missed the scent of his shaving soap—he used the grimy sand soap now. "I love you, Papa."

Lisel heard the smile in his voice. "I was worried, little one."

173

She looked up into his face, thin, lined and careworn. She knew she could not tell him about the air raid shelter, nor the shrapnel, nor her confrontation with the Polish slaves. She would not be another cause of his troubles. Lisel smiled up at him. "There was nothing to worry about Papa. I was stupid and missed my train. Then the tracks were destroyed and I had to take a few hundred buses home. One of them took us on a tour and showed us what the inside of a sewer line looks like."

Papa's gray eyebrows rose and Lisel saw the grimace beneath his mustache. It made her laugh. "And best of all, Papa, I got my employment booklet."

A wide smile lifted Papa's lips and his arms tightened around her. "Oh Lisel, our prayers have been answered."

Lisel wanted to agree, to share Papa's happiness but a question loomed in her mind. What about the rest of their prayers? That observation would have disturbed Papa so Lisel kept it to herself. For Papa, she brightened. "Now we must pray that I can find another job quickly."

Papa nodded. "We will trust in the Lord."

"And I will begin looking this afternoon."

As it turned out, Lisel slept through the afternoon. It was twilight when she finally woke. Papa used a few extra ration points for some raisins and nuts to celebrate. Even that small treat made their meal seem festive. Later, when Papa had turned to his old easy chair and his well-worn scriptures, Lisel picked up the *Volkischer Beobachter*. On the front page she read the headlines, "British Murders Sneak Attack On Early Train!"

The account cited a bombing attack on the morning train leaving the Wittenau station. One car had been completely destroyed and all passengers killed. Lisel's eyes darted over the list of victims. It included Oswald Hahn, Ursula Bonse, and Susanne Beckers.

Lisel stared at the familiar names until the print blurred into the paper. Then her hands began to tremble, the page to rattle. Carefully, she folded the paper and laid it down. All dead. Her brain refused to accept the fact. Their faces, their voices were still too vivid in her memory. She saw again Susanne's unself-conscious smile that showed her broken tooth. Long, homely Ursula

174

Bonse. Herr Hahn and his cocky walk as he moved up and down the aisles of workers.

She remembered her feeling of revulsion in Herr Hahn's presence. Now she would never know in what secret scheme he had involved himself or how she had threatened him. She remembered with gratitude the note of warning Ursula had left at her tray. The first day of work when Susanne had befriended her and that day when her first friend had turned away. She remembered bits and pieces: faces, voices, snatches of conversation. Even after she had been ostracized she had shared so much with the people of the Wittenau Munitions Works grenade room that she had become a part of them. But this one last thing she had not been a part of, had not shared.

Gradually, the question surfaced. Why was Lisel's name not among those on the list? Why had Lisel not been on that train? It was the train she always took. She always boarded the fourth car and sat on the second bench from the front near the window. The fourth car was the one that was hit. But she was not on the second bench from the front near the window. She was not there because she had missed the train. She had missed the train because . . . Lisel hesitated with that thought.

Had an unseen hand slowed her? Had the voice of inspiration warned her? Lisel searched her memories and a cold realization stole across her heart. She had missed the train because she had been slow getting to the railway station. She knew of no angelic hand, no still voice that influenced her. Though it might have been there, she had not felt it, had not heard it.

A hard knot grew in Lisel's stomach. When was the last time she had enjoyed the company of that guiding spirit? Last week? Last month? It was sometime at the end of last year, before Germany declared war on America, sometime before Marta was taken away from them. Like a sudden fever, her anger rose and brought out the sore memory of what the Wrobels had done.

They deserved their grief for sending Marta away, for the hurt it caused her and Lisel and Papa. She stole a glance at Papa. He was sitting quietly, his glasses on his nose, his chin on his chest, his eyes moving over the words of the holy text. Rhythmically, his index finger riffled the page corners from the back to the front of the book. The habit had rounded some of the corners and worn down others. He sat there in a blissful state of peace and composure. He had been a man without guile during the entire incident, even going to Friedrich Wrobel's funeral. That reaction had puzzled Lisel.

Marta's behavior seemed strange, too. Her letters were full of her new job in the military hospital where she said she felt her skills were of some use. She wrote of her coworkers and the five other nurses she shared a small apartment with, one of whom was also a Mormon. She wrote of her joy in explaining the gospel to her new friends, coworkers, and patients. She wrote that living in Frankfurt was "a marvelous opportunity" and she was grateful she had been sent there. The last paragraph was always about the future and how she looked forward to the time when the war would be over and Grant would, at last, come for her.

Lisel had thought the letters were Marta's way of comforting Papa. Of making a hopeless situation seem better. But now, Lisel was not sure. Was Marta really happy where she was? Was her being in Frankfurt a part of the Lord's plan, as she believed it was? Was Papa's lack of bitterness another gift of the Spirit? And what about Lisel?

Was her anger the element that had driven the Spirit from her life? Had made her prayers hollow and her faith become useless? The answer came like the sting of salt in a raw wound. Pain welled up in Lisel. Burning tears stung her eyes. And for the first time, she plainly saw the canker that had spread so slowly through her thoughts and feelings she had no knowledge of it until this moment. She wanted to tear it from her with her bare hands; but there was no physical way to reach the torment, the misery that made her whole being cave in on itself.

Her anguish brought her to her feet and she flew to Papa, knelt beside him and grasped his arm. "Papa, the paper said some of the people from the Munitions Works were killed in the air raid this morning."

He turned and looked down at Lisel. His blue eyes filled with compassion. "Yes, little one. I read the article. I am grieved for the families of those people, but I am grateful for the protection that kept you from such a fate."

Lisel put her head down on the arm of the chair, too ashamed to meet Papa's eyes. "But Papa, I missed the train only because I was late. I have been unworthy of any type of protection. I have been filled with anger and hate. I fear the Comforter has abandoned me. What do I do to get it back, Papa?" she cried. "Tell me what to do."

Lisel felt his hand on her braids. "This all began when the Wrobels denounced Marta?" Lisel nodded. "Then you must make peace with the Wrobels."

Lisel lifted her head and looked up at Papa. His eyes spoke his certainty, the touch on her hand, his reassurance. In that moment, the anguish of her heart was withdrawn as easily as a needle from a pin cushion. She knew Papa spoke the truth.

Lisel scarcely remembered running down the stairs to Frau Heidemann's apartment. Even though the repairs to the Wrobels' burned out apartment had been completed, the State declared a childless couple was only allowed twenty-six square meters. So a family of four had moved into the one-bedroom, upstairs apartment and the Wrobels had remained with Frau Heidemann.

Lisel paused at the door and ran her tongue over her dry lips. When she raised her hand to knock, she felt moisture in her palms and cold in her fingers.

"Lisel!" Frau Heidemann exclaimed. "I have heard you are unemployed. Such a reason to celebrate!" she laughed.

"Are the Wrobels here?" Lisel asked.

Frau Heidemann's face sobered. Lisel had not bothered to conceal her bitterness toward the couple and now she could see the wariness in Frau Heidemann's eyes. "Yes," she answered, "in the living room."

Lisel had not seen the Wrobels for several weeks and she was startled at the change in the pair. Elsa Wrobel's ample figure had diminished so her clothes hung limply from her now thin frame and Gustav Wrobel, once so erect, had withered to a stoop-shouldered old man. He sat with his pale hands, listless in his lap, staring at the air while she half-heartedly worked over a hole in the toe of a threadbare black stocking. Both looked up at Lisel with blank, disinterested eyes, and her heart recoiled. Had their grief made such an alteration in them?

Lisel sat down in Frau Heidemann's best chair. It was still warm and Lisel half suspected Frau Heidemann would shoo her out of it, but Frau Heidemann hovered, watchful, near the door.

"I have come to apologize," Lisel began. "I was angry with you for sending my sister away. I wished all manner of evil upon you. But I was wrong. I hope you will forgive me."

The Wrobels regarded her mutely, without recognition, as if she were a stranger who had said, "It looks as though we might have rain today."

"I also want to tell you how sorry I am at your loss."

Lisel saw she had touched something in them at last. Frau Wrobel's eyes began to glisten. Herr Wrobel's jaw tightened and his chin came out, but neither spoke.

There was one more thing Lisel had to say. It was something that might endanger her and Papa, but the calm feeling within Lisel encouraged and strengthened her resolve. "I wanted to tell you something about Friedrich." Lisel flicked a glance toward Frau Heidemann. Her face had gone very still, her eyes wide.

Lisel drew a deep breath and went on. "Several days after you received the news of his death, I listened to the German Language News Report on the BBC Channel Seven."

Both pairs of eyes riveted on Lisel. Frau Wrobel's mouth had come open in a soft "Oh," and a stain of fierce color climbed Herr Wrobel's neck.

"The BBC read a list of all those who had been shot down. They told who had been killed and who had been injured. They said Friedrich had been captured but that he was uninjured."

Herr Wrobel's jaw began to work. His face purpled. "Do you know the penalty for Black Listeners is death?"

"Yes."

"And still you admit this thing openly to us?"

Lisel lifted her shoulders. "I thought you should know the truth."

"The truth?" Herr Wrobel thundered. "The British are murderers and liars! They falsify even the most simple of facts to subvert the Reich!"

"Are you certain they said 'Friedrich Wrobel'?" Frau Wrobel broke in, as if she struggled with an unanswerable question.

Lisel turned to the older woman. "Yes, I am certain. The report said he is a prisoner of war in England."

"It is a lie!" Herr Wrobel burst out. Lisel saw the outrage in his mottled face, his clenched fists; but she was not afraid.

"But Papa, perhaps it is not a lie," Frau Wrobel argued. A fragile hope shone in her eyes. "Perhaps Friedrich is still alive."

"And perhaps snow will bake in an oven," he shot back vehemently. "The British make these announcements to deceive boys and foolish women."

"And the Nazis deceive only grown men?" she fired back, her eyes snapping.

Herr Wrobel looked as if he had been socked between the eyes. "Mama, this is treasonous speech!" he exclaimed.

"No, Papa," she shook her head. "This may, at last, be truth. I have wondered why we have not heard of any of our soldiers being captured. We have been told they all gallantly fought to the death. All of them, Papa. Does this sound like the truth to you? Or does it say our government does not want its people to push for a compromise in order to get our young men back? So they tell us they are all dead."

Lisel looked at Frau Wrobel in astonishment. She had never thought of the older woman as anything more than her husband's shadow. And from the look on Herr Wrobel's face, he had also not suspected otherwise. His mouth dropped open while he gaped at her, then his lips snapped shut.

"My mother's heart tells me Lisel has spoken the truth," Frau Wrobel said. "Our son is still alive and we should be grateful to her for having the courage to tell us." She turned to Lisel and squeezed her hands. Tears spilled over her lashes. "You will never know how thankful I am, my dear."

Lisel's heart soared. She leaned forward and pressed her cheek to the old, wrinkled one. "I am glad for you."

Herr Wrobel had limped across the room and stiffly lowered himself into a chair with his back to Lisel. She felt the wrench of his bitterness. "I will leave you alone now," she said. Frau Heidemann came up behind Lisel out in the hall, snatched at her arm and swung her around to face her. Her lips were compressed with anger. "What foolishness have you done now, Lisel Spann.

179

That old weasel will denounce you. You should have kept silent, like the rest of us."

Lisel's eyebrows rose in surprise. "You knew all along?"

"Of course I knew. Everyone on the street knew. But we also knew what would happen if anyone told. They are Nazi spies, a double reason to mistrust them."

Lisel laid her hand on Frau Heidemann's arm. "They will not denounce me," she said with assurity.

Frau Heidemann's eyes bore into Lisel's. "If Gustav tries, Elsa and I will poison him."

Frau Heidemann was so intent, so serious, it made Lisel laugh. "I am sure you would. But you will not have to." She made a move to go, but Frau Heidemann held her arm.

A new thought drew the older woman's mouth into a melancholy line; her eyes showed a hesitancy, but she spoke. "You have returned the Wrobels' son to them. Do you know anything of mine?"

Lisel covered Frau Heidemann's hand with her own. "I wish I did."

Frau Heidemann sighed and dropped her hands. "If only I knew he was well and safe." Her voice broke and she turned her head, but not before Lisel saw the shimmer of her tears.

After Frau Heidemann had gone back into her apartment, Lisel stood there for a moment in the dark, musty hallway. Wishing she had something to offer Kurt's mother. But she had nothing. She had no job and she was in danger of being arrested. Yet for all that, Lisel felt an ease of spirit she had not experienced for months; and when she moved up the stairs to her flat, it was with a light, optimistic step. She knew she could leave it all to the Lord.

Chapter 14

THE MID-SUMMER SUN WARMED LISEL'S HAIR. SHE COULD FEEL the heat down to her scalp and the moist warmth under the red braids wrapped around her head. All through the warm, sticky summer of 1942, she had thought of cutting her hair in a shorter style but always stopped before picking up the shears.

She fanned herself with the newspaper she had picked up as she left the office and looked down the street for the tram. Even when the streets were damaged, dependable Gussi Thorak, the conductoress on street car 5769, saw to it the tram was always on time. Today was no exception.

From around the corner and down the block, the tram rattled toward the knot of people at the stop where Lisel stood. The cars looked like shoe boxes—narrow and high with a rounded roof. The front of the first car was flat and Gussi sat in the driver's seat, square in the middle of the car, her thick fingers grasping the wheel.

Lisel raised her hand and sent a greeting to Gussi, who waved back. The gold buttons on her uniform strained across her bosom. Gussi was fortunate enough to have a brother still on the family farm who provided her with eggs, butter, cheese, and fresh fruit and vegetables—sometimes even meat. When she could spare it, Gussi shared bits of her good fortune with her passengers. An egg or two to one, a handful of green beans or a pear to another. More than once, Lisel and Papa had blessed Gussi over a bowl of strawberries or a slice of squash.

All of her passengers greeted Gussi by name and received a broad smile and a friendly word in return. Lisel slid into her customary seat near the front of the car and thought the tram ride was a good way to end her work day. Gussi's cheerfulness was contagious and everyone who rode the tram felt better for getting on.

Tall, bearded Herbert Biermann took his seat behind Lisel and thumped her shoulder genially, as he always did. Herbert Biermann was the perfect stereotype of a middle-aged Bavarian from his fun-loving manner to his befeathered felt hat and carved walking stick. "How are you today, Fraulein Spann?"

"Very well," she smiled.

Behind Herbert came Gregor Metzger, a blonde, broad-shouldered young man who had lost an arm in Holland. He kept his empty sleeve folded and pinned to his shoulder. Every afternoon when Gregor boarded, he looked straight at Lisel and soberly said, "Good day, carrots," then broke into a wide, teasing grin.

That grin always brought up the warmth in Lisel's face. "Good afternoon, Gregor," she returned with an equal amount of seriousness.

Of course, not everyone was as friendly. Some passengers sat silently during their ride, some read their newspapers. One, an SS man who rode only four blocks, everyone ignored because of his sour expression.

The last of the passengers boarded and with them, at the end of the car at the Jewish door, an elderly woman with her thin, white hair tied up in a scarf. She had a gold star of David and the word "Jew" printed over it in black, pinned to the front of her shabby dress. Since all the seats were taken, the woman stood near the back of the car, swaying with weariness.

Last year, on September 1st, the State declared all Jews must wear the star so they would be readily identified. That was because the State had discovered a plot, formulated by the Jews, to sterilize all Germans. And because President Roosevelt in the United States, whom the Nazis said was a puppet of the Jews, had declared all German-Americans must wear a black swastika on their sleeves.

That troubled Lisel. Were their missionary friends, people like Grant Nolte who had been born to German parents in America, being persecuted because of their German heritage? If her family had gone to America, would they now be persecuted like the Jews were here?

The America the Nazi press portrayed and the America the missionaries had told them about seemed two different countries. As Lisel thought about it though, she knew in her heart who to believe. No prejudice could exist in a land of such prosperity and happiness.

It had been a long time since Lisel had thought of America, had had the courage to remember her dreams of going there. Not since the announcement last December when her hopes were crushed. Somehow, still, the Wrobels were part of that disaster. But her heart lightened knowing she no longer blamed them. Lisel saw them occasionally. Frau Wrobel always smiled and said, "Hello," and she looked better, not so vacant-eyed. But Herr Wrobel coldly ignored Lisel. She wondered how Frau Heidemann and Frau Wrobel had managed to keep the man from going to the People's Bureau.

"Here, come sit here, star of my heart."

Lisel turned to see Herbert rising from his seat. He beckoned toward the elderly Jewish woman and gestured for her to sit down in his seat.

Fear widened the woman's eyes and pulled her skin tighter over her high, flat cheek bones and straight, bridgeless nose. She shook her head.

"The Jewish swine has no place among good German citizens," the SS man spat. "You must not offer your seat to one such as her."

Herbert's eyebrows rose, his chin came out. "And since when does one such as you tell me what to do with my own behind?"

The SS man's face reddened. He glanced around the car and saw the other passengers eyeing him. Then he clamped his lips shut and said nothing.

Herbert reached out and took hold of the woman's arm. "Come, my old darling, sit here."

Reluctantly the woman sat, smiled an uncertain thanks and watched the SS man out of the corner of her eye.

Lisel glanced up at Herbert; he grinned down at her and winked broadly.

Near the back of the car, Gregor thumbed through his newspaper as he hummed the popular tune, "I Know There Will Be a Miracle" from the movie, *The Great Love.*

Lisel and Grete had gone to the Marmorhaus Theatre when *The Great Love* played. Less than half-way through the picture, however, Grete became so restless she said she would leave. Lisel did not want Grete to go home by herself so both girls made their way out of the dark theater. Grete complained she did not care for musicals and after that, turned off the wireless whenever "I Know There Will Be A Miracle" or , "The World Will Not End Because Of This" played.

It seemed no one else in Berlin shared the same feeling. Everywhere that summer, someone was humming or singing snatches of the two songs.

The Nazi-despised Swing Music was still around, though performed and played in secret. Teenagers involved in the Swing Music movement earned no praise in Germany. Some were arrested and jailed. That news, reported in the media, troubled Lisel and she saw a new tension in Frau Heidemann. Was Kurt, ever the Jazz lover, involved?

Lisel turned and stared out the tram's open window. The building to the left had been hit by an incendiary in a raid last week. The roof had collapsed and above the glassless windows rose sooty, flame-shaped stains.

Every day, more and more buildings stood in blackened ruins. Now there were so many, crews were months behind in the repairs. It seemed to be the only thing capable of growing and thriving in burnt-out, bombed-out Berlin. Bright pink flowers topped the stalks and swayed happily in the hot breeze. They made a vivid counterpoint to the burnt, broken walls.

At the next stop the SS man got off, walking stiffly, his shoulders rigid; and everyone in the car relaxed. The Jewish woman dabbed the moisture from her eyes. Lisel stretched her legs under the seat ahead of her. She was tired of sitting. She never thought she would feel that way after those years of standing at the grenade trays. But now all she did was sit behind a desk at the Erwert Printing Company. Not that Lisel was ungrateful. She worked an eight-hour day, five days a week for an astounding forty-five marks a week—much more than what she was paid at the Works for working thirty-two hours a week more.

Her employer was Ludwig Erwert, a round, little man with a

purplish complexion and sparse black hair who always managed to keep a bottle of Schnapps in the filing cabinet. He was also Gunther Pinsel's nephew.

Professor Pinsel had turned up one night in February. Lisel and Papa were always glad to see the tiny, white-haired man and invited him to share their meager meal and spend the night. He had come, he said, on a happy but sad errand. Happy because he had completed the Spanns' research as far as was possible. He then turned over a thick stack of sheets, dating back to the twelfth century. And sad, he said, because he had completed the Spanns' research and would no longer be working for them.

Papa had laughed at the little witticism and told Professor Pinsel he would always be welcome in the Spann home and said he looked forward to a long friendship.

Professor Pinsel flushed a little. "Ah, but I may not be able to see you as much as I would like." Then he told Papa and Lisel he had been hired as the research director in one of the statistical bureaus where he had spent a good deal of time working on the Spann genealogy. Both Papa and Lisel congratulated him with enthusiasm, remembering his desperate circumstances the day Lisel brought him home to meet Papa.

The three spent that night poring over the documents Professor Pinsel brought them. Papa and Lisel exclaimed over the names and dates and places while Professor Pinsel told them stories of their ancestors and the places they lived.

At last, late in the night, Professor Pinsel pushed back his wire-rimmed glasses and rubbed his eyes. Then he frowned. "But, Lisel, should you not be at work?"

Lisel told him about her release from the Munitions Works and how she had, for a week, sought in vain for work.

Professor Pinsel looked thoughtful, then said, "My nephew's employer wants a reliable office worker."

"But I have no training in office work." Lisel objected. Her face grew warm. "I have not even finished school."

"Perhaps that will not matter as long as Herr Erwert knows you are reliable and I will be glad to speak for that."

The next morning, Professor Pinsel accompanied Lisel to the unpretentious two-story brick building in southwest Berlin. A

185

large white sign with black lettering declared it to be the home of the Erwert Printing Company.

Herr Erwert wanted Lisel to start right away. He made arrangements for her to take lessons in shorthand and dictation and sent her home with an ancient, cantankerous typewriter to learn the keyboard.

When Professor Pinsel left that afternoon, Lisel threw her arms around his neck and kissed his shriveled cheek. Tears stung her eyes. How greatly the Lord had blessed them all. She had a new, wonderful job. Her family had a marvelous friend. He had the position he had sought for so long. And the Spanns had their genealogy.

Papa took all the sheets Professor Pinsel brought and carefully put them in a leather satchel. Whenever the air raid sirens wailed, Papa grabbed his scriptures and his precious satchel before he went out the door to the basement.

For a while, early in the spring of 1942, the air raids seemed more of an inconvenience than a threat. The bombers came over at the same time every night and preferred to target the airport in south Berlin and the industrial area in the north. For the most part, they left the residential regions alone and, though Papa fretted, Lisel spent many air raids in her own room. One night she even slept through the sirens and explosions.

The tram jerked to a halt at the next stop. Lisel fished in her pocketbook and pulled out an envelope. She hurried up the aisle and down the car's steps to the van parked alongside the street. Since the main post office in Spandau, as well as a few of the branch offices, had been knocked out by fires and bombs, Berliners mailed their letters at post office vans that traveled throughout the city. Lisel shoved Marta's letter into the slot and ran back to the waiting tram.

Lisel wrote Marta several times a week. She still missed her sister and was greatly disappointed when, in June, Marta's vacation time was cancelled due to the influx at the hospital after the thousand bomber raid at the end of May.

Up until the thirtieth of May, no one had seen such devastation. Then, in a matter of only a few hours, over a thousand RAF aircraft bombarded Cologne, Hamburg, Bremen, Essen, and Frankfurt. The first of the squadrons dropped firebombs, then

came explosive bombs, incendiary bombs, and phosphorus canisters. Last were the heaviest explosives and aerial mines. The
bombers did not target only the cities' industrial regions but
assaulted residential areas as well. More than forty-thousand people were killed in that attack. Germany reeled.

It was several days before Lisel and Papa knew Marta was safe.
They had a short letter from her saying she could not yet come
home—the hospitals in Frankfurt were overwhelmed with the
wounded. Marta had written:

> I am so tired at night and sometimes I feel frustrated at the
> lack of medicines and supplies but I am happy to be of use, to
> ease the sufferings of others not as fortunate as I. There are so
> many terribly burned and maimed, and oh, the children!
>
> Almost all the children here suffer in some way. They are
> injured and orphaned. Some have lost their whole families. How
> I would weep for them if it would comfort the pain of their little
> bodies and ease their aching hearts.
>
> Indeed I am fortunate to have a loving papa, brother and sister.
> For being a member of the true Church and having the blessings
> of the gospel. For my Grant and knowing he will come for me
> and we will be together forever. Pray for me as I ever pray for
> you.
>
> Your loving daughter and sister,
> Marta.

Lisel and Papa had also had brief, terse notes from Michael. He
could not tell them where he was or even if he was well. He said
not to worry. But his handwriting wavered across the page and his
sentences rambled. Lisel and Papa did worry.

"What is this?" Lisel heard Herbert Biermann say. She saw him
frowning at something ahead on the street. Lisel straightened in
her seat to see. Up the street, a Black Maria stood at the curb
while two SS men struggled to change one of the front tires.

The vivid memory of her experience inside the truck, with its
odors of sweat and vomit and blood and the sounds of weeping
and swearing, brought a nauseous wave of fear up Lisel's throat.
Yet, for all her horror of the vehicle, she could not turn her eyes
from it.

As the tram drew closer, everyone in the car went silent, their eyes on the Black Maria. Then, as they passed, Lisel saw one of the back doors swing slightly open. A man slid out from underneath the door, dropped to the street and crouched behind the back tire. His head was shaved. He was dressed in the dirty, gray uniform of a prisoner.

"Someone is escaping!" she cried out before she knew the words had left her lips.

The prisoner turned as the tram passed then leaped to his feet and began to run toward the passing car with an awkward, limping gait.

Lisel jumped to her feet. "Help him!" she shouted. "Someone help him!"

The other passengers were on their feet, their faces at the windows, too frightened to call out to the man lest they draw attention from the SS guards, still working with the front tire.

The escaping prisoner came faster though his injured leg slowed him and made him clumsy. His arm reached out for the rail at the door. It was just beyond his grasp.

"We are going too fast!" Lisel heard Herbert shout. She glanced at Gussi who was watching her passengers in her mirror. If she did not slow, the prisoner would not catch them. If she slowed, she might attract suspicious attention. Lisel felt the slight slowing.

Still, the prisoner was falling behind. Leaving him in the street meant his death. Lisel ran to the back of the car. But Herbert and Gregor were already there. Gregor was leaning out the back of the Jew door with his one good arm and hand outstretched. "Come on, man, faster," he cried out.

The man made one more lunge for the door, an incredible effort. Lisel heard the grunt of pain. Gregor grasped his wrist. The prisoner stumbled and lost his footing. The tram dragged him over the paving stones but he clung to Gregor's arm. "Help me," Gregor panted. Herbert leaned over the top of Gregor and grasped the prisoner's sleeve.

"I'm slipping," Herbert shouted. Lisel grabbed his pants belt and leaned back, clutching the back of one of the seats. Her feet slid along the aisle.

Then the old Jewish woman was beside Lisel, also holding Herbert's belt and pulling backward.

"Everyone, pull now!" Gregor cried.

With a powerful, backward heave all four pulled. Lisel and the old woman fell into the aisle as Herbert, Gregor, and the prisoner came through the door. Lisel heard the cheering of the other passengers, felt the tram speed increase.

Lisel reached out for the old woman who had fallen beside her. They pulled each other up. The old woman smiled a little sheepishly. "Now that I am not so round, I do not bounce so well."

Lisel returned her smile. She looked back at the Black Maria, expecting to see the SS men coming after the tram. But the van still sat at the side of the road and the SS men still struggled with the front tire. Lisel bent over the prisoner on the floor. Herbert and Gregor knelt next to him while the old Jewish woman wiped the blood from his face with her head scarf.

The prisoner's pallid face was badly bruised and misshapen, one eye swollen shut, his lips split and his teeth broken. He lay there, gasping for breath, his thin chest heaving up and down.

"Can you speak, boy?" Herbert asked.

One blue eye opened and looked up at the four faces. Then, amazingly, he smiled, an odd kind of tired, lopsided smile in a way that was so familiar. His bloodied lips formed around a word. "Lisel."

Lisel could only stand there on her numbing legs and stare down at him. Her mind fought to remove the blood and the bruises, make the battered face once again the one she loved. Tears burned her eyes. "Oh Kurt," she wept and dropped to his side. She wanted to touch him, wanted to hold him, but she was afraid of hurting him.

Instead, he reached out to her and drew her down to him. "I thought I would never see you again," he said in a hoarse whisper.

Lisel pressed her face against his neck. He smelled of blood and sweat and worse. He felt so thin under her hands. "Oh Kurt, what have you done? What could have brought you to this? We have worried so about you. Your mother worries all the time. How could you have done this to yourself and to her and to me?"

Kurt pushed her away from him. He held her by the shoulders. "You always did talk too much," he complained. "Now see if you can listen. Is Mother all right? And Walter?"

Lisel told him. And she told him about Marta going to Frankfurt and about the Wrobels going to live with his mother.

189

"I am glad she is not alone, then, even if it has to be with them," he said. "I worried about her and Walter and I wanted to come home for them; but as you can see," he grinned again, "I was busy elsewhere."

"You will come home now, though," Lisel said.

He shook his head. "No, not now. Not yet. It would not be safe for anyone. Besides I have more work to do. But Lisel, when this is over I have great plans. First I have to go to Mother. I was wrong about so much. I was wrong about her. There was a spy in our group who told many seditious stories and I believed him. I have to apologize. Then I have to find that missionary of Marta's.

"Remember that day in the garden when he came to say good-bye? He said he was going to baptize me, remember? That's why I have to find him. He was right, Lisel; and so were you about so many things I did not see then. I have to find Elder Nolte, then I will have what you have."

Herbert interrupted. "Three blocks before the next stop. We will have to get you off there."

Lisel's heart dropped. Only a few minutes more. But she could not let him go again. "I will go with you," she declared.

She heard Kurt's grunt of exasperation. "Will you never get over being such a knuckle-headed girl? I will not drag you into this business. Do you not remember—"

"It will not matter what you say, Kurt Heidemann. You cannot manage this alone. I must go with you. I can help you," Lisel insisted.

"You can help me be arrested again, you mean," Kurt returned. "I have not been so good at taking care of myself, how can I see to you, too? Besides this is not a schoolgirl escapade. If you are even seen in my company, you will go back to Prinz-Albrectstrasse, and this time you will face the Blood Court and there will be no one to rescue you."

"But—"

"No!" His voice was so full of force Lisel flinched. "If I get off this tram, I will do it alone. And you will go home to your Papa and say nothing."

Lisel recognized his tone and the glare in his one good eye. She knew he would not be convinced. And he had called her knuckle-headed. So he would be gone again. Her heart contracted. Fresh tears burned her eyes. She dug her fingers into the coarse cloth of his shirt as if holding him tighter could make the time go slower.

Kurt's good eye closed for a second, wearily. Then he looked again at Lisel. "I have to tell you about something that happened at Prinz-Albrectstrasse."

Lisel nodded and swallowed hard, thinking of Kurt in that place.

He went on. "They moved me to a different cell. It did not look so different from the rest, you know how they are. It made me sick every time I thought of you in there, even for that one night." He drew in a long, ragged breath. "I was lying on the cot. They had beaten me pretty badly and for most of the night I did not know where I was. I kept thinking I was a little boy again at home and something frightened me in the night. I called out for Mother, over and over again. I cried until I had no voice left. And she did not come. Then, as I turned about on the cot, my fingers found a place on the wall where someone had scratched some words into the plaster. Someone had carved, 'I love you' into the wall. Can you imagine that, Lisel?"

The tightness in her throat kept back Lisel's words. She wanted to explain but she could only nod. "In my confused mind I thought the words at the tips of my fingers were words I heard. I thought I heard them in Mother's voice. Hearing that voice, hearing those words was like some wonderful potion. My pain disappeared. My fear faded. I was warm instead of cold. I was neither hungry nor thirsty. Just because I knew Mother was nearby and she loved me. That was all that mattered in the world. I slept then. Later, I saw the words were only words scratched out by some other prisoner who was probably just as delirious as I was that night."

Lisel opened her mouth to tell him but only a sob came out.

"What happened forced me to think. And I thought about the things you said the last time I saw you. Do you remember? You told me the love people have in their families was more important than any other commitment in our lives. I did not believe you then. I thought I was ashamed of Mother then. I did not know then. But I know now. Thanks to some lost soul who is probably dead now."

Lisel shook her head. "She is not dead, Kurt." Her voice came out as a squeak. "I wrote those words in the wall. I thought I wrote them to comfort me. I could not have known it would comfort you, too."

Kurt stared at her, then he grinned that wonderful lopsided grin again. "Oh, Lisel," he laughed and pulled her against him. She sobbed against his throat and felt his arms tighten around her. One of her braids had come loose and she felt his fingers curl around it, comforting. "I love you Lisel," he said hoarsely.

"I love you, too," she said.

"Well, I am glad we all love each other," Herbert interrupted again, "but we will be loving each other in heaven if we do not get this boy off the tram." Reluctantly, Lisel moved out of Kurt's arms and helped him as he pushed himself up.

"Getting me off could not be harder than getting me on," he said to Herbert. "I did not thank you," he said and extended his hand to Herbert and Gregor.

"Thank us when you are off," Gregor returned. "Our necks are involved now."

"We have trouble," Gussi called from the front of the tram. "There are SS at the stop."

Lisel stood and looked a half block ahead. Three black shirts stood at the curb. Fear trickled down her spine. "We must let him off before we reach the stop," she said.

"If we stop now," Herbert said, "we will draw their attention."

"Perhaps we can slow enough that he can get off without our stopping," Gregor suggested.

"Would you have him break more of his bones?" the old Jewish woman snapped. "We will disguise him. Then at the stop I will get out of the wrong door and the SS will notice me. He can escape then."

"No," Kurt put in forcefully. "You have already risked enough for me."

"Then we will just disguise him," Gregor said, taking off his own jacket. "I believe this will fit you well enough. One sleeve has never been worn and it even has a wounded veteran's pin," he said, pointing to the tiny insignia on the lapel.

"You will also need a hat." From the watching passengers an

older, bald man pulled off his felt hat and handed it to Kurt who put it on and pulled it down low over his battered face.

"Into your seats," Gussi called. "We are pulling up." Gregor helped Kurt to his feet and steadied him as he came up the aisle to a seat. Lisel felt a leap of uncertainty. How could Kurt get away if he could not even walk?

Herbert must have been wondering the same thing. "Here boy, if you wear a wounded veteran's pin and limp like a wounded veteran you must use a cane like a wounded veteran. He handed Kurt his carved walking stick.

Again, Lisel felt the prick of grateful tears behind her eyelids.

"Thank you, thank you all," Kurt said and Lisel heard the hitch in his voice.

The street car came to a stop. The three Blackshirts were watching the tram. One of the men was their former passenger, the SS man who berated Herbert for giving his seat to the old Jewish woman. "Perhaps they are here for me," she heard Herbert say in a light-hearted tone.

Everyone who was to get off at that stop stood. Lisel's heart was beating so hard and so loudly it made her ears hurt. Her mouth went dry. And though, every instinct in her made her want to get up and go with Kurt, she knew it would endanger him more. He might be noticed. She even had to fight not to turn in her seat, not to look back at Kurt. Swallowing back her tears, she remained where she was and hoped she looked as if she had just finished work and was on her way home.

Limping and leaning on Herbert's cane, Kurt made his way down the aisle and past Lisel's seat. When he paused next to her, she reached out and grasped his hand. "Where will you go?"

He smiled down at her. "I know a safe place not too far from here. I will be back when this is over." He bent and quickly kissed her mouth. She could taste the blood from his lips. Then he moved up the aisle. At the door Gussi slipped two peaches into his hand. Kurt grinned at her.

Herbert had climbed out of the tram before Kurt and Lisel saw the Blackshirts step up to the older man. Kurt limped past them and into the crowd on the sidewalk.

She saw the brief conversation between Herbert and the blackshirts. Herbert towered over all three men, laughed, and clapped one of them on the shoulder. The three glowered at him but did not stop him when he walked away in the opposite direction Kurt went. Lisel knew Herbert had gone the wrong way. But she also knew he did not want to risk exposing Kurt.

Up the street, Kurt turned a corner and disappeared. Lisel's relief was like a cleansing wash. He had escaped the Black Maria and outwitted the Blackshirts. He was safe.

"He will be all right now."

The old Jewish woman stood in the aisle beside Lisel. She knew the woman had been willing to risk exiting from the wrong door if it looked like the SS men had turned their attention toward Kurt's limping figure. The woman patted Lisel's shoulder. "We saw a brave young man today."

Lisel glanced around the emptying car. She knew what had happened that day would never go beyond the walls of the tram. No one had asked what Kurt's crime had been—Lisel did not even know herself. But everyone had been united in their purpose by their fear and hatred of the SS. A grateful lump formed in her throat. "We saw many brave men today, young and old. And even a brave woman." She looked up at the old woman. "I cannot thank you enough."

"You can thank me by passing on the deed to someone else who needs help."

For the rest of the ride home, Lisel's emotions were like one great, spinning carousel: relief at finding Kurt, horror at his condition, gratitude that he had at last come to an understanding of his mother, joy that he wanted to be baptized, sorrow at losing him again, fear that he would be caught. Out of all of that, however, one fact came clear. She would have to tell Frau Heidemann she had seen Kurt. But she would have to wait for a moment when the Wrobels were not there. Lisel felt a continued uneasiness over the Wrobel's loyalty and she knew the authorities would be looking for Kurt. She would have to lie about his physical condition. Not because Frau Heidemann would be upset, but because, instinctively, she knew Kurt would not want to have his mother know.

At the apartment house door, she paused and looked down the stairs to Frau Heidemann's door. The Wrobels would be at their weekly Party meeting until five-thirty, only a half-hour away. Lisel hoped it would be enough time.

Chapter 15

THE FIRST WEEK OF OCTOBER, 1942, SECOND-IN-COMMAND, Hermann Göring announced the worst was, at last, over. He promised fine food for Christmas and victory and peace in 1943.

The second week of October brought more good news. The State Defense Department announced the Sixth Army had wiped out the last pockets of Soviet resistance in Stalingrad. German military positions outside Leningrad had been enlarged and a certain victory was expected any day.

The German people received the news with relief and joy. The Russian enemy was defeated—the soldiers would be coming home. Hitler's power seemed even greater and more firmly established than ever.

Then the Gestapo began pressuring German civilians. In Hamburg a teenager was sentenced to death for listening to the BBC. In the west—Cologne, Essen, Herne and Wuppertal—Blackshirts raided individual homes and searched citizens on the streets, looking for subversive materials. Half of those arrested were sentenced to concentration camps.

Food lines grew longer, fuel scarcer, and the Germans more and more sullen.

The worst news since the beginning of the war came on Christmas Eve of 1942. The press announced: "The warriors at Stalingrad have been singled out by fate to give proof of Germany's honor and courage."

It was a flowery attempt to justify a shocking defeat. Stunned, Lisel and Papa heard the news. Michael filled their thoughts.

Hitler insisted his people fight to the death rather than give up. Did this new report mean the soldiers around Stalingrad had all been killed? Or had some disobeyed and surrendered?

Lisel shuddered. She yearned with her whole heart to know Michael was still alive but it horrified her to think of him as a prisoner of the Russians. The government was of little help—they could give the Spanns no information about Michael.

A dispirited 1942 gave way to 1943—the year of promised victories.

On February third, the State Defense Department announced: "The battle for Stalingrad is over. True to their oath to the last breath, the Sixth Army, under the exemplary leadership of Field Marshal General Paulus, succumbed to the superior strengths of the enemy and adverse conditions." A four-day period of national mourning and the closure of movie houses, theaters, and places of amusement was announced. Then, the second movement from Beethoven's Fifth Symphony was played.

The message could not have been more clear. The Nazi government considered the men of the Sixth Army dead. But Lisel could not accept it. "Michael is not dead," she insisted to Papa. "We would be able to feel it if he was. We would surely know."

Papa did not reply. He only sat in his chair with a wool blanket tucked around him, his face gray, and said nothing.

On February eighteenth, Propaganda Minister Joseph Goebbels addressed a huge audience at Berlin's sports arena. The speech was carried over radio. He claimed the 300,000 German soldiers at Stalingrad had not died in vain. They had stopped the assault of six Soviet armies, who at that moment, would have been swarming toward Germany. He said the dead had gone on to become beloved heroes in Valhalla.

Goebbels spoke with such emotion, he was able to fire the specially chosen audience into a frenzy. The effect impressed radio listeners to believe Germany was united as never before. And when Goebbels demanded the supreme effort for total war, the audience reacted with hysterical support.

New excavations began for construction of air raid shelters—one on Wilhelmplatz, in front of the Chancellery.

Germans were asked to give up anything that was not basic to daily life. Luxury restaurants and nightclubs closed. Beauty parlors and hair dressers closed. Confectionary shops closed. Professional sports competitions stopped. Press reports on amateur sporting events were curtailed. Fashion journals stopped publication and Erwert's Printing Company lost some clients. Most production of civilian clothing stopped. Markets were set up along the streets where people could buy, barter, or exchange used clothes and shoes.

New slogans appeared on posters and pamphlets, some of which came from the Erwerts. "Strenuous endeavor will beat every opponent in the end." "Half measures are no measures at all." "What cannot kill me, will strengthen me." "Better to wear patched clothes for a few years than run around in rags for centuries." "Total war is the shortest war." "One struggle. One victory." "The best protection is not concrete but a stony heart."

New food rationing was announced. Per week, each person was allowed one quart of nonfat milk, a little more than two ounces of margarine, half a pound of meat, and two pounds of bread. Potatoes and cabbage were available but only with ration cards. Most of the other vegetables, however, had been dehydrated and sourly dubbed "barbed wire." There was no sugar, no butter, no eggs. Germans were reduced to little more than fifteen hundred calories a day.

Grumbling, especially in the food lines, became a national pastime. Goebbels called it a laxative for the soul; but when he was confronted in the streets by an angry mob chanting, "For this we thank our Fuhrer," he had the more vocal grumblers arrested.

To help offset the Germans' growing discontent, once a month, civilians could buy a one-dish meal without their ration coupons from military kitchens, called goulash cannons, that were set up in the streets.

Goebbels also began a program called "strength through fear" in which he played upon the feelings of enmity that had existed between Germans and Russians from the beginning of history. With the Russians advancing on a thousand-mile front, Goebbels depicted Germany as the sole defender of all that was sacred in Europe. He called the Russians "sub-human." He told the Germans if the Russians were allowed to prevail over Germany,

German men would be carried off to slave camps in Siberia, women would be raped, and the children kidnapped. The allies, he said, would stand by, offering no aid, no mercy.

Then Berlin began its final program to sweep itself clean of all Jewish elements. Jews who still lived within the city were picked up and sent to labor camps.

In March, the first heavy air attacks hit Berlin. Thousands were killed and one hundred and sixty thousand people were left homeless. Lisel, remembering with sorrow the old Jewish woman on the tram, wearily looked over the smoking rubble of her neighborhood and wondered if the broom used to sweep away the Jews had refused to return to its closet.

The sky was still a smoky sulphur yellow that afternoon as Lisel picked her way down the last street to the apartment house. Her stomach growled. Lately, she had tried to still her hunger pangs by drinking more water but found, though she received some relief for a while, her stomach ached even more later. She glanced up at the apartment house with the warmth of gratitude in her heart. At least it had not been hit—so many had been. It seemed half the city lay in smoldering ruins.

She found Grete sitting on the front steps of the house. "It is too cold to sit out here," Lisel said.

"It is cold no matter where you sit," Grete answered, "unless you are sitting under a burning building." There was no emotion in her voice. Her face was pale, weary shadows underscored her eyes, and her hair hung in snarls, as if she had not combed it for a long time. There was a rim of black beneath her nails and a string gone from one of her shoes.

Lisel sat down next to Grete. The cold from the concrete steps came up through Lisel's old coat. "You are all well, then?"

"We are alive," Grete answered. "Have you heard any word of Michael?"

Lisel shook her head. "We inquire every week, but every week there is nothing."

A bitter smile twitched at Grete's colorless lips. "Oh they know about Michael. They just do not tell you. It is amazing the things they do not tell you—these people who run things. They are all liars and fakes!"

Shocked, Lisel glanced down the street, wondering if anyone had heard.

"They paint glorious pictures with their water-color promises. But just like everything else in this country of deceit and fakery, the picture is illusion and they are all liars." Grete swung her head around and pierced Lisel with a wild look. "He was not even handsome. Did you know that? He was tall and blonde and blue-eyed. Blue the color of ice. And his head the shape of a hatchet. When I would not, they tried to make me drunk. I only got sick and he hit me and hit me." Grete put her shaking hands over her face. "It was horrible. It was not glorious or patriotic. It was not romantic like they said it would be. It was degrading and it was horrible."

Lisel's heart softened and she put her arms around her friend, pulling her head down onto her shoulder. "Hush, Grete," she whispered, stroking her hair.

"All I could think of was how I argued with you the day you tried to tell me a person's eye color and hair color did not matter. You wanted someone who was the same as you on the inside, someone who had the same beliefs you had. It took me a long time to realize how right you were. How I have wished I had listened. How happy I would be to have one of your Mormon boys now." Grete's laugh was angry. "But who would want me?"

Lisel pushed Grete away from her and gave her friend's shoulders an affectionate shake. "That is ridiculous. You are a lovely girl. And you can have a Mormon boy and he will think you are wonderful." An idea leapt forward and onto Lisel's tongue. "When this war is over, Papa and Marta and Michael and I are going to America. You could come with us too, Grete. You could join our Church and come with us. There are lots of Mormon boys in Idaho; and when they see you, you will have to use a stick to keep them away."

Grete shook her head. "No. They will not want me when they know what I have done. When they know I can no longer have children."

"There are lots of children who need mothers. You do not have to give birth to all of them. The man who loves you will know that."

Conflicting emotions worked across Grete's face. Her pale brows came together in a frown and she rubbed away her tears with her wrists. "Perhaps if I had my child with me, perhaps if I had Joseph, that would be enough for a family."

Lisel smiled, relieved to see some hope return to Grete's face. "Perhaps it would."

"I must get Joseph from the Kurmack Home. We would be a family then." Her face brightened with a smile. For an instant, Grete resembled the schoolgirl who stood at the garden gate three years ago. She reached out and took Lisel's hands. "You have always been so good to me and I have been such trouble for you. I come here with gloom when you have your own sadness to live with. When you do not know if Michael is alive or dead." A chagrined look stole over her face. "I suppose I should not have spoken so bluntly."

Lisel made a helpless shrug. "But it is the truth. We do not know. We hope Michael is alive, but how can we wish him a prisoner of the Russians? And death? I wonder if that is such a horrible thing."

Grete's look was wistful. "It seems to me maintaining life is harder than dying." Her hand went to her forehead. "I am so very tired today. Last night, the house next door caught fire and we had to form a bucket chain to put it out. It took almost all night, then we had to help dig out some of the people who were trapped in the basement. Three of them were dead."

Lisel stared at Grete in shock, understanding now Grete's disheveled appearance and her embittered attitude. "That must have been horrible."

Grete smiled sadly. "For the dead it was easy. For those of us still alive it was horrible." Grete leaned forward and pressed her cheek against Lisel's. "You are a good friend, Lisel," she said, and then walked tiredly up the street.

Slowly, Lisel mounted the front steps, then the stairs to the flat. Where had the idea of going to America after the war come from? She had not allowed herself to think of that long ago dream; yet, somewhere in the corners of her mind the dream had not faded. Perhaps she needed to cling to it now with all of Germany going hungry, Berlin in ruins, her family torn apart, and her friends dispirited. It was the fulfillment of the promise in 2nd Nephi. She paused with her hand on the doorknob. Perhaps going to America would be possible. And Grete, too? Why not? If, at the end of the war, they were all still alive.

She found Papa on his knees, combing out the fringes on the carpet, softly humming "Lead, Kindly Light." He got stiffly to his feet. "I am so glad you are here, little one. I was afraid you would be too late. We are to have a visit by the brethren this afternoon."

Lisel hung her coat and hat on the pegs behind the door. "I suppose they will want to know if any branch members are in need after last night."

"Yes, that is probably so. We have not had members in our home in weeks, so this will be a special treat. I only wish we had something special to offer them."

Lisel put her arms around Papa and smiled up at him. "They will have to be satisfied with our special company."

Hans Ritter and Otto Sauerbruch showed up within the hour. Papa insisted Brother Ritter take the easy chair while he sat thirteen-year-old Otto Sauerbruch and Lisel on the sofa and he sat on one of the wooden chairs from the table.

Brother Ritter, a man in his late fifties, was of moderate size, though he had a wide chest and broad shoulders that made him appear to swagger when he walked. He had lost much of his still-dark hair. The wrinkles around his eyes and mouth were not so much wrinkles as soft folds of loose skin. With his wide, shallow-socketed eyes and thick, shapeless lips, his face resembled a kindly grandmother more than a master electrician in one of the largest electrical companies in Berlin.

Papa and Brother Ritter spoke of Michael and Russia, of Marta in Frankfurt, and Lisel's job with Erwerts. Papa reassured Brother Ritter that the Spanns were doing well, had adequate food and warmth—the usual report members made to branch officials whether it was true or not.

Lisel glanced at Otto. He was an awkward boy. Arms too long, legs too long, Adam's apple too big. Lisel could not remember his family being active, but because of bombings and evacuations and relocations, it was difficult to keep in touch with all the branch members.

Brother Ritter told Papa the Lanzingers had been bombed out and Sister Lanzinger and the littlest boy killed. The Hohlweins had evacuated to the country to live with Brother Hohlwein's sister. And President Johst had been called up to join a unit in Africa.

Lisel saw Papa's eyebrows rise. "But who will replace President Johst?" he asked. Lisel saw the flush in Papa's cheeks and realized how important the answer to that question was. Besides Ernst Johst, Papa was the only Melchezidek Priesthood holder left in the Branch.

A smile stretched across Brother Ritter's face. A tic started at the corner of his lips and Lisel saw a faint nervousness there. "The District Presidency has considered the matter very carefully." Brother Ritter cleared his throat. "In some parts of the country our members are being molested because of their association with an American church. So in order that we may appear more German, the District Presidency has chosen a man who holds a Party office. Egon Sauerbruch has been called to be Branch President."

Egon Sauerbruch was a stiff, uncompromising man, born and bred anti-Semite, an early Nazi party member of much devotion. Lisel shuddered thinking Brother Sauerbruch might lead the Branch with as much devoted attention. She glanced at Papa.

He looked as if his face had frozen. Then one eyebrow lifted. "I did not know Brother Sauerbruch had been advanced in the Priesthood."

Brother Ritter's smile stretched even wider and he spread his hands. "Well, this being such a special situation, special considerations had to be made. So even though President Sauerbruch is still a Priest, he was thought to be the best man to handle the job." Again, the tic twitched at the corner of Brother Ritter's mouth. "That is, he is the best man since we have the problem of being associated with the enemy. You must see how this is the best thing to do."

Lisel saw the tell-tale color rise on Papa's throat. She knew he would have objections about such a decision but Papa was too discreet to raise the question.

Instead, Papa turned to Otto. "You must feel very blessed to have such a high honor bestowed on your family."

Otto shrugged. "Father thinks he is better than the Fuhrer now," he muttered.

Lisel gaped at Otto. For a boy to say such a thing about his father was insufferably disrespectful. She glanced at Papa. His face ran full red.

"There is one other thing, Brother Spann," Brother Ritter continued. "President Sauerbruch has ordered a minor change in our regular meeting. When everyone has been seated, he will enter and walk to the front of the room. He has asked that everyone rise and remain standing until he is seated."

"But that is an honor reserved for the Prophet!" Lisel exclaimed.

Brother Ritter's bulging eyes came to her. His smile was patronizing. "That may be so in the American church," he explained, "but since we have no longer a connection with America, our Branch President will serve in the capacity of our Prophet." Papa shifted on the wooden chair. His lips thinned. Lisel saw the restraint with which he struggled. "Has this change been presented to the District Presidency?"

Brother Ritter spread his hands. "You know how it is, communication being so difficult now, but we are certain it will be approved before our next meeting."

Lisel saw Papa relax. She knew he was certain the District President would never approve of such a change. Calling a Priest as Branch President was unusual in itself, but then that he should insist on being treated as the Prophet was unthinkable.

It was not for another three weeks before Papa and Lisel felt it safe to go to their Sunday meeting. With the RAF flying daylight raids, the streets were just as dangerous during the day as at night.

The chapel was the upstairs banquet room of a restaurant a half-hour from the apartment house. It was a delightful April morning and as the Spanns rounded the corner, they saw several of their fellow branch members standing in a group outside the restaurant door. They looked up when they saw the Spanns approach.

"Good morning," Papa said as he and Lisel shook hands all around the group.

"Have you heard they excommunicated Brother Thaelmann?" Sister Ranheim said, her voice low.

"Why no," Papa exclaimed. "For what reason is this done?"

Sister Ranheim glanced up and down the street then lowered her voice even more. "He refused to stand when President Sauerbruch entered the chapel. Brother Thaelmann said he only stood if President Grant entered the room. President Sauerbruch claimed Brother Thaelmann was trying to subvert the priesthood. So they excommunicated him."

"Has the District President heard of this?" Papa asked.

"We do not know," Sister Ranheim replied.

"But how could President Sauerbruch excommunicate someone without the District President knowing about it?"

The small group broke up, going in to the meeting, and leaving Lisel and Papa standing in the street. She looked up at him. "Could this be true?"

Papa's mouth drew down beneath his mustache. "It is a detestable thing but I fear it must be so."

"What shall we do?"

"I suppose we must decide which is more important. Do we protest and lose our membership in the Church? Or do we stand to please a puffed-up Nazi?"

Lisel frowned with surprise at the harshness of Papa's words. She put her hand on his arm. "Perhaps we should go back home."

Papa looked down at her. She saw the struggle of thought in his blue eyes. From upstairs the opening notes of the hymn, "Lead Kindly Light," floated down to them. Even as badly off-key as the piano was, the strains of the hymn brought a certain peace to the Sunday morning street.

Papa's face calmed. He put his hand over hers. "I spoke too quickly, little one. When the Church told us to obey our country's laws, some of us were not happy with those laws but we did it to show our obedience to the Prophet. When we raised our hands to support our district president we were also pledging obedience. Now we must show our support to a branch president with whom we do not agree. And we will also do that to show our obedience."

"But Papa, what he asks is not right," Lisel said.

"We will let the Lord judge that. But we will be obedient and we will trust that the Lord will not allow a leader to guide us into wickedness." Papa patted her hand. "Besides, this standing, is it so tremendous a sacrifice?"

Lisel shook her head. "No, I suppose it is not." But in her heart Lisel was not so sure.

The meeting went as it always had except for the one deviation. When President Sauerbruch entered, everyone, including Lisel and Papa, stood. As Lisel waited for President Sauerbruch to sit, she sent up a silent prayer. "Father, I do this not because I believe President Sauerbruch is taking the place of our Prophet but because I would be obedient to the leaders thou hast set in place over us."

Since the daylight bombing started, no one stayed after church to visit. But, on the way out, Sister Ranheim took Papa's arm and asked quietly, "May I speak to you, Brother Spann."

Lisel waited at the door and when Papa joined her, she saw his face was stiff and pale. An instinctive dread tightened around her heart like a tourniquet. "What is it, Papa?"

He put his hand, heavy, on her shoulder. She saw the tension in his jaw and the soberness in his eyes. "You must be brave, little one."

She pulled up her shoulders. "What is it?"

He swallowed hard. "It is Grete. She is . . ." Papa paused as if searching for an easier word. But Lisel had heard it too many times to have it softened by gentle terms.

"Grete is dead. Is that what you are trying to say?"

Stiffly, Papa nodded.

Outside the window, Lisel heard a sparrow chittering in the eaves. A breeze lifted the curtains at the window and brought in a gust of cold air . . . so cold, her hands felt icy . . . so icy, they numbed at the end of her arms—as if they did not belong to her. A question rose to the surface of her mind and she thought it strange she could be so intensely aware of the coldness in her hands and of the room and the breeze and the birds in the eaves and still think of a question about her best friend who was dead. "How?"

"Sister Ranheim said she was drowned."

Had she heard the word right? Drowned? Lisel thought it should have been "Crushed beneath a bombed building," or "Burned," or even "An illness." So many suffered from the diseases of malnutrition. Should she not have died of an illness? But drowned?

Lisel blinked and Papa's face came clear. "How did she drown?"

"I do not know. Sister Ranheim said she heard three days ago but knew none of the details."

Lisel tried to think of what she was doing three days ago. Nothing out of the ordinary. Going to work. Coming home. What was she doing while Grete was drowning?

"Lisel?"

"Yes, Papa?"

"Do you feel strong enough to go see Grete's mother?"

Lisel thought of Frau Dengler. First, her husband taken. Now Grete drowned. She would be alone. "Yes, I suppose we had better see Frau Dengler."

Lisel did not remember the walk to Frau Dengler's apartment which was only two blocks from the chapel. At the door, an unfamiliar woman answered. Frau Dengler had moved, she told them. After her daughter's burial service, Frau Dengler went to her niece's house in Dortmunde. That was all she knew.

On the stairs, Papa and Lisel met Berta Hiller coming up. Frau Hiller had been the Denglers' neighbor for many years and knew Lisel well enough to speak to her by name.

"Ah, Lisel, what a sad thing about Grete."

"Yes, we only heard today."

Frau Hiller spread her hands and then clasped them together in dismay. "Frau Dengler was so distraught she probably did not think to let you know, poor soul that she is, you see. But let us not stand here on the stairs, you must come in so we can talk."

Lisel and Papa followed Frau Hiller into her tiny, two-room apartment, immensely overcrowded with furniture that came from an obviously larger house. Frau Hiller gestured for the Spanns to sit on a pillow-strewn sofa. "I wish I had something to offer you," she lamented, "some tea or something."

"Your offer is enough," Papa replied and Frau Hiller colored.

She was a plump, short-legged woman who had an obvious vanity about her thick, wavy brown hair and her delicate, long-fingered hands.

"Our poor Grete," Frau Hiller shook her head and rubbed away the moisture at the corner of her eyes. "I weep whenever I think of her."

"If you will excuse our asking, Frau Hiller," Papa said, "we can find no one who can tell us about how Grete died."

Frau Hiller's gleaming eyes widened. "Why, it was because of her baby. At least that is what her mother thought. You see, lately Grete had been trying to get her baby back." Frau Hiller's face reddened. "You know which baby I mean. Anyway, Grete went back to the Kurmack home. They put her off and put her off until finally, last week, Grete found out the little boy had been taken by a family. The father was a high official in the Party, you see. And they told Grete she could not have him back."

Lisel thought of the last time she had seen Grete, how the thought of getting little Joseph had given Grete something to hope for. And then, to have that hope destroyed—how Grete must have grieved.

"But her drowning?" Lisel heard Papa question.

Frau Hiller's eyebrows rose. "Did you not know Grete committed suicide? She threw herself into the River Spree."

It came at Lisel like a doubled up fist. The impact was like a blow to her ribs. The air rushed out of her lungs in a long, wrenching sob.

"Oh heavens!" Frau Hiller exclaimed. Her hands fluttered like distressed birds. "Lisel dear, please do not weep so. I have never been very good with words; I have told you very badly. But please do not weep so."

Lisel felt Papa's arms around her, knew her head was on his shoulder, her cheek against his scratchy woolen jacket. But there was no comfort there. Not now. Not when she knew she had been responsible for Grete thinking she had to have her baby back. Responsible for Grete's death . . . now guilt lay so heavily across Lisel's heart, she wished it had been her at the bottom of the Spree instead of Grete.

She felt Papa stroking her hair. "Lisel," he said. He seemed to understand that she for some reason blamed herself.

Through a haze of pain, Lisel heard the echo of Papa's voice.

"Each of us is given an agency to act for ourselves, to make our own decisions. Grete made hers. I fear she may have made it when she was not in her right mind. But it was her decision. Had you known she would have done this thing, you would have risked your own life to save hers. Is that not true?"

Lisel nodded.

"Are you sure that would have been enough to save her?"

Lisel tried to answer but her thoughts could not fight themselves free of the guilt and misery that ensnared them. "I do not know," she finally said.

Lisel felt Papa's worn handkerchief as he pressed it into her hands. "You may never know, little one. Knowing is not always the key to understanding. Acceptance is."

Lisel lifted her head. Through the blur of her tears she saw Papa's saddened face. "This is a hard thing to accept," she said with a tight throat.

"Yes, Lisel. For those of us who are yet mortal, death can be a difficult thing. But in these moments we must remember death is not an ending, only a change—that our eternal lives go on and on. We must remember our Heavenly Father loves each of us. He sees our struggles and knows of our pain. Mine, yours, and Grete's, too. She is as precious to him as any one of his children; and perhaps, at this moment, she is even more precious because she has returned in such a tragic way. And because we understand the glorious plan of salvation, we know she is in his arms now, in his loving care now, and he will not allow her to go on living in endless eternal torment. He will allow her a healing and a blessed peace. A healing and a peace she may never have found here."

There was solace in Papa's tender voice, in his tender words. And a comforting spirit of affirmation filled Lisel's chest, spreading and spreading, like a ripple across a pond, clearing a new, calmer surface on her heart. The hot tears on her face cooled. "Oh Papa, I know you are right. How could I doubt?" She looked up and saw Frau Hiller's twisted face. "I am sorry Papa, Frau Hiller." She wiped at her wet cheeks with Papa's handkerchief. "I have embarrassed you."

"No, no, Lisel," Frau Hiller said. "Grief is a part of life. Something all of us must go through. I remember when I heard my nephew had died in Poland—"

The long wail of an air raid siren stretched across the sky.

"Oh heavens," Frau Hiller exclaimed. "In the middle of a Sunday afternoon!"

After the all clear, Papa and Lisel said good-bye to Frau Hiller, thanking her, and started the walk back to the tram stop. In the distance, they heard the bells of the fire truck and within a block of the restaurant where they had attended their meeting, Papa frowned up at the black smoke spiraling in ragged plumes. "Could our building have been hit?"

Lisel thought the loss of a building was of little consequence, but she did not say it. Instead she said, "If it is not, it is very near the restaurant."

But it was the restaurant—their chapel. Lisel and Papa watched from a distance as a band of volunteer firefighters darted about the burning building, over heaps of rubble in the street, calling and shouting, trying to keep the fire from spreading to nearby structures. There was not enough left of the restaurant worth the effort to save it.

On the breeze, a black-edged sheet of paper floated to Lisel's feet. She glanced down at it. It was a page from a hymn book. The hymn was one the congregation had never been allowed to sing because of its Jewish composer, Felix Mendelssohn. Even his name was required to be blacked out.

Lisel watched the page as it curled and smoldered.

We'll sing the songs of Zion,
Though now in distant lands,
Our harps shall not be lying
Untouched by skillful hands.

Lisel put her foot on the burning paper and ground it into the cobblestone.

Chapter 16

O N A LATE AFTERNOON EARLY THAT JUNE OF 1943, LISEL DIS-
covered Elsa Wrobel at the door. Her face was flushed and perspiration stood out on her forehead and lip. "I do not know what to
do," the older woman wailed.

Lisel's first thought was that something had happened to Herr
Wrobel. Lisel took her hands. "Try to catch your breath, then tell
me."

Frau Wrobel pressed her hands to her heart. "It is Frau Heidemann," she sobbed. "We were in line outside the grocer's. I am
afraid Frau Heidemann was not being so very circumspect. She
said some things. Treasonous things. Some men came and
arrested her." She began weeping again. "I dared not tell Gustav
but I did not know what to do. I thought perhaps you would know."

Lisel did not know. She was not surprised at the arrest, consid-
ering some of the things Frau Heidemann had said and done in
the past. Perhaps if Lisel knew where the men had taken Frau
Heidemann, she would know what could be done. "Do you know
who these men were? Were they SS?"

Frau Wrobel's lips trembled. "No, I believe they were from the
Office of Loyalty and Patriotism."

"Then perhaps that is not so bad."

The apartment house's front door banged and Lisel heard the
sounds of sharp footsteps on the stairs leading down to the basement. She and Frau Wrobel looked at each other, then ran to the
banister and peered down the stairwell. At the bottom they saw
Frau Heidemann juggling parcels while she struggled to unlock
her front door. They also heard her muttered swearing.

Frau Wrobel allowed a small "Oh," to escape and Frau Heidemann looked up. Her face was flushed, her lips tight, her mouse-brown hair in disarray.

"What has this country come to when a person cannot even stand on the street without being abducted by ruffians?" she demanded. Her lock clicked and she kicked open the door.

Frau Wrobel looked to Lisel with her eyes rounded with surprise. "How has this come to be?"

"I do not know, but if we ask now, we might hear the version closest to the truth."

They found Frau Heidemann putting away her purchases and slamming cupboard doors. She turned to them scarlet-faced. "A woman is not safe on the streets of her own city anymore—not with such riff-raff about! Big, strong men, too, who should be out defending our country instead of kidnapping women in broad daylight!"

"But I thought you had been arrested," Frau Wrobel objected. "You had been saying things for which people have been accused of treason."

"That is not true!" Frau Heidemann shot back.

"What was it you said?" Lisel broke in.

Frau Heidemann looked at her as if surprised to see her standing there.

"She said we should put Hitler in a tub of cement and drop him in the river, just like they do gangsters," Frau Wrobel explained.

"That was a misunderstanding," Frau Heidemann grumbled. "I did not say we should do that to Hitler. No one heard me say 'Hitler'. Everyone *assumed* I was talking about Hitler." She lifted her chin. "I was actually talking about Roosevelt." Frau Heidemann's mouth twitched sideways a little sheepishly. "As soon as I made that clear to the Overseer of Loyalty and Patriotism, he had to let me go. He even apologized."

Lisel began to laugh. Frau Wrobel looked abashed and faintly unconvinced.

Throughout the summer of 1943, bombing raids increased. By July, more than a million homes and apartments had been destroyed. From the cities, people fled into the countryside. Bombs that hit the Tiergarten Zoo released tigers into the streets and alligators into the Landswehr Canal.

In August, the attacks came both night and day. At night the sky glittered with gunfire; and during the day, the sun was blacked out by smoke that layered everything with soot and ashes.

Looting, which began as a consequence of the bombing, became a common plague. Placards with red lettering in German, French, Russian, and Polish went up all over Berlin and warned of severe punishments to be meted out to plunderers. Those caught were sentenced to death.

By the end of the summer, everyone knew the supreme effort would not be enough to save the Reich. Berliners received flyers in their mailboxes advising them to evacuate to the country. Few did.

The night of November 22, 1943, the beginning of the RAF's Battle of Berlin, came like the end of the world. The morning of November 23, Berlin seemed one vast heap of rubble. Half of the downtown area was destroyed and a quarter of the residential areas were hit. The entire top floor of the Spanns' apartment house was gone. The exterior wall in Lisel's bedroom was blown out and the ceiling in Papa's broken in.

Special civil defense troops, made up of volunteers including women and the elderly, were formed to assist with repair work. They put out fires, pulled down walls of severely damaged buildings, covered unexploded bombs with bales of paper, installed double fauceted hand pumps in the streets to accommodate those who lost water service, helped slap together evacuee housing in the country, and set up centers for the homeless and displaced. Yet, for all of that, they could not keep up with the damage done by the attacks.

The volunteers also had the task of rescuing people trapped beneath devastated buildings. For some there was no rescue, however. The dead were laid out, row upon row, on gymnasium floors for relatives to claim. Others who were trapped could not be rescued and neighbors, relatives and passers-by heard with horror the weeping and knocking and moaning until there was no more sound.

Papa and Lisel considered themselves fortunate. Their precious genealogical records were safe, they had water and a gas jet with which to cook, and they were still alive. By bartering their sofa, they were able to replace their bedding with cots and straw-tick mattresses which they installed in the living room. But they were able to replace only a portion of their destroyed clothing and personal effects.

Many people lost their places of work, but the Erwert's Printing Company still stood and continued to put out posters, flyers, and pamphlets. The S-Bahn, the elevated train, was still running but other methods of transportation were unreliable so Lisel had to walk most of the way to work down icy streets. In the heavily bombed areas, government officials tried to bolster morale by putting up posters that proclaimed "One Struggle, One Victory," and "Adolf Hitler is Victory." The next day the posters were scrawled over with the words, "End the War!" and "This Mess is Hitler's Fault!" Walking through those streets made Lisel's legs heavy with sorrow; her head light with hunger.

Though the Spanns had potatoes Papa had planted in the back garden the summer before, their daily diet had come down to barley mush and dehydrated vegetables.

Rumors came wholesale. Brilliant German scientists were perfecting a secret weapon that would save them all. Hitler had an unrevealed plan of attack—they must wait for the most opportune time. The rumor that drove all that speculation was that the Russians were coming. Everyone knew the Russians, if allowed into the Reich, would strike with a fearsome vengeance.

The winter brightened when Marta received permission to come home for a visit. She was thin and threadbare just like everyone else in Germany, but she seemed cruelly older than her twenty-one years. Her soft brown eyes were weary and full of sadness and her complexion was pale. Her brown hair, though neat and clean, was lusterless.

Despite the unappetizing food, the heatless, cramped apartment and the bombing raids, the Spanns celebrated their reunion with joy and laughter. They only fell silent remembering Michael.

Marta talked of her coworkers at the hospital, her new friends, patients, and branch members in Frankfurt, some of whom, when they found themselves homeless, moved into the former Mission Home.

They talked about food, remembering meals of meat and

cheese, fresh vegetables and fruit, eggs and butter, and desserts made entirely of sugar.

And they spoke with hope of the end of the war and going to America and being sealed in the temple. And Marta talked of Grant and the time when he could come for her.

For Lisel, it was as if some of her dream had returned and she could, once again, imagine her family around her, the blessings of the temple enfolding them . . . and peace. For those three days, she closed the door on the actuality that life in Germany was an uncertain endeavor. No one knew from day to day who would be taken and who left behind. As Marta prepared to depart, the Spanns shared their final family prayer. In that precious, sacred moment together Lisel fought back an almost suffocating sense of foreboding. This time would be the last time.

The influenza epidemic of 1943-44 hit hard. Nearly everyone was undernourished and few medicines were available. Lisel missed a week of work but Papa's bout hung on longer. He developed a wheezing cough Dr. Kettel said was a result of the disease and the damage done to Papa's lungs when he suffered gas poisoning in the Great War.

Papa did not complain but Lisel saw his flushed and perspiring face and the chills that made him grit his teeth and huddle beneath his blanket. She sent out word among the branch members that Papa needed a priesthood blessing, but no one came. All of them were either in the military, displaced, or dead. And though Papa said not to, Lisel worried at work, even knowing Frau Heidemann would look in on him several times during the day.

One day, early in February, she came home to find Frau Heidemann and Dr. Kettel bent over Papa. "What is it?" she cried when Frau Heidemann blocked her from running to his side.

Frau Heidemann put a finger to her lips and drew Lisel across the room. "I found him much worse this afternoon," she whispered. "He was hot and in a delirium. I thought it best to call Dr. Kettel."

Lisel looked past Frau Heidemann. Dr. Kettel had turned Papa over and was thumping his back and frowning. Lisel's knees began to tremble so she could not stand on her legs. She lowered herself onto one of the dining room chairs with her hands clasped between her knees and waited for Dr. Kettel to finish.

Dr. Kettel moved Papa onto his back and pulled the blankets over him. Dr. Kettel rose with a heavy sigh and came to Lisel. "It is the old man's friend," he said. "Pneumonia."

Living with the menace from the skies and fearing starvation at every turn was nothing to the panic Lisel felt at that word.

"I fear it is a bad case," Dr. Kettel was saying, "and unfortunately there are no medicines available. But there is much we can do to help your father overcome this illness."

Lisel heard his voice as a faraway echo. She saw his frown. "Do you understand me?"

Lisel nodded.

"We need to keep his body temperature as normal as possible. If his fever rises, we must try to lower it by cooling him. If it goes down, we must warm him. You must change his bedding if it is damp. Give him a little liquid; water is best, especially if he is overheated. If he asks for food, let him have an unspiced broth. Keep the room as quiet and as dim as possible. An uninterrupted night's sleep would also help if you can find a way to convince the bombers to stay away."

Lisel saw Papa's pale, sweat-slick face, his glassy eyes, and heard the rattle in his breathing.

Dr. Kettel was frowning at Lisel again. "Can you manage this?"

"I will help her," Frau Heidemann put in.

"Good." Dr. Kettel picked up his case and moved to the door. Frau Heidemann followed, leaving Lisel behind on the sofa. "I will be back later this evening."

Papa seemed no better after Dr. Kettel's second visit that evening and Lisel sat up with her father that night, tending to him as Dr. Kettel had told her to. When the air raid came, Frau Heidemann and Elsa Wrobel offered to help move Papa into the basement but Lisel was afraid of taking him into that damp place. Instead, she sent the satchel of genealogy with Frau Heidemann. "Do not worry," Lisel told them. "The Lord will watch over us."

Frau Heidemann grunted. "I trust your American God also understands German prayers."

Lisel sat through the night of thunder and explosion with her arm thrown across Papa's chest, her cheek pressed to his, her lips to his ear. "It will not last long," she whispered. "Do not be frightened." But Lisel was not sure if she spoke to Papa or to herself.

Sometime in the night, Papa became delirious, calling out to unseen soldiers and shouting orders. In the morning, he was calmer. By mid-morning, Papa's temperature leveled and Dr. Kettel seemed somewhat satisfied.

"This is a good sign," he told Lisel, "but you must continue to be vigilant."

That afternoon, while Lisel was sponging Papa's face, he blinked. Then his blue eyes focused on her. "Lisel?" The word was but a reedy whisper.

Relief rose in Lisel's heart like a fountain. "Papa," she cried. "Oh, Papa. I was so afraid!"

"I had a wonderful dream." His voice was weary and faint. "There was a green meadow and a stream of clear water and trees in the distance. I could hear the birds. It was so beautiful."

"What can I do for you? Is there something you want?"

"Some water. I would like some cool water."

Lisel ran to the kitchen and took the bottle she kept on the ledge outside the window. Carefully, she spooned the water between his parched lips.

"How long?" he asked.

"Only since yesterday afternoon."

He nodded, then closed his eyes.

Frightened that he might slip away again, Lisel said, "Frau Heidemann said to tell you, when you are better she will roast a chicken for you. She said she would go to the country and steal the chicken herself."

The corner of Papa's mouth twitched with a smile. "Tell her I will look forward to it." His eyes opened a little. "I think I will sleep now. Do not worry."

"I love you, Papa."

Dr. Kettel was encouraged by Papa's small recovery but cautioned Lisel that his heart may have been affected. "You have nursed him well and he may have passed the worst but you must remember he is still very ill. He will continue to need constant care."

Papa improved each day. When he was awake, Lisel read to him from his worn scriptures. The sacred words seemed to ease his discomfort more than any other thing she did for him.

By the third day, he could take a little vegetable broth; and by the fifth day he was strong enough to sit for a few minutes. During that time, Frau Heidemann or Elsa Wrobel came to sit with Papa so Lisel could rest.

Lisel awoke one afternoon to voices; Papa and Frau Heidemann were talking.

"I have such fears for her." Papa's weakened voice. "If I am gone, how will she live? In wars, people alone are the most vulnerable. And if the Russians come—"

"Do not worry, Joseph. If you are gone I will see to it she goes to Marta. She will not be alone."

Lisel sucked in a shocked breath. How could Frau Heidemann speak so plainly to such a sick man?

"You have been a good neighbor," Papa said. "I would have no cause to worry if she is in your hands."

Lisel sat up and pushed the hair from her eyes. "Is Papa awake?" She tried to control the distress in her voice so Papa would not know she had heard.

Frau Heidemann smiled at her. "Oh yes, very much awake and asking for his roasted chicken."

Lisel went to him and took his hand. Each day he seemed stronger. Why did he talk of death? "Would you like something to eat?"

Papa smiled. "Yes, perhaps a little more of that delicious broth."

That night, he awoke Lisel. At first she was alarmed.

"Do not be frightened, little one. I only wanted to speak with you."

Lisel wrapped her blanket around her and sat down next to his cot. "What is it Papa?"

"Do you remember just after I was very ill I told you I had a dream?"

Lisel nodded. "The one about the meadow and the stream?"

"Yes. I had that dream again. I dreamed I was standing in the meadow. The green grass was high and full of wild flowers dancing in the breeze. A stream of the clearest, purest water flowed near my feet. At the edge of the meadow were tall, leafy trees and I heard the birds singing in happy voices. The sky was, oh, so blue, Lisel. Like it used to be before this war began." He paused. Lisel saw his chin begin to quiver, heard anguish crack in his voice. "Oh, that I have lived to see this day!"

Lisel laid her head against Papa's shoulder and held him close to her. Tears burned her eyes. "The sky will be blue again soon, Papa. I know it will."

She felt his hand on her braids. "Yes, of course, little one."

Lisel raised her head and smiled into his face. "Tell me more of your dream."

Though tears glittered on his eyelashes, Papa's eyelids lifted, wistfully. "In my dream, a path wound through the trees and skirted the meadow. It came up to an arched bridge made of gray stone. It was glorious to behold. As I stood there, I saw a figure come along the path through the trees. A figure in radiant white. She was still far from me but I knew her at once. I knew her as I have seen her every day in my memories."

Lisel heard the hard swallow in his throat, the struggle over his words, the catch in his voice. "It was your mother, Lisel. How beautiful she was. Her sweet face was full of peace. And she was smiling in that gentle way. That way that told you she loved you. And you had no doubt."

Tears welled up in Lisel's eyes as she remembered that lovely, tender smile.

"I wanted to go to her but my feet were like lead and I could not cross the bridge. I called out but she did not answer. She only continued to come closer. Still smiling. Then, she stopped. I could not go to her and she could come no closer."

Gently, Papa put his fingers beneath Lisel's chin and lifted her face. "The next time I dream this dream, little one, your mother will lift her hand to beckon to me and I shall cross that bridge." Lisel frowned, uncertain for a moment.

"But if you cross, that means you will die."

"Yes, little one. That is what I mean."

Lisel felt a chill up her spine. "But you cannot leave me!" She threw her arms around Papa's neck and pressed her face, hard, into his shoulder. "I cannot live without you!"

Papa patted her shoulder. "Yes, you will live without me, as all children must someday live without their parents. It is the natural course of life. I only tell you now because there are things I must do. I do not know when the dream will come again but I want to be ready—with no regrets. How I wish Michael could be here. And Marta. But how grateful I am for you, little one. How I love you. But I must ask something of you."

Lisel looked up at Papa and choked back a sob. "Anything Papa."

"Tomorrow, I will give you a father's blessing. This will be the last one—"

Lisel sobbed. "No!"

"Yes," Papa insisted. "And since it will be the last, I would make it one of great significance, one that will carry you through the rest of your life. I want you to think carefully about the blessings you desire under my hands. Whatever you ask, I will give you."

"I would ask that you stay."

"Even if I do not wish to stay?"

Lisel searched Papa's face. She knew he loved her. But now, looking into his pain-filled, world-weary eyes she knew his leaving was not a betrayal of that love, only a choice of rest and peace. Was her fear of loss more important? She felt very selfish then, but a calm assurance enveloped her. "No, Papa, I will not ask you to stay. I cannot. I am not mightier than the Lord nor will I question his will or your desires."

Papa nodded with a tired sigh. "You are an obedient young woman, Lisel. I greatly admire your courage and faith. Now, I would ask another favor of you."

"What is it?"

"Would you sing to me?"

Lisel's mouth dropped open. "But Papa, you know my voice. I cannot sing."

"To me, you have the most lovely voice in the world and tonight I would hear it. Sing to me. A hymn. Would you sing, 'Lead, Kindly Light'?"

So Lisel sang, holding her father's withered hand and watched until he fell into a tranquil sleep.

The next morning, Papa's color was better, though he seemed tired and preoccupied. Lisel was afraid he would ask what blessing she desired. But he did not. Instead, he asked for the Wrobels.

Elsa greeted Lisel with a warm smile but Gustav refused to acknowledge her. They sat down on the chairs Lisel had placed next to Papa's cot.

"How are you, Joseph?" Elsa asked.

"I am well for an old man," Papa answered. "But I fear I may not be with you for long."

Elsa reached out and took Papa's hand. "You must not say such things."

Papa smiled gently. "I must say such things because I do not wish to leave owing any account." He looked to Gustav. "We have been neighbors for nearly five years now. Some people said you came to this house to spy on us." Lisel saw Herr Wrobel's jaw tighten.

"For myself," Papa continued, "I do not care why you came. But I cannot, in good spirit, leave without asking, most humbly, for your forgiveness."

Lisel felt a rush of surprise. For what reason should Papa ask forgiveness? Was *he* not the wronged one? She saw Herr and Frau Wrobel start.

"But Joseph, it is we who should have, long ago, asked your forgiveness for what we did. Now, we know how wrong we were."

"That does not excuse my anger toward you," Papa said. "I am no longer angry but I have not told you this. I have allowed you to believe there was bad blood between us. Perhaps there was. But, for myself, there is no longer the anger I once felt. And perhaps when we meet on the other side of this life, we will meet as beloved friends."

Lisel put her fingers over her lips and squeezed her eyes shut to hold in the tears. When she looked up she saw Elsa also weeping and Gustav blinking back the moisture in his eyes. He reached out to Papa and took his hand.

"How foolish I have been." Herr Wrobel's voice splintered with emotion. "We have known nothing but kindness from you and we have repaid you with the thing we knew would hurt you the most. We separated your family. The greatest guilt is on us. It is we who should beg forgiveness from you."

"I bear no grudge," Papa said.

"Then I swear this thing to you now," Herr Wrobel added.

"Even as your daughter returned our son to us, she shall become our daughter. If you should die and we should survive you, she shall have a home with us and we will cherish her as you would."

Papa's glistening eyes came to Lisel. She read exultant joy there. He reached toward her and she went to him. He placed her hand into Herr Wrobel's. "I place in you, my beloved friends, my greatest trust."

Both Herr and Frau Wrobel embraced Lisel and she them. They drew apart and found Papa had slumped back against his pillow, his eyes closed.

"Are you all right, Papa?" Lisel asked.

He nodded. "Just a little tired."

"We will leave," Frau Wrobel said and bent and kissed Papa on the forehead.

Papa slept the rest of the afternoon and Lisel sat at his side and watched over him. She had no fear he would slip away from her in his sleep now. Not while he had not yet given her the blessing. That assurance kept her from thinking about what to ask for. As long as he did not ask, Papa was safely with her.

He awoke early that evening and seemed much improved. After he finished the bowl of vegetable broth, he lifted his eyes and asked, "Have you determined a blessing for yourself, little one?"

Lisel felt her heart stop. She paused midway between his cot and the kitchen, her back to him. Standing there, an eternity passed, and she hung on to the time she would not have to speak, would not have to let Papa go. At last she said, "It is hard to know what to ask for."

"Then perhaps you should think of the blessings I have given in the past and consider which impressed you the most."

She faced him. Lisel knew which blessing had touched her most. "It was not one given to me," she said. "Do you remember the blessing you gave Michael the first time he came home from the military?"

"Yes."

"I remember feeling Mama was here, too." Lisel studied the bowl in her hands. It was the last of Mama's china with the rosebuds around the rim. "That blessing was a great comfort to me, too."

"If it had not been for that blessing, we may not have been

prompted to collect our genealogy. What favors we have had from that, even through these years. And because of that blessing, I know your brother still lives and is being cared for." His look grew wistful for a moment. "Would you like a similar blessing?"

Lisel gripped the bowl, gripping the moment. At last she nodded. "Yes," she whispered. "That is the one."

"I will think about it for awhile."

Lisel moved around the flat carefully for the next hour, thinking Papa had again fallen asleep and fearing to awaken him. There had been no air raid that day and Lisel prayed for a quiet night. She lit the Hindenburg lamp and set it in the middle of the dining table.

"Lisel," Papa called softly. "Come here to me."

In the dim candlelight, Lisel knelt next to Papa's cot as he placed his hands on her head. They were so thin, almost weightless.

"Lisel Elsbeth Spann, by the authority of the sacred Melchizedek Priesthood which has been conferred upon me, I place my hands upon your head and pray for the Holy Spirit to guide me in giving this last blessing to you, my beloved daughter and companion. I pray that I may give you the blessing you need to see you through the trials of the rest of your life here on this earth until you, your parents, your sister and brother, and those others whom you so dearly love will be united in a glorious reunion."

Lisel expected him to pause here, waiting for the promptings as he usually did; but this time he went on. "I begin by telling you, you will survive the trials that are before you. You are needed to serve the Lord in many callings, the most important of which is to rise up as a mother in Israel. You will minister, not only to the members of your family, but to many others in need, sacrificing gladly to help fulfill those needs. You will be an instrument in helping to build Zion. This will be a great blessing to you but it will only come about by your diligence and faith and willingness to endure."

For Lisel, her entire existence came down to this moment. It was a familiar sensation, etched in other loving memories of other sacred blessings. Papa's voice in her ears, the touch of his hands on her head, and the hallowed spirit glowing within the room. The words wrote themselves into her heart.

"I admonish you to make the scriptures your constant companion. Turn to them often and you will have a sweet spirit of peace and comfort. Pray without ceasing with your heart and your voice. Do not hesitate to ask for those things you need and the Lord will lead you. Thank the Lord for the wonderful blessings of the gospel in your life, for your testimony, and for the great blessing of being allowed to live on this earth at this time."

Lisel flinched. Surely Papa could not mean that her life was a blessed one? Was he ill again? Fevered and wandering in his mind? She longed to reach up and touch his face.

"Now, my precious little one, you must bear your trials with humility and faith and endurance. Remember always God's great love for you. Christ's wondrous sacrifice for you. In your darkest hour you will be led and sustained and encircled about by the arms of his love."

Lisel could feel Papa's hands tremble and, for an instant, wondered if he were too ill to continue. Then she knew the trembling from his hands came not of weakness but strength and power. The spiritual power ran from his hands into her body, filling her chest, expanding her heart until she felt she could not breathe; need not breathe.

"Through whatever deprivation and affliction you must endure, remember he will lead you. Your family, though they be in spirit, will watch over you and be with you though your life be in peril.

"Remember all these things. Remember how your mother and I love you with our whole hearts. Your sister and brother love you. Know that we will love you through all eternity."

Tears, brought up by a spirit of great tenderness, burned Lisel's eyelids and trickled down her cheeks. Quietly, she wiped them away with her fingertips.

"And though we will be parted from you, we will pray for you always; and if you endure, we will be reunited in a better time and a better place and through the blessings of the temple, will never be separated again."

As with Michael's blessing, Lisel had a sense of her family, together again and whole, shining white, arms around each other, smiling into each other's eyes. Beyond that sacred circle was another circle. Grandparents, great-grandparents, aunts, uncles and cousins extending as far as she could comprehend. Lisel was filled with an overwhelming sense of oneness, of wholeness, of completeness—of total peace.

"Now, my beloved daughter, go forth with gratitude and rejoicing in your heart for the great blessings of the gospel. The Lord loves you and is joyful because of your willingness to serve him. He will lead you. The righteous desires of your heart will be granted to you. Remember these most precious things and cherish them always in your heart. Remember the testimony of your mother. Remember the testimony of your father.

"I humbly pronounce these blessings on you as your loving father and beseech the Lord to fulfill them as well as extend blessings to my other beloved children who are not present. I bless them that they will know my love for them and that I will always pray for them. I ask for these things in the name of Jesus Christ. Amen."

Lisel lifted her head. Through a blur of tears she looked into Papa's face. In the dimness, it seemed to be lighted from within. He smiled briefly through his own tears then wearily sank back onto his pillow. "I will sleep for awhile now."

Lisel wanted to stop him, fearing the dream would take him. Papa must have sensed her fear. "Do not worry, little one."

"I love you, Papa."

It was late into the night when he awoke again. When he called out to Lisel, his voice was but a whisper. She read to him for awhile by the dim light of the Hindenburg lamp, then, as he requested, sang his favorite hymn, "Lead, Kindly Light," until he slipped into a peaceful sleep.

With her hand still in his and reluctant to leave his side, Lisel sat beside his cot with her head on his mattress and slept.

Lisel awoke again a little later to the touch of his caressing hand on her hair. But when she lifted her head she saw she was mistaken. Her hand was beneath his fingers, which were cold now but at rest at last.

Chapter 17

MARTA COULD NOT COME HOME UNTIL TWO DAYS AFTER Papa's funeral. Silently, she and Lisel sorted through his few belongings. Not wanting to sell or barter Papa's clothing, they gave most of it to Herr Wrobel, wrapped the last of Mama's china, sold the furniture, and moved Lisel and the satchel containing their genealogy and Papa's scriptures down to the basement.

Marta promised to look for housing. "I will let you know when you are to come," she told Lisel. "We will hope it will be soon, though lodging space is just as rare in Frankfurt as it is in Berlin."

Living with Frau Heidemann and the Wrobels made parts of Lisel's life easier. By pooling their incomes and ration points, they ate better than people living alone or in pairs and they could afford more coal for heat, although, for Lisel, the basement seemed always cold.

Lisel was grateful for the company but, late at night, the sense of aloneness and despair tightened around her chest so that the rising and falling of normal breath became painful. During the day, her grief dragged at her shoulders and weighted her legs so that any kind of movement was like trying to walk upstream in a torrent. Her only relief came in prayer and scriptures—that sacred place she fled to when her pain threatened to overwhelm.

At first, she felt uncomfortable reading her scriptures in front of the others. Yet, she found Frau Heidemann and the Wrobels respectful of her worship and they even tolerated her soft singing when she sought to console herself. Every day, the one hope that buoyed Lisel was that she might receive word from Marta to come to Frankfurt where they could be a family again.

That spring was long and exceptionally cold; and even when, at last, the weather did began to warm, there were neither flowers nor birds. Most of the trees had been shattered in the bombing or cut down for fuel. In the streets, there were no children laughing, no barking dogs. The sky was a stinking, greasy dome of black smoke.

The talk on the street, on the radio, and in the papers was increasingly of invasion. To the east, the Russians had already crossed the Polish border and it was only a matter of time before the Allies came from the west. Day after day came and went in unending waiting. The talk was of "getting even with the Americans." "We will throw the Anglos into the ocean!" many declared. Everyone hoped when the Allies were routed on the Atlantic front, the tide of the war would turn in Germany's favor.

But Lisel knew better. She kept that knowledge to herself, however, and wished the invasion over with. "Please hurry. I am so sick of this war," she said to herself again and again.

During air raids at work, Lisel huddled in the cellar beneath the print room. Everywhere she stepped or turned, were bottles and buckets and pans and pitchers of water—in case the building caught fire. And, on orders of Herr Erwert, everyone had to sit on the floor with their backs to the wall. Then, when the first explosions were heard, everyone had to lean forward, breathing very carefully, and press their hands against their stomachs. Herr Erwert insisted this exercise would keep one's lungs from tearing. Lisel did not see the use of it, but she did it anyway. Herr Erwert was her employer after all.

In Frau Heidemann's flat, there were not so many rituals. Since it was her home, she insisted everyone sit on chairs, if it was possible. But since there were sometimes strangers from the street joining them, there were not always enough places to sit.

One of the strangers told of a safety device, wrapping a dampened cloth over the mouth and nose to prevent the damage of inhaling smoke and particles. From then on, Frau Heidemann and the Wrobels tied wet tea towels over their faces during air raids. In the dark, they looked like a trio of thieves.

At last, when news of the June sixth invasion at Normandy reached the Berliners, many cheered and called for revenge. Lisel heard the news with relief. It would not be long now. Marta would come home. And Michael. And Kurt. Then Grant would come and they would all go to America, to Salt Lake City. Never again would she be cold or hungry or frightened or alone. They would live in Zion in continual righteousness and peace.

On June 21, 1944, in retaliation for the Nazis' use of long-range guns on England, the worst daylight raid came over Berlin. It lasted for more than two hours. Afterward, ash and soot and plaster dust coated everything. The streets were two feet deep in rubble. The only light in the smoke-engulfed city came from the brilliant flames of unchecked fires. It was like some gothic hell.

Morale plummeted. Then came the assassination attempt on Hitler. His death would mean certain defeat. There were rumors of civil war. Rumania fell to the Russians.

Though a few cinemas, which were not greatly damaged, continued to show movies, all other entertainment stopped. Radio stations still functioned; however, listeners were able to hear little because of the Allied jamming of the signals. Ironically, at the end of the radio day, the German stations always managed to get through Maria von Schmedes singing, "Another Beautiful Day Draws to Its Close."

Railway and postal services were either curtailed or cut altogether. Sometimes Lisel went for a week or more without a letter from Marta. Lisel forced herself not to think of the possible. Marta had been killed in an attack, crushed beneath a building, stricken with a disease. At last, when Lisel did hear, she was relieved. Marta's letters offered little to hope for, however. She was still looking for a place in Frankfurt but housing was almost impossible to find. "You should go anyway," Frau Heidemann insisted. "This city is no place for a girl."

Lisel shrugged and reminded Frau Heidemann that being twenty-one no longer classified her as a girl. "Besides, who would keep *you* from getting into trouble?"

"That's right," Frau Heidemann scowled. "Your presence limits my activities. It must be all those prayers you say, all those hymns you sing. I am not nearly so tempted anymore."

Lisel smiled her disbelief. "Anyway, I have a job here, at least I am making some money. I would have nothing in Frankfurt."

Then the publishing industry failed. Nine out of ten magazines and newspapers stopped publication. There was less work at Erwert's. Lisel's hours were reduced as well as her wages. But Lisel decided some money was better than no money, so she stayed in Berlin.

At the first of August, the Russians crossed the Vistula River in Poland and a month later the Americans reached the German border at Trier.

One morning, that September of 1944, Elsa Wrobel complained of being too tired to get up. She lay in her darkened room for two days. "I'll be all right if I can just rest a little."

The third day she developed a fever and was delirious the fourth. Lisel, Frau Heidemann, and Herr Wrobel stood by in helplessness. Dr. Kettel had been called up weeks before and the pharmacies were all but abandoned by their owners. The three did what they could to strengthen Frau Wrobel but it was not enough. She died quietly on the fifth day.

They buried her, wrapped in one of their precious blankets, in the back garden near the stump of the shattered peach tree. It was horrible, putting her in the ground that way. Lisel remembered what a fuss Frau Heidemann had made when Herr Muller buried Maxi in the garden. Now they were burying humans there, and no one thought anything about it at all. Oddly, the closeness of Frau Wrobel's grave seemed to comfort Herr Wrobel.

For weeks afterward, Lisel worried for his life. At last, he began to return to them though he was, no longer, the same man. Aged and frequently lost in his mind, he sat staring at nothing, speaking to no one.

The Home Guard was established in October. It was a roundup of all men between sixteen and sixty to combat the coming invasion forces. Some Berliners wondered bitterly if this was Hitler's wonder weapon—units made up of the old, the lame, and the children.

It was the Home Guard, however, that healed a part of Herr Wrobel's despair. Because of his past history in the military and his support of the Party, he was put in charge of fifty men whose duty it was to begin fortifying the city of Berlin.

In the middle of October, the Bestial Bolsheviks, as the "Volkischer Beobacter" called the Russians, crossed into the Reich.

On the twenty-fourth, Aachen, the old imperial capital of Germany and the seat of Charlemagne, surrendered to the U. S. First Army—the first German city to fall into Allied hands.

Then the Russians invaded the German city of Nemmersdorf. They crucified the women and children who had remained in the city. The prisoners of the concentration camp at Nemmersdorf were so horrified at the Russians' cruelty, that they broke out of their prison and tried to protect the townspeople. The prisoners were also executed.

Germans, fleeing before the Russians, poured into Berlin bringing stories of rape and torture and murder. Frau Heidemann shook her head. "Well, what else can we expect. Did we not set the example?"

Christmas of 1944 brought a renewed optimism. A great battle, staged in the forest of the Ardennes was being waged against the Allies and won by the Germans. A victory seemed imminent. Berliners saw it as a reprieve. For the first time in many years, Christmas was a time of good spirits and confidence. And for the first time in many years, meat and a larger variety of food appeared in the markets. Frau Heidemann, who always seemed to hear all the gossip, said it was because Germany was bringing its produce from outlying areas to prevent it from falling into enemy hands.

The second week of January of 1945, Berliners heard the news with shock. The Ardennes offensive had failed, the western front collapsed. The ring was steadily closing in around them.

German ships carrying thousands of refugees across the Baltic Sea were sunk by Russian submarines. Train yards and railroad lines were destroyed by Russian fire. Germans fleeing the Russian onslaught in the east were coming into Berlin on foot, starved and frozen.

A refugee mother and her two small boys took shelter in what was left of the Spanns' abandoned apartment. Frau Kramer said her husband had been hanged by the Russians in their own barn. Her two older daughters were dragged away. They found the oldest partially buried in a snow bank two miles from their home. They did not know the fate of the younger.

Frau Heidemann drew Lisel aside. "You must leave here. There will be no protection for you at all if the Russians come."

Herr Wrobel overheard. "The Russians will not come," he insisted. "They will be turned back before they get to the gates of Berlin. We have important plans even now being formulated. Plans to make this city a great fortress." He lowered his voice. "And a marvelous secret weapon that will vaporize the Russian forces. You will see; they will not come."

"What eyewash!" Frau Heidemann retorted. "Everyone talks of a secret weapon but has anyone seen one? Why has it not been used? And as for this city being a fortress. That is rubbish! We do not even have a military unit to guard us, only old men and dotards. It would take the Russians just an hour and five minutes to get into Berlin. An hour to stop laughing and five minutes to push aside the Home Guard."

Herr Wrobel's face purpled and Lisel saw the flash of obstinate anger behind his wire-rimmed glasses. "You are not a patriotic German!" he blurted.

"No, only a realistic one."

Lisel broke in. "If the danger is that grave, we must all leave here. We must all go to Frankfurt.

"That would be pure cowardice," Herr Wrobel pronounced.

"But, Gustav, what about Lisel? Did we not promise to take care of her? I promised Joseph I would see she got to Frankfurt."

Herr Wrobel's face became thoughtful. "Yes," he replied slowly. "And perhaps I have not taken my responsibility as solemnly as I should have. Perhaps Lisel should leave."

"But I cannot go without you two," Lisel protested.

"I have my responsibilities here," Herr Wrobel said. "I must perform my duty. I must stay. But I would not find fault if you, Lisel, and Frau Heidemann, should decide to go."

"And leave you here alone?" both women asked.

"I am not alone," Herr Wrobel replied. "Elsa can take over the shopping and Friedrich will see to the vegetable garden. Then, perhaps later this summer, we will join you in Frankfurt and have a little holiday."

Lisel stared at Herr Wrobel. His expression was bland, logical. She exchanged glances with Frau Heidemann.

The older woman responded. "Lisel will go. I must stay here and help Elsa."

231

"No," Lisel shook her head. "If you stay, so must I." She smiled. "After all, I am the only wage earner here."

In the middle of February more than 120,000 people were killed in a raid over Dresden. The resulting firestorm was so hot it melted brick and stone. The dead were stacked on huge pyres and cremated.

At the beginning of March 1945, ration cards were no longer honored. The shops that continued to receive food had hours-long lines in front of them. Some people brought stools to sit on while they waited. Others assigned family members shifts, each taking two hours in the queue. So desperate were most, they refused to give up their places during the bombing, though some fled when low-flying fighters strafed the street. Of course, after the planes had passed over, everyone reappeared and assumed their original positions.

Most people scavenged and relied on rumors. "This shop was receiving a shipment of pudding powder." "That shop had tins of pickled pumpkin."

Frau Heidemann brought home some of the pickled pumpkin but no one could eat it. Too much brine.

While the Allies rained continuous death from above, the SS were searching the cellars for deserters, shooting them on the spot or stringing them up in the streets and inviting passers-by to twist the dead men's legs.

At the end of March, the British crossed the Rhine and Danzig fell to the Russians.

Hitler declared Berlin a fortress. That meant the civilians were responsible to defend the city to their deaths if necessary. The issued weapons were rifles from World War I with ammunition for the newest model K98.

Because of Herr Wrobel's responsibilities, sometimes he did not come home for two or three days at a time. When he did, he was filthy and exhausted, and growing more and more starved until Lisel could see the shape of his skull through his skin. Alarmed, the two women tried to convince him to stay with them, arguing he was too weak to go back. But he refused to heed them. He pulled on his helmet—a discarded coal shuttle—and picked up his ancient rifle that had no bullets. "It is my duty," he declared obstinately.

The Home Guard had blocked Berlin's main streets with abandoned vehicles and were digging a series of trenches that formed concentric circles around the heart of Berlin. The first, twenty miles out from the city center, followed the line of the autobahn. The second, ten miles from the city center, followed the elevated railway—the S-bahn. And the inner ring ran around the government quarter and the Tiergarten—an area designated as the Citadel.

The water taps in the apartment building dried up and Frau Heidemann or Lisel had to stand in line, braving attack by air, at the community street pump. Unfortunately, the pump had also suffered in the attacks. Its base was cracked so that it took two people to hold it together while one pumped.

The gas tap still worked, although with such a tiny flame it took hours to cook a pot of barley soup. The radio went dead and the only newspaper was a one-sheet affair with headlines that told of the atrocities perpetrated by the Russians.

Erwert's had been operating only a couple of days a week; and one day, when Lisel tried to get into the building, she found it locked. She banged on the door and called, "It is Lisel Spann! It is Lisel Spann!" until Herr Erwert came to the door. His clothes were rumpled, his formerly plump cheeks deflated. "We have decided to take a little vacation," he explained and counted out of the office box, Lisel's last wages.

With her Reichmarks in her hand, Lisel picked her way back home through the ruins of Berlin, past twisted rail tracks, bombed out yellow and red railway coaches from which dirty, tattered upholstery hung; past gutted automobiles and buildings that were no more than charred shells. She passed apartments exposed by bombs that had blasted away the walls—the wallpaper inside hung in strips. Someone still lived there as evidenced by laundry hung across the open space. She skirted mortar craters that had already filled with fireweed.

The people Lisel met were no more than mere shadows, dragging their wretched belongings behind them or pushing them in handcarts, hobbling, slack-jawed, empty-eyed, searching for shelter, searching for food. There never seemed to be enough, even when there was money. Everyone was hungry. Lisel stopped and looked down at the paper money in her hand. How could mere slips of paper have any value now? There was nothing to buy. And when the Reich fell, would whoever took Berlin honor the money? Would they give value to such small slips of paper?

Lisel opened her hand and allowed a spring breeze to carry them away, floating and fluttering until they came down in the rubble. She looked at her money for a moment, lying there. Then she realized she was not only looking at rubble but a pair of human legs sticking stiffly out from beneath the heap. Horror rose along her spine and up her neck. She put a hand over her mouth and staggered backwards, then she turned and ran, blindly, down a rubble-filled alley.

Unsteady on the loose lath and chunks of plaster, Lisel stumbled and fell, sprawling onto a heap. She lay there for a moment, stunned. Her head felt like a balloon. She rolled over and looked up at the sky, a gray, overcast roof, full of smoke and threatening rain, and wondered why she was alive. "Father in Heaven," she cried out in wretchedness, "for what good purpose hast thou placed me here? What have I done to be granted such a fate? I love thee, Father, but I do not understand. I do not understand!"

A tumult, sounds of shouting and running feet, made Lisel push herself up. She staggered to the end of the alley. A mob of people swarmed, pushed, and fought their way along the narrow passage.

"What is it?" she cried. "What is happening?"

"Hoarders!" a wild-eyed, wild-haired woman shouted back. "Those devils have been hoarding everything!"

The shouting mob swept past Lisel. With a surge of terror, she remembered another street mob from long ago. She flattened herself against a wall and fought to keep from being entangled in the swarm. But, like a leaf in a roaring, rushing stream, she was swept along. Down the alley, down a narrow flight of stairs, into a dark cellar. Around her people were groping and panting. Someone kicked her. Lisel shoved back, panicked. A curse. She tried to wrestle herself free and found herself on a dirt floor. On her knees, Lisel saw a crack of light in the wall and scrambled toward it. Someone stamped on her hand with a booted foot. Lisel cried out but kept crawling toward the sliver of light. It showed shelves of bread, stacks of tins, bottles. Food!

For an instant, Lisel could only stare at it. Then, wildly, she snatched at everything, filling her coat pockets, the skirt of her dress, fending off the wrestling people above her. She could carry nothing else. Lisel fought her way, hands and knees, across the cellar to the stairs. Her thundering heart gave her the energy to sprint up the steps. Someone at the doorway snatched at her coat. She heard the sleeve rip. She jammed her elbow into his stomach and ran on.

It took another twenty minutes to get home. She ran, stumbling, until her lungs burned and her head buzzed. Then, every time she stopped to rest, dizziness threatened her. If she fell in the street, passers-by would take her food. Lisel clutched her plunder and staggered on.

Frau Heidemann met her at the basement door. The color dropped from her face, her mouth opened with a cry of shock. "Blood!" Frau Heidemann was staring at the front of Lisel's coat.

Lisel looked down at the glistening scarlet mess, then dipped a finger into the stuff and tasted. The sweetness exploded in her mouth. Strawberry jam. She tried to smile. "I must have broken a bottle."

"What have you done?" Frau Heidemann demanded. Lisel shook her head to clear away the bursts of light. "I have become a thief. I just looted someone's cellar," she managed. How funny that sounded. She began to laugh. Weak, hiccuping sounds that sounded more like sobs. "What do you think they will do to me?"

Frau Heidemann rolled her eyes and pulled Lisel into the apartment, took the food from her arms and sat her down at the table. "What can they do to a cuckoo bird. Besides how can they do anything to you when they have not caught you. Nor will they. Let me get a compress for that bump on your head."

Lisel lifted her trembling hand to her forehead and flinched. The painful place was raised as big as a duck egg. How had that happened?

Frau Heidemann fussed and clucked over Lisel. "What other damage did you manage," she scolded. "I mean besides a concussion of the head and a ruined coat?"

Lisel had to think about it. "Someone stepped on my hand." Indeed, there was a bruise across the back of Lisel's hand in the clear shape of a boot heel and her thumb was swollen.

"Well, it does not seem to be broken," Frau Heidemann said. "Let us see what you have brought for us."

Two loaves of bread, a box of cocoa, two tins of kohlrabi, a tin of stewed chicken, a pocket full of carrots, a small turnip, a bag of dried peas and a box of Havana cigars. Frau Heidemann's eyes grew large. "How did you manage all that?"

Lisel looked at the hoard and felt her own surprise. "I guess I was hungry."

"My mother always said you should never shop when you are hungry," Frau Heidemann said, lauging. "Well, we can certainly use all this."

Lisel picked up the cigars. "I suppose we can give these to Herr Wrobel."

"Nonsense!" exclaimed Frau Heidemann. We can use those for barter or bribery." She picked up the tin of stewed chicken. "Well, shall we see what kind of meal we can make of this?"

"There is one other thing." Lisel hated telling her. "Erwert's is closed and I am afraid I behaved stupidly." She saw Frau Heidemann waiting for her to go on. "I threw away my last wages."

Relief relaxed Frau Heidemann's face. "Is that all? It was not worth anything anyway." She moved into the kitchen. "There is still water in the bucket if you want to wash up while I do something delicious with this chicken."

Lisel had just pushed herself from the chair when the knock came. She froze, half way up, and glanced back at Frau Heidemann. Had the authorities followed her? Had someone identified her?

Frau Heidemann bustled past. "Hide the food," she hissed. Lisel slid the food into her coat again and hid the coat in the closet. Frau Heidemann paused to see that Lisel did as she was told, then, slowly, she opened the door.

Beyond, stood an elderly man, his cap pulled down low over his stubble-covered face. His mouth showed a hardened bitterness. "Is this the home of Gustav Wrobel?"

Lisel felt the relief flow over her. She saw Frau Heidemann's shoulders relax. "Yes."

"We have brought him home." The man stepped aside and gestured up the stairs to the front door.

Frau Heidemann flashed a look of alarm at Lisel and both fled up the stairs and out onto the street. There, a boy no more than twelve, stood by a handcart, its contents covered by a ragged tarpaulin. Frau Heidemann leaned over it with her hands clasped against her thin chest, as if she were holding them back from the moment they would have to lift the canvas.

Sensing the older woman's hesitation, Lisel stepped forward and threw back the cover. The twisted body below resembled Gustav Wrobel no more than a bundle of sticks would a human being. His body was arched, one leg drawn up, an arm outstretched, the fingers clawed. His mouth was open but oddly drawn to one side of his face.

"We found him like that," the boy said. "He must have had some kind of attack."

"Apoplexy," Frau Heidemann murmured with finality. "He must have gone quickly. Thank God for that."

They buried him next to Elsa in the back garden. Lisel stood over the grave. She felt more tired than she had in her entire lifetime, as if all her blood had slowly seeped away. Maybe her weariness had something to do with the hollowness in her heart. She looked down at the newly turned earth. Should she not feel sorrow and loss for this man who had been a foster father to her? Had she thought so little of him that she had no tears to mourn him? Had she used up all her emotions? Or were they frozen? Frozen by all the daily horror she had to deal with so that, somehow, she was protected and steeled by her own despair?

"There used to be birds in the spring," Lisel heard Frau Heidemann say. She glanced at the older woman. Frau Heidemann was as gaunt and threadbare as Lisel had ever seen her. Her sparse, brown hair had thinned so much Lisel could see the sallow skin of her scalp. Frau Heidemann glanced at her, wiping the dirt from her hands. "We can leave in the morning."

"Leave?" she asked stupidly.

"There is nothing to keep us here now and I told your father I would see you got to Frankfurt. So we will go to Frankfurt. And we will do it just as everyone else travels these days. We will walk."

Chapter 18

GISELA HEIDEMANN AND LISEL SPANN ARE ALIVE AND HAVE GONE TO FRANKFURT.

LISEL DROPPED THE SMALL CHUNK OF PLASTER AND STEPPED back from the brick wall of her apartment house. She hoped the rain would not wash away the words. When it was all over, Michael and Kurt would want to know where the women were.

"We had best be on our way," Frau Heidemann said loading yet another bundle on the bicycle and tying it with an old scarf. The laden bicycle looked like a peddler's cart with pots and pans and bundles hung from the handle bars and parcels stacked high on the seat. Papa's satchel containing the genealogy, and his scriptures were wrapped in a piece of oilcloth and tucked between two blankets.

The bicycle had been Elder Parker's, the one he had left with them when the missionaries were evacuated nearly six years ago. Lisel swallowed back a sudden tightening in her throat. So much had happened. So much had changed.

"If only Kurt had not run off with the other bicycle," Frau Heidemann grumbled, "we could take twice as much. Here." Frau Heidemann handed Lisel a cooking pot while she slipped another onto her head and pulled the handle over her chin.

A few years ago the thought of wearing a pot might have been laughable but nowadays women set them on their heads and tucked up their hair just as naturally as they put on a pair of shoes. Had a woman used a regular military helmet, she might be suspected of harboring a deserter. So women wore their cooking pots and coal shuttles and no one thought a single whit about it.

Leaving on that gray, drizzling morning, Lisel forced herself not to look back at the building that had once been the home she shared with Papa and Marta, with the Heidemanns and with the Wrobels. That part of her life were gone now, never to be retrieved except in memory. Lisel preferred the memory to be untainted by a last look at the house, its top floor burned, the windows gone from the apartment where the Spanns had spent their last years together.

The two women headed south and west, often fleeing from one air raid shelter to another, waiting for the bombing to stop and then moving on. Even when the bombing ceased for a while, they could hear a low rumble, like thunder from the eastern skies. Someone said the sound was the Russian guns, "Stalin's Organs" they called them, only forty miles from Berlin.

While Lisel and Frau Heidemann continued to the edge of the city, they could still obtain some food—a few ounces of oats, a turnip, a handful of dried potatoes—but waiting in line wasted precious time, so Lisel and Frau Heidemann decided to live on what they had and what they could find in a hurry. As they walked they watched for nettles and dandelions and chestnuts, storing them in their pockets and in the pans swinging from the bicycle's handlebars. Close to the end of that first day, Lisel and Frau Heidemann reached the ten-mile ring of defense. Along the trenches, members of the Home Guard crouched on the wet ground, their heads on their knees, looking wretched and squashed. "The poor devils," Frau Heidemann whispered, "they have had it, too."

They also began seeing more posters. The old ones, "All This We Owe To The Fuhrer" and "Where the German Soldier Stands, No One Gets In" still hung tattered and yellow, faded and stained by rain. Alongside, the newer ones, handwritten in blue and red ink were tacked to crumbling walls and posts.

Once, when Lisel and Frau Heidemann stopped to rest, Lisel noticed one of the handwritten posters on a splintered acacia trunk. The poster was signed by Hitler and Goebbels. It warned Germans against foreigners and commanded every citizen to fight and not surrender.

Surrender? Who needed to surrender when they were already defeated? Bitterly, Lisel tore the poster from the stump, wadded it between her hands and threw it to the ground. The ball of paper fell next to a crudely fashioned cross—two sticks tied together with a bit of string—the grave of a person, who, in death had no name. Lisel reached down and plucked the paper from the grave. Was this to be her fate also? To lie in the ground next to some road?

In anguish, she lifted her eyes away and stared hard at the stump. Then she saw, breaking their way from the inside of the wounded acacia, tiny, unfurling buds. The leaves' translucent green and delicate points were like fragile, dainty lace. It brought to Lisel's mind memories of past springs, of red tulips and yellow daffodils, the scent of lilacs, the busy humming of bees. Such memories should have inspired feelings of hope's renewal just as spring brought life's renewal. But for Lisel, standing in the gray rain, in the midst of a devastated city, over the grave of some unnamed soul, she wondered if beauty would ever again be any more than a memory.

But Lisel, searching for hidden strength, knew she could not allow herself to yield to the despair that threatened to crush her into the ground. The very core of her spirit struggled against it. Against hunger that made people steal and lie and murder, against exhaustion that sucked away any desire to act, against despair that whispered, "Give up."

"Lisel?"

It was Frau Heidemann's voice. Lisel turned.

"What are you doing?"

Lisel tried to speak but at first she could find no words. Finally she said, "I was looking at this broken tree. It is growing leaves."

Frau Heidemann stepped closer and looked down at the tiny buds. "Yes, it is a miracle, isn't it," she said.

They spent that night in a community shelter. It smelled stale, of unwashed bodies and defeat. Lisel dozed with her head on her knees, conscious of the sounds of snoring from an old toothless woman in the corner while a mother rocked a small child and crooned. Overhead, the sounds of flak.

At daybreak, Frau Heidemann shook Lisel awake and, out on

the street, they sat down on the lee side of a wall, made a tiny fire, which they carefully shielded from the rain, and boiled a pot of nettles, thickened with a bit of flour. Because they had not eaten since the morning before, they also ate slices of raw turnip. "We must save the rest," Frau Heidemann insisted. "Who knows when we will have more."

At the edge of the city, the Home Guard had blocked the streets with cars, trucks and vans. The crumbling walls were scrawled with graffiti. "Keep Your Men At Home." "Down With War." "Enjoy the War While You Can—The Peace Will Be Terrible."

They saw troops in the street, trudging along from the west and the south, swept into Berlin by the storm of battle. Lisel and Frau Heidemann stepped out of the way to let them pass, limping, out of step, hollow-eyed. They no longer looked like German soldiers but more like Polish prisoners Lisel had seen that night of the air raid when she was caught in the street. Somehow it seemed like a logical reversal.

By the third day, they reached the twenty-mile ring. There, the dirty, weary Home Guard members, old men, boys and a few women, huddled in the trenches. One barefoot woman was building a cooking fire using the pages she tore from Hitler's autobiography, *Mein Kampf*.

The sky was still overcast, full of lead-colored clouds and rain. Lisel's coat had soaked through and her knit dress was heavy with the wet. She thought she would never be warm and dry again. A haze of hunger floated constantly before her eyes. She could feel herself growing lighter almost as if she were floating. Her legs ached from walking and running and pushing the loaded bicycle over and around masses of rubble. How she wanted to quit. To go home—even if home was just a hole in the ground.

During the worst moments, Lisel thought of the conversation between Papa and Frau Heidemann. How Papa was so frightened for her to be left with the Russians coming and how Frau Heidemann promised to see that Lisel got to Frankfurt. She thought of the sacrifice Frau Heidemann was making in fulfilling that promise, knowing that Kurt could return to the apartment house at any time and feeling that she should be with Walter, wherever he was now.

Lisel stiffened her spine and went on, concentrating on getting to Frankfurt, finding Marta and freeing Frau Heidemann to go to Walter, to wait at home for Kurt. Lisel tried not to think of the rumors—the Russians were only three days away and coming fast.

Panicked, many Berliners decamped, streaming west toward the advancing British or south to the American line. Lisel and Frau Heidemann joined the refugees thronging south out of the city. It was a miserable procession. Wretched, dirty civilians bent under the weight of the belongings strapped to their backs.

One stubble-faced man, his pants tied around his waist with a rope, his face shrunken as tight as a fist, eyed Lisel's bicycle. She knew he was not interested in their belongings. They would only slow him. But with the bicycle he could move ahead, put more distance between himself and the coming Russians. Lisel clutched the handles, wondering what she could do to frighten him away. Walking faster or slowing only made him change his pace. He never let them get too far ahead or too far behind. "What shall we do?" Lisel asked Frau Heidemann.

Frau Heidemann glared at the man. "There are two of us," she said loudly enough so he could hear. "He can do nothing." But the man followed and watched. And Lisel knew he would wait until dark before he made a move for the bicycle.

"Perhaps if we offered him something," Lisel said. "Maybe one of the cigars."

"No," Frau Heidemann insisted. "We will need those for something far more important than to buy off that little squirrel. We will watch him and be wary."

Lisel continued to worry. If he managed to steal the bicycle and things, how would they complete the trip to Frankfurt? What was there to do? The answer came so quietly and was so simple that she let out a little gasp.

"Come over here," Lisel said to Frau Heidemann as she guided the bicycle to the edge of the street. "Which sack is the large knife in?"

Frau Heidemann's eyes widened and then narrowed but she said nothing, only unpacked the knife.

Lisel hacked away at the front tire until she could peel the rubber away from the rim, then she did the same to the back tire.

"Are things not difficult enough?" Frau Heidemann snapped when Lisel handed back the knife.

Lisel jerked her head in the direction of the man who stood watching with an out-thrust jaw, his face full of angry color. "He can hardly outrun the Russians on a bicycle with no tires," she replied.

Frau Heidemann scowled. "We can hardly outrun them either."

The man faded into the crowd.

The procession filed out of the city and moved into open country. The road ahead was choked with people. Weary units of soldiers moving east. Diseased slave laborers and emaciated POW's trudged east, back to their homes in Poland, Czechoslovakia and Hungary. Germans fleeing east to escape the Allies. Germans fleeing west to escape the Russians.

The road they followed south was full of white, cordite-ringed bomb craters and pock-marked by the strafing the fighter planes had inflicted upon it.

Alongside the road stood burned out military vehicles and equipment, destroyed by the army as they fell back, unwilling to leave their hardware for the enemy.

Several times during that afternoon, Allied bombers flew over on their way to Berlin. The sounds of their engines filled Lisel with such fear it was as if a bomb had gone off in her chest, exploding into her limbs. For the first time she realized that though they were out of the city, there was no shelter from an air attack in the country. They were exposed and vulnerable.

Then came the fighters.

Lisel heard the angry buzz from a distance and the ratta-ratta-ratta as they strafed the road ahead. The procession halted. Everyone stood and listened. Lisel heard the fighters rise into the air and come back down again. The ratta-ratta-ratta drew closer. Lisel glanced around her. There was no place to run, except into the woods and there was little protection there. She dragged the bicycle off the road, dropped it in a stand of weeds and ran anyway. Frau Heidemann ran beside her, slipping on the wet ground. Out of the corner of her eye she saw the other refugees fleeing, casting away their goods. She heard them screaming. She heard the fighters coming down again, nearer yet. "Get down," she heard Frau Heidemann shout.

Lisel flung herself face first into the mud. The angry buzz became a roar. The firing bursts beat against her eardrums. She clapped her hands over her ears, gritted her teeth and prayed for it to stop.

The fighters rose away from the road. Lisel lay there with her heart beating a wild tattoo against her ribs. She was aware of the scent of the wet earth, cowslips, and blossoming hawthorne and thought that odd. The ratta-ratta-ratta continued down the road.

On shaking legs Lisel pushed herself out of the mud. Frau Heidemann was already picking her way back to the bicycle and swearing. "If my feet do not web from all this wet, we will know Darwin was a liar."

After the strafing, Lisel and Frau Heidemann decided to abandon the road and walk alongside it, in the trees. The ground was so wet, Lisel's cloggs sank into the freezing mud. The bicycle likewise sank and both Lisel and Frau Heidemann struggled to keep it moving forward. They had to rest more often but were loathe to sit down on the muddy ground, so they leaned against trees and struggled to regain their wind. Lisel lifted one foot and then the other in an attempt to ease the pain in her legs and back. She resented her exhausted body. Each moment they spent resting brought the Russians one moment closer.

In late afternoon, Lisel and Frau Heidemann stopped for the day. They used the large kitchen knife to cut brush and small limbs from the trees for their beds. Because of the rain, however, they were unsuccessful in lighting a fire to cook their meal. Instead, they soaked a handful of oats in a pot of water, made a salad out of dandelion leaves and tore one of the small loaves of bread in half. It quieted Lisel's hunger; but weak, exhausted and dispirited, a black depression crept back into her heart like a cloud full of icy rain. Sitting on her pile of branches spread with a wool blanket, Lisel drew up her knees and lowered her head. Why had she survived to have this happen to her? Why had she not been mercifully taken as Mama and Papa and the Wrobels? Death, as difficult as it was, must be easier than life.

"You have not read your scriptures today," Frau Heidemann said.

Lisel looked up to see the older woman standing over her. Frau Heidemann was dirty and disheveled, thin as a scarecrow, her eyes were shadowed with weariness. She extended Papa's book to Lisel. "You must do as you have always done. It will keep some normalcy in our lives."

Lisel considered her words for a moment. Then she took the book. It was heavy and Lisel's hands were so cold and numb she nearly lost her grip on it. She opened it to the place she had marked the night before, Alma 36, and riffled the upper corner of the pages as she had so often seen Papa do. She could almost feel the warm imprint of his finger there as if he had just put the book down. A comforting peace settled around Lisel's heart.

"What does it say?" Frau Heidemann asked impatiently.

Lisel lifted her eyes. Frau Heidemann sat on her pile of brush, watching Lisel with expectant eyes.

"This chapter is where the prophet Alma gives advice to his son Helaman."

"Well?" she urged.

Lisel read from verse 27. *And I have been supported under trials and troubles of every kind, yea, and in all manner of afflictions; yea, God has delivered me from prison, and from bonds, and from death; yea, and I do put my trust in him, and he will still deliver me.*

Frau Heidemann looked thoughtful. "You and Alma have a few things in common."

"Not many, I think."

"Do you put your trust in God?"

Lisel did not answer immediately. A moment ago she questioned her existence, doubted the Lord's judgment and murmured against it. Now she was humbled by Frau Heidemann's simple question. "Yes, I do put my trust in God."

Frau Heidemann's brows drew together. "Did this Alma survive his afflictions?"

"Yes."

"Good," Frau Heidemann pronounced. "Then we will survive, too."

Lisel was touched by Frau Heidemann's simple faith. She resolved to better keep Frau Heidemann's example.

From above them, in the evening sky, Lisel heard the growl of bomber engines as the aircraft flew toward Berlin. She looked up, expecting to see the sky filled with hundreds of the airplanes, but they were too high and the clouds too low. Lisel and Frau Heidemann were still close enough to the city to have heard the air raid sirens, if sirens had still been working. But they had ceased working months ago and now Berliners had no warning at all.

Lisel stood and walked toward the road, watching in the direction of the city. The pathfinders dropped their markers. They looked like huge fir trees, lit as if it were Christmas. They were bright, silvery things, hanging in the dome of the darkening sky, slowly floating to earth, showing the pilots where to drop their bombs.

Lisel wondered, what was there left to bomb? To what purpose did they continue to pound an already destroyed city?

Then came the explosions. She felt them in the wet ground beneath her feet. She saw the flash of light as the bomb lit. The sky glowed red. More fire, more destruction, she thought wearily.

Quietly, Frau Heidemann stepped up beside her. "It is the twilight of the gods," she said. Lisel heard the sorrow and the defeat in her voice.

Lisel took her arm. "Come on, let us see if we can sleep."

Though it was better than lying in the mud, the bedding was miserable—cold and uncomfortable. And there were sounds in the trees. Lisel heard rustling as if something or someone moved softly in the woods. Later, a scream. "Thief!" a woman's voice cried. "Help me!" The thud of running footsteps, crashing underbrush. A shot. Lisel saw the burst from the gun barrel. Voices, loud and angry. The sounds of pursuit moved away from them.

"Lisel," Frau Heidemann's voice whispered. "One of us must sit up and watch."

"I will do it," Lisel said and sat up, wrapping her blanket around her.

"Wake me, then, in two hours," Frau Heidemann replied.

Lisel wondered if she would have to. Even as weary as she was, she did not suppose she would be able to sleep.

Lisel awoke with a jerk. The gloom of night had just begun to lift. She sat up. Pain from her stiff joints shot through her like iced lightning. She gritted her teeth against the groan that rose in her throat. Lisel glanced at the sleeping Frau Heidemann. In the faint light, Lisel saw the older woman had her blanket pulled over her head so her thin ankles and booted feet stuck out. Lisel knew Frau Heidemann would have something to say about Lisel's leaving them unguarded through the night. Yet no harm had come to them.

Lisel glanced around the small clearing. The trees were ghostly in the gray morning and dripping. She frowned. Not far from where she sat, among the trees, she could see the figure of a man. A sudden chill of fear made a lump in Lisel's stomach. Through her fright, she forced herself to draw a deep breath and focused her eyes on the man—to see him better. But she could not see his face for he stood in the shadows, as if watching. "Frau Heidemann," Lisel whispered.

Frau Heidemann stirred and mumbled in her sleep. Then she was awake and sitting. "What is it?"

"There is a man."

Frau Heidemann followed Lisel's gaze. "How long has he been there?"

Lisel shook her head. "I do not know. I only just awoke." Frau Heidemann's widened eyes met Lisel's with alarm. "You slept through the night?"

Lisel glanced at the bicycle leaning against the tree. She could see the sack that held the knife, hanging from the handlebars. "He is far enough away that, if he approaches us, we have time to get to the knife.

Slowly, Lisel rose, keeping her eye on the dark figure. She turned and walked toward the bicycle, feeling a prickling down her spine. Then, Lisel heard Frau Heidemann's frightened cry. Lisel whirled.

A dim shaft of sunlight fell upon the clearing, lighting the figure in the trees. Lisel saw the squared shoulders, the gray jacket buttoned across the matching vest, the carefully knotted tie, the tiny clip with decorations from the World War, the baggy-at-the-knees creased trousers and the frequently blocked felt hat.

Lisel felt her heart stop. "Papa?"

As if a tiny flame flickered behind his face, his features came clear. The eyes, bright and blue, behind the wire-rimmed glasses.

247

The tender smile that lifted beneath his mustache. He raised a hand in greeting.

"Oh Papa!" Lisel stumbled toward him, her arms outstretched, sobs of relief and joy pumping in her chest. "Papa!" she cried. It occurred to her she had died in the night and Papa had come for her. She would be with Mama now, too. Lisel's heart leapt.

But when Lisel reached the place her father had been, the shaft of sunlight faded into shadow and Papa was gone.

She stood there, on the spot, for a moment. Confused. Disappointed. Hurt. Lisel glanced back at Frau Heidemann. She looked as if she had been frozen in shock, her face white, her jaw hanging, her eyes bulging. "Was it a ghost?" Lisel shook her head. "No," she said as she made her way back to their camp. "It was Papa."

"But how could this be?" Frau Heidemann was standing now, her face creased with confusion.

Lisel put her hand on the older woman's arm. "Before he died, Papa gave me a blessing. In it he promised that family members, alive and dead would watch over me. . . ."

She saw the amazement and understanding widen Frau Heidemann's eyes. "Is heaven so close then?" she asked.

Lisel lifted a shoulder. "I do not know. But Papa is." The knowledge warmed her. Bombers, rain, mud and hunger could not stop her if Papa was there.

Later, they ate their breakfast of four-day old bread and cups of water before they pushed on. The rain had stopped but the day was overcast and sultry.

The country they crossed was the lowland territory—a region studded with lakes, laced with streams, and intersected by canals. The terrain slowed their travel.

Along the road, small towns stood in ruins. The outskirts were surrounded by zig-zag trenches and marked by white-rimmed craters. Most of the houses were bombed or burned and every church steeple had been shelled—an Allied attempt to knock out observation posts. Signs warned of danger. "Unsafe," said one on a lone, two-story wall. Another declared "Typhus," and still another, "Cholera." At both ends of a street one said merely, "Gruesome." Those were the streets no one entered. It was there the dead had not yet been dug from a collapsed building. The entire block was permeated with the odor. The first time Lisel encountered it, it hit her like a fist to the diaphragm. It took her breath away and sent her stomach churning.

Yet, with all the destruction, soup kitchens functioned beneath camouflage tents, serving a thin gruel or dried pea soup once a day. And, most of the time, Lisel and Frau Heidemann were able to spend the night in some kind of shelter though sleep was difficult. Bombers targeted even the smallest towns.

Always, Lisel asked for news. The Russians, she learned, were only days behind and the Americans closing in. "If you continue south," one white-haired old woman told her, "you will run into the Yankees yourself. But better the Yankees than those filthy Russians."

Lisel began practicing her English.

"I hope you get to use it," Frau Heidemann said, frowning. "We must move faster now to keep out of Bolshevik hands."

Lisel and Frau Heidemann pushed on, moving as quickly as hunger and exhaustion would allow.

Toward the end of April, they came to a village that was no more than a smoking ruin. Not one building stood intact. Not one wall remained standing higher than Lisel's shoulder. Except for the crackle of flames, silence greeted the pair. No living thing stepped forward. Lisel and Frau Heidemann looked around in dismay. "There is no help for us here," Lisel said. "We had best go to the next town."

The rubble made the village streets impassable, so Lisel and Frau Heidemann had to walk through the fields around the town to reach the road south. It was there they heard the sound of vehicles.

They stood and watched as the small, square, open-topped vehicles came slowly up the road. They were painted a dark green with a white star on each door. In the lead jeep, a fat soldier in the passenger seat held, above his head, a loaf of bread in one hand and a block of cheese in the other.

"They are Americans," Lisel breathed.

Suddenly, the fields were alive. People rose from the ground, as wheat from the soil, running toward the road, shouting, calling, laughing. Women threw themselves at the soldiers, hanging about their necks, kissing their cheeks and weeping.

The Yankees set up a kitchen in the field and ladled out bowls of a greasy soup that had chunks of pink meat, potatoes, and onions floating in it. Lisel gulped hers down, grease and all. Within moments she felt a surge of strength in her limbs. It gave her a measure of courage.

She approached one of the soldiers. His young face was apple-cheeked, his eyes a bright, sparkling brown that painfully reminded her of Michael. He looked obscenely healthy. "Pardon me?" Lisel felt her face grow hot with uncertainty. It had been years since she had spoken English.

The young soldier frowned down at her without replying.

"Is the war over?"

"Not yet, ma'am. They say they are fighting house-to-house in Berlin."

Lisel thought of the friends they had left behind and her heart grew heavy and cold inside her chest. "Do you know where are the Russians?"

"Back up the road a piece, ma'am. About three days."

Lisel had to listen carefully to his speech. He drew out his words and slung them all together so she was not sure of what he said.

"They are coming here?" she questioned.

"Yes ma'am. We'll be hooking up with them on the Elbe River in a couple of days."

Lisel frowned. "The Elbe River is not south of here?"

"The Elbe River *is* south of here. We'll be pulling back and leaving all this territory to the Reds."

Lisel turned and hurried away to find Frau Heidemann. "We have got to go now," she told the older woman. "The Russians are on their way here. They are to meet the Anglos on the Elbe in three days."

Frau Heidemann's face drained. "Then we must get to the Elbe before they do."

The news spread quickly and within hours the road south was jammed with fleeing refugees. Lisel and Frau Heidemann no longer cared whether they spent the nights in a shelter. They slept in the furrows in a field or a ditch beside the road. Now that the days were warmer, mosquitoes swarmed and infested the woods at twilight and early morning. "I thought I would miss the big bombers," Lisel grumbled, smearing her face with mud—their only insect repellent. "But how can I do that when I have the little stingers?" Yet, she slept a sound, exhausted sleep, knowing Papa would watch over them.

When they found a soup kitchen, they stopped long enough to eat and hear the news.

"Where are the Russians?"

"About two days behind."

"How far to the Elbe?"

Other times they ate while they walked, spooning the last of their kohlrabi from the tin, eating the soft carrots and gathering nettles and dandelion leaves. It was dusk when the pair staggered into the town. An American flag flew over what had been the town hall. A dummy, dressed and painted to look like Hitler, was hanging by its neck from a dead tree. Here, the streets had been cleared for traffic and Yankee soldiers sped up and down in their jeeps. A few shops had reopened, some little more than stalls outside a heap of rubble. German civilians hurried along the street. Lisel stopped a man with one leg and a crutch.

Though he seemed anxious to be on his way, he told her the soup kitchen was closed and gave her directions to the shelter. "You must get off the streets," he continued. "After the 7 P.M. curfew, if the military police find you, they will lock you up."

Lisel and Frau Heidemann searched in vain for the shelter. As twilight fell, they became desperate. To be arrested would mean a delay; and with more than twenty kilometers to go before they reached the Elbe and the Russians only two days behind them, they could not afford to spend any time in jail.

At last Frau Heidemann suggested they give up looking. "The best thing to do now is hide."

They found a bit of shelter where the remains of two brick walls met. The wind rushed into it horribly; but from the street, no one could see in. Lisel and Frau Heidemann hid the bicycle and crouched in the shadow of the corner, amongst the bricks and broken plaster. They pulled their blankets over their heads and hardly dared breathe in the silent darkness.

It was not long before they heard the click of boots on the empty cobblestone street. It sounded like footsteps in a crypt. They heard the muffled voices of the soldiers and the crunch of their boots in the rubble outside their corner. Lisel squeezed her eyes shut and held her breath. "Please do not let them find us," she prayed.

Then she heard the voice. "Hey, Wally, what did I tell you? I find a couple of krauts here every night."

Lisel felt a sharp jab on her back. A gun barrel lifted the blanket from her face. A beam of light blinded her eyes.

"Hey, hey. It's a little redhead tonight. What's up Fraulein? You're under arrest."

Chapter 19

THE PLACE OF DETENTION TURNED OUT TO BE A NOISY, STINK-
ing, overcrowded school gymnasium. The MP directed Lisel and
Frau Heidemann to one side of the room. "Women there," he said.
"Men stay over there. You do not go together? Understand?"

Lisel nodded. She and Frau Heidemann threaded their way
through the masses: ragged, dejected refugees sitting and lying on
the floor. The two women found a spot near the far wall and
spread their blankets. Lisel put out Papa's satchel for her pillow.

"So they got you too."

Lisel turned and recognized a middle-aged woman who had
been among the cart-flight procession on the road out of Berlin.
"How long have you been here?" Lisel asked.

"Just since yesterday," the woman replied. "But that girl, over
there," she jerked her head in the direction of a teenager with a
bad complexion, "she has been here four days."

"Four days!" Lisel blurted. "What has she done to be kept here
four days?"

The woman shrugged. "She is a refugee. A displaced person.
All of us are displaced persons and we are to be kept here until
the Yankees decide what to do with us."

Did that mean the Americans would turn them over to the
Russians? Lisel looked at Frau Heidemann. "We have to find a
way out of here."

"Hah!" the woman said. "Everyone wants out of this pigsty." Her
mouth stretched out in repugnance. "Can you imagine making good
Germans stay in the same place with a lot of Serbs and Poles?"

Sleep was nearly impossible. Babies cried. Children whined. The sick groaned. A group of Lithuanians fled the far corner while five men grappled with bared fists, shouting and cursing. Someone played a mournful tune on a mouth organ. A woman sat nearby, telling her beads, ". . . who was scourged for us. . . ."

Lisel sat up and thrust her hands through her hair. Her scalp was wet with perspiration. The air was stifling and fetid. She would much rather have been lying in the furrow of some field and being eaten by mosquitoes than to be here in this hot, squalling, wretched mass of humanity.

"What is it?" she heard Frau Heidemann's voice.

"I cannot sleep. I cannot even breathe. Are there no windows? How can we get out of here?"

"Hush. We will find a way out tomorrow. Someone said they let us out into the yard in the morning to feed us. We will see then how we can escape."

"But I cannot stand it one moment more. I cannot stand the smell and the noise and heat. I must get out!"

Frau Heidemann put a hand on Lisel's arm. "What was that song your Papa was constantly humming?"

Lisel frowned. She knew Frau Heidemann was trying to distract her. "It was a hymn. 'Lead, Kindly Light. ' It was his favorite."

"I always thought the tune was lovely but I do not ever remember hearing the words. Perhaps you could sing them to me now. Just to pass the time."

"Me? Sing to you?" Lisel felt like quarreling and her tone was vinegarish. "You know what my voice sounds like."

"I am not talking about hearing your voice. I just want to hear the words to the hymn." Frau Heidemann smiled. "Please?"

After a moment, Lisel begrudgingly gave in. "Just to pass the time," she agreed. She began quietly.

Lead, kindly Light, amid th'encircling gloom;
Lead thou me on!
The night is dark, and I am far from home;
Lead thou me on!

The woman with the beads stopped to listen.

Keep thou my feet;
I do not ask to see the distant scene—
one step enough for me.

The player of the mouth organ picked up the tune and gave Lisel a soft background. She felt the sweet peace of the Spirit. It trembled inside her and sent her voice into the vaulted ceiling and beyond. The fighting in the corner ceased. By the last verse, a worshipful hush, felt even by the children, descended on the gymnasium.

So long thy power hath blest me,
sure it still will lead me on;
O'er moor and fen, o'er crag and torrent, til
the night is gone,
And with the morn those angel faces smile,
Which I have loved long since, and lost awhile!

When Lisel finished, the only sound in the dim gymnasium was the soft weeping of a woman. Lisel used the heel of her hand to wipe the wetness from her own cheeks. She felt cleansed, rejuvenated, her soul thrumming with joy.

Frau Heidemann's hand found Lisel's. "That was beautiful. I think, perhaps, we will all sleep now."

"Are you the one who was singing?" A young woman sat down next to Lisel. Her large brown eyes were luminous in her pallid face. Her dark hair hung down to her shoulders.

"Yes."

"Are you a Mormon girl, then?"

"I am."

The young woman smiled. "There is another Mormon girl over there." She pointed. "We were arrested at the same time, last week, but now she has typhus and will die soon. She asked that you come to her."

Frau Heidemann grasped Lisel's arm. "Typhus is infectious; you must not go."

Lisel smiled. Her inner calmness spoke. "No harm will come to me."

"In that case," Frau Heidemann replied, "I will go with you." The three women picked their way across the gymnasium. The girl dropped down beside a wasted figure lying on the floor and gestured for Lisel and Frau Heidemann to do the same. To the woman she said, "I have brought her."

The woman on the floor turned fever-bright, gray eyes to Lisel. Her cracked lips lifted in a smile. "I am sorry to be such trouble. Your song was beautiful. I am Trude Vinchow." Her voice was reedy and weak. "I am so grateful to have found you in time." She closed her sunken eyes, drawing up strength.

Lisel saw the perspiration on her face and in her matted hair. "How can I help you?"

She looked up at Lisel. "Are you an active Mormon? Do you have a testimony?"

"She is and she does," Frau Heidemann replied with conviction.

The sick woman's smile was fragile, fleeting. "From the mouth of a witness," she murmured, then continued. "I must ask you a great favor."

"I will do what I can."

"It is about little Jupp." Her eyes went to a small boy with huge blue eyes and pale golden hair who watched with anxiety on his small, pinched face. "He is such a wonderful boy. You can see what a wonderful boy he is."

"He looks like a good boy," Lisel acknowledged.

"I love him as if he were my very own son." Her eyes closed.

Lisel waited, thinking the woman had fallen asleep. Then her eyes came open again.

"You must excuse me. I am so weak and I have such a headache."

Lisel put her hand on the woman's shoulder. She could feel the bone through her clothing. "Then perhaps you must not talk."

"No, I must ask you. Will you take my Jupp?" Her face contorted, tears welled in her eyes. "They say the Russians are coming. I would not have them take my little Jupp. There would be no one to teach him the gospel." Her hands clutched Lisel's, beseeching. "You must say you will take him. Even if it is to deliver him into other hands so he can be raised in a Mormon home. Will you do that for me?"

Lisel glanced at the tiny boy. He would slow them down, perhaps prevent them from escaping this place and reaching the Elbe. Frau Heidemann would object.

"We will take him," Frau Heidemann broke in.

Lisel turned to her in astonishment.

Frau Heidemann scowled. "You would not leave him here for the Russians would you?"

"Thank you," the woman said. Tears rolled down the sides of her face and into her hair. "You do not know how I have prayed for someone to come. How grateful I am to the Lord for hearing me. I know he does not punish a little child for the parents' sins." She lowered her voice. "You must know he is from the Lebensborn Program. And it must not matter to you." Her grip tightened on Lisel's hand. "Does it? Does it matter to you?"

Lisel looked into the fevered eyes. "No, it does not matter," she replied and Grete's face flashed across her mind. Grete with her cornflower blue eyes and flaxen hair. In a burst of recognition, Lisel glanced at the boy. Was there a resemblance? Or did Lisel see it because she wanted to? "Can you tell me where he was born?"

Puzzlement crossed the woman's face. "I believe it was in a home outside Berlin. But he was such a sweet baby, he was adopted at once. A high officer in the Gestapo and his wife took him. It was the thing to do, you see. All their friends took Lebensborn babies. I was their maid and they left him to me most of the time. Then, when we heard the Russians were coming, they left. They were afraid to take little Jupp, for fear his past would condemn them. But I could not leave him." The woman's voice faded, her eyes fluttered shut. Lisel heard her labored breathing.

After a moment her eyes came open again. Her voice was weaker, hoarse. "His adopted parents are Kulle and Gitta Mehlman. He came to us named Joseph but we call him Jupp and he was four years old in December." She turned her head and beckoned to the boy. "Jupp, my darling, this is your new mama. She will take you to a wonderful home and love you just as I have loved you. You will have delicious food to eat and toys to play with. You must love your new mama and be a very good boy. Will you do that for me?"

The child nodded.

"You are such a wonderful boy." The woman reached up and fondly touched the boy's cheek. "You will always remember and never forget that I love you?"

The child nodded again.

"Good. Now take your new mama's hand."

The boy looked at Lisel. There was no fear in his eyes. No doubt. He laid his tiny hand on hers.

Hesitantly, Lisel closed her fingers over his. If only she had more time to think about this.

For the first time, a tranquility passed over the woman's face. She lay there for a moment. "I must ask of you one other thing." Her chest heaved up and down as if under great pressure. "My husband and I were saving money to go to Utah, to go to the temple, but then this war started. My Axel was killed in Russia. Now I will never go." Her hand reached for Lisel's and Lisel met it half way. "Would you do that for me?" the woman pleaded. "Will you see to me and my Axel?"

It was such a simple request. Asked with such sincerity. And Lisel understood Trude Vinchow's desire. Lisel gulped back the tightening in her throat and nodded.

Trude looked at her friend. "Will you get my papers?" She placed the sheets in Lisel's hands. "I know I can trust my eternity to you," she said. A peaceful sigh escaped her. "I can sleep now and awake to the smile of angel faces."

Suddenly, the woman eyes flew open, wide and horrified. She grasped Lisel's hands with alarming strength. "You must get out of this place! You must take Jupp away!" Her voice was high and shrill.

Frau Heidemann pushed the woman back down. "Hush," she said. "We will wait until tomorrow and see what can be done."

"No, I will tell you how to do it. I planned it all before I got sick. This is what you must do. . . ."

At dawn, American soldiers opened the gymnasium doors and the internees filed out. With Papa's satchel in one hand, Lisel turned and looked back over her shoulder. The disinfectant squad was loading Trude Vinchow's body onto a stretcher. The girl with the long, dark hair, the one who had fetched Lisel for Trude, stood by, blank-faced and holding Jupp's hand. He leaned his forehead against her leg and stuck a finger in his mouth.

In the yard, the refugees stood in line to receive a spoon and a bowl which was filled with hot soup. Afterward, the new internees were dusted with DDT, given an injection, and taken to a shower tent. Lisel soaped her skin from scalp to soles twice and, knowing what was to happen, scrubbed herself a third time. A Red Cross nurse in Khaki slacks and a white zippered jacket handed her clean underwear and socks. Lisel put her old, ragged knit dress back on and thought it a shame to put such dirty clothes on over her clean body. But she would only need the dress a few hours more.

Frau Heidemann sidled up to her. "Are you ready?"

Lisel nodded.

Frau Heidemann went first. Lisel saw her walk to the edge of the schoolyard where a row of shrubs grew in front of the women's latrine trench. On the other side of the trench, the Americans had erected a high, wire fence. A lone GI paced the area in front of the shrubs. A rifle hung from a lanyard around his neck.

Lisel saw Frau Heidemann glance at the GI. As soon as he turned his back she disappeared behind the shrubs.

Lisel waited a minute or two before she walked over to the girl with the long, dark hair and took Jupp's hand. Without a word, they moved toward the trench. Lisel could smell it from yards away and in the morning warmth, she heard the swarm of flies.

Lisel gave Jupp's hand a little shake and, dutifully, he looked up at her with accepting, blue eyes. His lashes were long and dark and made little spikes. Once again she thought of Grete. "Are you a very brave boy?"

He nodded vigorously.

"And are you also a very strong boy?"

Jupp lifted his arm and bent it at the elbow with his fist clenched to show off his tiny bicep.

Lisel squeezed it. "Yes, you are a very strong boy."

Jupp beamed and swaggered a little.

"I am going to ask you to do something that only a very brave, very strong boy can do. Do you think you can do it?"

Jupp looked uncertain for a moment. Then: "But I am a brave boy," he protested.

"Good," Lisel said. "Then you must do just as I tell you."

They walked past the tall GI. "Hi ya, Joe," Jupp called out.

"How ya doin' kid," the soldier returned with a grin.

Lisel held her breath and tried to move in a normal way, hoping the GI would not notice her fright. He continued his pacing, his back to her now. It would only be seconds before he turned again and started back toward them.

Lisel hurried Jupp behind the shrubs to the latrine trench. The smell gagged her. She could not bear to look down. Jupp began to unbutton his trousers. "No, Jupp. Not now. First we must climb down."

Jupp's eyes widened in horror. "That place stinks," he cried.

"Then we must plug our noses so we do not smell it," Lisel replied. She glanced toward the GI. He would be turning any second. "Like this," she said pinching her nose. "You follow me." Lisel climbed down into the ditch, holding Papa's satchel above the muck and crouched against the steep sides. The odor invaded her nostrils and her mouth. It made her eyes water. Disturbed flies swarmed around her. She could not look anywhere but up at Jupp. "Come, now!"

Jupp did as he was told and slithered down the side. "This place stinks," he complained, again. "Hush now. We must listen for the soldier's boots to pass by. Can you help me? Listen closely and whisper when you hear him walk by."

Jupp held still, listening. They both heard the boot crunch at the same time. "I hear him," Jupp whispered in excitement.

"What sharp ears you have!" Lisel exclaimed. "Now, we will play a little trick on Joe. I will push you up on the other side and you must crawl, very low on your stomach, over to that bush by the fence. But you must stay down on your stomach so Joe does not see you. That will be a funny joke on Joe. Then you must wait for me to come. Understand?"

Jupp nodded and smiled gleefully.

Lisel pushed him out of the trench and watched as he scooted along like a little crab to a patch of brush near the fence. Then Lisel waited until she heard the soldier pass again. When she knew his back was to her, she scrambled up the side of the trench and crawled. The brush where Jupp waited was just ahead of her. Only yards. But she was on weedy ground with not enough vegetation to hide her. If she made some sound, if the soldier turned now, she would be caught. Lisel glanced back over her shoulder. The soldier paced on. She scurried into the brush where Jupp waited.

"Oh, what a funny boy you are!" she exclaimed. "I think you have tricked Joe."

Jupp began to giggle.

Lisel put her finger to her lips. "Now let us see if we can wiggle under this fence. See this small hole?" Lisel pointed to an indentation in the ground beneath the wire. "Do you think you can get under there."

Jupp grinned, showing a row of tiny, white teeth. His speed surprised Lisel. "I am a very quick boy," he said proudly. The fit was a little tighter for Lisel but she pushed the satchel under first and then struggled through, suffering only a snagged sleeve and a few scratches on her arms and face. "Now, we must run and hide in that pile of bricks—do you see it over there?"

"I am a very fast runner," he declared. He showed Lisel. His little arms and legs pumped with all the energy of his thin body. From the broken wall, rosy-faced and grinning with pride, he looked back at her.

Lisel waved to him, nodded, and signaled for him to be quiet. She glanced back. She could not see the GI and supposed that he also could not see her. So she rose from her place and forced herself to walk, as if it was the most natural thing in the world, over to the pile of bricks. She found Jupp and Frau Heidemann sitting in the shade. Lisel dropped down beside them.

"Did anyone see you?" Frau Heidemann asked.

"No," Lisel returned, "but I am sure they will smell us, if we do not find a place to wash."

The place they found was an irrigation canal. Without soap, they did the best they could in the muddy water. Then they made their way back where they had hidden the bicycle. Lisel was certain it had been stolen; but there it was, just as they had left it.

Inside their corner, Lisel and Frau Heidemann pulled off their damp dresses and put on dry clothes from their bundles. "Next time," Frau Heidemann said, "we will see that we are not in a town when seven o'clock comes around. Ugh! I will never get this smell out of my hair!"

Even though the bombing was over, Lisel and Frau Heidemann decided to stay off the road. Who knew when an MP would come along and force them into another detention center. They met other refugees in the trees. "They said the Russians were a day and a half behind them."

That information sent a spike of panic through Lisel. "We cannot walk twenty kilometers in a day!" she exclaimed.

Frau Heideman shifted a sleeping Jupp on her hip. His head lolled on her shoulder. "Then we must trust your Papa to help us," she replied.

"Yes, we will rely upon Papa," Lisel returned. But walk like we rely on only ourselves, she thought.

They pushed on, only taking time to eat when Jupp became fretful and was too tired to walk farther. Lisel saw his face grow pale, his steps become shorter and slower. At this rate, they would never make it.

Thanks to a high, bright moon, they traveled into the night, taking turns pushing the bicycle and carrying Jupp. With each step his tiny body grew heavier. At last, exhausted, they stopped in an apple orchard. The sweet scent of blossoms was almost overpowering. "We will rest here for a little while," Frau Heidemann said. "But we must be moving again before daylight.

Lisel spread her blanket on the rough, hard ground, settled Jupp between herself and Frau Heidemann, and laid her head on Papa's satchel. She woke later to a gentle touch on her cheek. "Mama?"

It seemed strange, having this child call her Mama. She turned over to see Jupp's shining eyes, wide and worried, as he leaned over her. "What is it?"

"I am scared," his voice quivered. "There is a man over there."

Lisel sat up. The words of Papa's last blessing had stayed with Lisel. Sometimes, to make the unendurable walking easier, she repeated them to herself. And when she became frightened, she comforted herself by remembering Papa was watching her path. Yet, though he was constantly with her, this was only the second time she had seen him. He stood in a silvery light. He lifted his arm and pointed toward a dirt road that went over the brow of a hill.

"I am scared," Jupp said again.

Lisel turned to him. "Do not be frightened. That is our angel. He watches over us." Lisel reached over and touched Frau Heidemann's shoulder.

She sat up with a jerk. "What is it?"

"We must leave now," Lisel told her, getting up and folding the blanket. "Papa says we must take that road."

Frau Heidemann frowned, studying the road with her eyebrows drawn over her nose. "Do you know where it leads?"

Lisel tied the blanket onto the bicycle. "I suppose it goes south. Maybe a shortcut to the Elbe."

"We would need more than a shortcut now," Frau Heidemann replied. "We would need wings."

"I am hungry," Jupp said.

Lisel looked down into his pinched face. "We will eat as soon as we can find a soup kitchen. Perhaps we will have a big bowl of soup and a piece of white bread."

Frau Heidemann reached up and plucked a stem of pink and white apple blossoms. "How I would love an apple right now. Do you think we can eat *this*?"

Jupp's face became indignant. "Boys do not eat flowers," he insisted.

The sun came up, spilling a rosy glow over the trees. Lisel at first thought she saw fire on the horizon, then saw there was no smoke. She had mistaken dawn for destruction. The realization touched her with sadness.

The road wound around hills covered with orchards, a fairy tale land of frothy blossoms and intoxicating scent. The bounty of the scene contrasted so strongly with the desperation in Lisel's heart, the pain in her exhausted body, that she could not bear to look at laden trees.

She gritted her teeth so her jaw ached and she fought the physical sensations that would crush her spirit. The hunger, the exhaustion. She forced up the image of her Papa, her guardian. If she held the image, if she held the trust, she could ignore the despair that threatened her heart, the pain in her stomach and the ache in her legs. Tomorrow, perhaps, they would reach the Elbe and be safe from the Russians. Frankfurt and Marta would not be far away. Each step took her closer. Lisel looked down at her feet. Her clogs were so abused, the sides had begun to splinter. Soon she would be barefoot; but once she found Marta, it would not matter.

She trudged on through the hot, spring morning. How she longed to sit down. But she kept Papa's face before her, smiling, encouraging. One more step. One step. She could do another. One step was enough. Inside her head, Papa's voice rose in song. *Keep thou my feet; I do not ask to see the distant scene—one step enough for me.*

Lisel felt her leg stretch out just a little farther, her stride lengthen just a bit as if her spirit legs were pulling and pushing her physical legs. She almost laughed at the thought. Poor spirit trying to drag such a wretched body down this dusty road. "I can do this," Lisel said between gritted teeth. Just one step. One for Papa. One for Mama. One for Marta. One for Michael."

"What was that?" What are you saying?" Frau Heidemann snapped.

"I am talking to my spirit," Lisel replied unself-consciously.

"You are talking out of your head, you mean," she replied. "We had better rest before we collapse."

"Where is the soup kitchen?" Jupp whined. "I am hungry." He stumbled and fell face down. His little shoulders shook with his sobs. Lisel went to him, picked him up and let him weep against her shoulder. Slowly his crying softened and then with a shudder, he breathed deep and was asleep. He seemed to weigh nothing at all. Lisel and Frau Heidemann took turns carrying him as they slowly made their way south.

Along the hot road, they saw no one until just before noon. The sound came as a far off, grinding hum. Lisel and Frau Heidemann turned and watched the approach of the jeep. A ragged spume of dust rose from behind it. It was moving so fast. Incredibly fast. It would probably reach the Elbe in minutes while they would have to toil and struggle for hours. Lisel dared not think of those hours. The despair would return.

The pair stepped off the road as it sped past. They saw the black faces of the two GIs turn toward them. Thirty yards up the road, the jeep stopped and the soldiers spoke to each other, gesturing in argument. Then, the jeep began to back toward them.

Lisel felt a stab of alarm. Were they MPs, coming to arrest them? Or were they worse? Were American soldiers like the Russians? Lisel glanced around. There was no place to hide. She gripped Frau Heidemann's arm. They were both afraid, but neither moved.

"Perhaps they will arrest us?" Lisel asked.

"Perhaps," Frau Heidemann answered.

Then another thought came into Lisel's head. "Perhaps Papa couldn't get us wings so he sent us wheels."

Frau Heidemann turned and stared at Lisel. Then she smiled. "Perhaps," she said. The jeep drew up beside them. The GI in the passenger seat grinned. Lisel thought it remarkable how white his teeth and eyeballs were against his black skin. "You ladies need a lift?"

His words were slurred, his voice heavy as if it rumbled from deep within his chest. Lisel could make no meaning come clear from it. "I do not understand," she said in English.

The driver looked straight ahead with no reaction. But the other man smiled more broadly. "We will give you a ride," he said, mouthing the words carefully.

"We are trying to reach the Elbe River," Lisel replied.

"That's where we're headed. Hop in."

The GI climbed out. He was a huge man with wide shoulders and thick, muscular arms and legs. He strapped the bicycle over the spare tire, helped Lisel into the back of the jeep, took a sleeping Jupp from Frau Heidemann's arms and then, when she was settled, climbed in himself with Jupp cradled in his arms. He turned to smile at Lisel but his smile collapsed when he saw the tears streaming down her face.

"You have been so kind. We cannot repay you," she choked out.

He then did a remarkable thing. He dropped an eyelid in a good-natured wink. "You don't owe us nothing. Our folks walked many a dusty road and we were always grateful for those who made the way a little easier. We knew who sent them. This time, yessir, I'm counting on blessings from the Lord."

The jeep jolted over the uneven road for a half hour before Jupp woke up. His face blanched and his eyes and mouth both opened wide when he saw the black man who held him. The soldier forestalled the wail that threatened to erupt from the boy by dragging an oily paper bag from under his seat and taking out a round cake with a hole in the center. "You like doughnuts?"

Jupp liked anything that was edible and proved it by taking a huge bite out of the doughnut.

The black man threw back his head and laughed. He turned in his seat and handed the paper bag to Frau Heidemann with a wink. She scowled at him and inspected the contents of the sack suspiciously. Neither she nor Lisel had ever seen this type of confection before. Its sweetness exploded in Lisel's mouth and, without regard to any of her previous training, she wolfed down the doughnut. She even sucked her fingers.

The jeep pulled up outside a heavily bombed village. "We'll let you out here," the big soldier said. He unstrapped the bicycle. "Now don't you go telling folks we gave you a ride. The Major'd have our hides if he found out. You understand?"

Lisel only understood part of it. The two soldiers had risked getting in trouble to help her and Frau Heidemann and Jupp. "We will not tell," she answered.

"Right." The GI climbed back in the jeep. "The Elbe is straight up that road about half a mile. You can't miss it."

Lisel could smell the river's mud and moss. It had taken a little more than an hour to cover the distance that would have taken her and Frau Heidemann more than a day. She nodded. "Thank you."

The jeep leapt forward with a roar. The soldier tossed the sack of doughnuts to Lisel, winked and lifted his large hand. "See ya all in the funny papers."

They watched the jeep speed up the street. "Did he say why they were on the orchard road?" Frau Heidemann asked.

"No," Lisel answered.

Chapter 20

On the Elbe River, hundreds of refugees crowded the east bank. The bridge that had once spanned the river, stood in ruins with its center blasted away. "How are we to cross?" Lisel asked.

"We will ask," Frau Heidemann replied.

"You must wait for the hay ferry," a man with one eye told them and pointed to the ferry on the other side of the river. "Then if you have the price, the ferryman will take you."

"What is the price?" Lisel asked.

The man shrugged. "The highest price. You must offer something to him. If he wants it, he will take you. If he does not, you must wait until he is in a generous mood or you must find another way across." His wry smile showed toothless gums. "Perhaps you are good swimmers?"

Lisel and Frau Heidemann moved away from the crowd. The Russians were only hours away. They did not have time to look for another crossing. "What do we have to offer?" Lisel asked.

Frau Heidemann bent and ripped the hem lining from her dress. She opened her hands and revealed a gold watch. "It is worth fifty Marks," she said. "Perhaps that will be enough."

They went back to the crowd and watched as the ferry came up to the bank. The anxious refugees formed a line. The ferryman was a thin fellow with a narrow face and round, pale eyes. He surveyed the group without emotion, taking one person's offerings and rejecting another's.

One man, the father of three children, got down on his knees and, weeping, begged the ferryman. But he was not moved.

Lisel's hands were damp and trembling as Frau Heidemann approached him. She showed the watch.

The ferryman rolled his eyes. "I have enough watches now to open a jewelry shop."

Lisel felt her heart stop. It was the only thing of value they had. She glanced at Frau Heidemann and saw her face had gone red with indignation. "You cannot turn us away! We have a small child. We must get to Frankfurt!"

The ferryman's lips thinned. "So? Who does not? Stand aside. You are blocking the way."

"We will not stand aside!" Frau Heidemann insisted. "We must get to Frankfurt and a fish-face like you will not stop us!"

The man's face purpled. "This is my ferry. I name my price and my conditions. You, I do not want! Find your own way, if you can."

Frau Heidemann's fist came up. Lisel jumped between them. "Wait!" she cried. She dug into one of the bundles hanging from the handlebars and pulled out the box of cigars. "We have this."

She saw the ferryman's eyebrows rise with interest. His eyes moved to hers and narrowed. "My brother used to smoke but he had to give it up. They are of no use to me."

"But they are Havana cigars. Very expensive. Just look." She took one of them from the box and handed it to the ferryman.

He rolled it between his fingers, then lifted it to his nose and sniffed. Lisel saw the look of greed in his eyes but it was quickly replaced with shrewd assessment. "Well, perhaps I will be generous for the child's sake." He studied the cigar. "But this is hardly a fair payment for such a large group."

Frau Heidemann grabbed the box from Lisel's hands. "But there are only three of us and you may have the entire box. All the cigars for yourself."

"Very well. I will take the entire box but . . ." his eyes glittered and a sneer curled his lip, "the cigars will only pay passage for two."

Lisel felt the blood drop from her face. Only two of them could cross? One would be left for the Russians? If only they did not have to take Jupp. Guilt, sharp and piercing as a stiletto, stabbed at her. She grabbed at a straw. "What about the bicycle? You could have that."

The ferryman stared at the bicycle and then at Lisel. "You do not expect me to consider such a thing? It has no tires."

Lisel's mind spun in desperate circles, searching for an alternative. They had nothing more to offer him. "If you take all three of us across, I will return with whatever payment you name."

Impatience flashed across his face. "Are you coming or are you not? I do not have time to argue."

Something in the ferryman's tone told Lisel he would not reconsider, would not change his mind. This was her punishment for wishing herself rid of the child. She looked at Frau Heidemann. "I suppose you had best take Jupp and go," she said with resignation.

"What rubbish!" Frau Heidemann declared. "How would I explain that to Marta? Would I say, 'Oh excuse me, Marta, I went off and left Lisel on the banks of the Elbe. She so wanted to meet some Russian soldiers'?"

"Then none of us will go," Lisel announced. "We will find some other way."

"And cows chase rabbits!" Frau Heidemann retorted. She laughed when she saw the astonishment on Lisel's face. "No, Lisel. I promised your father I would see you to Frankfurt. This is the best I can do." She shot the ferryman a poisonous look. "Anyway, it is just as well we part now. You take Jupp and push on to Frankfurt. Marta will be there and your Mormon friends. I must find Walter. We will return to Berlin and wait for Kurt there."

"But the Russians—" Lisel protested.

"The Russians be hanged! I can handle a bunch of knuckle-headed Slavs. They could be no worse than my husband." She gave Lisel a little push. "Go on now. Get aboard."

"Not with that bicycle," the ferryman said.

"Hmph," Frau Heidemann grumbled. She proceeded to unpack part of the bicycle's load—Papa's satchel, Lisel's clothes, a blanket, a cooking pot and some utensils, the bag of dried peas, the box of cocoa and the sack of doughnuts.

"I cannot take all this," Lisel protested.

Frau Heidemann grabbed the paper sack, removed a doughnut and gave the sack back to Lisel. "That should make it lighter," she said with a grin. She bent and kissed the top of Jupp's head. "You must be a very good boy," she admonished.

"Hurry up now, move along," the ferryman scowled. "I do not plan to be here when the Russians come."

Lisel faced Frau Heidemann, suddenly realizing she must say good-bye. Perhaps the last good-bye. It was like being separated from her arms or legs. How could she get to Frankfurt as a cripple? She choked back the tears that tightened in her throat. "I cannot go without you, Gisela." Her voice squeaked.

Frau Heidemann's look was a combination of surprise and warmth. "That is the first time you have ever called me by my Christian name," she said and Lisel saw the glistening in the older woman's eyes, the trembling of her chin.

Frau Heidemann opened her arms and Lisel fell into them. "Oh, Lisel, how I will miss you and your foolishness. You nearly drove me crazy, you know. I would not be able to stand you for a moment longer." She held Lisel away from her. "Now, you are not to worry because I am not there to take care of you. You will be protected because you have your Papa and you will not be lonely because you have Jupp."

Frau Heidemann gave Lisel's nose an affectionate tap. "And, you will be resourceful because I have taught you."

Lisel sniffed and laughed at the same time.

"And when this is all over," Frau Heidemann continued, "you and Marta and Jupp must come back to the house in Berlin and we will all have a party and tell lies to each other and laugh."

Lisel nodded and rubbed her wrist under her nose. "Your lies will be best but we will be there. You will see."

"Of course you will. Now," she gave Lisel a little shake, "get going. I have some things to do and you are holding me up."

Lisel dredged her soul for the courage to face the moment and managed to force a smile. "Then you had best be going."

Frau Heidemann turned the bicycle and began to walk away.

"Just a minute," the ferryman's voice boomed.

Hope flickered in Lisel's heart. Surely the ferryman could not see her and Frau Heidemann parted.

"Where are those cigars?" he demanded.

Frau Heidemann's cheeks colored and Lisel saw the indecision cross her face. Then she shrugged and pulled the box from the cooking pot that hung on the handlebars. "There you are, you fish face!" she sneered.

Lisel found a place for Jupp and herself to sit on the crowded deck of the hay ferry. To quiet him, she broke one of the doughnuts in two and gave him the largest piece.

"Where is Frau Heidemann going?" he asked with his mouth full.

"She is going to see her son."

"Is he a little boy like me?"

Lisel looked down at the pink face. A breeze lifted a lock of pale hair from his forehead. She remembered when Walter had been a little boy, blonde and blue-eyed and full of tricks. He would be in his teens now. "No, Jupp, Walter is a bigger boy."

Lisel felt a bump on the bottom of the ferry and the rise and fall of the waves. She turned and looked back over the railing. Frau Heidemann was standing on the bank with the bicycle against her thigh. She raised her hand to wave and when Lisel waved back, Frau Heidemann lifted her other hand, high in the air. In it were three cigars.

Lisel did not realize how much she would miss the use of the bicycle. She put the cooking pot on her head, tied her bundles of clothes and utensils and food around her waist with Frau Heidemann's old scarf, slung the blanket across her shoulder, picked up Papa's satchel with one hand and took Jupp's with the other. After a half mile, she thought the weight would force her into the ground. Jupp was whining, wanting to be carried.

Because Jupp tired easily, they had to walk more and more slowly and stop more frequently. Lisel fought back her resentment. She tried to think of what Papa would say. She scolded herself, saying it was not Jupp's fault. It was Trude Vinchow's for putting her in this position. Perhaps she had been delirious. At any rate, Frau Heidemann should not have agreed. How was Lisel to take care of such a small child by herself? As slowly as they were moving now, they would starve before they got to Frankfurt.

They ate wherever they could find food—edible plants along the road, soup in field kitchens, and once an old farmer let them sleep in his shed and eat all the strawberries they could pick. Jupp got diarrhea and they had been delayed for a day.

They trudged on. Jupp quit complaining about being hungry and tired. He stumbled on beside her, pale, dull-eyed, and silent. Her own hunger felt as if it were eating her from the inside out, but for a small boy, Lisel realized his suffering must be agony.

"What am I doing with a child?" she asked herself over and over again. Frau Heidemann was better equipped to handle him. But Frau Heidemann was not here and Lisel had to keep going.

Rumors said Germany would be divided among the Russians, the British, and the Americans. Frankfurt was to be in the American section. If she and Jupp could get to Frankfurt before the division, they would be safe with the Americans. And Marta would take care of them. Marta would know an American family who would take Jupp.

Lisel hoped to hurry him along by distracting him. She told him stories about herself and Marta when they were children. When they lived in the big house in the country where they had a pony and a cart and a pond with ducks. She told them about the time the missionaries came and how her whole family was baptized in the pond. She told him about Joseph Smith and his wonderful vision. When she ran out of stories, she made them up.

Lisel and Jupp stumbled into the city in the late afternoon. The familiar setting of destroyed buildings and heaps of rubble and clumps of pink fireweed growing out of the ashes met their eyes. The Americans occupied this town, too and had cleared its streets and set about creating some kind of order. There were plenty of GIs in the streets but Lisel saw no Germans.

Lisel led Jupp toward the middle of town, hoping to find a soup kitchen still open. They approached two GIs sitting on a low wall. One elbowed the other and they both sang,

"Ven der Fuhrer says, Ve is der Master Race,

Ve Heil! Heil!

Right in der Fuhrer's face!"

After each "Heil" the soldiers stuck their tongues between their lips and blew, spraying their spittle across Lisel's back. Lisel straightened her spine and walked on. They called after her. "Hitler kaputt! Hitler kaputt!" they shouted with laughter.

That incident made her wary of approaching the MP who sat in a jeep outside a huge pile of rubble. He was scribbling something on a clipboard. His jaw was clenched, his chin outthrust as if in anger. For an instant Lisel thought to go past him, find someone else. But the time was growing late and there was no one else to ask.

"Excuse me?"

He looked up at her. Beneath his helmet, his eyes were dark below black eyebrows. His nose came down long and narrow to thin, shapeless lips. The stub of a thick cigar was clamped between his teeth. "What is it?" The hostility in his voice made Lisel step backward in surprise.

"We are looking for a soup kitchen," she said.

One side of his lip lifted in what looked more like a snarl than a smile. The cigar slid to the other side of his mouth. "A soup kitchen?" he asked softly. "Do you suppose we just give food away here?"

Lisel took another step backward. Jupp was clinging to her thigh. "I did not know. We have only just arrived."

The MP put down his clipboard and climbed out of the jeep. He straightened so he towered over Lisel. His eyes burned. "In this city there is only food for work. In this city there is only freedom through work."

An inner sense set the alarm. A prickle went up Lisel's spine. She eased her hand onto Jupp's shoulder and slowly turned him as she stepped backward. "We are sorry to disturb you. We are sorry for the mistake."

"Mistake? It was all a mistake?" His lips coiled and uncoiled around the cigar. "Was Dachau a mistake? What about Belsen? That was a mistake, too? Some kind of little goof-up on the part of your master race?"

Lisel's heart was hammering in her chest, her blood thrumming in her ears. For each cautious step she took back, he took one forward.

His eyes narrowed into slits. The cigar shifted again. "Does the name Weizmann mean anything to you?"

Lisel glanced at the tag on the MP's tunic. It said, "Weizmann." Lisel thought swiftly. She had been in school with a Ruth Weizmann but her family had emigrated to America in the late 30's. "Are you Ruth Weizmann's brother?"

"Would it frighten you if I said I was? Would you think I had come for revenge? What did you do to Ruth?" He pushed his face into Lisel's so his eyes were like two glittering moons above her. "Did you shoot her? Did you starve her? Maybe you just gassed her?"

Lisel drew back and stumbled. She caught herself. "I did not do anything to Ruth! She was my friend!"

"All you Krauts say that. You pretend to be shocked. You lie and say you were against the Nazis all along. Well, I don't believe you. You must pay for your evil." He drew the pistol from his holster and leveled it at Lisel's face. The barrel was like an empty, black eye staring at her. She felt the cold sweat start on her scalp.

Jupp began to whimper. Lisel pushed him behind her.

"You're wondering if I am going to shoot you." His lips twitched in a sardonic smile, lopsided because of the cigar. "Maybe I'm not going to shoot you just yet. Maybe I'm going to rough you up a little first." His hand shot out and caught Lisel on the shoulder with a sharp blow. She took two staggering steps backward, trying to avoid falling on Jupp. Lisel shoved him wide and went down on her back in the street. Jupp screamed.

The GI laughed. He threw back his head and laughed until the sound filled the empty street. Then, abruptly, he stopped and retrained his pistol. He was huge, standing over her that way. "So what do you think? Shall I shoot you now or not?" Lisel heard the click as he pulled back the hammer.

Would she be able to see the bullet spiraling down the barrel toward her?

The GI was watching her carefully, his cruel smile curled around the cigar. He seemed to enjoy her fright. It made him pull himself up taller. He was Herr Hahn over again. Lisel grasped at that idea. If she was to stop him, she must do it by conquering her own fear. Slowly, cautiously, she pushed herself to her feet. Then straightened and lifted her chin.

"You will not shoot me," she said quietly.

His face transformed from pleasure to anger. The muscles around his eyes squeezed his lids into dark slits. "You are very sure of yourself."

"And you are very unhappy about what happened to your people here. But they were not just your people. They were mine, too. They were not just Jews, but people of every religion and color. Some of them were not right in their bodies or their minds. Some of them only disagreed with the Nazis. But most of them were Germans. Good Germans. My friends, my neighbors, my countrymen. The worst things that were ever done in this war were the things we Germans did to ourselves. And even when this is long over, we will continue to bear the guilt for those who died because of our stupidity, whether they were German or not. And we will continue to bear the disgust we have earned from the rest of the world. I cannot excuse our behavior. But neither can you avenge it with all your hatred."

He made a sound of amusement under his breath. "Fraulein, I don't need hatred. I've got bullets."

"Then use them," she challenged. "You will fulfill your need for vengeance, you will absolve me of guilt, and you will relieve a starving, homeless woman and a four-year old child of their wretched, miserable existence. Kill us and right all wrongs."

He contemplated her for a moment, the corner of his lip twitched, flicking the cigar. He lowered his gun. "Perhaps you're right. You don't deserve an easy death. You don't deserve to see the one that gets you." He pointed with the barrel of his pistol. "That's the way out of town. Get going and wonder if I'm going to shoot you in the back."

With her head up, Lisel moved past him, pulling Jupp along behind her. Her knees trembled so she did not know if she could make it down the block, out of the pistol's range.

At the intersection, she glanced back. The GI stood in the middle of the street watching her with his fists on his hips. When he saw her glance he threw back his head and laughed. The sound filled the empty street.

Lisel picked up Jupp and ran.

When she was sure they were safe, she put Jupp down.

"Will we find the soup kitchen?" Jupp asked in a thin voice.

"No, Jupp. Probably not today."

"But I am hungry."

"So am I."

"That man was mean," Jupp said.

"No. Only very sad."

"He talked funny."

"That was English. Something you must learn, too." Only then did Lisel consider the things she had said. Yes, she meant them. Those words came out of her as if they had only been waiting for the right escape. But she wondered at the way they came out. With her minimal use of English and her disuse of it for so long, Lisel was astounded at the ease with which the words had leapt to her lips. She bowed her head. "Thank you, Father."

Lisel sat on a ditch bank. She and Jupp had stopped to rest for a moment and Jupp had fallen asleep, exhausted, in the grass. Lisel was too worried to rest, worried that she would fall asleep and not wake up until it was too late to look for food. Jupp must have something to eat soon. She had had to carry him the last half-hour and his tiny body was no more than a bundle of bones.

Lisel rubbed her weary eyes. She was so tired her eyes would not focus. Everything presented itself in pairs. And that haze of hunger was always there—especially today when they had had so little. Now she wondered if they dared go into the village just down the road. It must be getting close to seven o'clock.

If Frau Heidemann was here, she would know what to do. But it was only Lisel now and Jupp, and he depended totally on her. A surge of anger rose in her chest. How could Trude Vinchow trust such a small child to strangers, especially one who had no knowledge of children?

She heard Jupp whimper and turned. He was sitting up, his little chin trembling, his frightened eyes on a butterfly that had landed on his bare knee. The insect was a huge thing. Its bright yellow and black wings trembled and opened out flat, boasting their dramatic, shimmering design, their lacy edging.

Lisel looked at the creature and felt resentment. Resentment for its perfection, for its lack of need. How could it exist here and now without being somehow broken, somehow damaged and dragged down. She lifted her hand and debated smashing it.

"It is a Swallowtail," came a voice from the road.

Lisel glanced over her shoulder.

A woman in a pair of faded, men's overalls sat on a skeletal, sway-backed horse. Her iron-gray hair was scraped back from a high, narrow forehead. Her face was long, her nose and chin jutting. Her small, dark eyes flashed. "It does not bite. It is a gift from the angels and it only lands where an angel has kissed you."

Jupp stared dully at the woman, as though he could not comprehend what she had said.

The woman's frivolousness angered Lisel. She flipped her hand at the butterfly. It rose and, suddenly, she and Jupp were surrounded by a cloud of fluttering butterflies. Red Admirals, Peacock Fritillaries, Orange Tips, Camberwell Beauties. "You must be blessed indeed," the woman said, dismounting the horse. She walked toward them with long, easy strides, her thumbs hooked on the bib of her overalls. "Butterflies are one of God's most wonderful creatures."

"Can we eat them?" Jupp asked.

The woman's eyebrows rose. A smile creased her cheeks. "Only if you are a bird," she answered. "Are you a bird?"

Jupp shook his head. "I am a boy."

"I do not believe boys eat butterflies. Moths perhaps, but not butterflies."

"Can we eat that horse?" Jupp asked.

The woman turned and looked at the miserable animal. "I suppose you could if you were hungry enough. Are you hungry enough?"

Jupp nodded.

The woman smiled. She turned to Lisel. "Do you have the strength to work?"

Lisel got to her feet. She hardly had strength to stand up, but she would work all night if it meant Jupp would have food. "Yes, I can work."

"What can you do?"

Lisel thought fast. She could clean grenades. She could answer telephones, and write orders for posters. She could deliver messages. She could do shopping and housework. Somehow, looking at the woman before her, Lisel knew those skills were of little use. What could she offer? Then she noticed the woman's mud-caked work boots, her roughened hands. "I can turn soil. I can plant and hoe. I know the difference between a weed and a vegetable plant," Lisel replied. "And, once, I heard a lecture about root crops."

The woman's eyes twinkled with amusement. "Then, perhaps,

knowing those things you would consider working for me. I can give you a roof over your head, food to eat and, when the crops are in, wages."

When the crops are in? "But I must get to Frankfurt. My sister lives there and she will be watching for me."

The woman rubbed her chin and frowned at the ground. "I am in great need of help now. Perhaps you would consider working for this week only."

Lisel glanced at Jupp. His face was so pale, she could see the blue veins under his skin. His dark-shadowed eyes were sunken into their sockets. They were making little progress now so they would lose little time. And perhaps if they did not stop now, Jupp would not live to see Frankfurt. "I will work for this week."

Hanni Lang loaded Jupp and Lisel's belongings onto the horse. The boy leaned forward and put his head down on the animal's bony shoulder blades and was soon asleep. Lisel carried Papa's satchel.

Hanni was in her forties and had been a widow for three years. With no sons of her own, she had to rely on her nephews and men from the village to help with her farm. But the military came and took all the men. "I did not know how I would get my crops planted this week. I told the Lord I needed help and he told me to watch." She smiled a wide, bright smile that almost made her pretty. "And then the butterfly said I could trust you."

"The butterfly?"

"Most of God's creatures know who can be trusted."

"But I was going to kill it."

"No, your despair was going to kill it."

The road forked into a dirt track which forked again to a wide gate. On either side of the gate, someone had hammered signs. "Gruesome!" one exclaimed. "Leprosy!" said the other in English.

Horrified, Lisel drew back.

Hanni shrugged. "I have not been bothered here." She led the horse through the gate and they followed the track down the hollow through a thick stand of birch. At the bottom, a stream crossed the path. Lisel stepped into it. To her surprise, the water was warm.

"We have a warm spring here," Hanni explained. "It is a nuisance to irrigate crops when you have to cool the water first."

The track rose and curved around the outside of the hollow. Then, suddenly before them in a clearing stood a two-story stone building. Some of the shingles had blown off the roof, one window was papered over and the paint had peeled off the eaves and window frames.

All around grew apple and pear and peach trees. Some of the trees had blossomed but most were full of dead wood. Daffodils and pink tulips struggled up through the weeds that choked the neglected flower beds.

From around the corner of the building came a distant baying like a wolf pack in full cry. At least a dozen dogs flowed down the path toward them, yipping, leaping, wiggling, tails wagging.

Hanni greeted them with great affection. "There, there, lovely ones. I have brought guests. You must mind your manners." She turned to Lisel. "Poor things. Animals can be refugees just like humans. Only animals are not as cruel."

Lisel could not remember the last time she had seen a dog or a cat. Almost everyone she knew lost their pets in the bombing or ate them.

Hanni led the horse into the bottom of the building which was used as the barn. She took off its halter and scooped a scant handful of oats out of a rusted bucket that hung from a nail on the wall. "You are such a fine horse, Adolf," she crooned and ran her hand over the animal's back.

She led Lisel and Jupp up a flight of rickety stairs that opened into the house. The kitchen was a large, well-scrubbed room with a wood stove in the corner. The cupboards, table and chairs were country made, simple and practical.

Hanni opened a door off the kitchen. "It is not a luxury suite but it is clean."

Lisel stepped into the small bedroom. It smelled of carbolic and moth balls. The huge bed held a feather-tick mattress and was covered by a multicolored patchwork quilt. An ancient oak bureau with a small framed mirror was the only other piece of furniture. A crucifix hung above the bed. The fading sunlight sent the last of its rays through a small paned window and washed the room with gold.

For weeks Lisel had slept on the ground beneath a dirty blanket with nothing but rain-filled clouds for a ceiling. She felt her throat tighten. Even the King of England did not have such a glorious room.

"Do you want to eat first, or wash?"

Lisel turned. "I will work first."

Hanni smiled. "There is not so much to do on a farm after dark. You and Jupp go down to the wash house while I fix supper. Then we will decide what will be your chores."

Hanni gave her a huge bar of yellowish, homemade soap, two thin but white towels, her own flannel nightgown, and a blue striped shirt for Jupp that she said had belonged to her husband. She pointed out the wash house. It was no more than a shack, but inside, the spring bubbled up through a cement tank and ran outside through a rusty metal pipe.

Lisel pulled off Jupp's filthy clothes and her own and holding Jupp above the water, stepped into the tank. The warm water soothed her aching muscles, soaked away the filth from weeks on the road and turned her skin pink. Though she longed to linger, Lisel hurriedly scrubbed Jupp from top to bottom and back again, then soaped herself and washed her hair. Lisel braided it quickly and let it hang instead of pinning it up.

"What lovely red hair!" Hanni exclaimed when Lisel and Jupp returned. "My cousin Hans had red hair; and we all believed if you rubbed it, you would have good luck. Hans was nearly rubbed bald before he learned to fight."

Hanni laid a plate of sliced, white bread on the table. It already held a tall, metal pitcher of goat's milk, a jar of honey, and a bowl of boiled potatoes.

"I am sorry I have not better for you," Hanni said. "It is a good farm but I am afraid it does not produce so much with only one person to run it." She sat down at the table. "We always say grace before we eat," Hanni told them. The silent prayer Lisel sent up at that table carried the weight of all the thanks of a bursting heart, as well as a request for the safety of a woman who cheerfully faced an army of Russians to see Lisel to this place.

The next morning, Hanni gave Lisel her first lesson in milking a goat. Then she showed Lisel and Jupp how to gather eggs from the six chickens she had hidden in the cellar beneath the barn so the soldiers could not steal them. Of course, no soldiers ever came, but Hanni had kept them hidden anyway.

Lisel was frightened of the scrawny, red hens with their pointed beaks and their sharp claws. But Jupp seemed to know how to handle the fussy birds and could slide his little hand under them, grab an egg and have it out before the hen knew it was gone.

Within two days, the color came back into Jupp's face, his eyes were brighter and he talked nonstop about how he tricked the chickens out of their eggs and about the red tabby, named Siegfried, that had caught a bird.

As her own strength returned, Lisel went into the field with Hanni. She had hitched Adolf to plow; and while they turned the soil, Lisel came behind and picked the stones the plow brought up. Afterward, both women walked the furrows, planting seed.

The two shored up the walls of an old shed and rebuilt a pole fence. Hanni talked of the pigs she would buy with her first money from the harvest.

In the evening, as the light lingered, they put in a kitchen garden, planting onions, green beans, cabbage, carrots, chervil, borage, chives, and dill.

Then Lisel and Hanni pruned the fruit trees while Jupp picked up the branches and twigs that fell to the ground and heaped them in the corner of the yard.

Hanni fretted. "I am so late with the trees; I am not sure how well they will bear this year. But it could not be worse than last." She jammed her worn handsaw through a stubborn, dry branch and let it fall. "There are so many starving people in Germany today. If only I had the help to make this place produce better." She sent a glance of apology toward Lisel. "Not that I am not grateful for your help, Lisel. We are making great progress."

Lisel was uncertain of her contribution to the great progress Hanni insisted they made. She did not have the energy to do most of the work. She only helped when it did not require sustained strength. And she tired easily and had to rest. Hanni did not complain. She kept working, telling Lisel about her dreams to turn the run-down, dilapidated farm into something of wonder, something that produced enough food to feed half of Germany and support all the workers who wanted work. "There are too many starving," she would lament.

Sometimes, with the hoe or a shovel in her hands and the sun on her back, Lisel thought of another time when no one starved, in another place where she hoed and shoveled and weeded. She remembered Kurt in the back garden in Berlin, working in his undershirt, singing that silly C and A song and dancing among the tomatoes. She remembered the time Walter tricked her into the peach tree and the autumn afternoon Kurt had kissed her. Lisel had to turn her face away so Hanni would not see her tears.

Each night, after a hot bath, Lisel fell deeply asleep and did not dream. Neither did she wake again until she heard Hanni in the kitchen the next morning.

At the end of seven days Hanni wrapped two loaves of bread, a block of goat cheese and some small, wrinkled apples in a bundle, and handed it to Lisel. "Perhaps your sister would come here," she said. "There is plenty of work and we could make room."

Lisel saw the hope in Hanni's dark eyes and hated to put it out. "I cannot say, Hanni. I will ask her."

Hanni ran her hand through her hair. Her lips trembled and Lisel suspected she was trying to conceal her emotions. "Perhaps you would like to leave Jupp here. He loves it so and he is such a wonderful boy."

Lisel had considered that days ago. Traveling was hard on Jupp and she would be able to get to Frankfurt faster without him. Leaving him with Hanni, he would have protection, shelter, food and someone to love him and look after him. When Lisel got to Frankfurt, Marta would know an LDS family who would take him. How could anyone refuse such a wonderful boy?

The memory of Trude Vinchow leapt forward. She had thought Jupp a wonderful boy, too. Lisel's heart's voice reproached her. If she left Jupp now, Hanni would not be able to give him up later. It would be cruel to part them then. And Lisel had promised she would find an LDS home for Jupp. No, she could not leave him.

"I will bring him back to visit, if I can," Lisel said. "Here," she handed Hanni the box of cocoa. "I would like you to have this." It seemed a poor consolation.

"Thanks."

The two women stood together without speaking, avoiding each other's eyes. "I wish you would not go, Lisel." Lisel heard the quiver in Hanni's voice. "I had forgotten how lonely I was. I had forgotten what a truly joyful thing it is to share work and to share bread at the end of a day." Her voice broke. "I wish you would not go."

Lisel put her arms around Hanni. "I can never thank you enough for what you did for Jupp and me. You saved our lives. You gave them back to us. But our lives must go another way for now. I must find Marta. She does not even know if I am alive. Then, perhaps I will be back."

Hanni nodded and rubbed her knuckles across her eyes. "Yes, I know you must go. I am selfish. But I want you to come back. Will you? Will you come back?"

"I will see."

"God go with you."

Chapter 21

LISEL WAS SURPRISED AT HOW EASILY HUNGER AND EXHAUSTION returned. With Jupp in tow, it took another three days to get to Frankfurt. They had used up all their provisions except for the apples Hanni had given her. Yet for all her weariness, reaching the outskirts of Frankfurt lifted a mighty burden from her heart. For Lisel, it was like going home. This was the place Marta lived. This was the place she would be part of a family again. This was a place she belonged.

She did not expect the devastation she found there. Frankfurt was a city of broken stone and twisted girders and ash. It was a city of silence. A city of ghosts. Lisel had the feeling they were being watched from the caves in the rubble, watched and whispered about. But she saw no one. Heard nothing.

Most of the streets were completely covered with debris and red rubble. Footpaths wound around and through the ruins. Fireweed, already rooted and growing, choked the streets that would have been passable. Signs nailed to posts declared, "United States Property! Looting Forbidden!" What was there to loot? Who was there to loot?

Another sign, "Gruesome," made Lisel put her hand over her mouth and nose and pull Jupp along behind her.

There were no street names posted. No landmarks to judge by. How could she find the hospital? At last, she thought she heard a noise high up on a mountain of rubble. "Can you help me?" she shouted. "I must find the hospital."

A ragged child appeared and stared down at Lisel.

"Can you tell me where the military hospital is?"

He disappeared.

"Wait! Wait!"

Lisel sighed and looked around, frowning. This place might as well be on the moon.

"What do you want?" a voice shouted. A woman had appeared on the rubble, the child was beside her.

"I am looking for my sister," Lisel shouted and told her the address.

"Can you pay?" the woman replied.

Lisel checked the bundle tied to her waist. She had four apples left. She held up two.

The woman said something to the boy and he came scampering down the rubble. Lisel was shocked to see his left leg was missing below the knee. He used a crutch made of a tree limb. "Give me the apples," he said. His eyes were flat, expressionless.

"When you take me," Lisel answered.

The boy shrugged. "Follow me, then."

He moved with such speed, Lisel had to run to keep up. Jupp began to cry. Lisel scooped him up and lumbered on. Papa's satchel banged against her knees.

The boy stopped in front of a building that had had the top floors burnt off. The dark windows were glassless. The walls were riddled with bullet holes.

"Give me the apples," the boy insisted.

"How do I know this is the hospital?"

The boy shrugged. "Look for yourself."

Lisel set Jupp down on his own legs and approached the building. From the door, she looked in. The interior was cool and dark. When her eyes adjusted, she saw she was looking into a front hall. Rags, tin cans, bottles, coils of wire and spent shells littered the floor. "Is someone there?" she called. "Can anyone hear me?"

From deep in the back of the building, Lisel heard a boom, like the shutting of a heavy door, then footsteps. A woman came toward her. She wore the brown uniform of a nurse. "What do you want?"

"I am looking for my sister who works here. Her name is Marta Spann."

Lisel saw recognition cross the nurse's face. "Come this way."

Relief rushed through Lisel and she wanted to laugh and cry at once. She turned to the boy and put three apples into his hand. He looked up at her quizzically.

Lisel smiled back at him. "I have come a very long way to find my sister and you have helped me."

The boy shrugged, stuffed the apples in his pockets and sped off through the rubble on his one good leg and his tree limb crutch.

Lisel took Jupp's hand and followed the nurse through the dark entry hall. Relief made her giddy. "I have come from Berlin," she told the nurse.

She did not respond.

"Do you know Marta?" Lisel asked. "You must, if you work here. I have not seen her since our father died last year. I am afraid she does not know I am coming. It will be a great surprise."

Lisel stopped at the door on one end of the ward. The air was filled with stale cigarette smoke from the Lucky Strikes and Chesterfields the Americans were so generous with. A few patients had cots but most lay on the floor along the walls. They had waxlike faces and empty eyes; some had bandages crusted with dried blood. The nurse led Lisel to the end of the ward to another nurse who bent over an old woman with a bandaged head.

"This is Marta Spann's sister," the first nurse said. "She has come all the way from Berlin."

The second nurse regarded Lisel for an instant and then glanced down at Jupp. "Are you hungry?"

Jupp nodded.

"If you will go with this nurse, I think she can find a piece of bread for you." She nodded at the nurse. The first nurse took Jupp's hand and led him through a set of metal double doors.

The remaining nurse looked at Lisel. "Come with me."

Lisel was puzzled. "Is Marta off shift? If you would tell me where she lives I can go there."

The nurse opened a door to a small office and gestured for Lisel to go in. The office was small and without furniture.

The nurse shut the door and faced Lisel. She saw the haggard lines around the nurse's eyes and down the sides of her mouth. Weariness circled her eyes.

"Marta has been dead for more than a month."

Lisel thought the nurse had misunderstood. "You must be mistaken," Lisel said. "Perhaps you have confused my sister with someone else. I would know if Marta was . . ." Lisel groped for another way to say it. "I would know if something had happened to her." The nurse's face showed her patience, as if she had had to deal with this so many times she knew what to expect and how to handle it.

"Marta was living with two other nurses from this hospital. Their apartment was just a hole in the rubble. You understand?"

Lisel remembered the caves in the ruins.

"More than eighty per cent of the people here are without places to live. You must understand, we live wherever we can find shelter. Most of it is not very safe. Not stable."

Lisel nodded.

"The place Marta was living in collapsed. It was a day before we could dig them out. The other two nurses were already dead, but Marta lived for several hours."

"But how can you be sure it was Marta?" Lisel protested. "You could have made a mistake."

The nurse shook her head. "I was Marta's supervisor when she first came to Frankfurt. We have worked together these three years now."

Marta dead? Lisel struggled with the idea and lost. "But we were not informed," she said.

"How could we inform you? There was no postal service, no telegraph, no telephone." She ran a weary hand across her forehead as if wiping away a memory. "Marta left no personal effects. She had already lost everything but the clothes she wore, and we had to bury her in something. I am told the scripture book that was so precious to her could not be recovered. If you would like, I will show you where we buried her."

Lisel felt dazed, disoriented, as if someone had shone a very bright light into her eyes. A hum rose in her ears.

"You must understand. Even if we had had the largest hospital in the world and all the medicines in the world, we could have done nothing for her." The nurse looked down at her hands. They were red and raw. She looked up at Lisel. "Do you have someone you can go to here in Frankfurt?"

Lisel brought up a hand and rubbed at her temples. It was a strain to think of such trivial matters. "I do not know anyone here."

"No family?"

"My brother Michael is in Russia somewhere."

"And I suppose you have no place to stay?"

Lisel shook her head.

The nurse sighed tiredly. "Perhaps if you go down to the City Hall and register with the Americans as a displaced person, they can help you. They might even know where other members of your church are living."

"Is Marta buried far from here?"

"Come with me." The nurse led Lisel through the back of the building, through more wards with more wounded and dying, and out the back into what had once been an exercise yard. Rows of crosses made of discarded lath and nailed together stood along a crumbling brick wall. She stopped at an unmarked grave near a lilac tree. The dark purple buds had not yet unfurled.

"Since she was not Lutheran or Catholic, we did not know how to mark her grave. We put her here by the lilac."

Lisel stared down at the earth. There was not even a mound to declare the place. Where had Lisel been a month ago? How could she have been living her wretched routine while her sister was dying? Would she not know somehow? Yes, she would have known, she would have felt it. The nurse must be wrong.

Lisel turned to her. "Was Marta conscious those last hours? Did she say anything?"

"Yes, but I think she may have been delirious. Some of our patients, at the end, wander to a happier time in their lives, you understand. They appear to have conversations with family members. Sometimes they are family members who have already died. In her last moments, Marta thought she was talking to your mother and father. In her mind, they must have been trying to convince her to go somewhere for she kept saying, 'But Papa I must wait for Lisel. I will not leave without her.'"

Lisel's anguish rose in her throat. The first nurse had not introduced Lisel by her name, yet this nurse knew it from Marta's lips. There was no mistake.

"She was not disfigured," the nurse continued. "Her injuries were within her. She was crushed inside."

Marta was dead and Lisel had walked all this way, starving, motherless, fatherless to be with her only sister—her only family. Now there was no one and she was alone. Lisel felt the ground sway under her feet. The world spun round her. She put her hand to her forehead.

The nurse took Lisel's arm. "Are you all right?"

"Yes," Lisel lied. Then: "No, no I am not all right. I have nothing left to live for."

Lisel felt the nurse's grip tighten on her arm. "Selfish girl!" Her voice was harsh. "What about the boy? This is not the time to grieve. Grief immobilizes. You have a child to feed and shelter. What will happen to him if you are unable to act? The boy is what you live for."

Lisel covered her face with her hands. "But I do not know what to do."

The nurse jerked Lisel around to face her and gave her a shake. "You will do what you have to. You will put away your grief and you will concentrate on living. Find an American to take care of you if you have to. The more stripes on his arm the better. At least he will feed you and keep you from being preyed upon by other men. Or follow the garbage truck. Fight for scraps, if you can. But keep your child alive. Our children will be Germany's hope. We have no future if the children die. Do what you have to for your child. Your grief will wait. He cannot."

Through her shock and misery, Lisel knew the nurse had spoken the truth. She had to put away her grief and think of Jupp. Keep him and herself alive until she could find a proper home for him. Lisel lifted her head and looked into the nurse's eyes. "Where did you say I should go?"

For the first time, the nurse smiled, a brief, weary smile. She put her hand on Lisel's shoulder. "I will write down the directions for you."

Lisel took the paper, a small piece torn from a poster printed at Erwert's Printing Company, and thanked the nurse.

"There was one other thing Marta said just seconds before she died," the nurse said, as the two stood at the door. "It had to do

289

with that American boy she was in love with. His name was Grant?"

Lisel nodded. "Grant Nolte."

"Yes. Marta had been quiet for a while then suddenly she smiled. A big, bright smile as though she was very happy. And she said, loudly, 'Grant! You have come!' Then, she was gone."

Lisel bit back her tears. "Thank you for telling me."

She trudged through the rubble of brick and stone and mortar. She had her belongings tied about her waist, Papa's satchel in one hand and Jupp on her hip. His arms were slung about her shoulders and his head against her neck so she could feel his warm breath near her ear. Exhaustion and shock numbed her arms and legs so that walking was reduced to dragging one foot off the ground and dropping it in front of the other. She pushed on, blanking her mind so she did not think of Marta.

Occasionally, as if she were seeing through water, she caught sight of others, just as wretched as she. Some of them were hiding among the heaps of devastated buildings, some scuttled along other pathways, some picked among the mountains of debris. Frankfurt was more a wound than a city.

At last she came to a street that had been cleared by a bulldozer. The street was choked with people. People on weary feet with their goods strapped to their backs. People with handcarts and wheelbarrows piled high with bundles and boxes and suitcases. A grandmother lugging two babies in her old arms. Lisel had not seen a crowd like this since the cart-flight out of Berlin. An American jeep came through, hooting people out its way.

Lisel joined the throng and kept walking. They passed more debris, more destruction.

Up ahead, she heard a clamoring, like the voices of hundreds of shouting people. A man ran toward Lisel and dodged around her, carrying an armful of egg beaters.

The traffic along the street came to a halt. "What is going on?" Lisel heard someone ask from behind her. "Looting," came the answer from the front of the crowd.

Lisel knew what looting meant. A fighting, running, half-demented mob. If it came this way or if they were pushed into it, she and Jupp could be trampled. She had to get out of the street.

290

But the people behind were pushing forward. Lisel gathered Jupp into her arms and fought against the pressure from behind by moving sideways, elbowing her way toward the edge of the street to a recess in a head-high wall. But moving sideways through the jostling, shoving crowd, she and Jupp were also being thrust forward until she found herself on the very rim of the scene.

Men and women rolling in the gutters, ripping each other's hair and clothing, snatching at each other's loot. Raw knuckled fighting. Screaming. Cursing. Crazed people clutching their plunder to their chests, fighting off other plunderers, escaping wherever they could with whatever they could. More eggbeaters, cheese graters, pepper mills, silverware.

The crowd behind Lisel surged forward. Someone fell before her feet. She stepped wide, still edging toward the brick wall.

Jupp was bawling in her ear. The path to the wall was blocked. In desperation, Lisel jerked up Papa's satchel and, swinging it like a club, smashed at anyone in her way. The path opened. She leapt toward the wall, dropped Jupp and pushed him up against the wall then dropped Papa's satchel between her feet and flattened herself over Jupp so her cheek pressed against the brick.

Above the pounding of her heart, the roaring breath in her chest, she heard Jupp wailing, she felt the mob throng past her, forcing her away from her place. She dug her fingers into the mortar and held on. Her palms went wet and slick.

Then, from somewhere up ahead, two quick shots from a revolver. The roar of the crowd died. Lisel heard a voice bellowing in German. "Get out of here! Go now or I start firing lower!"

A murmur rose from the crowd. Two more shots. The crowd fell back with more pushing and shoving. With its own momentum, the retreating mob moved faster and faster. Lisel felt someone fall near her feet. A frustrated looter snatched Papa's satchel and jumped up.

Lisel glimpsed his face. A hideous face—wild eyed, open-mouthed. His breath smelled of sour wine. She looked down and saw his filthy hand gripping the handle of Papa's satchel. A strange, vile hand on Papa's satchel. The satchel that held her genealogy, Papa's scriptures.

"No!" she shouted, whirled and lunged toward him. He dove

into the crowd. Lisel grabbed at the back of his shirt. His collar ripped in her hand. The force of the retreating crowd carried her away from the wall.

"Mama!"

The child's shrill voice rose above the noise of the mob. Jupp! Lisel looked back. He was no longer at the wall.

Her heart thundered crazily. Her mind's eye saw him trampled beneath hundreds of feet, his tiny body crushed and bleeding on the street. "Jupp! Jupp!" she screamed.

"Mama!"

In a sudden burst of energy, Lisel twisted and clawed and kicked her way upstream through the running mob. "Jupp! Jupp!"

Blasts from a pistol shattered the air above her. "Halt! Halt!"

The effect was immediate. The mass became people again, frozen where they were. Except for Lisel. She ran along the street. "Jupp! Jupp!"

She found him, still and face-down in the gutter. "No," she moaned and threw herself beside the tiny body. "Oh Jupp," she sobbed. Carefully she turned him over. His eyelids were almost transparent, closed over his eyes. Tiny bits of gravel were ground into his forehead. A scrape on his cheek seeped blood.

Lisel thrust her hand into his shirt. His chest still rose in breath, his heart continued to beat.

"Is he alive?" a voice bellowed above her.

Lisel looked up. The rioters had formed a circle around her. They looked down silently with faces full of anxiety and concern. Above them, a GI stood on the seat of his jeep, his smoking pistol in his hand. He jumped down. The crowd parted. He came toward Lisel and knelt next to her. "Is he alive?"

Lisel looked into the GI's eyes. A flood of memories, precious and painful, washed over her. She caught back a sob. "Can you give him a blessing, Elder Parker?"

Lisel saw the recognition and astonishment in his eyes. "What is his name?"

"Jupp," she replied then corrected herself. "Joseph."

Robert Parker removed his helmet, placed his hands on Jupp's flaxen hair and bowed his head. Around them, the crowd silenced. "Joseph Spann," he began.

Within moments, Jupp's eyelids fluttered. His lashes lifted. He began to cry. A sigh came from the watching crowd. They clapped, then cheered. Clutching Jupp to her, Lisel bent over him and, weeping her gratitude, rocked him there on the street. She felt his little arms go around her neck, his face press against her throat and thought she had never heard anything as wonderful as the sound of his wailing.

Elder Parker put his hand on her shoulder and Lisel lifted her eyes. "Thank you," she said.

From the crowd, a man—a dirty, emaciated man—approached Lisel. He bent and placed Papa's satchel next to her. "I am sorry," he said in heavily accented German. Lisel nodded her thanks through her tears. The man faded back into the crowd.

Elder Parker stood up. "Move on now," he bellowed. "And this time, walk!"

The people in the crowd smiled wearily and moved off.

He reached down and helped Lisel to her feet. Jupp clung to her neck. "I did not expect to see you here," Elder Parker said.

"We have only come today," she replied.

"Where are you staying?"

"I do not know. I do not know anyone in Frankfurt." She thought of Marta but could not tell him, not now.

"I have friends here," he said, taking a pen from his shirt pocket and rummaging through his pockets for a scrap of paper. "They are LDS and they are living in the West German Mission Home." He handed her the paper with an address on it. "Tell them I sent you."

"But I have nothing to pay with," Lisel said. "I used three of my four apples already."

A smile twitched at his lips. "It won't matter. They will take care of you. And Jupp too. I will come later tonight and we will have a talk. Do you think you can find it?"

Lisel stared down at the address. "I will try."

"I am sorry I cannot take you myself but there are certain regulations—"

"Yes, I know about them," she answered before he could apologize more.

"I do not think it is too far to walk."

"No, it is not far at all."

Late in the afternoon, Lisel found the five-story brick and stone building. Remarkably, it had sustained little damage during the bombing, only a mortar shell in the courtyard. She banged on the front door. "Elder Parker sent us!" she cried. No one responded.

Carrying Jupp, Lisel walked around the building pounding and shouting at each door. "Elder Parker sent us! Elder Parker sent us!"

Just when she was about to give up, a door at the back opened. A man with suspenders over his undershirt looked out. "Elder Parker sent you? Then you must come in."

Four LDS families had taken up residence in the bottom of the Mission Home. The Schroeders, the Marquardts, the Elkens and the Zobels made twenty-two people in all. They were just as ragged, just as threadbare, just as thin as everyone else but faith and hope brightened their eyes. In their presence Lisel felt the despair flow out of her.

They gathered in the Schroeders' quarters, bringing fragments of food—a quarter loaf of hard bread, some soft parsnips, powdered milk for Jupp, and a bit of fish Brother Zobel had caught the week before and dried over charcoal.

They waited until Lisel had finished eating then asked her to share her story.

Lisel told them and saw their faces change—astonishment, awe, sorrow, understanding. And, as she told her story, some of her sense of loss, some of her grief lifted.

When she finished, Brother Elken asked. "What will you do now the war is over?"

Lisel turned to him in surprise. She had waited so long, she had given up hope of its ending. "The war is over?"

The assembled group smiled. "Yes," Brother Elken answered. "We heard May eighth. Hitler is dead by his own hand and the war is over at last."

Brother Schroeder sat back with his thumbs hooked in his suspenders. "Now she will ask, 'Who won?'"

Everyone laughed. Lisel smiled. She knew the answer. They had all known it for years. The glorious Reich that was to have lasted for a thousand years had lasted a little more than twelve. It was a relief to have it, at last, over.

"As soon as we can," Sister Marquardt put in, "we are going to emigrate to America. Perhaps you should do that too, Lisel. There is nothing here for you now."

Lisel amended the thought. If Michael did not come back, there would be nothing in Germany for her. But what would there be in America for her? Without Papa and Marta and Michael, she would attend sacrament meeting in the beautiful chapels alone. She would be among thousands of fellow Saints but she would be without family. Who would she share the peace with? Without them, of what value were those silly dreams about food and parties and beautiful clothes?

They sat in silence for a moment in the dim light of a lone candle. "You are a woman of great faith, Lisel," Sister Marquardt said at last. "All of us have struggled and suffered and we have known many who lost the struggle either in body or in spirit. But you have struggled so greatly and not lost."

The others nodded.

For what purpose? Lisel asked herself.

"The Lord chastens whom he loves, Lisel." Brother Marquardt had sat silently until now. His voice reached into Lisel's heart, his eyes seemed to see into her soul.

What sort of love was that? If the Lord loved her, he would have spared her these things. Lisel looked around the circle. She saw they waited for her to make a reply but she knew her answer would disappoint them. Her bitterness and hurt showed.

"Do you remember the story in the Book of Mormon where Nephi broke his bow?" Brother Marquardt asked.

Lisel nodded.

"Do you remember how those people had suffered in the wilderness. How hungry they were? So hungry that even Lehi, the prophet of the Lord, murmured?"

Again Lisel nodded. She knew what he was trying to tell her. She felt the hot prick of tears against her eyelids.

"Hunger makes people think and do and say things they would have never thought of before. Lehi found the strength to repent of that sin. You will find it too. And you must then forgive yourself. Then will your anguish be healed." His eyes were full of compassion.

Lisel's throat tightened so she could not make an answer. She pushed herself up from the table. "May I see to Jupp?"

Sister Schroeder led her into her children's bedroom—the Mission Office storage room that still held boxes of paperwork, files, letters, reports, and journals. Four of the children were nestled on two mattresses, their blankets kicked off, their arms thrown over their heads, their eyelids fluttering in dream. Jupp was not among them.

"He is here," Sister Schroeder said, holding the candle over two small bodies on the hard floor.

Jupp's fair head glowed in the candlelight. A bluish bruise had risen on his forehead and he wore dots of orange where Sister Schroeder had administered iodine. His little chest rose and fell in the deep rhythmic breath of peaceful sleep. Seeing him safe and well made Lisel's heart swell with gratitude.

"I suppose he is not used to sleeping in a bed," Sister Schroeder said.

"What about this one?" Lisel asked, pointing at the little girl who had curled up next to Jupp. She had her thumb in her mouth and was sucking it in her sleep. Her sawed-off brown hair lay across her eyes.

"Poor little thing," Sister Schroeder said. "We do not know who she is or where she came from. She followed us home one day about two weeks ago. We tried to find out but no one knew and she has never spoken." Sister Schroeder straightened. "The children named her Maria and she answers to it but she does not fit in with them. I am glad she has found a friend in Jupp."

Lisel looked down at Maria. "She followed you home?"

"The city is filled with orphans. They live in the rubble like wild animals. Some of them are maimed. All of them are malnourished. The Americans try to pick them up, but they have been frightened for so long and they know the rubble so well, it is hard to find them sometimes." She shrugged. "What can you do? There are so many."

Elder Parker showed up about an hour later. He brought day-old bread, a sack of limp carrots, a few tins of meat he called "Spam," and a box of powdered milk he called "klim." "It is not much," he apologized. The others shouted him down.

"You have only saved our lives with your pitiful gifts," Sister Zobel chided.

Then, sensing he had come to see Lisel, the others faded into their own quarters.

He asked and Lisel told him about Michael in the military, how they decided to collect their genealogy and how it led to Lisel leaving school and working at the Munitions Works. She told him of their dreams of going to America to be with the Saints and she told him about the day they discovered they were at war with the United States. She told him about Marta's going to Frankfurt, about Michael in Russia, and about Papa's death. She told him how she and Frau Heidemann outran the Russians, about Jupp and Hanni Lang. But she could not tell him about Marta. That wound was still too raw.

His eyes never left her face while he listened in silence. When she finished he sat back and rubbed beneath his glasses. Then: "I could have never imagined," he said and shook his head. "Do you know what you will do now?"

Lisel made a helpless gesture with her hands. "I suppose I must stay here. Berlin is no good and besides, I am not anxious to travel back through the Russian Zone. Then there is Jupp. I must think of him."

Elder Parker rubbed the back of his neck. "What about Marta?"

Lisel went cold. When she was able to answer her voice was quiet. "All through the war, she had never given up Elder Nolte coming for her." Until that moment, Lisel did not realize someone would have to tell Grant Nolte about Marta's death. "Where is Grant?"

She saw the stillness steal over Elder Parker's face. His eyebrows came together in a frown and he dropped his eyes to his hands. "Grant was always talking about coming for Marta. He was putting money away for a farm. Did you know?"

Lisel nodded. She remembered Marta's excitement. "Perhaps we will have a pond with ducks!" Marta had exclaimed. "And a kitchen garden for Papa."

"He had even drawn out plans for the house he wanted to build for her. That was all he talked about. Bringing your family to live in Idaho and marrying Marta. Then this war started." He broke off and both of them sat and remembered.

297

"Did you know we came into Germany in the same unit?"

Lisel shook her head. A suspicion, cold and dark, had begun to form in her mind.

"Grant was the lieutenant and last winter, after the Ardennes, we were told to take a road through the forest. It came down to hand-to-hand combat. They were just boys by then and old men." Lisel heard the bitterness in his voice. She heard the sorrow, too, and felt it herself. "Their weapons were no better than broom handles but they fought with great courage.

"By nightfall it was over. It was not a battle any of us felt any triumph in winning. And Grant kept worrying about the German boys. He kept saying, 'What if they are boys we taught?' I should have known he would go out that night. He took a flashlight and searched among the dead and the wounded. One of them had wired himself with a grenade and when Grant turned him over—"

Elder Parker gritted his teeth, the muscles along his jaw stood out in a ridge. He blinked rapidly but the tears overran his eyes. His head dropped between his shoulders and Lisel saw them lift in a painful sob.

She stared at him in horror, her fingers held tight over her lips.

At length, Elder Parker raised his head and wiped his eyes beneath his glasses. His voice was strangled by his tears. "I do not know how to tell Marta he is not coming for her."

Lisel swallowed hard. "You will not have to."

"No," Elder Parker shook his head, "It would be better coming from me. I was there."

"That is not what I meant." Lisel reached over and took Elder Parker's hand. "Grant has already come for Marta. She died last month. His name was the last she spoke."

Lisel did not sleep well that night. For most of the night she lay awake surrounded by a gray numbness—like the day they buried Herr Wrobel. It was an insulation that allowed her to see herself as if she were separate from herself, separate from all those things that had caused her pain.

Without her grief, Lisel found comfort in thinking of Marta with Papa and Mama. She found satisfaction in knowing Grant had kept his promise and had come for Marta.

She thought about Jupp and how willing she had been to lose the genealogy for which her family had sacrificed so much when she heard his frightened cry. She had resented him from the first, yet his life had come to mean everything to her. Why? Because of Trude Vinchow's dying wish? Because he looked like Grete and she still felt responsible for her death? Because he had been so brave and obedient? No, Lisel loved him because he needed her. And his needing her made her need him.

How would she leave him then? Even if she found a wonderful family like the Schroeders. How could she tear herself from him? An idea presented itself. Perhaps she could also stay here with the Schroeders and the Marquardts and the Elkens and the Zobels. The group was like a family, a very large one, and though she had only met them, they all had a great deal in common because of their beliefs and faith. Lisel felt she could fit in here and eventually be almost as comfortable as she had been with her own family.

Perhaps she could find a job here and save enough to take Jupp and herself to America.

Lisel drifted into sleep and a dream broke through the darkness.

She was standing under a sky of clear, bright blue in a broad meadow of high grass and dancing wild flowers. A forest of leafy trees skirted the meadow. She heard birds singing in the branches. A path came out of the trees on the other side of the meadow and up to a stone bridge that arched over a brook of sparkling water.

Lisel stood near the bridge and though she wanted to cross, she could not set her foot upon the bridge. She lifted her eyes and saw, coming toward her, Papa dressed in the brightest of whites. He stopped before he reached the bridge and smiled at her.

She wanted to call him to help her cross the bridge but the words would not come. Instead, she heard his voice.

"I have come to tell you good-bye, little one. You must not mourn for me. I am happy to be here."

Lisel's words came. "But Papa I want to be there with you."

His face turned stern. "Lisel, the Lord does not allow experiences such as yours without expecting that you learn wisdom, that you use that wisdom to lift a burden from another of his children. You still have great work to do."

Papa turned and looked off into the trees. For the first time, Lisel noticed other people, standing on the path that led into the trees. His eyes came back to her. "They are waiting for me, I must go." He turned away.

"Wait!" she called out. "Papa, I must know where I am to go, what I am to do."

His face filled with gentle reproach. "Be obedient to the commandments and go where you are needed." His smile lifted the corners of his mustache. "Farewell, little one. We will meet again soon."

He would not be called back. Lisel watched as he crossed the meadow and joined the group waiting in the trees. He paused, turned, and lifted his hand.

Lisel's dream stayed with her all the next day. Where was she needed? She remembered Papa's blessing. "You are needed to serve the Lord in many callings, the most important of which is to rise up as a mother in Israel. You will minister not only to the members of your family but to many others in need, sacrificing gladly to help fulfill those needs. You will be an instrument in helping to build Zion. This will be a great blessing to you, but it will only come about by your diligence and faith and willingness to endure."

The blessing did not tell her where she was needed. She knew she must find out. Perhaps she was led to Frankfurt because she was needed there. First, she must find a way to stay in Frankfurt. She must find a job.

Sister Schroeder did not know of any work to be found in Frankfurt yet she was sure there would be some soon. She suggested Lisel stay there, in the Mission Home, until she could find a job and a better place. Lisel saw no other alternative.

She pulled Jupp onto her lap and pressed her lips against the top of his head. His little boy hair smelled sweet. "Would you like to stay here in this big house and live with all these children?"

Jupp looked up at her. "Are *you* going to stay here?"

"Yes, I will stay here too. And we will be part of a large family. All these children will be your brothers and sisters. We will have family prayer twice a day and scripture reading and people we love to go to church with. Would you like that?"

Jupp studied his index finger. His moist pink lips pursed. "No," he answered slowly. "I want to stay with Hanni."

Lisel allowed her surprise to show. "But there are no children at Hanni's house."

Jupp thought about that before he answered. "But Hanni said I am better at getting the eggs than she is. She needs me to get the eggs for her."

Swollen clouds massed over the moon and made the night sky as black as the inside of a cast iron pot. Lisel trudged along the dark road knowing she kept to the road only because she had not fallen into the ditches on either side.

She stopped for a moment and rubbed her shoulder. The socket hurt from the days and hours of pulling the cart Brother Zobel had pounded and tied and wired together from parts scavenged from the rubble of Frankfurt. She glanced back at the cart's flat bed. Two tiny figures slept on the bundles that held their clothes and what was left of their food.

One of the children stirred. "Mama?"

"Yes, Jupp."

"I am scared. Are we lost?"

Lisel pretended she was not worried. "Everything is all right. I know the way."

The truth was, in the darkness, Lisel was not sure where she was. She thought she had turned off at the right fork in the road but now, it seemed miles farther and she could not find the other fork that led to the gate. If only she had not been so impatient, so sure she could find her way after dark.

But then, as if guided by an unseen hand, the clouds parted just a little and a finger of moonlight slid through the darkness. Not forty yards ahead Lisel spied the posts. On one, a sign that read "Gruesome!" on the other, a sign that declared, "Leprosy!"

"Look Jupp. We are here!"

Jupp sat up and shook Maria. "Wake up!" he cried out. "We are here!"

Lisel's relief came out in a long sigh. She hurried through the gate and down the path, careful not to bounce the cart and the children over the rough ground.

She laughed out loud as she splashed through the streambed and felt the warm water slap over her clogs.

The path wound around the hollow and there, in the silver-blue moonlight, stood Hanni Lang's two-story stone house.

Lisel heard first one bark then another and another. The dogs flowed from the barn and came, tails wagging, leaping, yipping.

"It is Lisel Spann!" she called out, laughing at the dogs. Hanni would never hear her with all their barking. "It is Lisel Spann!"

The soft light of a candle filled the window of Hanni's bedroom. Lisel heard Hanni's thumping footsteps and the door above the rickety stairs open with a bang. Hanni ran down, barefooted. The two women threw their arms around each other. "I knew you would come back!" Hanni laughed. "I told the Lord how much I needed you and he brought you back."

Epilogue

LISEL LEANED BACK IN HANNI LANG'S OLD ROCKER AND allowed it to sway back and forth, back and forth. The motion soothed her. She closed her eyes, savoring the day's last rays. They reached through the small window, touching her face with warmth like an old friend, casting a golden glow over her bedroom. She felt the comforting weight of Papa's scriptures on her lap and, absently, riffled the top corner of the pages with her finger.

From outside came the children's voices as they went about their chores; the humming of the electric milkers in the dairy, the popping of the tractor engine in one of the fields, a dog barking as it chased an outraged duck. She smiled when she heard Anna shout at the dog. "Bad Maxi! Bad Maxi!" Over it all floated the sound of rock music.

Downstairs the door slammed and Jupp called a good-bye to one of the children in the yard. "Will you be back to help me with my homework?" the child asked. It sounded like twelve-year-old Phillip.

"Maybe not," Jupp answered. "We are meeting with the high council tonight. You had best ask your mother."

Lisel heard Jupp's Volkswagen start and heard the engine sounds fade as he skirted the hollow and gained the paved road. He did not like her to call him Jupp any more. At least, that is what he told her when he was ten years old. Everyone called him Joseph now, or Papa, or President Spann. But every once in awhile Lisel got away with calling him Jupp. That is how she thought of him. Her little Jupp.

Out of a sense of obligation, Lisel had tried to find Kulle and Gitta Mehlman, the couple who had adopted Jupp from the Lebensborn Home, but even the Search Service of the German Red Cross and the International Refugee Organization could not help. The Mehlmans had disappeared.

Then, Lisel hired someone to search the Lebensborn records. She wanted to hear that Jupp was Grete's son and, at the same time, she wanted to hear he was not. But too many records had been lost in the bombing. No one knew who Jupp was or where his family might be. So Lisel petitioned the Allied authorities and, since they preferred to leave the child in its "present surroundings," she was allowed to adopt him.

Lisel followed the same process with Maria.

Lisel smiled to herself at the thought of her fun-loving, loquacious daughter who, even now in her forties, the mother of six, was frequently the source of comical antics and practical jokes.

Of course, Maria did not start out that way. For the first two years she lived with Lisel and Hanni, Maria did not speak. Then, one day, she came rushing into the barn where Lisel tended a sick goat. The little girl was out of breath and red in the face. "Jupp fell in the duck pond!" she wailed.

Without thinking, Lisel ran down the path toward the duck pond only to find an angry, dripping Jupp slogging up the path. He stabbed an accusing finger at Maria. "She threw me in!" he declared. Jupp claimed Maria had tricked him into climbing on a young tree she had managed to bend to the ground. When Jupp had straddled the slender trunk, Maria let go of the tree. It whipped upright and shot Jupp twenty feet into the duck pond.

Lisel sucked in her lips and bit down so she would not laugh. When she was able to assume a stern face, she turned to Maria. "Jupp might have been very badly injured."

Maria's head drooped and her bottom lip came out. She dug her toe into the dirt and said nothing.

"She wanted to drown me!" Jupp shouted.

"I think if Maria had wanted to drown you, she would not have come into the barn and told me you were in the pond."

Jupp opened his mouth to object. A thoughtful look crossed his face then his open mouth dropped even farther open. "She talked?"

Lisel nodded, angling a look at Maria who, by the look on her face, grappled with some internal question. "I think she has always been able to talk," Lisel said, prodding just a little. "But she just has not wanted to. Maybe today was an accident." She turned to Maria. "Was today an accident?"

Maria screwed her mouth around. "It was an accident for Jupp to fall into the pond," she said in a tiny, petulant voice. "But I do not know how I talked. The talking just climbed out my mouth by itself."

Lisel let her laughter rise then, full of delight and gratitude and love. She scooped Maria and Jupp into her arms and swung them around. They all laughed. From that moment, Maria had never been silent.

Of course, there had been other children on the farm. Brother Zobel brought a pair of twins boys he had found living like animals in the ruins. Once, when Hanni went into Frankfurt to see her brother, she returned with three ragged and filthy street children. Six different times in the remaining months of 1945, Lisel and Hanni found children huddled in the barn or wandering in the yard, as if they had been left there in the night. Other times, strangers brought children, saying they had heard the farm was an orphan home. Lisel suspected some of the little ones were brought by their own families, but she did not speak her suspicion. She only moved another child over to make room and was grateful the farm could feed the little mouths.

In the years after the war there were thirty-eight children on Hanni's farm. Two died despite Lisel and Hanni's best nursing care. Five were reunited with their families. Twelve were adopted by LDS families in the area around Frankfurt. And thanks to Robert Parker, seventeen went to LDS families in Utah, Idaho, Arizona, and Wyoming.

Several of those returned to Germany to serve missions and always managed to stop at Hanni's farm. Lisel's heart filled when she saw them, healthy and strong, doing what the Lord wanted them to do.

She remembered the day she had read from Papa's scriptures an Old Testament passage. The similarity of circumstance struck Lisel with such quiet force she read and reread it until she knew it from her heart.

In the days of Shangar of Beth-onath,
In the days of Jael,
Caravans plied no longer.
Men who had followed the high roads
Went round by devious paths.
Champions there were none, None left in Israel
Until I, Deborah, arose,
Arose, a mother in Israel.

There were certainly no champions left in Germany. The men were dead, disabled, or missing. It was left to the women to clear away the rubble and rebuild the cities and run the factories.

For Lisel's part, she plowed and planted, weeded and watered. And she saw to the lost children.

Was that what Papa had meant when he blessed her to be a mother in Israel?

Lisel had not thought about it then, but later, working in the fields, she realized Papa had not blessed her to be a wife in Israel. Of course, there were few young men available as husbands in those days.

In April of 1945, of all the Germans born in 1924, twenty-five percent had been killed and another thirty-one percent suffered from injuries sustained in the war. Most of the rest were too ill and too poor to support even themselves. In the American Zone alone, two million were homeless. Calorie intake dropped to less than a thousand per person per day. People did not think so much of making homes as surviving day-to-day.

Still, Lisel wondered what might have happened had Kurt returned. But he had not.

Kurt had been in Cologne with the Edelweiss Pirates, a group that had started out as Swing Youth and evolved into guerrillas, opposing the Nazis. They sheltered deserters, concentration camp escapees, and foreign laborers on the run. They armed themselves and raided military depots and installations.

The ringleaders of the Edelweiss Pirates were caught in 1944 and publicly hanged. Kurt was sentenced to a prison camp. Then, in the spring of 1945, with the advance of the Russians, the prisoners were mustered out. Sick with cholera and starving, Kurt joined the forces fighting the Russians and was killed defending his country. Lisel believed it was Kurt's death that, at last, brought Frau Heidemann into the Church. She and Walter were baptized in the fall of 1945.

Lisel tried to convince the Heidemanns to come to the farm, but Frau Heidemann insisted she was more comfortable in Berlin.

Lisel was not surprised. At the Elbe, when Frau Heidemann said she was going to find Walter and return to Berlin, Lisel did not doubt her. And indeed, Frau Heidemann had done just that. Of course, she told many tales of how she had constantly outwitted the Russians, miraculously found Walter, and made her way back to Berlin. Lisel suspected many of those tales were a little less than true but it did not matter to her.

Walter left Germany in the early fifties for Robert Parker's hometown of Heber City, Utah where he found a job as a mechanic. But Frau Heidemann stayed behind, living in the same apartment in Berlin's American Zone until her death in 1962. At her funeral she was eulogized as the most resourceful Relief Society President her Berlin ward had ever seen.

Michael was released from the slave labor camps in Russia in 1950 and found his way to Hanni's farm. At thirty-one, his hair grizzled and sparse, his teeth gone, his back bent with arthritis, his hands trembling, he was a man twice his age and so weak he frequently spent the day in Hanni's rocker, sometimes dozing and other times staring, lost in some world of his own. He rarely spoke of his years in Russia except once. He told Lisel about eating the bark from the trees and digging through frozen snow for the rotting leaves underneath.

Michael died peacefully in his sleep in early 1952.

In 1954, Friedrich Wrobel and his English wife came to see Lisel. He spoke German with an English accent.

"Mother?" Anna appeared at Lisel's door. Lisel's dark-haired daughter-in-law was a smiling, round woman. "Would you like a little dinner now?"

Lisel sighed. She was not hungry. Only tired. "No, thank you, dear, I think I will just go to bed."

"What about a bowl of bread and milk? You must eat something."

That made Lisel smile. She had spent most of her youth worrying about eating and now that she was old, she did not care if she ate or not. But Anna was persistent. "Perhaps later," Lisel said.

"Call when you are ready," Anna replied with a sweet smile.

Lisel heard her footsteps on the stairs. She remembered when those stairs had been rickety old things that led into the barn. Now the kitchen, dining and living rooms were in the bottom part of the house and Jupp and Anna's bedroom occupied the space where Adolph's stall had been.

Lisel, however, remained in the same bedroom with the same bed and the same ancient chest of drawers. She had even kept Hanni's crucifix on the wall, not for any religious reasons, but because it had been so much a part of the room. Lisel never stepped over its threshold that she did not pause and see it again as she had seen it the first time. And each time, her heart swelled with gratitude. That little room, Hanni Lang, and the farm had been Lisel's refuge and her healing. She thought of the farm as her own personal Waters of Mormon, a place where she had escaped the bitter world and washed away her anger and her grief.

The farm had changed in the last forty years from a dilapidated, run-down patch of clods and weeds to an efficiently run farm, dairy, and orchard. Much of that progress was due to Jupp's skills—he had gone to the University after his mission and studied agriculture—but a great deal of the farm's success had come from Hanni's dreams and diligence.

Lisel still missed Hanni though it had been in 1956 that she died of breast cancer. Lisel had wept with gratitude at Hanni's baptism only the year before, then as Lisel sat next to her bed and watched her friend wane and fade, she wept for gratitude again, knowing Hanni's glorious destination.

It was 1957 before Lisel at last grasped the goal her family reached for when they were baptized in 1934. Bearing Papa's battered old satchel, Lisel and Jupp and Maria entered the Salt Lake Temple. In the sacred ceremonies, Lisel felt the eternities gather around her, a sealing of past and present that promised an infinite future.

The Noltes were there, Grant's parents, to see their son's desire fulfilled. Lisel felt Marta's presence too, loving and joyous.

And Lisel received special permission to do the work for Trude Vinchow and her Axel.

Afterward, Robert Parker and his wife, Nancy, took Lisel, Jupp and Maria, to Heber City where they visited with Walter and his American wife, Carol, and their three children. The oldest boy, blonde and blue-eyed, had a lopsided smile and a crook in his nose, like it had been broken once and never set. Walter introduced him as Kurt.

Lisel shook his little hand, then turned away, embarrassed by her tears. Walter put his arms around her. "Have you heard the story about the man who went fishing with an alarm clock and a hammer?"

She smiled and playfully shoved him away. "I would have thought, after all these years, Walter Heidemann, you would have heard a new joke!"

Robert and Nancy took Lisel to a small apartment just down the block from their home. "We have paid the first month's rent," Robert told her, "and Nancy's father says he has a job for you in his grocery store. We want you to stay, Lisel. Say you will."

Lisel looked around at the gleaming appliances, the new furniture and the carpet that stretched from wall to wall. Was this not what she had wanted for years? To live with her family among the Saints?

She turned to Robert. "This is so lovely. And you are offering me something I have wished for most of my life. I want you to know how grateful I am that you have made it possible. But I cannot stay."

Robert looked surprised and a little hurt. "But the prophet has said all Saints who can come to America should come."

Lisel nodded. "I know." She put her hand on Robert's arm. "When I was a girl I thought I wanted to live in America because everyone was happy here, everyone had nice clothes and enough food to eat. I thought everyone loved each other and lived in a constant state of righteousness and peace. Now I know the place I was longing for was not America or Utah or Salt Lake City. It was the home I left when I came to this earth. I still long for that place. But for now, I must go where I am needed. And that is a farm in Germany."

"But Germany does not exist any longer," Robert reminded her. "It is chopped up and governed by other countries."

"I know that, too," Lisel replied patiently. "But we were a divided people long before the Russians came. Our government was so wicked and corrupt, even the good-hearted could not change it. It took complete destruction to root out the evil. It took fear and deprivation and death to humble us. Perhaps we are not sufficiently humble yet. I am happy for the German Saints who found a new life in America. But, I feel in my heart that Germany one day can be a free and great nation. I believe its future must be fostered by someone who has shared its past. I believe I am needed in Germany. I must go where I am needed."

The Parkers accepted Lisel's explanation though she did not think they understood or believed her.

So Lisel and Jupp and Maria went back to the farm in a country conquered, divided, poverty-stricken, and struggling.

And now, nearly thirty years later, in 1985, Germany had its own temple. Lisel had not thought she would live that long.

Lisel, Jupp, Anna, Maria and her Johannes crossed by train into East Germany to Freiberg. There they met Robert and Nancy Parker and Walter and Carol Heidemann. Together, they took the tour first through the new Stake Center, then entered the temple with its tall spire, gray slate roof, and stained glass windows. Though hundreds of Germans toured the temple that day, the atmosphere was one of deep reverence, peace, and serenity.

As Lisel moved through the sacred rooms, tears rose in her eyes and flowed freely down her cheeks. At last, Germany had a symbol of forgiveness and hope.

Now, more than a week later, Lisel rested in Hanni's rocking chair. She was still a little tired from the trip. With her head back and her eyes closed she felt the contentment and the light she had received at the temple in Freiberg. She rejoiced knowing that East Germany not only had a temple but already ground had been broken for another in West Germany, in Frankfurt.

This was the beginning of the final healing. In spirit, East and West Germany would, at last, be one again. Two Germanys, but of one heart, united in the blessings of the gospel.

Perhaps, sometime, those two Germanys would be allowed to be one country again, as well. Lisel prayed it would come soon.

Her rocker slowed and Lisel slipped into a peaceful sleep. A dream brightened her rest. She was in a broad, grassy meadow where wildflowers danced and bobbed in the breeze. Around the meadow stood tall, leafy trees and Lisel heard the song of birds in the branches. Overhead, the sky was clear and a bright blue.

A path wound out of the trees, across the meadow and to a bridge that arched over a sparkling brook.

Lisel remembered this place and was not surprised to see Papa, dressed in the brightest of white, coming toward her. He paused at the bridge and smiled. "We are waiting," he said and gestured to the path in the trees.

Lisel turned her eyes and saw them all, dressed in white, smiling. Mama, Michael, Marta and Grant, Frau Heidemann, and Hanni. And Kurt. Everyone she loved.

"It is time to come home," Papa said.

Without hesitation, Lisel lifted her foot and stepped onto the bridge.

About the Author

"When I was little, my mom said, 'What do you think you'd like to be when you grow up?' I think she was expecting me to say, 'A mommy just like you.' Instead I popped off with. 'I'm going to be a writer.' I can still remember her face. 'Well, don't you think you need to be able to read first?' I didn't think so.

Terry Montague is a full-blooded American who doesn't have to look back very far to find the ancestors who came to America from another land. Her ancestors are mainly Germans who lived in Russia near the Black Sea.

Terry grew up in Rupert, Idaho, and in that small community was part of an even smaller but very active German community. She says all her neighbors spoke German, their church services were in German, and they made their own sausage and ate cheese dumplings on Sundays. While growing up she remembers being very sensitive about shows such as "Combat," where every one who spoke German was a "dirty Kraut." Terry says, "I just couldn't believe my tiny grandmother could be a 'dirty Kraut.'" It was being an American while trying to understand her German heritage that led her to write *Fireweed*, a novel dealing with life in World War II Germany.

After high school Terry went to a girls school in France, near St. Malo, where she saw lasting scars of the war, long since over. Her heritage, along with that experience, made a deep impression on her. She attended BYU where she met Quinn Montague, whom she later married.

Presently they reside in her girlhood town, Rupert, Idaho, where they own two Ace Hardware franchises. Terry and Quinn have one daughter and a variety of pets. In addition to writing, Terry is the public relations representative for Minidoka County Hospital. She has previously published *Mine Angels Round About* (a book of missionary experiences in WWII Germany), written for the *Ensign,* and won second place in a national fiction contest.